THE SAGA OF THE BARNES' CLAN, MOUNTAIN MEN

TERRY GROSZ

WOLFPACK PUBLISHING

Print Edition

© Copyright 2018 Terry Grosz

Wolfpack Publishing
6032 Wheat Penny Avenue
Las Vegas, NV 89122

ISBN: 978-1-62918-670-2

Library of Congress Control Number: 2018966491

DEDICATION

To the "All Seeing One" who 'rode' and 'worked His magic through me' on the adventures you are about to read about, I tender special acknowledgment... Many long hours were spent at the computer recalling and writing about aspects of American history from my memory banks, classic research history books, 'historical revelations', natural history resources, and a number of personal natural history experiences. However, as is the case in every writer's experiences and in one's efforts at writing, there always comes a time when the writer runs into a 'blank wall'. Many times that happened to this writer and so many times within seconds if not just scant minutes, a 'light' of sorts would come to me and off I would go proceeding with the adventure I was trying to commit to print in adventurous, interesting and believable detail. For almost 20 years during my writing labors after I retired from a 32-year career in wildlife law enforcement, I never fully realized such 'lights' were being provided by a wonderful "Coauthor" 'riding' by my side. 'Riding' at my side in my feeble human efforts to convey a point or 'speaking through me' recounting a special adventurous moment in time, even though I had never physically lived such an exciting event because of my place in geography, history, grace or time.

Being human with all of my flaws, it took some time realizing that the "Copilot and Coauthor" always 'riding at my side and many times speaking through me', was none other than the "Master Author of My Life"! So without further ado, it is to my "Coauthor" of this and all of my other literary efforts when "HE" rode "Copilot" with me during those 24 literary "Creations" that I dedicate this book and say a heartfelt THANK YOU! A THANK YOU for allowing me to bring into my readers' lives American and natural history, along with a little bit of adventure and humor that hopefully brightened up each of those readers' days...

CONTENTS

CHAPTER ONE

MISSOURI "MOONSHINE-MADNESS"

RUFOUS BARNES, hard bitten Patriarch of the Barnes Clan, watched his five hardworking boys from the easy chair on his farm's front porch in St. Charles County, a farmstead that is immediately adjacent Daniel Boone's homestead and property in the State of Missouri. Rufous, a rugged West Tennessee Irish-American and twice wounded veteran of the 1813-1814 Creek Indian War or Red Stick War, rested his bad back and badly damaged right leg from wounds previously received at the battles of Tallushatchee and later at Talladega. Sitting there in his heavily padded wicker chair in the warming Missouri sun and rubbing his bone-damaged right leg from a Creek Indian's lead ball, he let his mind drift back to his younger days during those war-

1

ring years. A war he had not wanted because of his close personal relations and friendships with many of his Creek Indian neighbors. However, when a number of native Creeks or "Red Sticks" as they called themselves, attacked a white settlement at Duck River and later at Fort Mims, where over 200 Tennesseans and friendly mixed-blood Creeks, including Rufous's wife, Martha, were killed, he had gladly gone to war with a vengeance! Heeding the Governor's call for 3,500 state volunteers even before the Federal Government had authorized going to war with the Creek Nation, Rufous Barnes had gladly joined up to avenge the loss of the love of his life of many years, his beloved wife Martha.

He along with a number of his West Tennesseans like Davy Crockett and Sam Houston, under the leadership of Major General Andrew Jackson, had immediately marched against the Creek Nation, initially destroying several entire Indian villages. Then they had defeated the Red Sticks in the battles of Tallushatchee and Talladega, followed up in the fall of 1813 by administering the death blow to the Red Sticks at the battle of Horseshoe Bend.

Having been wounded twice, crippled up even more from later infections and now unable to continue in his Tennessee family's logging business, along with losing his wife, Martha, to the Creek Indians in the attack at Fort Mims, Rufous gathered up his five sons and headed west into the "Louisiana Purchase" lands to begin their lives anew. Rufous later settled near the current-day Missouri town of Matson on 600 acres of rich bottomland, which after a lot of hard work clearing the land, finally became a prospering corn and wheat farm. Since that date, Rufous and his five sons had raised wheat and corn, but because problematic wagon transport over rough country roads into crop-glutted markets in the St. Louis area did not provide what he considered a sufficient living, he and his sons had successfully branched out in later years into another industry in order to make a better living. In so doing, they had branched out into the legal making and sale of Rufous Barnes's family recipe product of high class West Tennessee "Moonshine". West Tennessee Moonshine that was more economically transported by wagons of the day and quickly sold into the nearby vast markets of St. Louis and surrounding areas. Once those marketplaces experienced the Barnes Clan's exceptional brand of "Shine", their 600 acres of wheat and corn production hardly sufficed in meeting the annual demand for the baseline ingredients for the making of that fine whiskey product!

Reaching down from his wicker chair, Rufous retrieved a gallon stoneware jug of his special brand of high class Shine, tilted it back and let its silky-smoothness slowly slide down the back of his throat with great satisfaction. Putting the cork back into the mouth of the jug and tapping it lightly with his hand to make sure the jug was sealed, he placed it back down beside his chair for later retrieval when his bad leg began bothering him once again as it always did come every late afternoon. He then silently cursed the mushroomed lead ball still lodged in his thigh bone next to the top of his knee, as he leaned down once again and rubbed that area producing the constant and offending pain in his leg. When he did, he also felt the sharp pain in his chest every time he leaned down and compressed his insides upon reaching for something lower like his knee, the floor or the ground. However, he just figured the chest pain was caused by his damaged back, also from a previous bullet wound received in battle with the Creeks, and tried ignoring its oftentimes searing pain.

Sitting back up in his chair, he yelled at Wallace, his oldest son, to make sure the jugs of Shine he was loading into the back of the wagon had plenty of hay spread all around so the stoneware jugs would not bang against themselves on the long and rough ride on the dirt roads into the St. Louis area. "No use traveling all that damn way just to arrive with broken or cracked jugs," yelled Rufous. "If you do and those saloons or river boatmen turn to another supplier because our Shine has run out into the bottom of the wagon after the jugs have cracked or broken open, you will have to answer to your brothers for your carelessness after all of their hard work producing it at the still site," he continued.

Wallace just grinned over his father's caution-ary words yelled from the front porch of their farmhouse. He had heard those words of caution many times before and just shook his head. His dad had taught his sons well and there was no need in reminding any of them to be careful with their 'liquid' livelihood. Then Wallace turned to his other brothers bringing jugs of Shine out from their "still house", and helped Otis, Cedrick, Sterling and Oliver finish loading the last two wagons with their latest run of Moonshine all nestled in stoneware jugs among the piles of hay to prevent breakage while being transported in wagons to St. Louis and surrounding areas.

Rufous watched his boys loading the remain-der of the Shine and then calculating the number of jugs loaded, figured with those latest sales he could just about pay off his debt to the bank for his new farm, making it free, clear and finally his own. That brought a smile to the old man and in so doing, caused him to reach down once again for his jug of "white lightning" for another long pull... *It will be a cold damn day in hell be-fore that greedy damn banker ever gets my farm! he thought. Then he remembered bitterly that the U.S. Government had yet to pay him for his service to the country during the Creek Indian War. Money that he could damn well use in helping to pay off his farm's mortgage and operating expenses as well...* That last thought elicited another long pull on the jug of Shine comfortably resting at his feet.

One week later, found the Barnes boys filling gallon stoneware jugs once again with their newest batch of Shine produced from their five small stills operating in their still house located in their barn. Once again, Old Man Barnes sat in his favorite chair on the front porch of his home watching the boys exiting their still house carrying gallon jugs and loading them into hay-filled wagons for transport to the saloons and river men in the St. Louis area who seemed to have an insatiable appetite for the smooth West Tennessee style of Shine made by the Barnes Clan. *1822 was going to be their best year out of their last three because of the Shine made from his old family recipe,* thought Rufous with a smile.

About then, Rufous noticed his local sheriff and two other men he had never seen before riding into the front yard of his farm. "How-do, Rufous?" asked Sheriff Bill Clemmens.

"Be doing fine, Bill. What brings you out this-a-way?" asked Rufous.

"I brought these two Federal Revenuers out to meet with you at their request and also that of our new and first governor. It seems according to these two federal men, that you ain't never paid any federal excise taxes on your fine brand of whiskey. I mention that because since we have just now become a state for this here United States, we fall under a number of their federal laws. And one of those laws is the "Whiskey Excise Tax Act of 1791". In case you don't know about that federal law, that was a tax law brought about because money was needed to help pay off the cost of our Revolutionary War. These Federal boys have been doing some nosing and asking around about you and your family Moonshine business and as a result, especially now knowing about the reputations of your Irish hot-tempered five sons and their liking to fight, have some bad news for you. As such, they have asked me along to keep the peace once they share that bad news with you," quietly said Sheriff Clemmens so as not to raise the ire in the old and stove-up Irishman.

"The hell you say! Keep the peace for what reason? My boys have not been off the farm raising hell ever since we brought in our wheat and corn crops last year. They have been busy minding their own business planting this year's crops and making Shine for the markets in St. Louis and that ain't breaking any law I know of. Anyway, let them two fellas say what they have to say and then they can get their federal asses off my land," said Rufous, sitting up in his chair remembering the federal government's non-payment for his military service in the previous Creek Indian War. However, when he up and bowed his neck, he felt the old familiar pain in his chest rising up inside him once again. When it did, that pain caused him to once again reach for his comforting jug of Shine by the side of his chair.

"Mr. Barnes, my name is Agent Thompson and I am a Federal Revenue Officer. You and your boys appear to be quite busy so I will be quick with my business. In 1791, the Federal Government established a 25% excise tax on all alcoholic spirits produced and sold in order to help pay off the debt caused by our War of Independence. Under the Associate Justice of the United States Supreme Court, James Wilson, a ruling has been asked for by the Federal Government and rendered regarding this Whiskey Excise Tax and its legal authorities. Under the Associate Justice's ruling, the Federal Government has the authority, by military means if necessary, within all state boundaries, to collect the 25% whiskey tax on all spirits produced and sold. Since Missouri became a state of this here union in August of 1821, within its boundaries all production and sale of spirits produced by United States citizens are subject to the 25% Federal Whiskey Excise Tax. If necessary, the governor of the great State of Missouri can order state militias to assist the Federal Government in the collection of these taxes. With that being said, it has come to our attention through our office and our subsequent investigations, that you have been producing whiskey and selling the same in St. Louis to houses of ill repute and saloons, and along the Missouri and Mississippi Rivers to boatmen for some time now. It has also come to our attention that there is no State of Missouri or Federal Government records showing that you have complied with the requirements of the Federal

Whiskey Excise Tax. If my information is incorrect, Sir, would you please so advise."

For the longest time Rufous just stared at the officer in disbelief over what he was hearing being said. He had never heard of this Whiskey Tax 'thing' nor was he interested in taking any of his hard-earned money and giving it to the Federal Government so they could just piss it away! Then Rufous got his 'Irish' up! To his way of thinking, he had sacrificed his body for his country in the Creek Indian War! Then he had lost his beloved wife in that war as well as his logging and lumber business back in Tennessee due to the lingering physical effects he had received in that war. Lastly, he was never paid by the U.S. Government for his military service, had gone bankrupt because of his war wounds and as a result, had been forced to move on in order to begin life anew for his sons and himself. Now here was that same government with its hand out for even more of what little he had left to offer!

"BOYS!" bellowed Rufous and moments later five burly men stumbled out from their whiskey making still house expecting the worst. Upon seeing Sheriff Clemmens, they slowed their running to just walking trying to figure out why their father had yelled at them for some sort of family assistance. When they arrived at the porch, Rufous said, "Throw those two government son-of-a-bitches wearing those goofy hats off our farm! The sheriff claims they are called

'Federal Revenuers' who are claiming we owe them a 25% Whiskey Tax based on all of the whiskey we produced in previous years and are now producing by the sweat of our brows and are selling in St. Louis."

"Now wait a minute, Rufous! These government men have every right to be here on official business. Truth be known, if you don't pay what the Federal Government says you owe, they can confiscate your farm, sell it and settle up the bill you owe for your back taxes! This they can do because of the whiskey you and the boys have produced and sold over these many months since your arrival and now, especially since Missouri became a state last year," said Sheriff Clemmens, trying to keep a lid on the peace and avoid a killing of the government men or any of the Barnes Clan if Old Man Rufous got any hotter under the collar!

Otis, always the thinker of the group of brothers and one of the best fighters among the Barnes Clan, saw red in what he was hearing but kept his Irish temper in check…for now. He then said, "Dad, if what they say is true and there is a government whiskey tax, it looks like that is something we may have to pay now that Missouri is part of the United States. How much do we owe according to them?" he asked Sheriff Clemmens.

"Agent Thompson, what do you figure the Barnes Clan owes the government for this Whiskey Tax thing?" asked Sheriff Clemmens, still trying to keep a lid on a possible violent explosion erupting between the two factions.

"Well, our sources tell us that the Barnes Clan brings in at least two wagonloads of gallon jugs of whiskey a week into St. Louis and leaves with empty wagons every time. As near as we can calculate since Missouri became a state in '21 and this is a year later, we roughly figure the Barnes Clan owes the Federal Government at least $3,000!" said Agent Thompson. "Being that our records are not that exact, I have been authorized to accept $3,000 as settlement for back whiskey taxes, providing the Barnes's stipulate in writing that they will in the future comply with the new federal tax law in full. Comply in full, which means, the Barnes Clan must start keeping records on how much whiskey they are selling so the proper amount of taxes can be levied based on what they are producing and selling," continued Agent Thompson.

"Three thousand dollars, three thousand dollars, and if we don't?" said Rufous trying to hold back his temper over the economic disaster he could see unfolding in front of him and facing the rest of the Barnes Clan!

"Then the government will immediately foreclose on your farm, sell it for the back taxes owed and you will be out and on your ear," said Agent Thompson, now dropping any civility he may have earlier harbored seeing he was up against a hard-headed Irishman and not making much progress in the mission he was trying to accomplish.

"Rufous, I suggest you somehow comply. If you don't, the governor will be requested by these here federal fellas to send in the state militia and they damn sure will take your place no matter how much you and your sons decide to try and stop them!" said Sheriff Clemmens. "So, I suggest you find a way to settle up and pay these back taxes and start keeping records in this matter or you and yours will lose everything you all have worked so hard for."

With those stinging words coming from his much-respected friend and local sheriff, Rufous staggered up from his chair, removed a plug of "Brown's Mule" chewing tobacco from the front pocket of his overalls, tore off a bite, and nestled the chunk of black tar looking-like chew between his cheek and gum. Moments later, he spewed a long line of spit onto the ground in front of the porch near the boots of the federal men, grabbed the front of his chest, pitched over the porch railing and died from a massive heart attack! Instantly there was a mad scramble for the Barnes Clan Patriarch, but what the entire Creek Nation could not do during the Creek Indian War, the 25% Whiskey Excise Tax and a worn-out heart did…

That evening the five Barnes boys dug a grave for their father and after a few last words from each son, Rufous was lowered into the ground on what at that moment in time was still his farm. Also lowered into the grave went two one-gallon jugs of his fine West Tennessee whiskey, just in case… Then the boys got rip-roaring drunk on their whiskey that evening since they did not have the $3,000 to pay off the Whiskey Tax and the rest of the bank's loan on the farm as well. The following morning, Wallace, who had also been a trapper back in Tennessee in order to earn extra money for the family, ringing head and all from the big drunk the evening before, took their last wagonload of whiskey into St. Louis to sell. He purposely took their final load into town because the boys needed the money, and he had remembered a posted newspaper ad in the *Missouri Gazette and Public Advisor* newspaper advertising for trappers to form up a brigade and head west into the unexplored frontier to trap beaver. Wallace figured since they were going to lose their farm to the back taxes and the bank, the brothers may as well look for some way in which to support themselves and having trapped beaver back in Tennessee as a young man, that new adventure out on the frontier was as good as any place to start making a new life and good name for all of them…

CHAPTER TWO

THE ODYSSEY BEGINS

THAT EVENING WHEN WALLACE RE-TURNED to the farm after selling their last load of Shine to the saloons in St. Louis, he found all of his brothers sitting on the front porch nursing a gallon jug of their dad's West Tennessee Shine. Hitching up the team to the hitching rail out front of the farmhouse, Wallace walked up onto the porch, took the much-used jug and without a spoken word, made sure he was making up for lost time as well. Finally after several long moments of silence among the Barnes Clan, Wallace said, "I need to read this here newspaper article from the *Missouri Gazette and Public Advisor* to all of you to see what you think." Hearing no dissent from his four brothers who were still mulling over the recent and untimely

15

death of their father, Wallace commenced reading the newspaper article out loud in order to get through any 'haze' his dad's Shine had left in his brothers by saying, "To enterprising young men. The subscriber wishes to engage 100 men to ascend the river Missouri to its sources, there to be employed, one, two or three years as fur trappers. Interested parties are to inquire of Major Andrew Henry near the lead mines in Washington County." Then Wallace advised the brothers that the newspaper's subscriber was none other than their new Lt. Governor, General William Ashley. That caused a number of his brothers' eyebrows to shoot up in surprise over their new Lt. Governor being involved in such an enterprise of 'daring and do' out on the largely unexplored, dangerous Indian and grizzly bear infested frontier.

"Well, my brothers, what do you think? We will soon lose our farm and home here to the Federal Government for non-payment of back whiskey taxes since we have no money to pay those taxes off in the time frame they have left us. So here is a chance for all of us to see some new lands, start anew and make an honorable living based on the Barnes Clan's work ethic and Irish luck. What say all of you to this opportunity for us to begin a new life of our own out in the unexplored West?" asked Wallace, ever the one of the brothers with the most wanderlust.

"I ain't never done any trapping and wouldn't even know where to start," said Cedrick quietly, as he took another nip from their communal jug of Shine.

"Well as all of you know, I have trapped beaver, muskrat and mink back in Tennessee when our family needed the extra money and could teach all of you on how this trapping thing is best done," said Wallace hopefully.

"What about leaving Dad 'here' on this place which is no longer ours?" asked Otis, a younger brother and the deeper thinker and best brawler of the group. "I sure as hell don't want whoever buys this place to plant a damn old pig farm over his grave."

"Well, to Dad, this was his home. I suggest we leave his grave unmarked. That way no one will know where he is buried and desecrate it, whoever ends up buying this farm for the back federal taxes owed. Besides, if we all are successful in this beaver trapping thing as I think we will be, we can save our money and when we return to Missouri, maybe we can buy this place back from whoever purchases it out under from us for the owed back taxes," said Wallace.

Looking down the line of his still long-faced brothers over losing their father, farm and distillery all in the same day, upon hearing no dissent, Wallace said, "Alright, here is what we all are going to do then. I say we all stay together as a family and join up on this trapping thing out west. I say we take what belongs to us here on the farm, take it into St. Louis, sell it off and use the proceeds to procure what we will need in the way of extra gear in order to do this 'fur trapping' thing up right and proper like. However, that newspaper ad in the Missouri Gazette I just read to all of you has been advertised for a few days now and another ad just like it has been advertised in the *St. Louis Enquirer*. So if we want to be considered and be able to go as a group, we need to get our butts out to the lead mines, look up that Major Andrew Henry, examine the deal offered and if we all like it, sign up as a family so we can all stay together," continued Wallace. With that decision made in typical Barnes Clan fashion, the jug of Shine was passed all around to each of the brothers once more as if to symbolically seal the deal on this new adventure just discussed, for better or for worse.

The following morning, Wallace took the reins of the horses pulling one of their "Whiskey Wagons" as the clan called it, as the rest of the brothers clamored in and sat in the wagon box full of loose hay with a jug of Shine and enjoyed the ride into St. Louis and then out to the adjacent lead mines. There the five brothers of the Barnes Clan met with Major Henry and after much 'cussin' and discussin', began the process of exploring the terms and conditions associated with signing up with the American Fur Company for a three-year stint as 'company fur trappers'. As the brothers discussed the terms and conditions of the American Fur Company's company fur trappers' contract, Major Henry provided even more details on any questions that arose.

During those contract discussions that followed, Major Henry advised that they would become American Fur Company 'company fur trappers' and would be paid in 'halves'. That meant the fur company would supply each man with a horse, saddle, tack, rifle, camp ax, and six beaver traps. In return, each 'company fur trapper' would be entitled to half of what he caught and the American Fur Company was to receive the remaining half of the furs trapped annually by company trappers in return. In so doing, each trapper would be obligated under the terms and conditions of the contract to sell his entire catch to the fur company at the contract prices offered per pound of fur in any given year. Also, the company trappers would have to purchase all of their supplies from the American Fur Company at company-dictated prices or what would soon be known among the trappers in the intermountain west as "Mountain Prices". Mountain Prices meant the fur trapper purchaser would be paying anywhere from 700-1,000% more for an item out in the intermountain west than that same item would have cost the purchaser in St. Louis! Major Henry further advised the brothers those higher prices charged for needed goods and supplies were because of the anticipated losses suffered by the American Fur Company supplier. Losses suffered due to Indian attacks, horse wrecks, drownings and other losses when bringing those supplies all the way from St. Louis into the dangerous frontier and then bringing the valuable furs back to the American Fur Company's fur house in St. Louis.

That was when Otis asked Major Henry if he could have a few minutes alone with his brothers and discuss an issue 'sticking in his craw', which was so granted. Walking off to one side and out of earshot of the Major, Otis said, "I smell a rat in this contract if we were to sign it as written! What the Major is advising is that we will have to sell our furs to the company for what they decide to offer and will have to buy our coming year's supplies at the price they want to charge. That could lead to our ruination if we aren't careful."

"What else are we going to do?" asked Oliver. "We soon will have no place to live and out there on the frontier at least we will be able to make a go of it based on our abilities as trappers and hard workers. I say as a group, we are pretty damn well self-sufficient in what and how we go about doing things, so we should be alright no matter what we do. We really don't have much choice if one really takes a close 'gander' at it. Dad put all of our money into paying off the farm and making his brand of Shine. As a result, that didn't leave us with much in our "Posthole Bank" because he was looking long-term and living as well. To be quite frank, those damn revenuers pretty well sunk our planning regarding the long-term operational thinking about what we were going to do with our farm. I say we take the deal since it appears to be the only one on the 'table', make the most of it and knowing this family's abilities, we will make it on our own come 'hell or high water'. Besides, if this doesn't work out, we will have our horses and tack and can leave anytime we choose after our three years under the contract are done. What do the rest of you say?" asked Oliver.

No one else had much to say so the brothers returned to Major Henry, signed on for three years and were told when and where to go and get their promised company supplies needed for the coming crosscountry travel into the largely unexplored American West. That evening the brothers returned home and assessed what they had in the way of personal gear and what they could sell from the farm's stocks. This they did in order to purchase more of what Wallace was advising they would need, since the frontier held no ready supply sources once they got out there and were basically on their own.

The next morning, the brothers loaded up all of their stills into their three wagons and took them over to their friends working on Daniel Boone's farm who were also from Tennessee and sold them to their breed of "Moonshiner". Later, all of their wagons were sold to another neighbor who had also purchased all of their remaining wheat and corn farming equipment as well. However, the brothers kept all of the farm's horses which provided for each of them their own familiar riding horse as well as one good extra riding horse in case any of their animals were injured or killed while out on the 'horse-starved' frontier. Otis and Wallace figured since the fur company had promised each man a riding horse, they would just keep those extra animals as packhorses since they had good dependable riding stock of their own that they could use from their farm. That way the brothers figured they could take along more provisions on the extra horses. That they would do because four of the brothers were large men and what Otis called 'eager eaters'. So with their farm stock, they figured the extra company supplied horses could pack more food supplies into the field and hopefully, bring back to the American Fur Company extra heavy loads of beaver fur. Additionally, that meant right off the bat they would not be in debt to the fur company by having to purchase additional horses as pack animals on which to carry extra needed goods and their furs back to be sold.

Then taking their riding horses into town along with four pack animals, the brothers went shopping for extra gear Wallace figured they would have need for once out in the wilds of the frontier and away from any ready supply source. A trip to two gun shops provided a Lancaster

.54 caliber flintlock rifle for each brother, as had been recommended by Major Henry. That way each man would have a rifle heavier than the lighter caliber Pennsylvania rifles they currently possessed. Pennsylvania rifles which the brothers then traded in against the purchase of the heavier caliber Lancaster rifles which were more appropriate for the larger big game animals and predators they would encounter out on the frontier. That way, when the fur company provided each man a rifle, even if it was inferior to a Lancaster, the brothers figured 'a little bit was good and a lot more was better'. Hence the extra single-shot flintlock company rifles they each would be carrying while afield in Indian country in addition to their heavier caliber Lancasters. Since the fur company said nothing about carrying a pistol, the brothers taking some more of the money earned from selling a large amount of their remaining equipment from the farm, each man purchased two .54 caliber smooth bore pistols. Two smooth bore pistols each that were purchased so they could be used to fire a solid ball, buckshot, or buck and ball together for close-in work if an occasion arose whereby they were close to being overrun by attacking Indians or a mean-assed grizzly bear.

The brothers had learned that defensive lesson of carrying extra firepower from their Dad and his learned experiences while fighting Indians during the earlier Creek Indian War back in their previous home in Tennessee. He had always advised his boys that when in Indian country, carry every bit of armament possible because when the Indians came at you with evil intentions, they usually would only do so if they outnumbered who they were attacking. Therefore, he always advocated making sure one had lots of firepower, a tomahawk and a knife when it came to fighting Indians if one wanted to avoid 'going under' or 'losing his hair'.

A week later, the word went out to the 100 men who had signed up with Major Henry and when they were all gathered together, the men were allowed to pick out the riding horse, saddle and tack they preferred, as the Major had promised his American Fur Company would provide. Then each man was surprisingly issued a specially built, expensive .54 caliber Lancaster flintlock rifle with a shortened barrel to facilitate riding in heavy timber on a horse so the rifle barrel would not be hitting the trees and always be in the way. While the brothers looked over their new rifles, they had a chance to meet several other members of their newly organized party of fur trappers, namely Jim Bridger, Jedediah Smith and a rough and tumble, coarse speaking 'river man' named Mike Fink. The brothers also quickly discovered that they took a liking to the easygoing Jed Smith and Jim Bridger. They also found they had little use for the coarse mannered and rough speaking 'river man' named Mike Fink, being that all of the brothers had been raised to be good Christian men. The men were then advised they would be supplied with the rest of the gear they would need before being disbursed out onto the frontier to start trapping in the fall from the supplies at the small fort they were going to build up on the Yellowstone River. The small fort Major Henry was referring to was soon to be built and located on the eastern side of the Yellowstone River where it met the Missouri River, in the current-day State of Montana. According to the Major, that fort was to be built in such an area because it would be in the heart of beaver trapping country and adjacent to several tribes of Indians.

And locating the fort in such an area would allow fur trading to occur with the Indians who were doing the vast majority of fur trapping out on the frontier. That the Indians did because of their major use of animal furs and skins for their own livelihood, but also because they could trade animal furs of what they considered of low value in order to acquire 'white man's' goods which they considered of higher value and of great use within their own communities.

The 100 men selected by Major Henry for the American Fur Company, or "Ashley's Hundred" as they were historically to be called, were then given three days to say their good-byes to family members and take their last opportunity to 'paint the town red' before heading out to the north and west into the frontier. On May the 8th, 1822, the

100 men under Major Henry's command, headed up the Missouri River towards the faraway confluence of the Yellowstone River where a small fort and trading post was soon to be built. From there once the fort was built and established, the men would be fully outfitted and then head out onto the many adjacent trapping grounds to get home sites situated and prepared for the fall and subsequent spring beaver trapping seasons.

For the next 30 days, Ashley's Hundred and their supply caravan of men, horses and mules slowly traveled northwesterly up the Missouri River and then turned and headed along the sandy and shallow flowing Platte River. Along the way, the men were almost in constant sight of small groups of Indians who always kept a respectable distance away from the large contingent of heavily armed men. As expected, Major Henry ran the column of men and heavily loaded horses and mules like he would a small military contingent. There were always scouts and outriders leading and flanking the long column of men and valuable livestock, as well as a well-armed group of men at the rear of the column. The men at the rear of the column were picked for their frontier experience in dealing with the Indians' favorite mode of attack, namely from the rear of any such group so encountered. That favorite method used by attacking Indians was one of a quick strike into the rear of such a column. There they killed off the stragglers riding 'drag' and when the rest of the column being attacked circled up for the protection the defensive circle represented, the attacking Indians would then run off the 'tail-end Charlies' of the group being attacked, be they horses or mules. With that, they would then quickly disappear into their familiar surroundings, richer for their efforts and not concerned with any form of effective pursuit on what the Indians considered their home grounds.

Come time for making their daily evening encampments, Major Henry allowed opportunities during those times for the horse and mule herd to be unloaded from their heavy packs in order for them to graze and water. When he did, the livestock had double guards posted around the feeding herd to avoid theft from marauding Indians following the column. Then come the evening hours and the cover of darkness, the horse and mule herds were brought back into the encampment, double hobbled or if picketed, the picket pins were driven deeply into the soil, precluding easy theft by the Indians. Then guards would be posted around the valuable animals rotating on four-hour shifts throughout the evening and into the morning hours. Come daylight, the regimen would be instituted in the reverse for the livestock. They would be allowed to graze and water for an hour and then curried to preclude pack sores from developing. Then after the men had eaten their breakfasts, they would be repacked with all of the goods and provisions carried from the day before, lined out and once again hit the trail en route their Yellowstone River destination.

In between such close coverage of the very valuable livestock, the 100 men were broken up into 25-man groups with each group having a separate campfire and set of cooks. Prior to establishing camp each night, several of the outriders would kill two buffalo in front of the oncoming column of men and livestock and upon arriving at the kill sites, there camp would be made for the night. That made it fairly simple for the camps' cooks to have a readily available supply of meat right adjacent to their campsites and shortly ready for cooking. Cooks' helpers would gather up driftwood from along the Platte River for the cooking fires and if that was unavailable in sufficient quantities, then the men hustled around their campsites gathering up the ever-present and readily available supplies of dried buffalo chips scattered about the prairie for their cooking and campfires.

Meals at the end of each day as well as breakfasts usually consisted of staked buffalo meat, fried bacon, Dutch oven biscuits and coffee. On Sundays, Major Henry allowed the men and animals a day of rest so the animals could graze as long as they wanted and fatten up. In so doing, that allowed some of the men not on guard duty to get some extra sleep. Additionally those Sundays of rest allowed other men to bathe and shave along the river, and the cooks would have the opportunity to soak beans so they could be cooked and added to the men's meals as an extra treat. However, because of the ever-constant sightings of roving bands of Indians, many times tailing the column of trappers for days, the men always carried their weapons everywhere they went, even when they went to the bathroom out on the prairie.

One Monday morning after the livestock had been brought back into camp for packing and saddling, Sterling, youngest member of the Barnes Clan, was in the process of currying down his horse prior to its saddling. Standing by a piece of driftwood, Sterling kicked it aside so he could come under the neck of his horse and curry it from the other side. When he did, a disturbed rattlesnake lying hidden underneath the driftwood, crawled out, quickly formed itself into a coil and began making his angry presence known through its set of rattles! Sterling quickly stepped away from the dangerous reptile but his horse, upon hearing the angry snake's rattles underfoot, spooked and broke for the nearby shallow and sandy Platte River! When Sterling's mare broke and ran, its reins were jerked from his hands as the panicked horse spooked off kicking and bucking! When that happened, Sterling was dragged off his feet and ended up in a heap almost under his horse's hooves and right next to the coiled and angry rattlesnake!

Quickly rolling away from the snake, Sterling

leapt to his feet and took off chasing his run-away horse before she got lost out on the prairie or found herself in the hands of an Indian. As his horse splashed into the Platte, Sterling, in an attempt to cut off the horse's escape across the river and out onto the vast prairie, took a shortcut across the water in an attempt to inter-cept his frightened horse and bring her back to camp. Five steps into the river going at a dead run, STERLING SUDDENLY FELT THE SANDY FOOTING GIVING WAY AND QUICKLY FOUND HIMSELF PLUNGED UP TO HIS WAIST IN QUICKSAND!

"HELP!" screamed Sterling, realizing what had happened and the danger he was now in! In an instant, the entire camp upon hearing his desperate cries for help, exploded into a mass of men moving for their near at hand weapons and looking around for the danger! Men were instantly arming themselves figuring Indians were close at hand and in those moments of dis-organized scrambling around, Sterling sunk up to his armpits as his life-and-death struggles to extricate himself did nothing more than sink him even more deeply into the deadly quicksand! By the time Otis figured out that his brother's calls for help were coming from the Platte River, he dropped his rifle and broke for the waterway. By the time he arrived, Sterling was almost up to his neck in quicksand and the look on his face said it all! Sterling continued thrashing around, not realizing in his panic that he was only making himself sink even more quickly into its clinging depths! Otis, upon seeing his brother's plight and without thinking, plunged into the sandy shallows to save his brother, only to find himself in the quicksand's deadly clutches as well! Realizing what was happening and being a very strong swimmer, Otis tried 'swimming' out from the deadly peril, only to find he was sinking quickly under its deadly clutches as well! Then Oliver, upon realizing what was happening, grabbed a rope off his horse and sprinted for the bank of the river. Arriving seconds later, he attempted to throw his rope to Sterling first, who by then was up to his chin and now screaming and thrashing around in terror! Oliver's first toss of the rope caught on some sagebrush behind where he stood and as a result, fell too short. By the time he had retrieved the rope for another throw, Sterling was up to his terror stricken eyes, which were now showing an inordinate amount of white…

THEN IN THE BLINK OF AN EYE, HE WAS GONE AND THE ONLY REMAINING VESTIGE OF WHAT HAD ONCE BEEN A HEALTHY AND STRAPPING SIX-FOOT MAN, WAS HIS WIDE-BRIMMED FELT HAT SLOWLY SWIRLING AROUND IN THE THIN SHEET OF WATER FLOWING OVER THE DEADLY PIT OF QUICKSAND! Oliver stood there for a second in shock over seeing his brother disappearing into the life-grabbing sands before his eyes and being unable to help! Then three other men arrived with ropes and managed to get several loops under Otis's arms and bodily dragged him from the deadly 'clutching' quicksand and onto the safety of the river's bank. When Otis found his feet upon solid ground, he quickly scrambled away from the river's water on 'all fours' still in terror over what lay hidden in the shallow river behind him. There he lay gasping for breath over his near-death experience, as his heart rate slowly began returning to normal now that the danger was past.

Then the only sound heard for the longest moment of time was that of a scream from a nearby circling golden eagle, as if heralding a simple horse-chasing event that had turned deadly. Meanwhile, Sterling's mare, now realizing it was away from the rest of the horse herd and not liking being out there on the prairie all alone, crossed back across the Platte River missing all other nearby quicksand beds, and quietly rejoined the rest of the horse herd... Then Sterling's floating wide-brimmed hat that he wore to keep the sun's rays from his eyes, caught a slight bit of current in the shallow waters and drifted off slowly downstream never to be seen again, just like its previous unlucky owner...

About then Major Henry rode up into the group of men standing around the river's edge looking on in wide-eyed shock over what had just occurred to one of their own. He bailed off his horse and figuring out what had just happened since all the men were looking towards the shallow flowing river said, "Who did we lose?"

For the longest time, no one wanted to mention the name of the man just lost 'to the ages' in the quicksand out of shock and then quiet respect for the dead. Then Otis turned facing Major Henry and said, "We just lost my brother, Sterling, to the quicksand."

"Damn," said Major Henry, "Sterling was a damned good man and had a lot of potential. My condolences go out to the rest of you Barnes boys over the loss of your brother to the shifting sands in this here river." Then turning and facing the ever-increasing gathering of trappers from the other camps, Major Henry said, "Let this be a lesson to the rest of you men. The frontier will kill any one of you in a heartbeat if you drop your guard. Let this lesson of 'quicksand' be a lesson as well to all of you when it comes to this river. This here river is full of patches of quicksand ready to take any of you who are unwary to meet your Maker just as quickly as a speeding lead ball or the flight of a steel-tipped arrow! From now on, anytime any of you are messing around on this river, make sure you are doing so in pairs. That way if something goes wrong, one or the other of you will have some help. Now, we have a powerful piece to go this day and we need to get going. So, say your last words to the unfortunate loss of a damn good man and be done with it. Welcome to the frontier, Gentlemen…"

Then the Major being all business and 'military' said, "However, after saying your last words and before you load up, I would like the company's blacksmith and livestock man to take another gander at each and every animal you men are riding or packing. I hand-picked Steve "Cooter" Krentz as the American Fur Company's lead horse and blacksmith representative because he is one hell of a damn good livestock man in addition to possessing dynamic skills as a blacksmith. None of us can afford to lose a single animal on this trip, so before you saddle up or pack any of your animals today, I want Steve to examine each animal for saddle or pack sores, loose shoes or anything else that may cost us the health of an animal down the line. So with that in mind, let us get going because we have a fair piece to go this day and I mean to get there afore dark if at all possible. That and may the good Lord take a liking to Sterling. Now we are burning daylight, so let us get our livestock inspected by Cooter and hit the trail," continued Major Henry. That behavior the Major just exhibited in his commands to his men, he did so because of his military training and in order to rid the men of the shock they were feeling over the very real loss of a comrade. That and getting their minds back on the trail and into the needed frontier survival mode of thinking.

Later sitting there on their horses on the banks

of the Platte River near where Sterling had met his fate, Wallace, Otis, Oliver and Cedrick, each in his own way, said 'So Long' to their hapless younger brother. Then realizing they were holding up the column of trappers, turned their horses and pack animals westward and fell into line with the rest of the column of 'horseflesh and humanity'. However, that did not stop the many backward glances at that deadly spot of 'disappearance' in the Platte River by the rest of the Barnes Clan where their younger brother had met his Maker, as they traveled out of sight and into the rest of their new lives. Meanwhile downstream, a small fish-eating bird, a belted kingfisher, sat on the crown of a felt hat slowly floating down the shallow and slow-moving Platte River. Thereon, the kingfisher used his perch to aid him in his hunt for a stray and unwary breakfast minnow, ignorant of the lethal moment in time that had just given him his convenient floating perch...

For the next month-and-a-half, Major Henry and his band of trappers headed westward and then northward until they arrived at the Yellowstone River. Then they turned easterly and followed it until they arrived at its confluence where the Yellowstone met the mighty Missouri River. There Major Henry picked a spot that could easily be defended in the case of an Indian attack for the location of their small fort and trading post soon to be constructed. Typical of Major Henry, he once again organized his group of men into their specialties. Cooter Krentz organized a crew of men to level the ground for their new fort, as well as established a group of well-armed men to watch over and manage their horse and mule herd. The Barnes Clan, having come from a logging and lumbering family back in Tennessee, was organized into a timber-falling crew, while another group of men were responsible for, with the use of their mules, hauling the logs and cut timbers down to the new fort's location where a building crew began construction of their new home and fur trading post. By the end of August, the small fort had been constructed, all of their packs of provisions safely ensconced within its walls in storehouses, Cooter Krentz had his blacksmith shop up and running, and Major Henry was almost ready for business. But first things first, as Major Henry prepared to outfit his trapping parties so they could head out into the wilds, establish their base camps and then begin trapping beaver once the colder weather set in and the beaver came into their prime during the coming fall trapping season.

Come the 'anointed' day for the trappers to 'provision up' and make their individual group plans to head out into the backcountry, Major Henry gathered his company trappers all around him and outlined his plans. "Men, here are my plans for the organization of our trapping parties. To those of you who have organized yourselves into the largest parties of men for the protection it offers and economy of labors, I will have you provision up first. I do it this way because with larger parties of men, you have bigger needs and can better protect yourselves. With that, I want those groups to be able to travel the greatest distances out into the wilds to ascertain the beaver trapping opportunities now and for the future of this fur company."

"That being said, I will start alphabetically as we would do in the military with the Barnes Clan since they have four men in their group. For that group, I want them to trap a river almost due north of here coming out of Canada called the "Big Muddy". According to Vasquez's journals, an early fur trapper and trader in this area when he was here in '07-11, that Big Muddy River system is loaded with beaver. However as a word of caution, that river system is deep within Blackfeet Indian country and according to Vasquez's records, he did not trade with them, especially with firearms, because he felt they could not be trusted. As a result of those trading-denial actions on his part at his Fort Raymond trading post located where the Big Horn River meets the Yellowstone River, the Blackfeet are now hostile to all white men! That is why the four of you men from the Barnes Clan will be assigned to trap that area because you men will be better able to protect yourselves because of your numbers and good shooting abilities witnessed by me on our trip up here. Additionally, since you have such a distance to travel from here to get there if you head clear to the Canadian border, by outfitting you first, that gives you more time to get there, get a cabin built for the four of you and begin trapping before winter sets in. Oh, and one other thing. According to Old Man Vasquez, you might be confronted with other fur trappers coming down from Canada stealing what should be our beaver by trapping in our country. Those trappers will be working for the Hudson's Bay Company and are as cutthroat as they come when it comes to pushing us out and trapping in our country. Lastly, the Hudson's Bay Company according to Vasquez's notes, has a "Partisan" whom you may run across in trapping on the Big Muddy, especially on its upper reaches near the Canadian border. In case none of you are familiar with the term Partisan, that person is a Hudson's Bay Company leader on any kind of a field expedition such as a group of trappers at a rendezvous or large field trapping operation. Just for your information, this Partisan's name according to Vasquez's journal is "Pierre 'The Wolverine' La Gren" and he is meaner than a stepped-on snake in the hot sun! That Pierre La Gren fellow is reported to be the best rifle shot in all of Canada, is a master in the use of knives and tomahawks, and has no problem in using them against white trappers from the United States. In fact, it has been reported this Wolverine fellow is such a rifle shooter, he can split a playing card in half with his flintlock rifle with just one shot at 20 paces! So, I would suggest if any of you Barnes's get into a shootout with what you figure is this chap, you had best 'mind' yourselves by shooting first and asking questions later! That is all of the information I have for you four for now. However, once I have a chance to read Vasquez's field notes in more detail, I will have more definitive information for the four of you if I find any information relative to your trapping area on the Big Muddy. Now, I suggest you get over to our storehouse and provision-up before everything you might need is all gone once these other trappers are turned loose to provision up as well," continued Major Henry.

Heeding Major Henry's advice, the four Barnes brothers headed over to the storehouse holding most of the fort's provisions to be utilized by the American Fur Company's contract trappers. Led by older brother Wallace, the natural leader of the group and former fur trapper back in Tennessee, the four brothers trooped into the warehouse and hooked up with a fur company Clerk. Following that, they began the process of selecting enough provisions for the four of them to last for what they figured would be the better part of a year. Since Wallace was the only experienced family trapper, the rest of the brothers opted to let him take the lead in shopping for what he figured they would need just as long as they could chime in every now and then with suggestions as they saw the need.

That leadership issue settled, Wallace first led the brothers over to that portion of the fort's warehouse holding all the shooting accessories. There Wallace selected four eight-pound sheet lead, corked, airtight canisters holding four pounds each of DuPont's best FFg gunpowder valued at $1.50 per pound of powder. By picking that known brand and powder size, that powder could be used for either their rifles or their big bore pistols. As it turned out, Wallace had selected such pure lead powder-holding airtight and waterproof containers for several reasons. First of all, they were airtight and waterproof which was necessary for the life and full strength of anyone using black powder. Second of all, when empty, the sheet lead containers could be melted down and cast into additional balls for their weapons. Then he picked up an additional 20 one-pound metal tins of Du Pont's best FFg powder (coarse grain), which were easier to carry in one's 'Possibles bag' on a daily basis, and another 20 one-pound tins of DuPont FFFFg (fine grain) for the priming mechanisms (striker pans) for their rifles and pistols. When he did, his brothers gave him the looks of "why so much" powder? Turning, Wallace said, "The Major advised we are going into the country of the white man-hating Blackfeet Indians. That being the case, I don't want to lose my life because I am out of rifle powder in a fight." The questioning looks from his three brothers' faces quickly disappeared with those words of survival wisdom being uttered. Then Wallace selected 50 pounds of lead pigs and 400 precast lead balls in caliber .54 for their rifles and pistols at $1 per pound. He selected the precast lead balls selected because it would be some time before the men had the time to sit down, melt some of their lead pigs and cast more rifle balls. And since they were going into the country of the deadly Blackfeet almost immediately, well… Walking over to the next section of the warehouse, Wallace selected two pig lead smelting kettles and three bullet casting mold blocks, caliber .54, at $4 each. As he did and looking at the prices the fur company was charging, Wallace just shook his head in disbelief. Otis had been right earlier when he had questioned the fur company's contract requiring the trappers to buy only from the American Fur Company at their prices. The fur company's prices were higher than a 'dog's back in a three-way cat fight' he grimaced, running at what he had been told by Major Henry at a 700-1,000% profit over the prices in the St. Louis area for the very same items because of the costs of getting such items safely out onto the frontier! By now, Wallace could see that his brothers were not challenging any of his selections. That was because they were beginning to realize that where they were going to trap beaver may mean they would have to fight their ways in and out in order to be successful and live to tell about it! Additionally, in order to make a go of it by their own means, they may also have to fight like wildcats just in order to even stay in country once there! But Wallace knew the Barnes Clan had one important thing going for each of them. Their dad had demanded that each son become a 'crack' rifle and pistol shooter when they were growing up, based on what he had seen during his previous Creek Indian War experience as a soldier. To date, Wallace also knew as a result of their earlier training with firearms, it would not be wise to stand in front of any of the Barnes Clan if they were shooting at you.

Then Wallace moved over to the next counter where he selected an ample supply of gun worms or wipers, ball screws, extra parts for replacing the locks on their flintlock rifles or pistols in case some were damaged in a fight or horse wreck, tools to repair their firearms, extra powder horns for each brother, twelve canisters of patches, extra ramrods for their rifles in case any were broken while afield, and a number of fire steels and flints because they were easily lost or misplaced. As he continued selecting provisions needed to survive for a period of a year for four men, Wallace no longer looked at the Mountain Prices being charged. He just figured he would let the Clerk following them around recording what he selected continue to do so, hoping he and his brothers would be able to trap enough beaver to pay for what they needed and were in the process of selecting for purchase.

Walking over to a log walled-in bin filled to overflowing with beaver traps, Wallace passed on by. Then turning because he could once again see the inquiring looks on his brothers' faces as to why he had passed on the beaver traps since they were there to trap beaver, Wallace said, "We normally would only need about six to eight traps per trapper. Since each of us has already been issued six traps of the St. Louis-style of beaver traps, those are all that we will need as a group. Where we are going, we will need two of you sitting on your horses providing protection for the two of us designated as trappers for the group in the water or on the ground. That in mind, we already have a total of 24 company-provided beaver traps to set or re-set on a daily basis. That should be more than enough for us to catch a world of beaver if they are there in the numbers on the Big Muddy as the Major has reported. However, we will need three spools of wire with which to tie our traps to our anchor poles out in the deeper waters, and Otis if you will, grab that many and set them over next to our pile of selections. Besides, just catching the beaver is only half the work. Then we have to skin them out on-site, take their pelts back to our cabin and remove any fat or meat still remaining on the skins. Then we have to gather in a mess of green willow limbs, so we can make hoops in which to stretch the fresh pelts so they can dry and be made ready to fold and transport back to the fort to sell, so we can pay off our debt for all of these provisions. That as well as set aside some money so when we return to civilization, we can purchase some land and settle down once we tire of being fur trappers, or just 'plumb' wear out. Now I think all of you can see that with the traps we have and if we have any luck in catching beaver, we will have more than enough to do with the complement of traps we now possess."

Then Wallace walked over to the trap section holding all the other kinds of traps from the small-in-size marten traps to the giant toothed, evil-looking bear traps saying, "However, we do need ten of these Newhouse #14 wolf traps. Once we freeze out in our beaver trapping operations come winter, we will be pulling our traps and waiting until spring comes along and the ice goes out once again. That means our winter is free to hunt and trap wolves, which will bring us a pretty penny back at the fort come our summer get-together. I plan on buffalo hunting for the meat during the winter and using what is left of their carcasses to set our wolf traps around. That way we can add to what we take and increase our money returns once we sell all of our furs."

Moving on to another section of the warehouse, Wallace turned and said to Cedrick, "Cedrick, since you are the designated cook in the bunch because you always were the best family cook followed by Otis, you need to select out what we will need in the way of cooking implements." With that, Wallace stepped aside and let Cedrick move into the cooking section of the warehouse.

Standing there for a few moments letting his eyes scan the assortment of goods lying before him, Cedrick finally made his move like a man on a mission. A man on a mission because he knew his brothers were all eager eaters and if he made a mistake here and did not select the right kinds and numbers of cooking implements, he would never hear the end of it!

Then without any hesitation, Cedrick selected six sheet iron kettles at $2 per pound, three six-quart Dutch ovens at $3 each, three sets of cooking irons to hang cooking pots over an open fire at S2 each, and eight metal cooking rods used to skewer and hold chunks of meat over an open fire at $1 each. Those selections were quickly followed by selecting an assortment of stirring spoons, steel plates, coffee cups, bowls, forks, knives, eating spoons, wash pans, three 16" cast iron, three-legged frying pans, and two large two-gallon coffee pots, all priced for a total of $16. Then as an afterthought, Cedrick also selected a number of fire starting steels even though some had been already set aside in their pile of soon to be purchased items. Finally Cedrick 'ran down' on his cooking implement selections needed to care for his brothers' needs, nodded his head that he was done with what he figured he would need, and stepped aside.

Then Wallace, after looking around a bit like he was looking for something in particular, he led his brothers to another implements section and turning to Otis said, "Odie, you need to select what we will need to build our cabin, cut wood, use to split the chest and pelvis of a buffalo or elk when butchering, and the like." Without a word, Otis, the best builder in the family, stepped forward and selected two square-nosed shovels, two four-foot-long single buck saws, three heavy axes, six files, two heavy duty hammers, a smaller rip saw, a 25-pound keg of long nail spikes for cabin building, a six-pound maul for wood splitting, and a 20-foot heavy logging chain for log hauling behind a team of horses, all for $18.

Those selections out of the way, Wallace headed for the next section of the warehouse which garnered a huge smile on his weathered face. At first it was apparent that Wallace did not approve of the quality of what he was looking at as he stood there, all 6'-4" in height and frowning the whole time. Then he said, "THERE THEY ARE!" Picking up his pace in excitement, Wallace walked over and pointed to a section of knives on display saying, "Look at that bunch of knives over there, boys. Those are the kind of knives we need to carry as sheath knives and use for general work. Those are some of the best butcher and scalper knives made from the finest Sheffield steel the English have to offer! Remember, boys, a trapper always has a need for a good knife or knives that are style-wise country made, heavy duty enough for chopping, yet small enough to be used as a 'scalper' or general purpose knife. Those Thomas

Wilson knives we are looking at are some of the best ever made! I am going to pick out a number of these knives, namely for skinning, butchering and what I call cooking knives. Good knives of this quality are essential to a trapper and if the truth be known, equally as valuable to an Indian as well." With that and much evident enthusiasm, Wallace gathered up a number of fleshing, butchering, sheath and general purpose knives for the group to use during their everyday duties. Then he spotted another shelf holding a number of specialty knives. "Well, lookee-here! I am also going to take three of this type of knife. I will have Cooter Krentz our blacksmith and in fact from what I have observed, is an artisan as well, get him to grind these three knives so the bevel is only on one side of the knife for the purpose of safely skinning out the beaver we catch. That way with that type of blade configuration, that will reduce the danger of 'holing' our fresh pelts which will subtract from their values back here at the fort," exclaimed Wallace. With that, Wallace gathered up three of the knives he wanted re-ground as well as three butcher's steels and four heavy whetstones in order to help keep the edges on their knives and other edged instruments when in use.

Following that at Wallace's request, the Clerk led the men over to the extensive clothing and blankets section of the warehouse. At that section of the warehouse, Wallace picked out eight two-and-a-half point blankets at $7 each, 16 horse blankets at $6 each (figuring his group would be riding or packing at least a total of 16 horses), eight heavy woolen capotes at $5 each for the men's use in extreme winter weather, blue cloth at $4 a yard for clothing repairs, and four heavy woolen blankets for more clothing repairs or as use for extra coverage around one's shoulders in the extreme winter weather expected in the northern latitudes in which the men would be working (little did he realize buffalo robes worked better). Then Wallace selected two dozen pairs of wool socks making sure they fit his brothers, two pairs of heavy gloves each and then he surprised the brothers with his next selections. Walking over to a bin full of buckskin leggings, he selected two pair that even fit his big, long-legged frame. Then he had Cedrick pick out two pairs as well. Seeing Cedrick's questioning looks on his face, Wallace explained, "Since I have trapped beaver before, I will be our group's main beaver trapper. However, if something happens to me where I cannot trap beaver any longer, it will fall to you Cedrick, to continue our trapping program. The reason we have selected leggings is because it is easier to wear those when we are waist deep in the water running and setting our traps. Additionally, we will need to fashion ourselves several breechclouts to wear as well when we are beaver trapping. Then when we exit the cold water and mud, we can change out into our regular warmer clothing and let our leggings and breech-clouts dry out as we ride back to camp." Lastly, Wallace picked out eight "Linsey-woolsy" shirts for his brothers and himself.

The brothers, knowing from living and working out on the farm, gave questioning looks at their older brother over the purchase of English-made shirts. English-made shirts that had a reputation for wearing out fast under heavy outdoor use. Wallace just grinned over his brothers' questioning looks then replied, "These shirts will be worn during the summer months when the wearing of buckskin shirts will be too hot to wear. Additionally, these same shirts will be worn underneath our buckskin shirts during the winter months for the added warmth they will bring." With those explanations, Wallace could see the questioning looks fast disappearing off his brothers' faces. Lastly, Wallace went to a shelf holding a variety of hats. There at his bidding, each of the men selected an additional wide-brimmed felt hat to wear in the summer months, in addition to several kinds of heavy fur hats with ear flaps needed for the colder weather yet to come when working in the northern latitudes, especially when out trapping wolves.

Then it was off to another part of the warehouse where Cedrick, Otis and Oliver began making food and cooking provision selections that would have to hold the four brothers for almost a year without chance of re-supply. There the two men selected 40 pounds of brown sugar at $1 a pound, three 50-pound bags of green coffee beans at $1.25 per pound (needed to be cooked or charred in the bottom of a Dutch oven and then ground before making good coffee), 20 pounds of raisins at $1.25 per pound, and on it went for the anticipated needed amounts of flour, salt, black pepper, red pepper flakes, dried beans, rice, other cooking spices like their mother, Martha, had used, cinnamon, three jugs of honey, steel moccasin awls, spools of thread, spurs, spool of brass wire for repairing cracked gunstocks, bolts of gray cloth for clothing repair, six kegs of Fourth Proof rum, iron buckles, leather strapping for repairing packs, pack saddles, panniers for their packhorses, 100' spool of cotton lead rope, more fire steels (easily lost or broken), dried fruit, two bags of hard candy, washing soap, straight razors, (Author's Note: Contrary to belief, most Mountain Men shaved. There was a head lice epidemic in the general population in those days and by shaving, that kept the head louse habitat on one's body to a minimum), shaving soap, several tins of bag balm to treat pack and saddle sores on animals from rubbing leather gear and as applications for all minor injuries to humans, two crocks of bear grease (cooking base used in Dutch ovens when making biscuits), and finally, 12 "carrots" of James River chewing and smoking tobacco (Author's Note: Tobacco in those days in order to facilitate easy measurement for valuation and safe travel when packed in horse or mule packs, was tightly rolled and wrapped with a heavy twine until the lump of rolled tobacco resembled a long, large wrapped carrot weighing about three pounds). Satisfied all of the goods purchased, augmented with buffalo, elk, bear and deer meat, would carry the four men from the Barnes Clan for the year afield, they gathered up their provisions and left the fort's warehouse. As such, all provision costs were kept on the books and if the trappers survived their time in the field, their lot of beaver skins trapped during that first season would be levied against their previous fall's provision bill. However, if they failed to survive, their initial cost of such provision acquisitions were 'eaten' by the American Fur Company.

Then at Cooter Krentz's earlier bidding, the Barnes Clan led all of their horses over to the new blacksmith shop and there Krentz and his helpers removed their old horseshoes and replaced them with new shoes for the coming year's trapping ventures. Also while the men's horses were there, Steve checked all of their teeth and 'floated' those which needed to have their teeth floated. Then Wallace approached Krentz and had him regrind the three skinning knives he had specially purchased so there would only be a bevel on one side of the knife to facilitate safer skinning of the beaver pelts by Cedrick, who was also the designated one to skin all trapped beaver while in the field.

When the Barnes Clan was all through shopping for the provisions they figured they needed for the coming trapping seasons and having all of their horse herd looked after by Cooter Krentz, the company Clerk advised the men they 'were into the company' for $866.33½ cents! At first the men blanched over such high costs for the small amount of goods they had purchased and for goods that were generally of a cheaper quality than they could purchase in St. Louis! That grumbling carried on until the company Clerk pointed out a thing or two to the four men. With a big grin over the men's reaction to the high costs of the items purchased, the Clerk pointed out to the men that a First Class Beaver *"Plus"* (pronounced 'plew') or "Made Beaver" was bringing around $6 that year! That and the Big Muddy's waterways into which the Barnes Clan had been assigned for beaver trapping, were reportedly crawling with the large-in-size furry rodents. With that 'down-to-earth' information coming forth, the 'hackles' went down on the Barnes Clan and were replaced with wide grins knowing and having faith in their abilities to produce a quality work product based on their historical work ethics and a little bit of the 'good ole' Irish luck! (Author's Note: A Made Beaver was a measurement and medium of exchange at most trading posts. A Made Beaver was a prime quality skin from an adult beaver. In most trading posts and at later rendezvous, it was considered a standard unit of trade. For example, ten Made Beaver could be used to purchase one Indian Trade rifle, or a keg of Fourth Class rum. Or one Made Beaver could trade for 1½ pounds of powder, a hatchet, a good coat, a brass kettle or two pounds of cone sugar or the like.)

The following day, the Barnes brothers were up at four in the morning filling their packs with all the goods and supplies they had selected from the warehouse the day before so they would be ready for loading on the horses. It wasn't until around the noon hour that they had finally completed their tasks. Covering their packs against the afternoon thunderstorms with tanned deerskins, the brothers spent the rest of the day tipping cups of rum and celebrating with a number of Ashley's Hundred full well knowing the next time they gathered together, there would be less than a 100 of them because of the nature of the business they were in and the odds of survival they were facing out on the often times dangerous frontier facing hostile Indians, horse wrecks, drowning, grizzly bears, freezing to death, and even starvation…

CHAPTER THREE

TRAPPING THE "BIG MUDDY"

COME THE DAY AND HOUR OF DEPAR-
TURE for the Big Muddy River by the Barnes
Clan, Major Henry walked out to the standing
there quietly ready to leave caravan of brothers
and gathered them in closer towards him with
a wave of his hand. Standing alongside the four
Barnes men, Major Henry once again advised that
they should be more than careful in the country
into which they were now going to trap beaver.
With that cautionary, he reminded the men of
the extreme Blackfeet menace throughout the
area in which they would be trapping and then
paused. Looking up at Wallace, the designated
leader of the group of men, Henry said, "Wallace,
best also watch out for that French-Canadian
fellow named Pierre 'The Wolverine' La Gren,

especially if you lads end up trapping on the extreme northern reaches of the Big Muddy near the border of Canada. According to Manuel Vasquez's ledgers and reports that I just finished reading derived from some of his trappers reports upon their return from the field, a number of his company men paid dearly for not heeding Vasquez's earlier warnings about that "La Gren" fella. In two of his reports, Vasquez advised that La Gren sneaked into and robbed the cabins of several of his trappers of not only all of their furs but the rest of their much-needed provisions as well. This he had done while those trappers were afield running their trap lines. La Gren did so Vasquez figured, in order to run off his Hudson's Bay Company's beaver trapping competition from the Americans. So keep a sharp eye peeled because after that quicksand episode on the Platte with Sterling, I don't need to lose another of you Barnes's," grumbled an obviously concerned Major Henry over his pretty much 'green' crew of company trappers.

With a nod of his head in acknowledgment over the Major's warnings about La Gren and a wave of his arm, the men saddled up and moments later, Wallace led the Barnes Clan out from Major Henry's small fort and trading post into what was to become an adventure of a lifetime. Continuing north and then westerly as they had been instructed by the Major, the men first traveled along the southern edge of the Missouri River. Keeping an eye out for the confluence of the Big Muddy where it entered into the Missouri from its northern side of the river, that point of travel was finally reached. Sure as Major Henry had advised his men, the very first river they ran across draining into the northern side of the Missouri would be the Big Muddy River, as had been described to the Major in the Vasquez's journals. Stopping for the night along the south side of the Missouri opposite the confluence of the Big Muddy, the men's horses were unpacked, checked for any pack or saddle soring developed during the day's travels, double hobbled and let out to water and graze in the river bottomland's rich grasses under Oliver's watchful eyes. As Cedrick set up their camp, Otis and Wallace began sawing down a number of dead trees in the area in preparation for making a log raft in order to be able to cross to the northern side of the Missouri River. Two days later, the log raft had been completed and the men in shifts had safely paddled across all of their supplies, saddles and packs to the northern bank of the Missouri River. Then a final trip was made crossing the Missouri with Oliver, naked as a baby bird, riding one of their horses bareback and 'swimming' the rest of their herd of horses across, as the other three brothers paddled their raft alongside the horses shouting encouragement until all were safely across and on the northern side. Then the brothers, with the help of a team of horses, dragged their log raft up high onto the northern shore and tied it onto a tree above the flood plain so they would have it to use upon their return during the following year's summer months en route the fort and trading post, hopefully with a load of valuable furs.

That first evening the men made their camp on the western side of the Big Muddy River and ever-mindful of Major Henry's Blackfeet warnings, camped in the riverside's deep brush fields where they were out of sight from the wandering eyes of any Indian buffalo hunters or war parties. There the horses were picketed and double hobbled once again to prevent easy Indian theft of their valuable life-giving herd, camp was set up and Cedrick began preparing their evening meal of coffee, Dutch oven biscuits and the last of their buffalo meat hung over the open flame of the fire on steel roasting irons to merrily roast away.

For the next five days, the brothers headed almost due north as they traveled alongside the western side of the Big Muddy looking over the beaver trapping opportunities along the way. Then each evening, camp was once again made along the Big Muddy in the riverside's dense brush fields to avoid any problems with all of the reported, mean as a bunch of stepped-on snakes, Blackfeet Indians. However, throughout each day's travels, only lots of unshod pony tracks were seen as evidence of the Indians being in the area hunting buffalo. But plenty unshod pony tracks did they see as a reminder that they were deep in Blackfeet Indian country! As the men continued traveling northward, they observed tremendous evidence of beaver activity in the forms of beaver slides, cut down trees, beaver houses, numerous beaver dams and beaver actively building even more dams, along with many signs of swimming beaver even during the daylight hours! Additionally, the men encountered numerous herds of buffalo at every turn in the trail, vast herds of antelope, numerous prairie wolves following the buffalo herds, a small number of grizzly bears, and herds of lordly elk scattered throughout the prairies. (Author's Note: Elk were originally a numerous prairie grassland species in the early years of the American West and found all the way across the country into many of the eastern states. As a highly desirable big game species and major source of protein in the eastern states, they were quickly shot out of existence. As for the prairie-loving species of elk, heavy hunting pressures from the Indians and later the settlers eventually drove those elk from the prairies into the rugged mountain chains found in the western United States where they primarily reside today. Today in a number of eastern states that were originally home to the elk, they have since been successfully reintroduced with some hunting seasons now being allowed.)

Finding the northern prairies a veritable animals' paradise, the Barnes Clan delightfully feasted every night on a different species of game animal for their suppers. But when game was killed, only Otis, the clan's best shooter, killed game for each of their suppers. His sure eye and shooting ability allowed for only one shot to be heard in case the dreaded Blackfeet were nearby. That way the group figured there would be less interest in the sounds of only one shot being heard versus many. However, meat from the buffalo soon proved out to be the group's favorite and most preferred type of meat, cooked medium rare of course…

Finally near the location of modern day Plentywood, Montana, the brothers stopped their northward exploratory migration along the Big Muddy looking for the best beaver trapping grounds upon which to build their cabin nearby and make ready to begin their fall beaver trapping operations. Seeing so many signs of heavy beaver infestation along the many waterways, in awe they had continued traveling into the very upper reaches of the Big Muddy to see where all the activity would end. In so doing, they finally found themselves just somewhere slightly below where they figured ran the Canadian border! Throughout their earlier travels along the Big Muddy, the men figured the beaver sign was so promising that they would go as far north as possible. Once there, then would stop and make their camp so they could begin trapping beaver in that location. Then once that extreme northern area was trapped out, they figured the following year they would start lower on the Big Muddy and trap out the lower portion of that heavily beaver-laden river as well. That way for the coming two years, they could trap in familiar country, harvest out the beaver and still not have far to travel to Major Henry's fort and trading post at the confluence of the Yellowstone and Missouri Rivers in order to sell their furs and re-supply. Little did the brothers realize that ever since they had left the fort, that facility had been almost under constant attack by the Arikara Indians, not wanting to suffer any fur trade competition with the white men. That and from the Blackfeet Indians just not wanting the white men trespassing on the sacred lands of their forefathers for any reason after Vasquez had denied them trading privileges with his company's first trading post located at Fort Raymond years earlier.

Pulling their pack strings into a heavy grove of cottonwood trees later one afternoon not far from the Big Muddy River, Wallace stopped the brothers and just sat there on his horse thoughtfully looking around. All around him were numerous small herds of feeding and resting buffalo using the shade of the nearby cottonwoods and relaxing alongside a small stream running out from the foothills and eventually into the Big Muddy. Additionally, all around him were just the criteria of what he had been looking for in a potential campsite. Right off the bat to his way of thinking, there was plenty of cover for building a cabin off the beaten path and mostly out of sight from any casually passing Indians. Importantly, there was an abundant supply of water in the little stream running through the nearby meadow upon which a cabin could be built close at hand. There also appeared to be plenty of good grazing in the surrounding area for their large horse herd if the feeding herds of buffalo were any kind of indicator. Then shifting his weight in his saddle and looking around even more closely, Wallace noticed that there was a good cabin site at the head of the draw with plenty of room for a near-by horse corral that would also be pretty much out of sight once constructed. Then looking even more closely at the surrounding terrain, there appeared to be plenty of nearby firewood and the entire area was sheltered from the northwest winds from whence came many of the worst storms in the northern latitudes by heavy stands of timber and several long ridgelines.

"Here is where I suggest we build our cabin and horse corral next to this little stream. We are not far from what looks like one hell of a lot of damn good beaver trapping, there is plenty of nearby timber for building our cabin, not to mention plenty of horse graze with firewood close at hand and in good supply. I say we set down our roots in this location and get busy making our new home 'ship-shape' and livable before the winter weather finds us. What do you think, my brothers?" asked Wallace, as he turned in his saddle and faced his kin looking for their replies. When he did, he could see that they were also giving the location a good 'look-see' as to the possibility of that becoming their next 'home place' as well.

Otis was the first brother to respond to Wallace's question about the campsite's possibilities, quietly saying, "Looks good to me. Plus there is a lot of nearby right-sized timber for us to build our cabin in such a location that it would be out of the way of most anyone passing by. Additionally in so doing, the saw-timber we need to remove in order to build our cabin will not reduce our 'cabin cover' that much either, based on the lay of the land and the other stands of nearby timber. Your choice looks pretty good to me, my brother."

After a pause and looking around some, Cedrick said, "If we put our cabin next to that small bluff of rocks, that would give me a great place to build our outside campfire area where it will be out from the north wind and immediately adjacent to our front door opening. That way you 'galoots' wouldn't have so far to walk to get your chow or warm up by the campfire."

Oliver, being one of the better shooters of the brothers and the quietest and most introspective of the bunch, just quietly looked around, finally saying, "Sure gives us a great field of fire if we build our cabin by that bluff of rocks, plus we can keep a good eye on our horse corral if we were to put it over there by that small stand of pine trees."

"Then it is agreed. Here we will put down our roots for better or worse and call this our home for the coming months," said Wallace, as he stood up in his stirrups and continued looking intently all around his place of choice as if to validate his decision as the group's leader.

With that, the men tiredly dismounted after their many hours in the saddle and rubbed their sore knees from their legs being carried at an awkward angle for such a long time in the stirrups. Then the brothers led their pack string over to the nearby stand of pines, unloaded the packs from their horses and arranged them in a defensive circle around the base of the trees for the protection that offered against any surprise Indian attack. As they then watered their horses in the small stream, the men checked them for any sores caused by the packs, hobbled them and let them out to graze in and among the nearby cottonwoods. By so doing, the life-giving and valuable horse herd could be closely watched by the rest of the brothers even as they busied themselves about. As the rest of his brothers tended to the horses, Cedrick walked over to where he figured they would build their cabin, paced off the distance from the soon to be front of their cabin site to his cooking area, and with his shovel began digging his outdoor firepit. Once the pit was dug to Cedrick's satisfaction, the brothers began hauling in rocks from the nearby streambed in order to build a proper fire and Dutch oven cooking area. Then as Otis and Oliver began hauling in firewood that lay scattered about under the trees, Cedrick and Wallace began hauling over to the firepit their cast iron frying pans, a coffee pot, two Dutch ovens, steel hanging rods, and individual roasting steels. Then after he had assembled and dug in his hanging irons, Cedrick built a fire so he could have some coals later on in which to use his Dutch ovens to make the men's favorite meal item, namely biscuits. As he did, Wallace picked up his rifle and walked off into the timber behind their campsite like a man on a mission. Within minutes Wallace had quietly disappeared into the surrounding pine trees and sagebrush like he had never even been there...

Twenty minutes later, a single shot was heard from his rifle and about 30 minutes later, Wallace walked off from the small foothill behind their potential cabin site dragging a freshly killed mule deer doe. "Hear you go, Cedrick. See if you can work your magic on this," said a happily grinning Wallace as he dragged the deer alongside the firepit and laid it down. Then Wallace ducked a handful of elk turds playfully tossed at him by a very pleased Cedrick over his brother's 'meaty gift' for their supper. Later that evening when Oliver, Wallace and Otis were bringing in their horse herd and tying them off onto a makeshift picket line strung between two trees, Cedrick made the last minute adjustments to his supper and then with a low whistle, summoned his now tired brothers to their evening meal of coffee, biscuits and chunks of venison backstrap roasted over an open fire. As the men dragged in their saddles to act as temporary chairs around the campfire, Cedrick ladled onto their plates heaping mounds of freshly roasted venison, medium rare of course as most trappers liked their meats, two biscuits each and a cup of black tar looking-like coffee. Without a word, the tired brothers sat down and feasted. The quiet around the campfire that evening was interrupted only by the smell of something glorious baking away in one of Cedrick's other Dutch ovens, namely more biscuits, loaded with raisins and covered with now crystalizing brown sugar, nutmeg and cinnamon! Glorious smelling sweet biscuits that Cedrick had made special in his Dutch ovens for his brothers in celebration of their locating a new home site and the very real beginning of their new life style. Later that evening after enjoying a cup of rum and a smoke in their pipes around their campfire, the four men adjourned to their circle of packs, sleeping blankets and saddles now hauled back from the firepit area to act as 'pillows', and one by one, they tiredly drifted off to sleep.

The next morning, Otis, Oliver and Wallace awoke to the rustling of pots and pans around the campfire, as Cedrick filled one sheet iron kettle with water and a mess of pinto beans to soak. He followed that by taking another kettle loaded with dried rice, filled it with water to soak and fluff up as well for their coming supper. As for breakfast, the smell of brewing coffee filled the air and competed for the attention of the men's noses with the smells of freshly baking Dutch oven biscuits and roasting venison. Soon everyone had rolled out from their blankets, were streamside washing up, shaving and looking their best under the circumstances, all the while, hungry as a 'team of mules after pulling loads of heavy logs out from the forest all day long'…

Breakfast went quickly that morning as the men realized they were now 'burning daylight' when it came to getting the day's work done. As Cedrick cleaned up the breakfast pots and pans around the campfire, Otis and Wallace, being the two stoutest of the brothers, each sporting a four-foot-long single buck saw laid over their shoulders and a rifle in hand, headed up behind their bluff of rocks and onto the adjacent timbered foothills. Soon the sound of their saws could be heard, followed shortly thereafter with the crashing of falling pine and Douglas fir trees. As for Oliver, he was busy at the proposed cabin site with a square-nosed shovel scraping the ground down to the mineral soil layer in order to make a level pad satisfactory for a cabin's floor with wall logs soon to be laid upon. Once Oliver was finished and Cedrick was squared away with his duties as camp cook, those two men with rifles in one hand and long-handled axes in the other, headed for the sounds of the two sawyers sweating away with their single buck saws dropping the logs needed for their new cabin. Moments later, the sounds of saws were seconded with the ringing of axes removing the limbs from the recently felled trees slated for building a cabin large enough to comfortably hold four fairly good-sized men, up to a year's worth of supplies and hopefully eventually numerous bundles of valuable beaver pelts.

When the sun was high, Cedrick returned to his firepit, drained the water off his previously soaking pinto beans and added more clean water to the pot. After that, into that pot went various amounts of black pepper, red pepper flakes, which aside from their unique flavor brought to bean dishes, helped keep the men 'regular' along with several handfuls of just recently discovered on the rocky hillside and dug up, delicate tasting wild onions. Then that bean pot was set on the coals at the edge of the fire to slowly cook. Finished with that chore, the pot of rice water was also drained off, reloaded with several handfuls of dried raisins so they could plump up, cinnamon, nutmeg, a cup of rum, a handful of brown sugar, and more fresh water, all of which was set on the edge of the coals to slowly simmer away in a cast iron pot as a supper dessert. A supper desert that was designed to satisfy the 'sweet tooth' desires of all of his brothers.

Following that, Cedrick returned to the 'timber crew', now leading two horses pulling a logging chain. Soon, the first of the logs cut to lengths for the walls, began coming down off the foothills and decked near the proposed cabin site. Each time Cedrick brought in a number of logs, he took the time to add more firewood and water to his slowly cooking bean pot, along with a stir or two when tending to his sugary raisin and rice creation. Then back up onto the hill for another set of logs cut to length for their cabin. One hour of hauling later, Cedrick added more wood to the fire to replenish the coals slow cooking the beans and rice dishes, only that time, fresh chunks of venison were added to the bean pot, stirred in and soon great smells began filling the air as more and more logs came off the hillside and were laid near the future cabin site.

Come the late afternoon, Cedrick brought down another set of logs and after being hobbled, let all of their horses off their picket line so they could water and graze. Then it was back to the firepit to add more wood, pre-heat his Dutch ovens and smear their insides with some bear grease from an earthenware jug for his biscuits to come. Their coffee pot full of water was then set on a hanging iron to boil, as Cedrick took another of his steel kettles, shoveled in several handfuls of green coffee beans and roasted the same over the coals. When the beans had been roasted, into another empty Dutch oven they went and were carefully crushed with a flat river rock so they could be placed into the coffee pot for the final brewing that was to follow. By now, Cedrick's firepit smelled not only heavenly but sent those odors to the Heavens, as the tired logging crew now came off the hill and headed for their campsite stream for a long drink and to wash up for what portended to be a great-smelling supper. After a supper feast, a cup of rum for what ailed them and a pipe full of aromatic smelling James River tobacco, four tired men headed for their sleeping area and a good night's rest for tomorrow portended of another long and hard day sawing down and cutting logs to length for their new cabin and the placement of the same...

Two weeks later found the cabin walls up, a front door and two window openings cut out, and the building roofed in and covered with almost two feet of soil. Soil of which was added to reduce any threat of fire from an attack by the Blackfeet, extra insulation during the coming winter weather and protection from the rains and melting snows. Additionally, the postholes had been dug, corral posts had been set, the rails strung and a hell-for-stout meat pole now hung in the nearby grove of pine trees capable of holding two elk or one buffalo. Additionally, two sets of smoking racks had been constructed adjacent their cabin so their tender could keep the birds and bears away while the meat was being processed into great tasting jerky for later use when out on the trail. Following that, additional dead trees had been dropped, hauled down adjacent the cabin and while more trees were being cut, Otis sawed those logs already hauled into shorter lengths, then split and stacked the wood for future fires in either the inside fireplace or the outdoor firepit. He then cut four of the biggest logs in circumference into short lengths and hauled them with brute force over to the firepit where they were positioned around as sitting logs for the men to sit upon. Sit upon as they ate or just sat around the outside fire during nicer weather with a cup of rum in hand, a pipe full of James River tobacco, all in the company of the ever-present swarms of mosquitoes of course…

As the summer days grew 'long in the tooth' and the weather began turning colder, one morning found three of the brothers hauling in all of their packs and provisions into the now completely finished large cabin for safer keeping away from the rodents, insects, bears and always willing to chew on everything leather tasting of salty sweat, porcupines. Cedrick on the other hand, busied himself with the camp cook's duties until breakfast was ready. Following the end of breakfast, Cedrick announced that he was fresh out of meat and unless they went hunting, they were down to biscuits and beans for their next set of meals.

Later that morning found the four brothers afield with three of their packhorses carrying panniers alongside three recently killed buffalo and butchering out the same. Later back at camp, the men began boning out much of the meat. A large portion of which was cut it into inch-thin strips and hung on the meat smoking racks after being properly salted and peppered to the men's taste. Then while Cedrick watched the smoking fire to make sure it didn't get too hot and cook the meat on the smoking racks, the rest of the brothers went forth, cut down and brought back to their campsite more mountain mahogany wood appropriate for the smoking of the meat just brought in and for future meat smoking details.

While Cedrick prepared the men's evening meal of buffalo meat, beans and biscuits that afternoon, Oliver, Wallace and Otis adjourned to their cabin and began drilling holes into its inside walls and installing wooden pegs onto which to hang dry goods and other items up off the floor. Following that, the brothers built bedframes strung with rope webbing so the men would not have to sleep on the cold and damp dirt floor. Finally the next day, Wallace, the brothers' best carpenter next to Otis, put the finishing touches on a set of log chairs and a table he had been working on during his spare moments ever since the cabin's initial construction had begun. Tables and chairs which were to be used while inside the cabin during inclement winter weather.

As the three brothers hammered and banged away inside the cabin the following day, Cedrick prepared the biscuit dough for their supper and adjusted the cooking irons holding large chunks of fresh buffalo meat roasting over a low fire. He then walked over to their stream, filled the coffee pot with fresh water and then walked back to his campfire to tend to the skewered and cooking buffalo meat. After roasting and grinding the green coffee beans, Cedrick loaded the crushed product into their two-gallon coffee pot. The pot was then set over the hottest part of the fire to bring it to a rapid boil because his supper was almost ready and without hot coffee for every meal, he knew his brothers would grumble like 'smashed cats'.

Once the coffee came to a rolling boil, Cedrick pulled it off from the lower hanging irons and prepared to hang it onto a higher hanging iron in order to reduce the boil and let its contents cool down somewhat for drinking. Just as he did, he became aware of some unusual movement catching his eyes in the meadow below their camp and looking up, was surprised to see an INDIAN LEVELING HIS INDIAN TRADE RIFLE RIGHT AT HIM FROM JUST ABOUT 20 FEET AWAY! CAUGHT OFF GUARD AND STANDING UP IN COMPLETE SURPRISE WHILE HOLDING THE COFFEE POT HIGH IN HAND IN FRONT

OF HIM, CEDRICK SAW IN ALMOST SLOW MOTION SMOKE ERUPTING FROM THE END OF THE INDIAN'S RIFLE BARREL AND THEN HIS ENTIRE WORLD LITERALLY EXPLODED!

WHAM! WENT THE INDIAN'S BULLET RIGHT INTO CEDRICK'S CHEST! BUT NOT BEFORE SMASHING INTO AND DRIVING CLEAR THROUGH THE FULL STEEL COFFEE POT, BLOWING UP ITS TWO GALLONS OF BOILING HOT CONTENTS, THEN SMASHING OUT THE FAR SIDE OF THE COFFEE POT AND INTO CEDRICK'S CHEST! FORTUNATELY, THE SOFT LEAD MUSKET BALL, MOSTLY SPENT AFTER HAVING BEEN DRIVEN THROUGH SO MUCH COFFEE POT METAL AND TWO GALLONS OF BOILING HOT LIQUID, DROPPED AS A SMASHED-FLAT LEAD BALL ONTO HIS FOOT INSTEAD OF BEING DRIVEN CLEAR THROUGH HIS CHEST!

"YEOWEEE!" SCREAMED CEDRICK, AS THE BOILING HOT COFFEE BLEW UPWARD AND OUT THE TOP OF THE POT FROM THE BULLET'S IMPACT INTO THE SIDE OF THE COFFEE POT! IN SO DOING, IT SPLASHED ITS BOILING HOT CONTENTS ALL OVER CEDRICK'S BUCKSKIN COVERED CHEST, EXPOSED NECK, FACE AND TOP OF HIS HEAD! THAT AS WELL AS KNOCKING HIM BACKWARDS THREE STEPS UPON RECEIVING THE IMPACT FROM THE BULLET!

CEDRICK INSTANTLY FOUND HIMSELF DROPPING AND ROLLING AROUND ON THE GROUND IN AGONY, FRANTICALLY RUBBING HIS SCALDED BODY PARTS, WHILE SIMULTANEOUSLY ATTEMPTING TO GET HIS BREATH BACK! GETTING HIS BREATH BACK AFTER THE INDIAN'S LEAD BALL HAD FORCEFULLY STRUCK HIM DEAD CENTER IN HIS CHEST AFTER BLOWING CLEAR THROUGH THE FULL COFFEE POT! THIS IT HAD DONE AFTER EXPENDING MOST OF ITS ENERGY AND FLATTENING OUT AS IT TORE THROUGH ONE SIDE OF A STEEL COFFEE POT, BLOWING THROUGH TWO GALLONS OF LIQUID, SMASHING THROUGH THE STEEL BACK SIDE OF THE POT AND THEN STRIKING CEDRICK'S BONY STERNUM, BEFORE DROPPING EXPENDED AND FLATTENED OUT ONTO HIS FOOT!

Scant seconds later after the Indian had shot Cedrick in 'the coffee pot', a white puff of black powder smoke erupted from the trappers' cabin's open doorway as Otis, who just happened to be coming out from the cabin to attend to a call of nature, saw the danger his brother was in by the cooking fire. Quickly transferring his rifle from being carried in his left hand up to his right shoulder, Otis 'face-shot' the Indian trying to kill his brother, dropping him like a stone! Then he dropped his rifle to the floor of the cabin and grabbed another Lancaster rifle laid purposely against the inside wall next to the door for just such unforeseen kinds of emergencies. A second Indian had immediately raced forward after his partner had shot the hated white man, with tomahawk upraised to strike the death blow and count coup! Otis seeing the threat, instantly cocked the hammer back on the rifle just grabbed from the inside wall, raised it to his shoulder and snapped off a shot all in one fluid motion, just as the second Indian began the death plunge of his tomahawk into the head of the still rolling around on the ground and screaming in pain, coffee pot-scalded brother!

WHACK! went Otis's fatal shot into the side of that Indian's head trying to deal a death blow with his tomahawk to the badly hot coffee-scalded Cedrick, still rolling around on the ground in agony! However, fortunately for Cedrick and unfortunately for the attacking Indian, Otis was a crack rifle shot. The impact of Otis's headshot on the Indian, along with his forward running motion trying to tomahawk Cedrick, flipped him clear over the top of Cedrick, sending him sprawling and landing him face down over one of the men's sitting logs by the fire.

BUT THE BATTLE WAS CLEARLY NOT OVER! Two more Indians from the original four-Indian attacking party, fired their rifles simultaneously at Otis as he stood exposed in the cabin's open doorway! That they did, just as Wallace yelled at Otis upon hearing the shooting close at hand, hurled his loaded Lancaster rifle to his brother from clear across the cabin! When Wallace yelled at Otis, he had fortunately turned and upon seeing Wallace's already poorly tossed rifle in the air coming right at him, bent down to catch it before it hit the ground inside the cabin! When he did, both Indians' just-fired shots at him whistled right over where he had been standing fully exposed just an instant before! Had Otis not bent over to catch Wallace's poorly tossed rifle, he would have been killed outright where he stood!

NOW THE 'SHOE' WAS ON THE OTHER FOOT SINCE OTIS HAD ANOTHER LOADED RIFLE IN HIS VERY CAPABLE HANDS! The two Indian shooters, realizing they had just missed killing the trapper standing in the open doorway and that they now were now in possession of two harmless empty rifles, took off running for their lives! Quickly taking aim, Otis dropped the fattest Indian, who unfortunately turned out to be the slowest, with a shot between his shoulder blades and into his spine! Dropping Wallace's tossed rifle, Otis took Oliver's Lancaster rifle now just handed to him from inside the cabin, cocked the hammer and shot the last running away Indian from the four-Indian attacking party with a headshot! When Otis's bullet hit that Indian running for his life, the .54 caliber bullet's impact blew out the entire front portion of that Indian's head, spewing his essence ten feet in front of his frantically running for his life, self… A run for his life that the Indian would not find self-fulfilling because of a fast-moving half-ounce slug of lead fired by a crack rifle shot named Otis…

Then aside from Cedrick still wiggling around on the ground in agony from having two gallons of scalding hot coffee blown all over his exposed neck, face and head, and still gasping for air after having a nearly spent bullet striking him dead center in his chest with such force that it knocked the wind from his lungs, the campsite was now quiet. Well, except for the crackling campfire, burning buffalo meat still skewered over the fire and smoke being emitted from Cedrick's Dutch oven now holding biscuits burned beyond recognition…

As Wallace knelt at the streamside, he took some of the woolen cloth from their provisions and kept dunking it into the cold water and tenderly applying the 'cooling wet' to Cedrick's badly scalded and now water-blistered, pockmarked neck and face! In the meantime, brothers Oliver and Otis now reloaded and ready for 'bear', after locating the now dead Indians' horses tied off in an aspen grove some yards from the campsite, loaded their bodies onto those horses and used them to carry their dead masters away from their campsite. Riding their own horses and trailing the Indians' horses carrying their dead masters a few miles downstream on the Big Muddy, Otis and Oliver finally stopped. There they took their knives and opened up the dead Indians' bellies 'from stem to stern' so their bodies would not later bloat and float under the two men's planned disposals. Then they picked up rocks from the nearby prairie and filled the Indians' body cavities with them. Stripping down to his naked self, Otis waded out into the deepest portion of the beaver pond the brothers had selected for disposal carrying the rock-loaded Indians' bodies one at a time. This he did while Oliver stood guard over the grisly work being done. Taking each body, Otis anchored them deeply under water. This anchoring was done with sharpened willow stakes driven through their bodies and then with the stakes being driven even more deeply into the bottom of the pond to hold them forever in place. That they did in case some of their own kind came looking for their long-lost kin. If they looked in that particular beaver pond, they would be unable to find any of their lost souls because the snapping and mud turtles, crawdads and fish would have finished with the edible parts, making discovery problematic. After Otis had finished with his grisly task and redressed, the two brothers rode about five miles away from their camp and individually released the Indians' horses so they could run freely and not be found by the kin of the now dead and deeply staked-out Indians. Staked-out Indians in the bottom of a beaver pond, as it turned out currently feeding two very happy alligator snapping turtles…

Making their ways back to camp after hiding the bodies and releasing their horses out onto the vast prairie, Oliver and Otis discovered how the Indians had come upon what they had thought was a fairly secluded campsite. Riding by the remains of the dead buffalo the trappers had killed earlier, they clearly found where four un-shod ponies had also discovered the suspicious, dead and butchered-out buffalo carcasses. Then the unshod pony tracks had 'mirrored' the shod horse tracks of the trappers and their pack animals right back to their campsite. Those unshod horse tracks were then followed into the aspen grove where they were originally tied off and hidden from the trappers' view. With Otis dis-mounted and Oliver leading his brother's horse, he backtracked the four now dead Indians' moc-casin prints right into their campsite where they had waylaid Cedrick while he was unsuspect-ingly cooking his brothers' next meal and had fortunately shot him right in the 'coffee pot'...

That evening, Cedrick, still stove up from the burns sustained when he was 'shot through his coffee pot' by an Indian warrior and splashed with the scalding liquid, fixed his brothers an-other meal. That was, after he had visited their stash of supplies in their cabin and retrieved their second new coffee pot purchased back at Fort Henry earlier, brought along just in case some-thing was to happen to his old coffee pot... Well, that and one of their tins of bag balm normally used on their livestock for minor sores, cuts and abrasions but now liberally applied onto those parts of Cedrick's badly burned body.

However, little did the brothers inexperienced with Indian cultures and dress realize the recent battle of 'the coffeepot' was far from over! Little did any of the brothers realize that in their recent battle, due to their inexperience in being able to identify Indians by their dress, they had fought four Northern Cheyenne warriors! Four Northern Cheyenne warriors, who had been looking for their wives and children, previously captured by the Blackfeet and whisked away into captivity. Four Indian warriors who had inadvertently stumbled upon the Barnes Clan and looking to do battle with anyone in the territory of the hated Blackfeet, managed to leave their bones in the bottom of a beaver pond in an alien land. But once again, the Barnes's, inexperienced in Indian culture and dress, had recovered the attacking Indians' valuable Indian Trade rifles and were now mixing them in with their own firearms and using them as further added protection while out running their trap line. Further protection in the form of being carried out in the open and in each packhorse's panniers as extra firepower in the case of being attacked by overwhelming numbers of Indians while afield.

In the aftermath of the 'coffee pot battle' and still in the emotion of the moment, all four Indian Trade rifles from the dead attackers were scooped up and planned on being used as extra protection against any future Blackfeet Indian attacks as well. However, when those rifles were picked up, reloaded and prepared for use, none of the Barnes Clan took the time to examine the stocks of those rifles. As it turned out and not understood by the brothers because of their cultural newness to Plains Indian cultures, each of those Trade rifles retrieved was extensively marked with the placement of brass and steel tacks. Steel and brass tacks, which to every rifle picked up on that field of battle that morning, told a very distinct story. A story in brass and steel tacks that upon discovery would soon place the Barnes boys in a fight for their lives against even greater odds...

Come the early fall's colder weather when the beaver were going into their prime, found the Barnes Clan beginning the setting out and running of their trap lines. However to avoid any problems with discovery by Blackfeet Indians searching for what the Barnes Clan figured were their four long-lost kin along, with their Christian values, the trappers avoided the beaver pond holding the four Indians' bodies still staked to the bottom of the pond. To the trappers' way of thinking, there was just something wrong about trapping in a beaver pond soured by four Indians' decomposing bodies... Plus, the Barnes Clan was just a little spooked over the thought of the idea of trapping so 'close to the dead'.

After several trips checking the many waterways along the Big Muddy, the men had decided on initiating their trapping activities along one particularly long string of adjacent beaver ponds. Beaver ponds that were heavily evidenced by numerous long and well-kept stick and mud dams and conical mud and stick houses dotting the numerous ponded areas throughout. Loading their pack animals early one fall morning, the trappers led by Wallace, left their campsite and headed north along the Big Muddy. A short time later at their previously scouted out designated starting spot for their first trap line adjacent the Big Muddy, Wallace and Cedrick dismounted and headed for their two pack animals for the materials they would need to begin trapping. There Wallace removed his warmer woolen pants and put on his leggings and breechclout, which he favored to use when trapping immersed in water. In the meantime, Oliver and Otis, the two best shooters of the group, remained mounted and vigilant so the two defenseless men on the ground doing all of the trapping would remain protected. The brothers, heeding Major Henry's earlier cautionary words about the Blackfeet menace when trapping along the Big Muddy, made sure they were 'loaded for bear' when it came to their defenses!

Both Oliver and Otis carried a rifle across their saddles with an extra Lancaster rifle in scabbards on their riding horses. Additionally, each man sported two pistols carried in their sashes along with a tomahawk carried behind their backs in a belt. As a matter of interest, pride and practice, Otis and Oliver had been throwing tomahawks since they were old enough to do so under the tutelage of their Creek Indian War-experienced father. Anyone within 20 feet of an angry Otis or Oliver and facing one of their thrown toma-hawks would quickly learn if he was going to a place in 'Heaven or Hell'... As for Wallace and Cedrick, they were prepared for 'Hell or High Water' as well. Each man's riding horse carried two Lancaster rifles in scabbards. Additionally, each of the two packhorses brought along to facilitate their trapping activities, was now car-rying two fully loaded Indian Trade rifles loaded with buck and ball. Trade rifles removed recently from the four Indians, what had been figured were Blackfeet, who had made the mistake of attacking the four trappers at their cabin site... *However, little did the trappers realize those Indian Trade rifles were a dead giveaway as to ownership and would cause all of them future deadly troubles!*

Wallace being the only experienced beaver trapper in the group took the lead as the group's main trapper. Cedrick, in addition to his duties as camp cook, would act as Wallace's support man on the ground and trapper-in-training in case something fatally happened to Wallace down the line. That way even with the loss of Wallace, the brothers could still continue trapping as a livelihood by using a now-trained Cedrick as their trapper. Wallace then removed one five-pound, St. Louis-style beaver trap from the packhorse's pannier, a hand ax and a pre-cut length of wire which he wrapped around his wrist. Wallace then unwound the chain from around the trap and sat it down on the bank of the beaver pond. He then depressed the trap's springs on each end of the rectangular-jawed trap simultaneously with his feet and engaged the trap's 'dog' in the 'pan's notch'. The beaver trap was now an instrument of death to any beaver unfortunate enough to place a foot or feet onto the pan…

Turning around and heading for the first beaver pond, Wallace said, "Come on, Cedrick. You can give me a hand and learn the beaver trapping trade all at the same time." Cedrick, carrying one of the previously pre-cut, 2" in circumference, dried four-foot willow poles removed from one of their packhorse's panniers, trotted after his older brother who was already bent over and examining the muddy ground around the edge of the beaver pond. As Cedrick trotted after his brother, he was harshly reminded of the burning pain now felt in his 'coffee scalded' neck, face and the side of his head that the foot-jarring of trotting induced. Mindful of that pain trotting induced in his now much water-blistered neck and face received from the scalding coffee, he slowed to a gentle walk in order not to further irritate his already messed up features.

By that time, Wallace called Cedrick over and pointed out a well-used beaver slide area entering the water, dotted with numerous tracks of the large rodent indented into the soft mud. "Here is what to look for, Cedrick. Where there is a much-used slide like this one, that is a good place to set a trap. Here, let me show you how it is done once you have found a good solid spot on the bottom of the pond onto which to best place a trap. Like I said, it is important to look for a good solid piece of ground onto which to place this here trap. Notice that I have already set this trap before I get into this damn cold water, so all I have to do is carefully lay it down on my solid piece of ground so the trap will spring the right way when a beaver steps into it. In so doing, I make sure the trap is placed in only about 4″ of water. Then watch this little trick an old-timer back in Tennessee taught me," continued Wallace, as he swirled water with his hand over and around the now well-placed trap until it was covered and out of sight with just a slight film of mud. "When you do this, make sure it is just a film of mud over the trap and not gobs of mud, otherwise it might screw up the trap and allow the animal to escape when initially trapped," continued Wallace.

"Now comes the important part. Notice how carefully, without moving my now set trap, that I walk out into the deeper water until I reach the end of the trap's chain. When you do this, make sure you don't jerk your trap off its solid piece of ground upon which it is sitting covered with a film of mud. Because if you move the trap and the mud film covering the trap is disturbed exposing the trap, the beaver will see it and may not step in it. Now, throw me that dried wooden anchor stick. As I explained to you earlier when we were cutting these, I use a dried stick as my anchor pole, because a beaver once trapped will not attempt to chew through it. However, if you use a fresh green stick as your anchor pole, many times a trapped beaver will chew right through a fresh stick and escape with your valuable trap. Remember, we saw back in St. Louis when these traps were issued to us, the company had a price tag of $9 on each trap distributed to us company trappers. So we sure as hell don't want to lose any out here in the field. Additionally, if you don't anchor this dried stick in deep enough water, the beaver if he can get his feet on the ground, may just chew off his trapped foot and there goes your pelt." Wallace, then careful not to drag or disturb the previously set trap, passed his wooden stick through the steel ring on the end of the trap's chain and then placed the end of the stick and the trap's ring on the bottom of the pond. Taking his hand ax, Wallace then drove the dried anchor stake into the bottom of the pond. Removing the wire tied around his wrist, Wallace made sure the steel ring on the end of the trap's chain was tightly tied to the wooden anchor pole. That way, if the trapped beaver somehow dragged the anchor pole out of the mud, the weight of the five-pound trap would still eventually drown the beaver. Later when looking for the trap, it would be discovered still tied to a floating anchor pole and could be recovered without the loss of the valuable trap.

(Author's Note: The Author in college for a parasitology class trying to amass a larger collection of parasites during a required lab project, ran a beaver trap line in order to catch beaver and recover unique fur and intestinal parasites from such animals. In so doing, in one of my traps I caught a 109-pound beaver! Hence the reason for having such a stout anchor pole at the end of one's trap chain.)

Walking back to where he had set his trap in the shallow water near a patch of willows, Wallace took out his sheath knife and cut off a green willow twig about two feet long. He then peeled all of the green bark off the twig so the beaver would not attempt to eat it. Wallace then had Cedrick hand him the bottle of castoreum that he had been carrying. He then dipped the end of the twig into the foul smelling liquid made from the 'castors' (glands) of beaver and then stuck the dry end of the twig into the bank, allowing for the end dipped in the castoreum to hang diagonally out over the water just over the trap. As did, he could see that Cedrick was looking at his 'stick placement' actions with a questioning look on his face. Grinning over his brother's innocence, Wallace said, "Cedrick, beaver are very territorial. If they smell the scent of an unfamiliar beaver in their area, they will come right over to investigate. The way I just set that trap, the resident beaver should come over to investigate the strange beaver smell in his home waters. When he does, he will swim to the end of that stick I just dipped in the castoreum, stand in the bottom of the pond so he can reach up, and pull the stick over to his nose for a smell. When he drops his feet down in order to stand up, reach out and grab the end of that stick in order to smell the castoreum I daubed on its end, the trap will snap closed and we will have a beaver with one or both feet caught in that trap. In a panic, the beaver will swim away from where the trap just slammed shut on his foot or feet and will head out into what it thinks is the safety of the deeper water. However, the beaver can only swim the length of the six feet of the trap's chain and no further. That is because the heavy wooden stake that I drove into the bottom of the pond will keep the beaver from swimming no further than the length of that trap's chain. There he will continue trying to swim away in panic, all the while being held from escaping because of the trap's chain being fastened to that wooden stake. Soon the five-pound weight of the trap and its chain will cause the beaver to become exhausted, dragged underwater and drown. When we return, if we have set the trap just right, we should have a $6 beaver drowned and hanging dead in the trap. So ends the first trapping lesson and in the case I am not able to trap for some reason, it will be up to you to duplicate what I am showing you so you can carry the fortunes of the group instead of me as the main trapper," said Wallace with a big grin.

By around four o'clock in the afternoon, with Wallace teaching and assisting Cedrick in the fine art and procedures of trapping beaver, between the two of them they managed to set all 24 of their company's beaver traps! When 'scalded face' Cedrick tiredly emerged from the cold water and even colder mud at the bottom of the trap setting waters, he discovered his brother Wallace closely watching him with a huge grin of approval. Then the two men walked around on the prairie in the fall's warming sun, pleased with their trap-setting efforts, as they warmed up while eating some of their tasty buffalo jerky. In the meantime, Otis and Oliver dismounted, joined their brothers and visited, but still kept a 'peeled set of eyes' looking all around for any signs of danger as they did.

About then Cedrick started to change out of his soaking wet leggings and breechclout back into his warmer wool pants when Wallace stopped him saying, "We ain't done yet. I would bet a cup of that rum we have back at our cabin that if we checked the traps just set, we will have a beaver or two already hanging dead in them because they are so territorial. That plus there are so many in the area we can't help but catch some." With those words, Cedrick pulled his cold and wet leggings and breechclout back on, shook his head and mounted up for the wet ride back checking their previously set trap line. On the way back as Wallace had predicted, the men discovered eleven of the very territorial dead beaver already hanging drowned in their traps! When they did and after Wallace had waded out and retrieved the first of the beaver carcasses, a 90-pound specimen, Cedrick's next lesson as a trapper began.

Standing there on the bank, Wallace told Cedrick, "Since you are also to be our chief skinner and have never done this before, let me do the first one so I can show you how it is to be done. Do it otherwise and it will cost us big money when we get back to the fort and the company's graders and sorters take over." With those words of caution, Wallace grabbed up the 90-pound beaver just retrieved and laid it out onto the nearby grassy bank on its back. Then he took out one of his specially ground Thomas Wilson knives previously altered by American Fur Company blacksmith Cooter Krentz just to be used for skinning, since it only had the one bevel which reduced fur cutting mistakes. Then looking over at Cedrick, Wallace said "There is a right and wrong way to do this beaver skinning thing. I will show you the way I want it done and the way the old trapper back in Tennessee taught me how to skin a beaver properly. Now watch carefully how I slit the skin of this here beaver down the entire length of the animal's belly. That cut made and done, I will now make transverse slits along the insides of each beaver's legs and then I am now going to cut off each of the animal's feet. OK, now I am going to cut off the tail and toss it into a pannier because once roasted, they are a real treat because of their fatty content and flavor. Try to remember this little tip of the trade since you are the clan's cook. The colder it gets, the more fat we will need in our diets in order to help keep our body heat up. Since we will be retrieving beaver each day, remember to keep a mess of their fatty tails come the colder weather to cook for us so we can help keep warm in this damn cold trade we find ourselves in. Besides, the tail's outer skin will make a very good knife sheath if one is in the need for one." Then Wallace paused and looking at his brothers said, "Beaver meat is a real treat. What say, all of you, that I introduce you to a roasted beaver supper tonight?" Only hearing silence from his kin in return to his rather unusual question to those 'unwashed' who had never partaken of such a rodent delight, Wallace smiled inwardly and then kept proceeding with Cedrick's skinning lesson. "Next watch carefully when I skin this critter and do so carefully because once again, if you cut through the side of the pelt other than along its edges when we hoop them and for every cut you make in the wrong place, it is a dollar off the value of your pelt! Also, a beaver has a heavy fat layer between his body and his fur. That is what allows him to live and swim around in such cold water, even comfortably swimming in the frigid waters under the ice. Again, using one of these specially made knives, I am going to carefully remove the skin from this here beaver's carcass and when done, will toss the pelt into the pannier."

Within moments, Wallace had his beaver skinned out, the carcass and the pelt tossed into the pannier carried by one of their packhorses and then the men moved on. As they did, Oliver and Otis continued riding so they could see further from atop their horses as they looked for any signs of danger. However, Cedrick and Wallace walked along the edge of their previously set trap line so they could warm up after spending most of their day immersed in the cooling waters found occurring during the fall season. Upon arrival at the next trap, another beaver carcass awaited. That time it was another rolling fat adult weighing about 70 pounds. Following his brother's lead, Cedrick copied what his brother had shown him when he had skinned out their first beaver and being the quick learner he was, did so much to his brother's delight and satisfaction! Once again, because his brothers were eager eaters, Wallace tossed the 70-pound beaver into a pannier for their evening's supper as well. Then Wallace informed Cedrick that any further beaver caught would be left a distance away from the trap site because they had more than enough beaver meat for supper and by dumping the carcasses in the field, that was where they would keep any hungry grizzly bears occupied, instead of having them feasting on any carcasses piled up around their cabin.

Finished checking their last trap and having skinned out their eleventh beaver, the men headed for a large patch of willows where they cut and filled one of their packhorse's panniers with the very flexible green willow limbs for the "hooping" work yet to come. Later back at their cabin, Wallace instructed all of the brothers in the proper fleshing technique when it came to their eleven fresh pelts and then followed up with lessons on the correct way to hoop a beaver skin. As Otis, Oliver and Wallace continued with their fleshing and hooping duties, Cedrick left to build a fire so he could attend to his cooking duties. Supper that evening for the tired trappers consisted of hot coffee, Dutch oven biscuits, beaver cooked over a spit and Dutch oven rice and raisin delight that more than satisfied every brother's appetite and sweet tooth. Adjourning to their cabin later that first night of the fall beaver trapping season, the last man in bed made sure the leather inside door latch was in place so that no surprise attacker could just come busting through their front door. However, all the brothers realized that if a grizzly bear wanted into their cabin, the leather latch would be a thing of the past...

The next morning, the brothers were rudely awakened by the sounds of many hundreds of grunting and shuffling buffalo right outside their front door. Jumping out from their beds, the heavy smell of numerous close at hand buffalo bodies, fresh dung and air filled with the dust from several thousand shuffling feet had already filled their cabin. Releasing their inside door latch and opening the front door, the men were greeted with a 'sea of brown', as several thousand buffalo shuffled through their campsite on their way to the far side of the meadow next to the trappers' cabin. **BOOM!** went Cedrick's rifle from the cabin's open doorway, dropping a cow buffalo right next to their firepit! That sound of a close at hand explosion sent the herd of buffalo quickly on their way into the meadow beyond, save for a single dying cow buffalo kicking her last right next to 'Cedrick's kitchen'. That morning the men were late in checking their traps as they had the not so small chore ahead of them butchering out a buffalo in their front yard. When they finally left that morning to check their beaver traps, a fresh buffalo meat breakfast had been had by all, a quartered-out freshly killed buffalo hung from the men's meat pole in the nearby pine trees cooling and glazing, and the guts, hide and head now resided in a distant aspen grove, soon to be covered by happy crows and black-billed magpies having their breakfast as well.

For the next month, the daily beaver trapping regimen became the same. An early morning's breakfast, checking their trap line, removing and field skinning dead beaver, the resetting of traps, and a constantly moving trap line as beaver were quickly trapped out from each area trapped. Then a quiet return to their willow patch for more hooping material, fleshing and de-fatting of fresh beaver pelts in the evening, hooping the same so they could dry, a quick, almost the same every night supper and then tiredly off to bed to await the next day's activities. Fortunately for the trappers, hardly 'hide nor hair' of a hostile Indian was seen. That was soon to change...

One morning in early November just before freeze-up, found Wallace in the water next to a beaver dam setting one of his traps. As he did, he heard a low whistle coming from Cedrick. In a hurry to get out from the near freezing water, Wallace continued setting his trap and ignored Cedrick's whistle. Then Wallace heard Cedrick's whistle once again, and that time it sounded more urgent. Turning, Wallace's throat tightened as he observed ten mounted Indians slowly riding towards his brothers, Otis and Oliver, who were on guard and now on high alert! One of the mounted Indians had his right arm raised in the sign of peace as the group of winter-dressed warriors continued riding toward Otis and Oliver, who were now turned and faced the oncoming riders. Wallace instantly ducked down below the beaver dam where he had been setting a beaver trap and moving bent over, made for the dense willows lining the bank and hiding from view Cedrick, their lone packhorse and their two riding horses. Pulling himself up into the dense patch of willows, Wallace moved swiftly and quietly towards the still-hidden Cedrick and their horses. Still hidden from view from the ten slowly oncoming Indians, Wallace grabbed his Lancaster rifle from off his riding horse and an Indian Trade rifle out from the nearest packhorse's pannier. Cedrick already was holding his Lancaster rifle removed from his riding horse in his right hand and one of the Indian Trade rifles from the packhorse's other pannier in his left hand as well. Both men then leaving their tied-off horses sneaked towards the edge of the dense willow patch hiding them so they could better see what the intentions were of the ten oncoming Indians. Then each man laid down one of their rifles on the grassy bank close at hand for quick retrieval, and made ready with their other in case there was trouble when Oliver and Otis finally confronted the ten mounted and very serious-looking Indians.

That was when Wallace and Cedrick clearly heard one of the Indians speaking in broken English talking to Otis and Oliver. Fortunately, the ten mounted Indians had yet to discover

Wallace and Cedrick. At first, the discussion between the trappers and the Indians seemed cordial enough in nature. Then one of the mounted Indians all of a sudden quickly reached down and grabbed out one of the Indian Trade rifles from Otis's packhorse's pannier and began intently looking at something that had caught his eye on the rifle's stock! Then he began talking very excitedly in his own language as he kept pointing to the brass and steel tack designs on the Indian Trade rifle's stock. It was then when several other Indians moved their horses over and began looking at the Indian Trade rifle just removed from the packhorse's pannier that the talk went from the calm to the dark and foreboding! Dark and foreboding sounding with lots of angry hand gestures being made by the now very excited and highly agitated group of Indians yet unknown as to tribal affiliation!

That was when Wallace leaned over to Cedrick and whispered something. Immediately, both men quietly laid down their Lancaster rifles, picked up the two Indian Trade rifles loaded with buck and ball, had them shouldered and quietly pointing them in the direction of the now highly agitated Indians. Largely outnumbered with the discussions seemingly going badly between the two mounted trappers and the ten Indians, Wallace figured no good was coming their way and fast! Then he heard the Indian doing all of the talking in English demanding to know where was the owner of the rifle just jerked out from the packhorse's pannier? Then from the English-speaking Indian, it became apparent that the Indian Trade rifle's owner was a friend of the man, based on its tack designs in the rifle's stock and forearm! With that information out and into the now heated air, he was demanding in no uncertain terms, where was the owner of that rifle! Unfortunately, the owner of that rifle was one of the four men who had shot Cedrick in the 'coffee pot' battle and was now dead, shot and killed by one of the trappers now confronting him, namely, Otis!

It was then that Wallace and Cedrick saw two of the Indians confronting Otis and Oliver at the back of the pack of horsemen, surreptitiously fully cock their Indian Trade rifles as if getting ready to surprise-shoot the two trappers off their horses sitting in front of them! Otis and Oliver also saw the furtive movements made by the two Indians in the back of the group of mounted Indians, and it was then that Wallace saw Otis shoot him a quick 'knowing' glance over at his place of hiding, plainly 'spelling out' that he felt that evil would soon be coming and 'it' was riding ten horses! It was then that Wallace saw the two Indians with their cocked Trade rifles start moving their horses subtly to the forefront of their group of mounted horsemen, as if getting ready to surprise and kill the two trappers still quietly sitting on their horses to their front! It was also apparent to Wallace from the ten Indians' actions, that they had no idea there were also two heavily armed trappers hidden in the nearby willow thicket watching on and waiting...

Wallace leaned over to Cedrick with whispered instructions and then quietly and still unobserved, the two trappers slowly raised their Indian Trade rifles loaded with 'buck and ball' designed to be very deadly at close ranges on massed targets and fully cocked their rifles! "NOW!" shouted Wallace and when he did, both he and Cedrick fired their rifles almost simultaneously! Their fired twin shots from the cover of the willow patch did what they were intended to do! As planned by Wallace and Cedrick, those two shots of buck and ball immediately blew seven crowded together Indians from the rear of their group off from their horses and onto the ground in a jumble of dead and dying bodies! Both Cedrick and Wallace then quickly dropped their Trade rifles, grabbed up their Lancaster rifles lying alongside in order to continue in the fight. This they did, as the almost instantaneously shooting between Otis and Oliver and the remaining Indians roared forth with many quick shots now being exchanged at close ranges! After firing their rifles into the bellies of the two closest Indians to their front, Otis and Oliver quickly dropped their rifles, drew their pistols and continued firing into any surviving Indian to their front now enveloped in a huge white cloud of black powder smoke! As it turned out, the single remaining uninjured, but still horsed Indian tried to ride off and escape the fury of firing surrounding him. When he turned to ride off, he was hit simultaneously by two heavy .54 caliber lead balls fired from Otis and Oliver's pistols simultaneously! Upon those .54 caliber lead balls' impact, that Indian was literally exploded from his saddle, tossing him under the nervous hooves of his compatriots' now rearing and bucking horses! However, being killed even before he had hit the ground with the possibility of being stomped by numerous horses' hooves was now the least of that dead Indian's worries. Then all was quiet in the beaver's marsh, which was now dotted by several whitish clouds of black powder smoke drifting silently off into the vastness of the prairie winds.

Seeing no further horsed Indian targets, Wallace and Cedrick laid down their rifles and quickly grabbed up their reserve pistols from their standing nearby riding horse's holsters. Then Cedrick and Wallace ran forward to continue the battle if needed. However upon their arrivals, all that was left to do was dispatch five of those Indians cleared from their saddles earlier with non-lethal but still deadly crippling strikes from the 'buck and ball', which were swiftly and lethally attended to! Turning to Oliver and Otis, Wallace saw that both men were slightly wounded! Both had taken flesh wounds to their legs when they had quickly with their off hands, grabbed the ends of the two Indians' rifles in front of them and had immediately depressed their muzzles downward and away from them. Simultaneously, both trappers using their strong hands, had gutshot those same two Indians off their horses with their Lancaster rifles which had been lying across their laps! However when they did, since the two Indians to their front already had their fingers on the triggers of fully cocked weapons, both depressed rifles went off, striking the two brothers slightly in their legs! Fortunately, the two trappers only had flesh wounds and bad powder burns from taking such close-in shots alongside their legs. Additionally, when the bullets had grazed the legs of Otis and Oliver, they had continued on and had grazed the bellies of both of the men's riding mounts as well. Once again, fortunately only the skin was split away from the meat and ribs of their riding horses and with a lot of bag balm, some stitches and time away from daily beaver trap checking, those two riding horses would eventually recover from their painful flesh wounds.

Now the trappers faced a real dilemma. They had just killed ten Indians and were once again confronted with what to do with their bodies so other Indians would not discover them and come looking for who had done such a killing thing. That and being there were shod horse prints in abundance, the Indian-killing culprits would be fairly easy to track down and more than likely, face swift retribution if ever caught! That evening the bodies of ten dead Indians 'graced' the Big Muddy, for better or worse. As the last Indian's body bobbed out of sight downstream, the trappers took stock of what had just happened. When they had been approached by the ten Indians, the one speaking English had identified themselves as Northern Cheyenne Indians from far to the south. Northern Cheyenne who were looking for four of their tribal elders who had come north earlier looking for their wives and children who had been taken captive by the much-hated Blackfeet when most of the Northern Cheyenne menfolk had been away hunting buffalo. Then when one of those Indians discovered a rifle in a pack animal's pannier from one of the four men they were looking for based on that rifle's tack pattern in its stock, that made all of them mad at the trappers, figuring they had been the ones who had killed their fellow tribal members. Then Oliver spoke up saying, "Those damn Indians were all peaceable-like until they discovered that rifle with all of the brass and steel tacks on the stock in our packhorse's pannier. According to the Indian who spoke passable English, those tacks identified that rifle as one from one of their chiefs they had been seeking. Once that got out and into the air, they all went 'haywire' and that started all the shoving, shouting and shooting!" With those words, Otis just nodded his head in confirmation over his brother's wise observation and words.

About then Cedrick, who had been examining all of the Trade rifles after hearing what Oliver had said about identifying the owner by the tack patterns on the rifle stocks, just shook his head in disbelief. "Guys, every one of those Trade rifles is greatly decorated with all of those brass and steel tacks differently. I don't know what they all mean but you can bet they all belonged to other important tribal members as well. That being the case, I say we keep these rifle out of sight for the most part or we may find ourselves in another mad mess of Indians and that next time, not fare so well when all of the black powder smoke has drifted away. Or at least maybe remove all of those tacks so the rifles look all normal like for any other future Indian's eyes to feast upon if and when such an occasion arises."

"Well, those Trade guns just saved our bacon and I say we keep them and keep them handy as well. No matter how we look at it, we four are always going to be outnumbered and we need to keep our heads about us, keep a sharp eye peeled and every rifle and pistol we own loaded and ready for bear for whatever the good Lord brings our way," said Wallace quietly. "After all, this is the lifestyle all of us have chosen and if we want to survive out here on this frontier, we need to be more than ready and meaner than any others who might want to take us on. Besides, remember all of those packs of high quality furs that we now have back at our cabin. I would say we have done something right if those fur numbers have anything to say about our choice of lifestyle and levels of success," continued Wallace who was still coming down emotionally from his recent killing high.

"I agree," said Otis. "We came by those Trade guns fair and square and I say no matter whom they belonged to, we need every bit of firepower we possess and then some as we saw here today. Thank God they didn't initially see Wallace and Cedrick behind all of those willows and thank God they were using those Trade guns filled with that saddle clearing 'buck and ball'. Otherwise, we all would have had our hands full and I doubt all of us would have been here now had it not been for Cedrick and Wallace when they intervened and how they did it. The only other thing I have to offer is we had better get the hell out of here afore them damn Blackfeet, after hearing all of that shooting, now maybe come for a closer look-see as well. Also, I hope all of you looked closely at what them damn Indians were wearing. We need to get better on being able to identify who we come across or cross swords with when it comes to these different groups of Indians. Best we learn and learn fast so we have the edge in all future confrontations or we may end up like these ten poor bastards."

That afternoon after they had finished checking and clearing their traps, the Trade guns went home with the Barnes Clan as did the ten valuable Indian horses. Horses that once placed in the corral were washed clean from all of the blood spatters and distinct painted marks on the horse's shoulders and flanks left by their now dead owners. That evening as Otis, Wallace and Oliver 'defatted' the skins from the daily take of beaver and hooped the same for the drying to follow, found Cedrick doing otherwise. As Cedrick's evening meal was cooking around the outside campfire, that found Cedrick after much examination and consideration, sitting on a sitting log prying off the telltale tack patterns from all of their Indian Trade rifles with his knife and throwing the tacks into the fire. Henceforth, any Indian examining those four Trade rifles taken after the battle of the 'coffee pot' and now with those Indian Trade rifles taken from the Northern Cheyenne 'searchers' battle', would only see cheap Indian Trade rifles with bare and heavily scarred butt and fore stocks. Then those guns were secured in their cabin after being reloaded just in case a need for their use ever arose. Like had been said earlier, they would always be outnumbered and better to be over-gunned and alive than under-gunned and 'cooling out on a windy prairie' as a 'scat' from a grizzly bear, prairie wolf, coyote or a black-billed magpie…

(Author's Note: Brass and steel tack patterns on a number of the Plains Indians' rifle stocks were highly individualized and carried many specialized meanings. "Togia" or the special- ized placement of tacks and their patterns on a number of Plains Indians' rifles, meant 'to talk or write' the 'strong language', in many instances of a "Wakan" (holy man) using "Oowa" (marks). Tack patterns on rifle stocks were special as was the placements of steel versus brass tacks. It was culturally important that any tack patterns be placed on the stock's right side and the symbols outlined by the tacks represented the picto- graphic or cryptic language of many of the Plains Indians. In the above case of one of the Northern Cheyenne Indian Trade rifles picked up after the battle of the 'coffee pot', there were two symbols outlined by tack patterns on the right side of the stock. One was of a large cross which indicated the owner was of the Northern Cheyenne "Dog Soldier" society. Below the larger cross was an- other one, only smaller, which indicated the ri- fle's owner was the head of such a society. Lastly, on the wrist of the stock on the left side was a Togia symbol for a chief or "Thunder Being"! When the above tack symbolism was discovered on the rifle residing in the pannier by one of the ten Northern Cheyenne Indians who had inter- cepted Otis and Oliver as being that of a rifle belonging to a chief from their band, it was no wonder the group had gone from being civil to that of killers. Such a rifle discovered belonging to a highly regarded chief, one who would never relinquish such a rifle for any reason other than in death, and now being discovered in the hands of two white fur trappers, was bound to excite ill will and bad feelings among those Indians in the 'know'!)

Just before freeze-up, the brothers pulled their beaver traps ending their first fall trapping season on the Big Muddy. Then it was out to hunt buffalo for the start of their winter meat supply. Three cow buffalo later lay on the ground and then the work started. Just before dark, the men had butchered out the three cows and their four packhorses now had all the fresh meat they could carry. Back at their cabin as Cedrick began preparing a celebratory supper of fresh buffalo steaks, pinto beans, biscuits, coffee, and a rice and raisin mixture in another Dutch oven, the other three brothers hung the buffalo quarters with difficulty from their two meat poles in the pine trees. Otis and Wallace then threw a buffalo skin over the hanging quarters of meat in order to keep many of the now winter fat and meat hungry black-billed magpies, Steller's jays and chickadees at bay. Then they washed up and headed for their outdoor cooking fire from whence all the great supper food smells were emanating.

After such a supper and as a cooling wind blew in from the northwest, the men sipped their cups of rum and filled the air with the rich smell of their James River pipe smoke. Sitting around that evening relaxing were four very full and happy brothers. Happy brothers because their cabin was stacked clear to the ceiling with bundles of high quality beaver furs, many of which were 'blanket-sized' (from the largest of beaver), fresh quarters from three cow buffalo now hung from their meat poles, all of their horses were healthy including the two slightly wounded in the 'searchers' fight' with the ten Northern Cheyenne over the rifle discovered in the packhorse's pannier with all the damning Togia brass and steel tacks on the butt stock, they had ten extra valuable horses, and all of them still had their hair. Not only that but the men realized that after inventorying their stock of beaver furs and looking forward to their spring catches, figured they would more than need the ten extra horses picked up from the killed Northern Cheyenne Indians to transport their extra bundles of furs to Fort Henry come the summer. Then as Otis got up to refill his coffee cup with more coffee prior to adding some more rum, a large and very wet snowflake landed on his hand. Turning, he said, "Boys, I think we need to get our outside cooking area squared away and moved inside in order to make ready for the first snowfall of the season." Half an hour later amidst a swirling wet and heavy snowstorm, the men had finished squaring away their campsite, put away all of their tack from out of the weather and had adjourned to the warmth of their cabin from a roaring fire in the fireplace.

Opening the cabin's front and only door the next morning, found the land covered in about 10" of freshly fallen snow, a brightly shining sun and an outside temperature hovering around 30 degrees. As Wallace hobbled and released their horse herd so they could feed in the nearby meadow, including the ten recently acquired Indian horses, Cedrick prepared a breakfast of biscuits, fried buffalo steak, coffee and a new treat, thick gravy made from the drippings in their two three-legged frying pans. This he did inside their cabin at the fireplace as the rest of the brothers prepared for their first day afield getting ready to begin their wolf trapping season.

That afternoon a mile or so behind the foothills hiding their cabin, the brothers shot three buffalo from three different small herds, opened them up for the odors of death that would create and then set out their ten wolf traps using the buffalo carcasses as bait. Finding that none of them had dressed warmly enough for horseback riding out in the winter weather, they all headed back early to their cabin to warm up and 'tip' a cup of rum or two in celebration of the new trapping season. Arriving later in the day, the brothers brought in the rest of their horses from the meadow, only to discover fresh grizzly bear tracks in and around their vacant horse corral! Then the men discovered the bear had 'winded' the cow buffalo quarters hanging on the meat poles in the pine trees and had been able to reach one of the partial carcasses and had torn it down! All that was left of that partial quarter of the buffalo ripped from the meat pole were a lot of the larger rib bones scattered about and part of a much-chewed upon spinal column.

Otis, upon looking at all the rest of the giant paw prints underneath the rest of the hanging carcasses, looked over at his brothers saying, "This is not going to do. For that bear it is too early to go into hibernation and he will be back for the rest of our meat unless we hunt him down and kill him. As you all remember too well, when we had black bear problems back in Tennessee and they got into a meal, they would eventually be back for more until we killed them or they cleaned us out."

The other brothers said nothing, realizing what Otis had just said about the great bear coming back until all the buffalo meat had been consumed or he invaded their cabin looking for something to eat, made sense. That after-noon with the brother's best tracker in the lead, namely Otis, the hunt for the great bear began. Each man had changed out their pistols from buck and ball to just straight balls in case the bear got any of them trapped in a bad and dangerous spot requiring them to use their pistols at close range. As for their rifles, everyone had loaded them with as much powder as they could safely hold and shoot behind a massive .54 caliber lead ball! They all knew about how dangerous a grizzly bear could be, especially one that had been wounded. So great care was taken to be prepared for the worst when 'tangling' with the bear and all hoped for the best.

Just before dusk, Otis had tracked the great bear to a rocky outcropping a mile or so from their cabin, with a small cave at one end. The many grizzly bear tracks led right to the entrance of that small cave and then disappeared inside. Without making a sound, the four men arranged themselves alongside one side of the cave and in so doing checked their rifles once more, making sure they were more than ready to fire. As Otis gathered up some dry wood in order to make a torch to be thrown into the mouth of the cave and hopefully bring the bear out from inside, a light but wet snow began falling once again. By the time Otis had fashioned a torch for throwing into the cave, the amount of snowfall had increased substantially. Using his fire steel, it took Otis many long minutes to finally get a fire started in the air heavy with dampness but soon he had a torch making much fire and smoke.

Walking over to the side of the mouth of the cave so he would be out of the line of fire from his brothers if the bear came charging out unexpectedly, Otis became aware of the bad odors coming from the mouth of the cave. Looking up and down the row of his brothers all standing with their rifles upraised to quickly fire, Otis slowly walked up to the cave's entrance, took a quick look inside, tossed in his torch and then ran back away from the entrance so when the bear emerged, he would not be in the way of the bear or the firing that was to come. For the longest time, nothing happened. Then with a loud roar, out from the mouth of the cave came the huge grizzly bear at a full charge, looking for whatever had disturbed it from its late afternoon nap as it slept off its dinner of trappers' buffalo meat filched from their camp's meat pole!

Otis being the closest to the mouth of the cave, swung his rifle as the bear raced out from the cave and fired. **BOOM!** His shot flew true and the great bear dropped like a stone, ONLY TO QUICKLY RAISE BACK UP ON ITS FEET, TURN, AND CHARGE OTIS IN LESS TIME THAN IT TAKES TO TELL! Oliver next in line and the second best shooter of the brothers, calmly swung his rifle at the bear's head, now lowered and coming at Otis in a full charge, lined up his sight on the bear's nose to allow for its forward speed and pulled the trigger. **POOOFF!** went Oliver's Lancaster whose powder had gotten wet in the heavily falling snow, causing a misfire!

Simultaneously, Wallace swung his lead on the charging bear, pulled the trigger and **POOOFF!** went his rifle as well, when it also misfired because its powder had also gotten too wet to fire in the heavy moisture-laden falling sleet and snow!

By now, the enraged bear was within ten feet of Otis, who was now drawing his pistol down on the bear's head in desperation, when Cedrick pulled the trigger on his rifle. **BOOM!** went Cedrick's rifle and when he fired, its ball hit the bear in its left shoulder and broke the enraged animal down in a flurry of flying snow and wet dirt when it hit the ground! However, in a split second, the badly injured and now adrenalin-fueled bear was up on its hind legs roaring its defiance loudly enough to almost cause the men's horses tied 30 yards away in a grove of trees to bolt! **POW!** went Otis's pistol from just ten feet away from the enraged beast, shooting it in its head! However, all his shot did was knock the beast sideways, as its bullet blew the animal's jaw into a dozen flying splinters of bone, teeth and bloody froth from its destroyed mouth!

Seeing their brother in imminent danger, without hesitation, all three brothers drew their pistols simultaneously and took off running right at the staggering bear just feet from reaching Otis, drawing him into its muscular grasp and crushing him! **POW–POW–POW!** went three quick pistol shots from the brothers fired from just four feet away! Two of the balls just fired struck the bear in the side of its head, dropping him to the ground! Then with a yell to **"RUN!"**, all four brothers, now with empty firearms, took off running for their horses like the wind in case the great bear somehow arose and pursued them! The already spooked horses smelling the air heavy with the smell of an enraged grizzly bear, upon seeing all four men running right at them, panicked, broke free from the branches onto which they had been tied and headed for the safety of their corral in a flurry of flying hooves, clods of flying dirt and snow kicked up by their fleeing hooves!

Finally sanity reigned once again, as the brothers stopped running in what they considered the safety of the trees knowing the bear could not climb, took the time to still their heavily beating hearts and quickly reloaded all of their weapons. That they did as they all kept their eyes on the great tan mound of an 800-pound boar grizzly bear lying in the snow some 30 yards away breathing his last. Then once all of the men had either cleared their misfiring weapons or had reloaded, in a line abreast, slowly approached the now dead bear. Cedrick, ever the realist, after poking the bear with the end of his rifle barrel held ready to fire if the bear moved, ended up poking the bear several more times just to make sure. Upon finishing, Cedrick said, "One of you needs to go back to camp and bring our horses back. I am sure by now they have fled clear back to the safety of their corral and away from this bear smell. When you do, remember to bring back that big buckskin packhorse. He is tamed down enough to carry bear meat and not go crazy over its smells, as well as a set of panniers. Looking at this bear, I can see that it is rolling fat. We need to butcher it out and replace its carcass for the buffalo it ate. Besides, we could use a bear rug back at the cabin as well as this bear's intestinal fat which is the lightest for my cooking, especially when I am making our biscuits."

Just before dusk that day, found four tired, dirty and covered with blood, bear grease, hair, bear smell and bodily juices brothers riding and leading a heavily loaded packhorse with the shoulders, hams, backstraps, ribs and hide of a monster in size remains of a grizzly bear. Additionally, the men were carrying in their arms great gobs of now winter-cold congealed bear leaf lard removed from the animal's intestines to be used for their cooking. As they did, each man was very careful not to make any sudden moves, especially with all of their horses smelling the heavy smell of a bear nearby from all of the blood and bodily juices on the men's clothing. That evening, fried bear backstraps in bear grease, along with biscuits and coffee graced the brothers' supper table as the winter snows once again swirled around their cabin. Thus passed a long and cold winter of wolf trapping, caring for the furs of those wolves trapped, hunting buffalo for fresh meat, casting small mountains of lead balls for their lead-eating Lancaster rifles, cutting wood, tending to their horses needs and waiting for the spring thaw so trapping of beaver could commence once again.

As "Old Man Winter" finally began passing the 'torch', the brothers began seeing the first vestiges of the new year to come. Aspen buds began swelling, grasses began poking up their first green shoots of spring, there was mud everywhere, open water began appearing around the edges of watered areas, and many times numbers of buffalo could be found in the nearby cottonwood groves rubbing their thick winter coats off against the tree's rough bark. Another sure sign that spring and summer would soon be upon the brothers were their efforts in beginning preparations for the upcoming summer trip back down the Big Muddy and rafting across the Missouri en route Fort Henry to sell their furs and acquire the provisions the men would need for the following trapping seasons. For a full week, the brothers took their remaining dried beaver furs, folded them with the fur side in and with protective tanned deerskins for each pack of furs, placed 60 furs to a bundle. Then using a chain, pole and a sapling press contraption, compressed each bundle of furs into packs weighing about 90-100 pounds. Then they tightly tied and laced the tanned deerskins around each pack of dried pelts for the protection that offered against dirt or tearing when going through dense brush during their travels back down to Fort Henry. Those packs would later be loaded two packs to a horse for transport to Fort Henry to be sold at Mountain Prices (sold low), which would hopefully fetch around $300-600 per pack of Made Beaver (adult-sized beaver). Then those monies derived from the sales of such beaver and wolf pelts would then be used to once again purchase at Mountain Prices (purchases made at higher prices) provisions for the next year's fall and spring trapping seasons. Those higher Mountain Prices reflecting the business investors' concerns against the potential loss of the furs being transported all the way back to St. Louis. Historically, some entire fur caravans returning to St. Louis were wiped out by the deadly Arikara or Blackfeet Indians, prairie wildfires, river crossings, buffalo stampedes, or losses of horses off steep mountain trails and falling into the canyons below!

CHAPTER FOUR

THE DAY OF THE "WOLVERINE"...

FINALLY SPRING CAME later than usual and when it arrived, it found the Barnes Clan more than raring to begin their spring beaver trapping. Especially since the beaver had been living beneath the ice all winter long and as a result, their coats were the thickest and most luxuriant during anytime of the year. That being the case, those winter beaver pelts brought the highest monetary returns for the trappers once sold. With that, the brothers spent the first weeks of spring smoking their beaver traps to rid them of the man smell, currying their horses daily to rid them from their excess hair from their heavier winter coats, casting more bullets, cutting wood, and adding several more cow buffalo to their spring meat larder in preparation for the intense work and long days required during the coming spring trapping season.

Come the first day to begin spring beaver trapping as decided by Wallace, Cedrick had the brothers up early, fed and in the process of making their animals ready for that first lengthy day in a never previously trapped area. As luck would have it, the men departed their campsite in a driving snowstorm! However by around noontime, the short spring storm had subsided and Wallace was found up to his waist in near-freezing waters setting his last trap! Stomping out from the icy cold waters after making his last set, Wallace staggered up onto the bank surrounding a large beaver pond and took off fast-walking across the prairie trying to get some life back into his near-frozen legs after all of his morning-long immersions. (Author's Note: The invention of rubber wearing apparel like rubber boots did not come about until around 1832. Hence beaver trappers prior to that invention coming on line had to brave the icy waters with their bare flesh and maybe only a pair of buckskin leggings as covering. As a result of those frequent immersions into the icy waters, many trappers quit trapping early on due to cases of the early in life onset of extreme cases of rheumatism.)

Pausing in his fast-walking about on the prairie trying to get some life and warmth back into his feet and legs, Wallace became aware of a 'rumble of thunder'. Looking skyward figuring another spring storm was on its way, he saw only blue sky. About then, Wallace felt the ground vibrating beneath his semi-frozen feet as he just stood there wondering what the hell was happening. That was when Otis was seen riding his horse and trailing Wallace's, moving like the wind as he headed directly for his brother standing alone out on the open prairie! Arriving moments later, Otis yelled as he rode up, "Mount up, Wallace, we have one hell of a buffalo stampede coming our way and unless you want to be made into 'hoof soup', you had better get your carcass into this here saddle and be off with the rest of us!"

Trying to swing his almost lifeless near-frozen legs up into the saddle and not being successful until his third attempt, Wallace and Otis finally headed off across the open prairie and back towards the beaver ponds just trapped. As they did, the still snow-covered prairie from the morning's spring snowstorm behind them turned from white to a heaving mass of brown! A mass of brown flooding across the prairie of rumbling, stumbling, heaving with their tails held high into the air, aggravated buffalo in a full-blown stampede and coming their way over the hilltop just left!

Frozen legs and feet now forgotten by Wallace, the two brothers raced across the prairie back towards the beaver ponds just trapped to the shouted encouragement of their remaining two brothers huddled on their horses in a large willow patch along the bank. Just then, the stampeding masses of furry beasts turned as if on command and headed right at the two fleeing men! As the beasts neared the two racing-away men, most animals could be seen running in terror with a large amount of white ringing their eyes! As Otis and Wallace now streaked across the prairie, near-frozen feet and legs on the part of Wallace became forgotten as the stampeding buffalo quickly closed the gap between the front of the herd and the two fleeing men.

Finally, the race was won as the two fleeing trappers rode their horses full speed into the shallow waters of the beaver pond, ONLY TO FIND THEMSELVES STILL BEING CLOSELY PURSUED BY THE TERRIFIED BUFFALO EN MASSE INTO THE WATER! By then, Otis and Wallace had been joined by Oliver and Cedrick after they had been flushed out from the comforting cover of their willow patch, who now found they were riding for their lives out across the beaver pond closely pursued by thousands of terrified and fleeing buffalo as well! Stopping their horses directly behind a large beaver house, the men dismounted 'on the fly' onto the beaver house and began shooting into the front of the seemingly unstoppable oncoming herd! Upon dropping the first four buffalo from the front of the mass of oncoming buffalo stampeding across the beaver pond, that portion of the obviously panicked herd split and seamlessly flowed around the mud and stick beaver's house. As they did, they barely left untouched the trappers standing on the beaver house with their nervous horses standing behind it!

Now firing their pistols into the flowing herd of buffalo as they continued swarming around the beaver house with the trappers' horses directly behind it using it for their cover as well, the men after a short period of time could finally see the end of the herd nearing their location. THEN THE MEN SAW WHAT HAD STAMPEDED THE HERD OF BUFFALO RIGHT AT THEM… As they stood on the top of their protective beaver house hurriedly reloading their rifles, the Barnes Clan could just barely make out through the upraised dust from the stampeding buffalo what appeared to be about a dozen riders sitting on their horses trailing a number of pack animals on a distant ridgeline! THEN IN A BLINK OF AN EYE, THE MYSTERY RIDERS WERE GONE JUST AS FAST AS THEY HAD MOMENTARILY APPEARED STRUNG OUT ALONG THE FAR RIDGELINE!

"Who the hell do you suppose those riders were and what the hell were they doing trying to get us killed by stampeding those damn buffalo right at us?" asked Cedrick as he continued reloading his rifle and two pistols.

"I don't know but they sure as hell messed up all of the traps we set in this here ponded area when that herd of buffalo about ran over the top of us and them too. I sure would love to get my hands around their damn scrawny necks and squeeze the hell out of those riders for what they just did to the four of us," said Oliver quietly.

"No use sticking around here now that the danger is gone. I say Cedrick and Otis butcher out some meat from those four dead buffalo in front of this here beaver's house and Wallace, since he is now all warmed up and I see if we can recover any of our previously set beaver traps in this here pond. Those traps are so damned expensive we can ill afford to just leave them. So I say we try our hand at finding them if at all possible," said Oliver as he mounted his horse with both of his rifles now loaded as well as both of his pistols.

An hour of looking later over the hoof-pounded ground and muddied ponded area that the buffalo had finally left produced nary a single trap of the four that had been set in that specific area! Truth be known, the traps had been stomped into the mud and out of sight by the several thousand buffalo that had tromped through the area. In the meantime, the sun had warmed up the area and much of the snow that had come earlier in the morning had since begun dissipating, leaving muddy and hoof-pounded ground throughout in its wake. However, of the remaining 20 traps previously set in other nearby ponded areas not touched by the buffalo's stampede, 12 already contained lifeless beaver hanging at the end of the trap's chain in the deeper waters. With that kind of success hanging in the traps, the dozen unknown men who had stampeded the buffalo seemingly intentionally right at the Barnes Clan, moved to the back of the men's minds but were not forgotten… As Cedrick skinned out the 12 recently trapped beaver, Wallace dressed back into his warmer clothing after retrieving the last beaver from the icy cold waters, mounted his horse and waited for his brother to finish his skinning detail so they could return to their cabin and he could warm up even further in front of their indoor fireplace.

About an hour later, the men turned the corner into their secluded meadow and began their ride towards their cabin at the head of the draw. About halfway up the long draw leading to their cabin, Wallace stopped his horse and signaled for his brother, Otis, to move forward on his horse. When Otis moved up alongside his brother's horse, Wallace pointed towards the cabin. There off in a distance stood their cabin with its only door wide open! "Looks like maybe a grizzly has visited our cabin while we were out trapping from the looks of that wide open front door," said Wallace disgustedly. "Best you and Oliver move forward and see how much damage it has done," he continued with a shake of his head once again in disgust. "We will stay back until you kill the damn thing if he is still in the cabin and that way we won't have our horses spooked all over the hillside," Wallace continued as an afterthought, pending any grizzly bear action taken. "Just be careful," said Wallace, "spring bears just out from hibernation can be meaner that a snake because they are so starved and hungry."

With that, Otis and Oliver dismounted, checked the pans on their flintlock rifles and began the long slow walk towards their cabin and a possible altercation with a cabin-occupying grizzly bear. Sitting there at the end of the meadow with their horses, Wallace and Cedrick watched their two brothers pull a sneak on the cabin hoping to surprise the bear instead of it surprising them. After quietly taking up their positions just outside the cabin, Otis beat on one of Cedrick's steel pots hoping to put the bear on the run outside their cabin where it could be safely killed. When he beat on the side of the steel pot with a metal cooking spoon, no bear emerged from the men's cabin. After a long wait, the two brothers approached the cabin with their rifles held at the ready and then after a quick peek through the open front doorway, both men entered in a rush!

Moments later, Otis exited through the open doorway and gestured for his brothers to make their approach. As they did, Otis walked over to their outdoor firepit and sat down on one of the sitting logs spaced around the campfire, aimlessly poking one of their meat skewers into the now long-out coals. Dismounting, Wallace walked over to Otis saying, "What is up with the open front door?"

"Go take a look for yourself. But when you do, be prepared to be pissed off!" replied Otis with just a touch of 'deadly' rising up in the tone of his voice. "While you are at it, you might take a look over your shoulder at our corral as well." With those words, Wallace turned and looked in the direction of their corral located in a stand of aspens. It was then that he noticed for the first time that the corral gate was wide open and every valuable horse was gone! Wallace turned back around and from the look on his face over seeing an empty corral, someone was going to die! Then realizing he could do nothing at that moment over the theft of their livestock, he walked over to the cabin and entered slowly through its open front doorway.

"DAMN IT!" bellowed Wallace from within the cabin. Moments later, all four of the brothers were gathered around the outside firepit with dark looks on all of their faces. "Those son-of-a-bitches who stampeded those buffalo into us as we ran our trap lines have just cleaned us out!" said Oliver with more than just a touch of 'deadly' in the tone and tenor of his voice.

As Oliver spoke, Otis, the group's best tracker, walked over to their now empty corral of all packhorses, dropped to one knee and began examining the ground closely. Then he rose and walked off a short distance obviously tracking a cold trail of shod hoofprints down through the stand of pine trees where their meat racks, previously hung with several hindquarters from buffalo, now hung empty as well. "That did it!" Otis uttered under his breath as he turned and walked back to the cabin and the rest of his brothers.

"Near as I can tell, they cleaned us out completely! Whoever it was, they knew what the hell they were doing. They took all of our pelts, every keg of gunpowder, our bags of flints, our kegs of rum, every bar of lead, and every knife and ax that we had in the place! In short, we have been pretty much abandoned and left 'afoot' with only what we are carrying in our 'Possibles bags'. Near as I can figure it, unless we get lucky, we are 'dead men walking' without what they took!" exclaimed Wallace.

An hour later found the Barnes Clan with Otis as lead tracker, returning to where the mystery men had first been spotted stampeding the buffalo directly at the brothers earlier in the day. From there, Otis easily picked up the men's trails and on foot or horseback depending on the terrain, went after those who had done them wrong and were now going to have to atone for their sins, just like the Good Book decreed... But doing so was going to be a bit of a chore. The Barnes Clan collectively had one small bag of jerky, a one-pound tin of DuPont black powder between the four of them, 12 flints, a small bag of patches made from ticking, 32 lead balls, their heavy winter clothing and a powerful heap of Irish American gumption, 'going to do unto others for what had been done unto them'...

By that evening come the dark and cold, Otis

had figured there were 13 riders on shod horses trailing eight packhorses all deduced from their hoofprints in the spring's soft earth. Additionally, the horses were heavily loaded and appeared to be heading due north towards Canada. Later that night as the four brothers huddled together under the boughs from some dense fir trees for the warmth their bodies collectively offered, Cedrick all of a sudden exclaimed, "Damn, it is that damn French-Canadian, Pierre "The Wolverine" La Gren! I will bet that is who we are tracking. If I can get my hands around that bastard's throat or the blade of my tomahawk into his skull, you can damn well figure he will have seen his last sunrise! Who else could it be? We are near the Canadian border, the Major warned us about keeping our guard up when trapping on the upper reaches of the Big Muddy near Canada and he took all of our most important supplies needed for survival by any fur trapper. That is exactly who took our furs and supplies! Just like the Major said before we left. That Wolverine fella would strike when we least expected it and make off with everything of value that we had. Well, he may be a wolverine but I don't think he knows who he is messing with. Especially when we are out here freezing our butts off instead of being back at our warm cabin tipping a cup of rum."

"Speaking of freezing our butts off, how about you get back into our huddle under this damn tree so we all can stay warmer?" said Oliver, the skinniest brother of the Barnes Clan...

The next morning right at daylight found the Barnes Clan hot on the trail of their furs, provisions and horse thieves. As they did, Otis soon discovered that the thieves, figuring no one was now on their trail, were now walking their heavily loaded packhorses. That let Otis know the men being cold-tracked had a long way to go so they were now taking it easy on their horses. The rest of that day, the Barnes Clan put one of their brothers out in front on foot to reduce the chance of being inadvertently discovered hot on the thieves' trails. Another cold and sleepless night soon rolled around and it was then during that time that the brothers got a break. Out gathering pine and fir boughs to make a warmer bed for all the men, Otis paused and stood stock-still for the longest time. Returning with his pine boughs, he knelt by his resting brothers saying, "Take a deep smell, my brothers." Realizing that Otis was on to something, all of the brothers began sniffing in big 'snootfuls' of the cold night's air and discovered a slight smell of pinewood smoke in the air!

About an hour later, after tracking down the faint smells of smoke leading to a distant campfire, found the Barnes brothers peering into a camp full of men laughing and speaking in a language they did not understand but figured it to be French! Additionally, the camp full of men was finishing off the next to last keg of the Barnes brothers' rum, which to their way of thinking, made that a killing offense in and of itself! Having seen enough, the brothers slinked off further back into the darkness to formulate their plans for taking back what was rightfully theirs. There they figured taking a man's packhorses, provisions and furs was akin to a killing offense! Two hours later with their bellies full of roasted buffalo meat and stolen rum, the men in the camp of thieves settled down into a noisy snoring slumber. Little did any of them realize just how deadly the night was soon to become for those of their 'stealing one's horses and livelihood' ilk...

Positioning themselves in a line abreast so there would be no crossfire concerns once they figured the shooting started, the Barnes brothers sneaked in from the darkness into the fading light of the suspected French-Canadians' two slowly dying campfires. Walking quietly right up to the line of men snuggled away in their sleeping furs around the two fires, Wallace looked over at his brothers making sure they were ready to sow a healthy dose of 'hellfire and brimstone' into and among the stealing Frenchmen! As he did, he noticed that each of his brothers had already cocked his rifle and each of their two pistols loaded with buck and ball for close-in shooting carried in their sashes! There was no two ways about it, the devil was about to get his due...

"HEY!" yelled Wallace, as rifle fire followed by eight pistol shots ringing out so fast into the once sleeping and then startled upwards to their feet Frenchmen, that it was more like a single roar of sound followed by a rolling cloud of white black powder smoke enveloping the dead and dying! Twelve suspected Hudson's Bay Company Frenchmen died that evening in a fusillade of shots fired by the Barnes brothers! The thirteenth Frenchman, somehow untouched by 'shot or shell', leapt up and being the experienced frontiersman that he was when danger abounded, bolted off into the night much like a wolverine, wearing only a flapping in the cold night air nightshirt... That man fleeing into the darkness of night wearing only a nightshirt represented a piece of fleeing civility among the just-experienced 'Code of the West' being coldly carried out!

The next morning after feasting on the remains of the Frenchmen's buffalo supper, the Barnes Clan quietly left the scene of death. When they did, they left the bodies of the Frenchmen where they had fallen without being graced with a Christian burial for the beasts of the forest upon which to feast. However, the Barnes Clan found themselves 13 horses richer for their efforts, which they trailed back to their camp for eventual trailing back to Fort Henry for barter, sale or trade. Additionally, they recovered all of their stolen furs, horses and provisions, not to mention 13 rifles and a smaller number of pistols from the Frenchmen who no longer had a use for any of them...

That evening as Cedrick prepared the men's evening meal the other three brothers unloaded all of their packs of stolen furs and provisions and hauled them back into their cabin for safe-keeping. Then as their expanded herd of horses fed in the nearby meadow, Otis, finishing with his plate, stood up from his sitting log and put his dinner plate into the wash pan. Turning, he loaded up his pipe with smoking tobacco, lit its bowl's contents with an ember from the camp-fire, sat down on his sitting log saying, "I have a suggestion. What say the four of us up and leave this area just as soon as the beaver leave their prime or we trap all of them out? We early on figured we would trap out the upper reaches of the Big Muddy and then come the next trap-ping season, trap out the lower portion of that same river. But here is what I am thinking. Soon as the beaver 'prime out' or are trapped out, we pack up our gear and head for the lower reaches of the Big Muddy. That way we get a jump on our next trapping season by building another cabin on the lower reaches of the Big Muddy and when we return for the fall trapping season, we will almost be ready to go and not have to worry about building another cabin. Also by doing it that way, if that Wolverine fella recovers from his fright and comes looking for us with more of his fur-stealing friends, he will find that we are already gone and maybe we won't have to worry about him come the start of the fall trapping season. What do all of you think about my plan?" asked Otis, as he filled the cooling evening air with his rich-smelling pipe smoke.

Oliver had just finished his supper and with what his brother had just said, replied, "Sounds great to me. I would rather build us another cabin during the early summer months than have to fuss with all of that as the beaver trapping season and winter comes upon us in the fall. I say we start packing now so that when we either trap out this area or the beaver go out of prime, whichever comes first, we 'hit the deck a-running and spin the guns around'."

Cedrick and Wallace just nodded their support for Otis's idea as they happily finished the last two Dutch oven biscuits from the Dutch oven. With that decided, Otis, ever the thinker, sat back and enjoyed the remaining bowl of his smoking tobacco. Especially when his cloud of mosquitoes left him because of the offending pipe smoke and descended upon the remaining three brothers still sitting around their campfire...

Three weeks later, the last of the beaver were trapped out on the upper reaches of the Big Muddy. Two days later found the Barnes Clan on the move further south into the lower reaches of the Big Muddy looking for a suitable area in which to trap beaver and the building of another cabin for their coming fall and spring trapping season. After three days of slow travel examining the beaver trapping possibilities, the brothers drew up alongside a large lake on the eastern side of the Big Muddy. Just about opposite the lake's outlet river into the Big Muddy River, the brothers discovered a meadow area in the nearby foothills that provided a suitable location for their new cabin. They did not have the running water like in their last location on the upper reaches of the Big Muddy, but the new area promised a rather nice spring once the water source was dug out and developed with a little shovel and rockwork. There were sufficient nearby stands of timber from which to build a cabin and set of corrals not to mention two nearby meadow areas sufficient enough for the size of their considerably expanded horse herd in which to graze.

Pulling into their new home site, Cedrick stepped off the distance from the proposed cabin site and commenced building his new outdoor cooking area knowing his brothers' penchant for eating on time. Otis, once the cabin site's location had been determined, grabbed a shovel and began digging and developing their soon to be spring box, which he later rocked up. Following that, Otis began digging the postholes for their new and within watching distance corral. The next day, the stout Irishman walked up into the nearby stand of timber with a single buck saw and began cutting down what he figured were the right-sized trees for their new cabin. This he did to the sounds of another saw cutting down timber for the cabin and the sounds of two ringing axes limbing the freshly cut logs.

By the second week of the brothers' occupation of their new cabin site, found the walls of the cabin up, the corrals built, a nearby water source developed from a more than adequate ground seep, and an outdoor cooking area up and functioning. One week later found the roof up on the cabin, all the packs and provisions moved inside the cabin's protective walls to prevent Indian theft or damage from the many summer rains, and work beginning in making the interior of the cabin 'homey'.

Come the first week of July found the Barnes Clan 'caravanned up' once again and heading south on the Big Muddy en route the mighty Missouri River. Days later found the brothers retrieving their raft hidden in the brush built the previous summer along the Missouri so they could safely cross that river, and two days later all their packs had been paddled across. Then all that remained was for Oliver, bare naked as a baby bird, safely swimming their entire horse herd across the Missouri River as well. Tired from all of their labors, the men made camp for the night on the south side of the river.

Early the next morning, the men awoke to the faraway 'popping' noises of sporadic gunfire coming from further east along the Yellowstone in the direction of Fort Henry! Hurriedly breaking camp, Otis was sent on ahead with instructions to find out what all the shooting was about and report back to the rest of his brothers. In the meantime, they would be moving their caravan slowly along until the return of their brother with information relative to all of the questionable and suspicious shooting coming from the direction of Fort Henry. Later that afternoon, Otis came riding back 'hellbent for leather' with word that Fort Henry was under attack by a number of Indians! With that information in hand, a 'council of war' was held by the brothers. There they learned from Otis that about 20 Indians had circled the small fort and had it under desultory fire from all sides! That was when Wallace, quiet up until that time, came up with a plan. Wallace surmised that they needed to get into the fort in order to trade off their beaver skins and extra horses so they could resupply and then continue trapping in the fall and spring of the coming year. However, there were lots of 'looks of concern' from his three brothers as Wallace laid out his rather daring plan.

The next day with the Barnes Clan's horse herd picketed and hidden deeply in the dense river brush along the Yellowstone, the brothers made their dangerous move. Each brother sported a riding and packhorse as they left their new campsite. Then taking their four Indian Trade rifles from the battle of the 'coffee pot', their own arsenal of firearms and all of the firearms seized from the Frenchmen who had robbed their cabin, the four Barnes's figured they were ready for 'bear' and Wallace's battle plan! Taking all 24 of the rifles the Barnes Clan now had in their possession, each man was issued a total of six rifles. Then with their own pistols and what they had recovered from the thieving Frenchmen, the Barnes Clan had a total of 15 pistols among the brothers! Then all of the rifles and pistols were loaded with buck and ball for what they considered would be 'close-in work'. The plan was that the Barnes Clan would divide up into two teams of two men, with each team taking an adjoining side of 'besiegers' circling the small fort and ambush them from behind! With only 20 Indians besieging the fort from all sides, Wallace figured if the brothers could kill at least four Indians on each side of the fort that they attacked with such multiples of firepower, that would cause great concern among the Indians. So much so that it would cause them, not knowing the forces surrounding them, to melt off into the vastness of the woods and disappear. Otis thought the idea was a little crazy and a lot could go wrong but being a hard-headed Irishman, any fight no matter the odds, would be a good one!

Come nightfall, the Barnes's original battle plan had already been changed. Otis, more Indian than Irishman, had located the camp where the Indians camped at night along the Yellowstone near Fort Henry. With that discovery, a change of plans was made once again and set into motion. Since the now identified Blackfeet Indians had left just four of their own to remain around the walls of the fort at night to continue some desultory fire to keep those trapped inside thinking they were still heavily surrounded, the rest retreated back to their camp to eat and sleep. That way, the rest could also live to fight another day against the much-hated white man, his fort and trading post located right in their own backyard.

Come the deep of night at the Blackfeet Indians' campsite, only one Indian sat around the campfire keeping it tended while the rest of his kind slept. The impact from the heavy lead balls hit the Indian campfire tender dead center in his back! The kinetic energy from the close at hand fired buck and ball blew the campfire tender off his sitting rock and splayed him across his well-tended campfire, to slowly roast away and stink up the air with the smell of a burning human being! With the sound of that shot, the camp of 15 sleeping Indians exploded up from their sleeping furs, only to be struck by a 'blizzard' of 'buck and ball' fired from the close at hand four trappers' numerous rifles and pistols. Of the 15 previously sleeping Indians, only two made it into the nearby river and a welcome escape from the 'lead hell' being dished out back at their campfire! Then for the next 20 minutes or so, silence reigned around the Indians' campfire, except for the burning and crackling of the body fat from the first Indian killed and splayed across his well-tended fire after being back shot. Then the four Indians who had been left back at the

fort to keep up harassing fire all night, upon hearing the explosive firing back at their campsite,
left the fort's surroundings and moments later,
slowly stalked into the light of the campfire with
arms at the ready to see what had just happened.
What had happened earlier at the Indians' camp
'happened' to the four Indians returning to their
campsite to see what the hell had just happened to
their brethren! Realizing all the Indians had been
taken care of except for the two that had escaped
into the river, the Barnes brothers saw to it that
the remaining dead joined the two Indians who
had managed to make it into the river to escape
as well… That way, maybe all the floating bodies
discovered floating in the river might just serve
as a reminder for others to abandon their future
plans to attack the Fort Henry Trading Post.

The next morning to avoid any unnecessary
mistakes as to their identity, the Barnes's waited
until full daylight before they made their grand
entrance into the fort much to the surprise of the
somewhat beleaguered fort's few inhabitants.
Suffice to say after an explanation by Wallace as
to the previous night's events, the rum flowed
freely that evening at the fort and the Barnes
Clan not surprisingly, did not have to pay for a
single drop they consumed…

The next day around noon when heads had
cleared somewhat from the previous night's celebrations, the Barnes Clan surprisingly also received top dollar for their furs even though they

were only contract trappers! For the next week, the Barnes Clan were celebrated several times by the fort's inhabitants and by those fur trappers arriving daily still carrying their 'topknots', who became aware of what had happened several nights previously! While there, Major Henry advised the Barnes Clan that the fort had been attacked by the Blackfeet and Arikara Indians at least four times every month! Henry also advised that if the level of attacks continued, he was going to recommend that the fort be abandoned and they go to a supply system whereby the company would come to the trappers in the field at a place to be annually determined, instead of having the trappers come to an easy to attack central fort or trading post. Then the central trading and supply location in the field would also be determined by the number of friendly tribes of Indians in the area, as well as a site central to the best beaver trapping. There both the trappers and the friendly Indians could be supplied with provisions and the company could gather up the furs brought to the gathering for shipment back to St. Louis and eventually the ever-hungry European markets. (Author's Note: The numerous historical Blackfeet and Arikara Indian attacks upon Fort Henry forced the realization that a small stationary re-supply fort was not the most practical answer, and eventually brought about the very successful "Rendezvous" supply system practiced during the fur trade for the next several years. That Rendezvous system was successfully practiced for a number of years until the trappers had basically trapped out the beaver and a social change had been made, whereby the societal desire for the beaver hat changed to that of the silk hat. With those two factors in play, the beaver fur market died as did the famous Rendezvous system of trade and supply.)

For the next two weeks the Barnes Clan celebrated with their friends at Fort Henry. Also during that period, Steve "Cooter" Krentz was approached by the brothers and asked to select out the 16 very best riding and packhorses gathered up from the battles with the Frenchmen and Northern Cheyenne as well as those owned by the Barnes Clan. Those remaining horses not selected were then sold to Major Henry as replacement horses for less fortunate contract and Free Trappers. Additionally, Cooter Krentz saw to it that all of the brothers' horses were reshod with new shoes free of charge for what they had done to break the earlier Blackfeet siege of the fort.

By the end of July, the Barnes Clan found they had celebrated with their friends and fellow trappers enough and found the frontier and beaver trapping opportunities at their new location on the Big Muddy calling. They had sold their extra horse herd, all the rifles seized from the two battles they had with the Northern Cheyenne and the French-Canadians, and their furs as dictated by their contract being that they were contract trappers. Half of the furs were taken by the American Fur Company as dictated by their contract signed in 1822 and the rest they sold. All totaled after they had paid back what they owed to the American Fur Company for being provisioned the previous fall, the brothers still had $1,803 to the good from their horse, rifle and fur sales! That in mind, Major Henry cut a Letter of Credit to the brothers for that amount to be redeemed once the brothers were back in St. Louis at the American Fur Company fur house. Two days later, fully re-supplied, packed and ready, the Barnes Clan left Fort Henry for another fall and coming spring trapping season on the Big Muddy. Only this time, instead of trapping on the upper reaches, they had chosen to trap out the lower portion of that river's system adjacent their new cabin site located in the foothills opposite the confluence of the Lake River which flowed out from the western end of Medicine Lake into the Big Muddy.

Once again, the brothers recovered their log raft from the year before and ferried all of their provisions, saddles and packs across the Missouri River. As done in times past, Oliver stripped down naked as a jay bird and riding one of their horses bareback, 'swam' the rest of their 15 horses safely across the Missouri River to the other side.

CHAPTER FIVE

RETURN TO THE "BIG MUDDY"

AFTER CROSSING THE MISSOURI, the brothers camped along the northern side of the same river deep within one of its brush fields for the protection it offered against inadvertent discovery and Blackfeet Indian attack. The next morning around noontime, the brothers had finally loaded all of their animals for the trip that lay ahead. Then the Barnes's headed almost due north along the Big Muddy for whatever the good Lord had set aside for them in the way of life's further adventures... True, they were heading into the land of the dreaded and killing Blackfeet but being four strong and heavily armed with the dreams of many 'blanket-sized beaver' whirling around in their heads, they figured their chances for success and survival were good. Besides, the Barnes Clan, good shooters one and all, figured if one worried about catching a bullet that was a waste of time. After all, they believed to a man, why worry about catching a 'speeding bullet' since destiny had already decided that outcome for each of them at birth by a Supreme Being...

Three days later of slow travel keeping close at hand to the Big Muddy's brushy river bottom to avoid any unnecessary clashes with the dreaded Blackfeet, the brothers arrived at their new and previously built cabin site just north of the current-day town of Homestead, Montana, and on the western side of the river. Turning into their secluded meadow holding their new cabin, as the men moved closer into the actual site, they noticed that the door was wide open. Stopping their horse caravan a short distance from their cabin, Oliver and Otis moved forward on foot with their rifles held at the ready in case a grizzly bear had taken up residence in the brothers' new home. Because if one had, he soon would be gracing their supper table, his bear grease would be saved for making biscuits, and his fur would soon become a winter robe for one of the men. However, once a careful look had been taken inside, only a porcupine had taken up residence in their new cabin and he was soon hustled out the front door and sent on his way.

Shortly thereafter, the horses had been unpacked, unsaddled, hobbled and now fed quietly in their nearby meadow. As for life back at the cabin, it was all a-bustle. All their packs were now being unloaded and put away on the pegs and shelves that had been installed earlier that summer to prevent spoilage or being eaten by the ever-present rodents. Meanwhile, Cedrick, the camp's faithful cook, already had a fire going making a bed of coals for his famous biscuits, with biscuit dough rising alongside in the fire's warmth, and a pot of pinto beans soaking away in a pot of water adjacent the fire. Once the provisions were put away, the saddles and packs were then put up in their covered structure adjacent their cabin up and away from any salt-hungry porcupines looking for sweat-soaked leather to chew on. Then their damp horse blankets were arrayed along the corral's rails in order to dry as the hardworking trappers then took a breather.

Shortly thereafter, Oliver and Otis left the cabin with rifles in hand and about an hour later, were back at their cabin with a field dressed buck antelope for Cedrick to work his supper magic upon. That evening, the men supped upon freshly roasted antelope, biscuits, coffee and a fresh Dutch oven apple cobbler made from dried apple slices soaked in warm water and loaded with nutmeg, cinnamon, raisins and brown sugar. Suffice to say, the always 'eager eater' Barnes brothers left the outdoor campfire that evening more than fully satisfied with their first day at their new campsite and the bountiful grub consumed. Especially now that they knew they did not have to get into a big rush and build their winter cabin since they had done so earlier in the summer.

The next morning found the men making a long, 'hell-for-stout' meat pole near the horse corral and in the afternoon, cutting and stacking a small mountain of dry wood for Cedrick's outdoor cooking fire. Then for the next two days, the men cut and hauled dry logs to the cabin site for their winter's wood supply. With the entire antelope consumed by day three, the men saddled up their horses and two packhorses, went forth and killed a cow buffalo from a nearby herd. That cow buffalo was shortly afterwards butchered in the field and the four quarters brought back to the camp's meat pole and hung in order to cool out and glaze. Following supper that evening of roasted buffalo, biscuits, coffee, Dutch oven pinto beans, and a Dutch oven rice dish heavily sprinkled with raisins, dried apricots, dried apple slices, cinnamon, nutmeg and brown sugar, the men sat back around the campfire barely able to move after eating so much and just happily relaxed. Later once the mosquitoes got bothersome, the men headed for their sleeping furs with dreams of the morrow afield looking over the nearby beaver waters for their quarry soon to be taken, skinned, hooped and made ready for transport back to Fort Henry come the following summer.

After a hearty breakfast the next morning and attending to a call of nature getting rid of the previous evening's rich and heavy meal, the men saddled up and headed for the Big Muddy. There they rode to survey the fall beaver trapping water adjacent their campsite previously chosen for the coming fall's trapping ventures. Starting out near the confluence of the Lake River where it entered the Big Muddy from the east, the men came upon a pleasant surprise. Slowly riding along the Big Muddy near a sandy shallows taking in the amount of beaver activity as evidenced by all the beaver slides, willow, cottonwood patches and tree cutting activities, the brothers chanced upon hearing much laughter coming from their side of the river. Laughter and other noises sounding of women and children enjoying themselves!

Remaining mounted and hidden behind a dense patch of willows, the men continued riding near an active beaver dam and soon discovered the approximate location from whence was coming all of the happy noises and laughter sounding of women and children at play. Moments later after much looking and surreptitious scouting along the edge of the willow patch, the men discovered the exact source of such sounds of merriment. There on a sandy spit below along the river were four naked Indian women bathing and as they did unawares of the trappers' close presence, watched their children playing in the nearby shallows. All of the women appeared to be young mothers out for a quiet outing with their children. Then the men noticed a number of "Bull Boats" anchored on their side of the river at the edge of the sandbar. For the longest time the men watched with obvious interest the beautiful Indian women bathing and cavorting along the sandy spit totally unaware of the four onlooking and still-hidden white men fur trappers.

Then Otis, the brother with by far and away the best eyes in the group, noticed something unusual that caught his visual senses. About a quarter-mile below where the naked Indian women played in the river's waters with their children, were six horses tied off in a dense stand of willows. Not seeing any of those horses' riders, Otis quickly warned the brothers of the potential danger the six riderless, most likely Indian horses, represented! With his quiet warning of the possible nearby danger, the still remaining hidden trappers quickly checked their rifles and then let their eyes carefully sweep the brush alongside the Big Muddy near the bathing, seemingly unwary Indian women. This they did, figuring the riders of the nearby hidden Indian horses may very well be stalking the same women the trappers were watching bathing along the shore of the Big Muddy with evil intent in their minds...

At first, the brothers spotted nothing out of the ordinary moving along the brushy river's western shore except that of a few local disinterested birds. Then once again, Otis's sharp eyes discerned just a slightly unusual movement of the willows directly below the trappers and slightly behind the bathing Indian women! Intensifying his examination in the area holding the slight disturbance in the brush alongside the river near the women, Otis finally spotted potential danger! Directly behind the Indian women in the dense patch of willows, Otis spotted six younger looking male Indians sneaking up behind the Indian women! Alerting his brothers as to the possible dangers the Indian women faced, the four trappers quickly dismounted, tied off their horses and began making their ways towards the six unsuspecting Indians making their ways towards the unawares Indian women and their children.

Because of the distance between the trappers and the Indian women, the six Indians sneaking up on the Indian women were able to strike first before the trappers could intervene! Bursting forth from the edge of the dense patch of willows, the six Indian men immediately attacked the four naked Indian women bathing at the river's edge! SCREAMS IMMEDIATELY RENT THE AIR AS THE INDIAN WOMEN WERE QUICKLY OVERRUN, GRABBED BY THEIR LONG HAIR AND TOSSED TO THE SANDY BEACH! AS FOUR YOUNG INDIAN MEN BEGAN MAKING SIGNS OF MOUNTING THE FOUR NAKED WOMEN, THE REMAINING TWO ATTACKING MEN WITHOUT AN

ADULT WOMAN IN THEIR MIDST, RAN FOR THE GROUP OF CHILDREN PLAYING AT THE WATER'S EDGE! SOON TERROR SPREAD ACROSS THE SANDY BEACH AS THE UNKNOWN INDIAN MEN BEGAN MOUNTING THE FOUR INDIAN WOMEN FIRST CAUGHT, AS THE TWO MEN RUNNING FOR THE CHILDREN, GRABBED TWO TEENAGE-LOOKING INDIAN WOMEN FROM AMONG THE YOUNGER CHILDREN AT PLAY AND BEGAN MOLESTING THE YOUNGER GIRLS, SOON TO BE ADULT WOMEN, AS WELL! BY NOW THE REMAINING CHILDREN WERE RUNNING SCREAMING DOWN THE BEACH IN AN ATTEMPT TO GET AWAY FROM THE UNKNOWN MEN ATTACKING THE SEXUALLY MATURE WOMEN OF THE GROUP...

First to reach the beach unobserved was Otis, who grabbed the first Indian man he came to, dropped his rifle in the sand, jerked him up off the female he had pinned under him on the beach, snapped the man's head upward and lifted his body clear off the woman lying struggling under her attacker! Then the powerfully built Otis slammed his man under the river's adjacent waters and held him there until he quit struggling and showed no signs of life! Meanwhile, Wallace, the second Barnes running onto the beach, grabbed the next Indian man in line violently raping the screaming woman under him!

Jerking the rapist upward with his tremendous arm strength from off the female, he broke the man's neck with a quick and violent twist of the man's head! Then without a single wasted motion, Wallace took two steps down the beach, kicking the next Indian in line raping the woman under him in the ribs, causing him to jump up in pain and alarm over being surprised by a white man! Wallace then shot the man in the chest from such close range, that the man's flesh was rent with flames from unspent black powder and residual white black powder smoke from such a burning close-in shot!

Cedrick, next of the brothers to reach his raping man on the beach, already found him starting to lift himself up off the woman he was sexually assaulting because of his awareness of the now attacking fur trappers. In his anger of the moment over what the man had been doing to the defenseless young Indian woman, Cedrick quickly clubbed him to death with the butt end of his rifle! Oliver, the last of the brothers to reach his assaulting Indian male, also found him raising up in alarm over being surprised by the close at hand white men and shot him in the head from such close range that the man's head exploded, splashing the woman he was sexually assaulting with the essence from the man's exploded brain case! The sixth Indian, now alerted and also alarmed over the arrival of the attacking white men, quickly rose up off the young girl he had been raping and went for his rifle lying close at hand on the beach! When he did, he was shot dead by Otis, now that he had risen up from drowning his Indian attacker, had picked up his rifle and sighted it on the next standing Indian attacker! When that Indian fell after being shot by Otis, he fell back down upon the young Indian girl he had been raping. She, figuring he was attacking her once again in all of the killing of the moment, did not settle down and quit screaming until Oliver had lifted the dead Indian off her and tossed his body into the river with a big splash!

Moments later, the six Indian women assaulted by the men from an unknown tribe who had attacked them, were standing naked as all get-out in a huddled and frightened mass upon now seeing the four white trappers standing nearby. Not speaking the language but having learned some 'sign language', Oliver signed, "The white men were friends and there in peace." That didn't seem to have any calming effect on the just assaulted and terrified women! Then the Indian women realized they had children frightened out of their wits and scattered up and down the beach still crying and running about in panic. With that, their instincts as mothers took over and disregarding the four white men standing there not knowing what to do next, found the women scampering all around gathering up their children and trying to calm them down. Then the Indian women hustled all of their kids into the

Bull Boats, shoved them off from the shore and frantically paddled across the Big Muddy River for the far Medicine Lake shore, not even taking the time to get dressed they were so frightened! Reaching the far side, the women hustled their children onto the backs of their tied-off horses and soon the entire contingent of naked women and their children rode off like the wind towards Medicine Lake without any looks backwards to where the 'awful' event had occurred on their previously quiet and isolated sandy beach during a pleasant mid-morning swim and frolic with their friends and children...

Kicking the last of the dead Indian men into the Big Muddy to take their bodies hopefully to the Missouri River for its eventual disposal of the same, the brothers quietly walked back to their horses crowded with their private inner thoughts over what had just happened. There they quietly mounted up without any words being spoken among them since none were needed. Then with a final look backwards towards the direction where all the women and children had disappeared making sure they were still alright, the brothers rode down to where Otis had previously spotted the Indians' tied-off horses. There the trappers gathered up the Indians' valuable horses and with no further thoughts of checking out the beaver waters to be trapped in the near coming days, rode back to their camp quietly after having just experienced such a violent moment of time in their lives...

Here the brothers of Christian faith had just killed six men with no thoughts of remorse, and then had calmly tossed their bodies into the Big Muddy River so they would soon hopefully float into the Missouri River and be lost forever somewhere along its reaches. Riding quietly back to camp, the men soon found their thoughts turning to brighter images in life such as what Cedrick would soon be fixing for their supper. After all, sometimes the occurrence of such violent events and the killing that followed, were normal out on the frontier. The brothers had only done what their Christian father and faith had taught them to do under like circumstances. Suffice to say, in the Barnes brothers' minds, they had done nothing more than killing some vermin that truly needed killing, and had done so!

The next morning right at daybreak, Cedrick awoke having to 'see a man about a horse' and went outside to take care of his urgent call of nature. Finishing somewhat later, he walked over to their spring box, took a deep drink of the icy cold spring water, washed his face and then lathered up his face with shaving soap. Taking his straight razor to the communal razor strap hanging on an aspen tree limb, he hit it a couple of licks with his straight razor to better set the edge on the blade. Then he adjusted the communal mirror on an aspen limb to better fit his height and began shaving off his two-day-old growth of whiskers. Washing off his straight razor in a pan of cold water after making a couple of swipes with the blade, he looked back into his mirror, and ALL OF A SUDDEN SAW A BRIGHTLY PAINTED RED-AND-YELLOW INDIAN'S GLOWERING FACE LOOKING AT HIM FROM CLOSE BEHIND AND SO NEAR, THAT HE WAS NOW SEEN 'SHARING' THE MIRROR!

Whirling and dropping his straight razor in the same motion, Cedrick went for the pistol he always carried in his belt. When he did and before he could draw it from his sash, he saw that his 'one Indian' observed in his shaving mirror had now multiplied into three, and every one of them was facing him from no more than six feet away with their rifles fully cocked and aimed right at him waiting for him to make a move! Realizing he was a 'dead man' if he even tried drawing his pistol and defending himself at that moment in time, he slowly raised his hands above his head in the universal sign of surrender. When he did, his pistol and sheath knife were immediately removed from his person and with a rifle barrel jabbing him in his back, was 'directed' in which direction the Indians wished him to walk...

Otis, staggering out from his sleeping furs in the cabin somewhat later and REALLY 'having to see a man about a horse', raced out from the cabin and ran for his 'sitting log' over at the nearby latrine behind the cabin. Arriving, he dropped his buckskin pants and with an 'internal explosion', made sure the rich supper Cedrick had served the men the night before was a problem no more. Then another problem arose which immediately 'stoppered' him up 'tighter than a tick' with the continuation of his bodily functions in a heartbeat! Melting out from the elderberry bushes behind the cabin walked two heavily armed and yellow face-painted Indians with leveled rifles aimed right at him! As they did, there he embarrassingly sat, all bare-assed naked and helpless as a newborn elk calf in front of a hungry grizzly bear! Slowly raising his hands in surrender, Otis was 'told' to stand up and raise his buckskin, with the Indians gesturing such silent commands with the ends of their rifle barrels! Moments later, Otis joined his brother Cedrick over by the spring box where a dozen or more heavily painted Indians obviously on the warpath, collectively glowered at the two white men trespassing on the Indians' home ground…

Somewhat later, out from the cabin staggered Oliver as he headed for the nearby outside cooking fire. Not really paying much attention to his surroundings and just looking for his 'morning wake-up' cup of coffee, he went to his sitting log expecting to be served his favorite cup of brew by Cedrick, the camp's cook. Suffice to say, Oliver was soon 'woken' up 'Blackfoot Indian' style, when he realized the five humans approaching him from behind the cabin and walking towards him were all armed Indians heading straight for him! Oliver soon joined Cedrick and Otis now being held under five Indians' leveled rifle barrels. Indians who looked grouchy enough like they had just swallowed a great horned owl who did not want to be swallowed and was biting and clawing all the way down...

Half-an-hour later, Wallace emerged from the cabin, stood in front of the door of their cabin, yawned widely as he rubbed the 'sleep' from his eyes and then realized upon blinking his eyes back open, there were at least 30 painted and heavily armed Indians sitting on their horses looking right at him from just 20 yards away! Realizing to reach for his pistol was pure folly based on their numbers and from looking at their fiercely painted faces, he did the only thing that he could do and that was to raise his right hand and arm in the universal Plains Indian sign of peace. As he did, he wondered, *where the hell were his kid brothers and why hadn't they given him any king of warning as to the closeness of the danger now at hand?*

For the longest moment no one moved on either side. Then a very tall and rugged looking specimen of an Indian slowly but gracefully dismounted and began striding towards Wallace. Stopping right in front of Wallace, the fierce-looking Indian slowly looked him up and down as if trying to decide what to do with the white trapper who was obviously trespassing on sacred Indian lands. As the two men stood there eyeing each other up and down, Otis, Cedrick and Oliver were brusquely shoved into view from behind the horse corrals where they had been held captive, over to where Wallace was standing in front of the important-looking Indian. An Indian still coolly looking him over like a rattlesnake would do when looking at a close at hand and petrified deer mouse dinner soon to be...

When the four trappers were finally gathered together in front of the important-looking Indian standing in front of Wallace, all under heavy guard, the distinguished-looking man with the regal bearing finally spoke. When he spoke, he spoke in perfect English! Perfect English which the trappers surprisingly later discovered, that he had learned from the "Black Robes"! Learned from the Black Robes when they had come through the country after Lewis and Clark had returned to the United States. Then Lewis and Clark had fulfilled one of their promises by sending such personages back to teach the friendly Indian tribes the ways of the white man.

"Are you men of the Hudson's Bay Fur Company from the northern lands of the Queen or from the white men in the little fort by the great river called by you white men, "The Yellowstone"? Called The Yellowstone because it comes from the smoking lands to the south with the hot springs, bad smells and has the yellow stone throughout?" quietly asked the distinguished-looking Indian standing in front of the now captive Barnes brothers.

The brothers were amazed to be addressed by an Indian who spoke perfect English if the looks on their collective faces said anything as to their levels of amazement. After getting over their shock of the fact that the Indian standing before them could speak English, by eye contact and head nods, they 'designated' older brother Wallace to speak for the four of them.

"We four brothers and fur trappers are from the small fort to the south of us located along the Yellowstone River and who might you be?" asked Wallace rather bluntly and 'gutsy', in light of the rather poor situation the four brothers now found themselves in.

Approving of Wallace's courage and blunt demeanor in the face of being surrounded by a large number of his armed warriors and with a nod of his head, the distinguished Indian standing in front of the brothers said, "I am called "Gray Wolf", Chief of the Medicine Lake band of Blackfeet by your people. I want to know what gives you four men the right to build a cabin and get ready to trap beaver in our sacred lands?" asked Gray Wolf, with a face looking as if it was carved in granite stone.

Realizing he and his brothers were trapped with that question, Wallace figured honesty, under the conditions they were facing was the best policy, quietly replied, "We four trappers heard beaver trapping on the Big Muddy River was very good so we asked no one and just came in peace in order to trap the beaver. We also built a cabin so we would have a place in which to live in comfort, especially when the winter snows came."

"Who said you could kill and eat our buffalo, drink our water, cut our trees and build your cabin on our Father's sacred lands?" quietly asked Gray Wolf, without an ounce of emotion showing on his face or heard in the tone and tenor of his voice as he faced Wallace.

Realizing he and his brothers were trapped once again and there was no way out from the direct line of questioning Gray Wolf was taking and figuring it was just a short matter of time before all four of them became 'dead men walking', Wallace's Irish heritage and temper began surging forth. With that he replied, "We did not think the Great Blackfeet Nation of people would be angry if we killed a few buffalo among the many, cut a few trees where there are more of them than blades of grass, and drank a little water from all of the water found throughout this great land. Since we came in peace, we figured the Great Blackfeet Nation would allow us to live in peace as well."

For the longest time, Gray Wolf just stood there looking at the four men without any emotion showing on his face over the responses he had thus far received. Then Gray Wolf's tone and tenor of voice changed slightly when he asked, "Was it you four white men who attacked the Arikara war party who were attacking our women and children yesterday on the Big Muddy River and killed all of them?"

Sensing a glimmer of change in the demeanor of Gray Wolf and his line of questions, Wallace replied, "Yes, it was us."

"Why did none of you then take our naked women and have your way with them, like the other fur trappers we find in our land always do?" Gray Wolf quietly asked.

For the longest time Wallace mulled over his answer before he responded because he was not sure what Gray Wolf was looking for in his response. *True, they could have 'taken' the helpless Blackfoot women and had their way, but that was not how they had been raised as Christians and of the Catholic Faith*, thought Wallace. With that in mind, he once again responded to Gray Wolf's direct question as to why they had not 'feasted' upon the helpless women when the Arikara war party had not been so reserved. "We white men and brothers were not raised to treat helpless women and children in the manner in which they were being treated by those you called the Arikara. In our world and the way in which we were raised, a white man needs to marry a woman before he 'beds' her. Those women along the river yesterday were not our wives so we did not bother them, but let them return to their husbands unharmed by our hands," quietly replied Wallace just as impassively faced as was that of Gray Wolf.

"Then why do you trap our beaver, drink our water, kill and eat our buffalo and cut our trees? Those do not belong to the white man just like our wives did not belong to the white man," asked Gray Wolf, with a look that indicated he had now cleverly trapped the white man.

By that time, Wallace's 'Irish' was now flowing mightily through his veins! With that and his rising temper at being caught 'flat-footed' with their guard down and now being grilled by an Indian Chief who did not appreciate the presence of the brothers on his land, a land big enough for all, brought his temper to a head, outnumbered or not! "We did so because we did not feel the Great Blackfeet Nation would miss so little of what we took, and because "The Great Spirit" made so much. We just figured what little we took would not be missed by a generous people like the Blackfeet," said Wallace, realizing those words may or may not salve Chief Gray Wolf's concerns or questions but at least he was being honest in his response.

"White man, I can tell from the look in your eyes and your responses to my questions that you are a courageous, truthful and honorable man. You did not lie to me today in order to save your lives. You spoke with a 'straight tongue' and because of that and what you and your kind did yesterday to save our women and their children from the hated Arikara, you shall live in peace in the land of the Medicine Lake Band of

Gray Wolf's Blackfeet. You shall live in peace as long as I am the chief of the Medicine Lake Band of Blackfeet and will be welcome to share in our land and what The Great Spirit has provided for all of us to use and enjoy. I also personally thank you and your kind for saving my sister from a life of shame which she would have suffered and had to endure had you not arrived when you did. You and yours are now our brothers in the land of the Blackfeet." With those words, Gray Wolf said something to his warriors in his native tongue and immediately all of the weapons taken earlier when the brothers were disarmed were then returned. Then in a surprising move, Gray Wolf stepped forward and personally shook the hands of all of the brothers without saying another word. But the look in his eyes as he shook the hands of each brother said it all... Following that, he mounted his horse, whirled it around and with a wave of his right arm to his outlying warriors, left just as suddenly and quietly as they had arrived. For the rest of that 'rather interesting' morning, the brothers found themselves busy around their cabin. However to a man, they all took time to say a short "Thank You" to "The Old Boy Upstairs" in their own way for not letting that morning's events turn deadly and become their last...

For the next month-and-a-half after the beaver came into their prime, the Barnes's trapped beaver as they moved their trap lines further and further south down along the Big Muddy with great success. Almost on a daily basis, they found their traps full of beaver, with many of them being 'blanket-sized', showing that the Big Muddy was a long way from being trapped out. One early morning during the first week of November before the waterways had iced up, found Cedrick fixing breakfast and warming himself, especially his legs by the campfire. He, like Wallace, was finding the waters getting colder and colder by the day as he helped in their trapping endeavors. Come the afternoons of setting and checking their traps in the icy waters, their feet and legs were getting so cold that even by the next day they had troubles warming up their lower extremities. Had troubles in that their feet and legs were still icy cold come the following morning and many times, both brothers doing the trapping had to sit close by the fire in order to get some sort of the feeling back into their extremities! They were finding that wading in the northern latitude's waters, sometimes up to their waists, was not the grandest thing they had done in their lives... But it was their chosen lifestyle and both Cedrick and Wallace suffered in silence for having such an opportunity doing what they enjoyed in the wild and beautiful land that they loved.

Saddling up their riding horses and equipping two packhorses with their packs adjusted to carry panniers, off the men went one frosty morning downriver from their cabin site. They had now trapped out about three miles of the Big Muddy next to and below their cabin and were now forced to travel further and further south on the river in order to keep their traps catching beaver. Stopping along the northern end of their newest trap line, Wallace dismounted, removed his wool pants and slipped on his buckskin leggings and breechclout for the wet and cold endeavors lying ahead when it came to setting and tending his traps. As he did, Cedrick began preparing the gear Wallace would need and began dragging out from their panniers several four-foot-long, dry anchor poles as needed for the individual traps along their trap line. Then when a dead previously trapped beaver was retrieved, he would skin out the animal, toss the hide into the pannier, the trap would be re-set and the group would then move on to their next trap. By mid-afternoon, Wallace had 'frozen' out in the cold waters and Cedrick had taken his place as the trap tender while Otis and Oliver, even though assured they were safe in the land of the Blackfeet according to Chief Gray Wolf, still remained mounted and kept a wary eye when it came to watching over their immediate surroundings. This they did because all of them remembered the day they had killed the Arikara messing with the Blackfeet women and children and if they had come that far north that time, they could do so once again. Especially now that the brothers were trapping further and further south on the Big Muddy and in essence, bringing them closer and closer to the lands the Arikara commonly roamed. A land in which the Arikara called their home and would kill every hated white man they ran across given just half a chance.

Little did the Barnes Clan realize that years earlier, the United States Government had invited one of the most famous, beloved and influential Arikara chiefs to visit Washington, the seat of power and home of "The Great White Father". The official thinking in that day and age was that the Arikara chief would be so overwhelmed with the power and magnitude of the white man that he saw on his trip, that he would return to his people with such intimidating information and in so doing, would assure that the warlike Arikara nation would then sue for peace with the white man. By suing for peace, allowing the further expansion of the white man and his interests without having to continue fighting the Arikara Indians. However, soon after his arrival, the great Arikara chief caught a white man's disease and died! Fearful of having to tell the Arikara peoples that their great chief had died under the hands and care of The Great White Father, nothing was said to that tribe for over a year about his untimely death! When the Arikara nation and her peoples were finally told what had happened, there was great angst among them and the distrust of the white man soared!

As a result, instant war ensued between the now deadly Arikara and the white man across those Indians lands and continued until the United States Civil War! By then the great hordes of the white race had overrun the historical lands of the fierce Arikara and that and disease depleted their ranks to the point that they became inconsequential, and were finally settled on a reservation in North Dakota with two other tribes of displaced Indians where they remain to this day.

By late afternoon and nearing the southernmost end of their trap line, Cedrick spied a small herd of buffalo herded up and looking down towards the watered beaver ponds and dams over something that had caught their interest and concern. Thinking nothing of that odd behavior, Cedrick continued walking his trap line as Wallace walked along behind him trying to get the circulation back into his feet and legs after wading around in the icy waters most of the morning on the upper portion of their trap line. Behind the two walking brothers rode Otis and Oliver watching all around them for any signs of danger from either man or beast and leading the trappers' riding horses and packhorses.

Rounding a dense and elongated patch of willows, Cedrick could see what the small herd of buffalo up on the hill were looking at. Lying close to a beaver pond was a dark lump on the prairie. Looking more closely, Cedrick could see covering the mysterious dark lump which turned out to be a dead buffalo, were a number of crows, ravens and black-billed magpies feeding on the remains of the dead animal. As Cedrick got closer, he spooked off the feeding birds and since he had to walk close to the dead animal to get to his next beaver trap, he took a closer look at the dead buffalo. It appeared to be a fresh kill and from the looks of the side of the critter, all ripped apart and all, it had been recently captured, killed and partially eaten by a grizzly bear.

Stopping to get a closer look, Wallace walked up to Cedrick and looking more closely at the dead buffalo as well, said, "Cedrick, this being a fresh kill and being that we are short on meat back at the camp, what say we four roll this animal over and remove the meat for ourselves that has been untouched by the bear on the other side?"

Cedrick ever the 'cook', looked the animal over more closely and said, "I think that is a fine idea. Since "Mr. Bear" has left the far side totally untouched, I say we help ourselves to the meat and that will save us from having to waste precious powder and ball on killing one for ourselves. However, let me tend to this trap first and then we can quarter out the remains of this fresh-killed buffalo, load the meat in the panniers, take it back to our cabin and hang it up on our meat pole so it can cool out and glaze."

With those words, Cedrick slipped into the late fall icy cold waters of the beaver pond to remove a dead beaver hanging in one of their traps. Removing the beaver and re-setting the trap as well as re-scenting the bait stick with a touch of castoreum, he exited the pond and tossed a rather large beaver over to his brother Wallace, who was now doing the skinning. When he did he said with an 'I am damn glad to be out from this cold water' grin, "Brother, this one is all yours to skin out."

With that, Cedrick took off fast-walking across the prairie in order to get his blood circulating in his now almost frozen-stiff legs and feet. In the meantime after taking another long look all around the area for any sign of danger, Otis and Oliver dismounted and walked over to examine the grizzly bear's freshly killed buffalo's remains as well.

"By Gum, she ain't all that bad. That bear has left fully one-half of this here critter and we sure as hell can make use of the other half," said Otis approvingly, as he looked the dead buffalo over more closely.

Laying down his rifle, Oliver rolled up the sleeves on his shirt in order not to get it bloodied and sticky in the butchering process to follow saying, "When Cedrick gets back from his foot-warming, I say we roll this here cow over onto the bad side where the bear has chomped it all to hell and start skinning her good side out. Near as I can see, we should be able to save a shoulder, her backstrap, one side of her ribs and the hindquarter. That will last us for a few days providing Otis doesn't go hog wild come dinner time and eat the whole damn thing at one sitting," he said with a big smile over pulling a 'funny' on his brother.

Typical Otis, he just gave a "Harrumph" over what his brother had just said, figuring he would get even when Oliver wasn't expecting it. Getting even like taking something 'brown and gushy' out from the latrine trench and putting it into the toe area of Oliver's moccasin when he was asleep and not looking…

About then Cedrick came walking back into the group of men standing around the dead buffalo waiting for Wallace to finish skinning out the beaver. Ten minutes later, Wallace had skinned out the beaver and tossed the pelt into one of their packhorse's panniers. Then after washing off his bloody and greasy beaver fat-covered hands, he walked over to give the brothers a hand at rolling the buffalo carcass over onto its mostly eaten-off side so the remaining good side of the buffalo could be reached and butchered out.

With that, the four stout Irish brothers each grabbed a piece of the dead animal and with a loud "Heave Ho!" from Wallace, the men rolled the carcass over onto its bad side, exposing its still edible side. **"URRRRGHHHH!"** roared a grizzly bear, aroused out from its day bed in a nearby dense willow thicket sleeping off a meal of buffalo, who had just heard Wallace's loud

'Heave Ho' yell! Upon waking and hearing that close at hand shout, the bear with its poor eyesight, stormed forth towards the sound of a man yelling and rounded the dense stand of willows at a dead run just mere feet from the four brothers in order to protect its remaining buffalo carcass and meal. Four brothers who unwittingly were still congratulating themselves over their feats of strength when it came to rolling over the buffalo's half-carcass!

Otis being the closest to the charging bear drew his pistol and fired just as the bear 'paw-slapped' him so hard for having the audacity to shoot, that he went flying 'ass over tea kettle' into the nearby beaver pond! Cedrick next in line of the bear's angry charge, jumped over the buffalo's carcass in order to get away from the huge and open mouthed bear, only to have five 6"-long claws raked and slapped across his 'retreating' bottom, ripping long slashes into the hind end of his pants and deeply across the soft tissue of his rump! Oliver in surprised desperation had drawn both of his pistols and fired them into the bear just as the bear, continuing his furious charge, bowled him over onto his back, pounced upon him and began biting and ripping at his chest with his teeth! When the bear's first bite found something substantial, like the meat on Oliver's chest and the front of his buckskin shirt, he snapped his head back and upward, tossing a limp as a dish rag Oliver over his rump to crash and then lay still on the prairie behind him! Wallace in the meantime, standing closest to the pile of the men's laid-down rifles, grabbed one up and while the bear was involved with tossing Oliver over his back, managed to cock the rifle and just had time to jam the rifle's long barrel down the open mouth and throat of the now still oncoming and furious bear. When he did, the bear bit down hard on the barrel of the rifle and that was when Wallace out of desperation pulled the trigger!

BOOM! went Wallace's rifle and **WHOMP!** went the bear onto the ground, dying with a lucky spinal shot as its heavy bullet blew itself upward through the bony column! But not before his mad as a hornet charging forward energy smashed over the top of Wallace, and flattened out dying while lying on top of Wallace with its 700 pounds of now dead weight crushing down on him!

That was when Otis, now back from his unplanned 'grizzly bear assisted dip' in the beaver pond with his remaining good arm, the one not damaged by the bear's initial paw-belting strike, managed to lift the bear's head off his brother's face which just moments before was starting to suffocate Wallace. Starting to suffocate Wallace, as the now dead bear's digestive system involuntarily vomited up about 30 pounds of acidic covered and partially digested slime-coated buffalo meat and digestive juices all over his face in a massive flood! Then Cedrick arrived and between Otis and him, managed to roll the bear off to one side and move its crushing weight off Wallace so he could remove the 'blanket' of bear's vomit covering his face, breathe and be able to see once again when his eyes were finally wiped somewhat clean.

That evening a sad looking caravan of beaver trappers smelling strongly of grizzly bear rode their skittish horses into their campsite. Sad looking because only Otis and Wallace had the energy to round up their spooked-off horses after the bear had made his 'somewhat testy' presence known back at the beaver ponds. Then Wallace had to boost Otis into his saddle because he had such a badly sprained left arm and shoulder from when the bear had clubbed him for being so bold as to shoot the bear in the neck with his 'piss-anty' pistol! Cedrick on the other hand could not ride his horse. He had four 2"-deep gashes slashed all the way across his entire bottom where the bear had 'paw-slapped' him across his last part over the fence! Understandably, that made for a sore as hell and bloody mess of what had once been a perfectly good hind end! So, not wanting to plant his bloody hind end into the leather of his saddle, he chose to walk all the way back to camp. As for Oliver, having been badly bitten in the chest and then tossed like a rag doll clear over the back of the bear, Wallace and Otis with his one good arm, had to help him up and into the saddle of his horse. But there was one good thing that came out of the mess of messed-up trappers. The two packhorses, because of damn hard-headed Irish determination, were packing the quarters, ribs and backstrap from the bear's buffalo carcass. As for salvaging the bear, he was left behind for the critters to finish off. As it turned out, the bear was old, rangy and in bad body condition, which in part probably accounted for its 'mad as a wet hen' behavior. That being said, the unfit for human consumption bear's carcass was left behind for other prairie quadrupeds and avian critters of the air to enjoy.

Supper that evening back at the trappers' camp consisted of a number of cups of rum for each of the injured men. That was before Wallace sewed up Cedrick's claw-slashed hind end to a lot of howling and wiggling all over the place every time the sewing needle entered too deeply some of the badly damaged fleshy part of his 'last part over the fence'! Then that 'frontier doctoring' was followed with the sewing up of the bear's toothy gashes in Oliver's chest as he laid there under the painful needle quietly taking the pain unlike his younger brother. Lastly, Wallace wrapped up Otis's arm and shoulder with a long swatch of their gray cloth normally used to patch up the rips and tears in the men's clothing. As for Wallace, a trip to their spring box and several pans of soapy water were needed to get all of the bear's vomit involuntarily spewed all over him, into his ears and throughout his thick locks of hair, somewhat cleaned off. Spewed bear's vomit after the animal had convulsed and died after being shot through his mouth and having the heavy lead ball blasting into and lodging into his spine just as it had attacked and flopped on top of the shooter.

For the next week after the 'battle at the buffalo', the trappers continued running their trap line. However, in order to do so, Cedrick did a lot of walking because the gashes, even though treated with warm soapy water and splashed with rum daily, became infected which did not allow him to ride a horse comfortably for a two-week period of time. Oliver on the other hand, still rode sentry duty. However, he had to be lifted up onto his horse so he could ride and provide protective cover. For him to try and lift himself into the saddle of his horse, found that it kept tearing the twine stitches loose. So assistance in getting into his horse's saddle was called for if the men wanted his additional rifle for the protection it offered. Otis could also ride after being boosted into the saddle by Wallace and being as strong as he was, still provided protection because he could shoot his rifle very accurately with just his good arm and hand.

So Wallace ran the trap line while everyone healed up, and Cedrick still did the skinning and cooking since a damaged hind end did not interfere with those duties. However, everyone else chipped in doing what they could when it came to hooping the beaver pelts on a nightly basis. However, by so doing and everyone being in so much pain, the rum supplies took a big hit... As for the buffalo quarters, they supplied the necessary meat for the four brothers throughout the healing up ordeal and kept them alive and from having to go on the hunt once again. Two weeks later came freeze-up on the Big Muddy and that allowed the men, except for a buffalo shoot or two in the interim, to completely heal up fully except for their bruised egos and many scarred parts.

Come the two coldest months of the winter found the men hauling and cutting wood, and breaking the ice over their spring box so the horses could water instead of eating snow for a change. Then it was on to casting a small mountain of bullets for their rifles and pistols, bundling up the 313 beaver skins for transport to Fort Henry come the summer, hunting buffalo, wolf trapping, and tearing down all of their rifles and pistols, replacing worn parts and deep cleaning the trigger mechanisms to avoid any misfires in the future. The men also made it a daily habit after firing any of their rifles, to thoroughly clean their barrels of any black powder fouling which in so doing, enhanced the shooter's long-range accuracy.

One bright spring morning, Cedrick made and served the men their breakfasts being made in their fireplace. While feasting away on coffee, biscuits coated with brown sugar, roasted buffalo meat and pinto beans, Cedrick reminded the men they were eating the last of their buffalo from the meat pole. For the longest time quiet reigned and then Oliver spoke up saying, "Well, guess there is no time like the present." With that, he got up from his log chair, walked over to his sleeping area and began dressing for the cold outside weather. Moments later without a word being spoken, all the brothers did the same, realizing cold weather or not, if they wanted to eat what they loved eating the most, the hunt was on.

Getting ready to leave their campsite a short while later, Wallace, in a surprising move, walked out from their cabin carrying the Indian Trade rifles and a number of the rifles taken from the Frenchmen that they had decided to keep instead of selling at Fort Henry. When he did, Otis asked, "Why all the serious hardware?"

"Don't know but my sixth sense has been roiling up in me ever since Cedrick reminded us we were out of meat. I just figured with a day like this one, every Indian short of meat will be out killing buffalo. I guess with that in mind, if we run into the wrong kind of Indians, being better armed and surviving is better than losing our hair and going under," replied Wallace.

"But why so many guns?" persisted Otis, realizing how common sense-minded his brother always was and now sensing something serious was in the wind. "We are good enough shooters that we can take care of ourselves and kill all the buffalo we need with just our 'old faithful' rifles that we always carry," said Otis almost as a 'searching' afterthought.

"Don't know why but just like I said earlier, my insides are all a-roil over going out this day. Since we will be going out for four buffalo and trailing four packhorses, I figured we would carry one extra rifle in each animal's pannier from our arsenal. That way if things go all "crookedly", we will at least have enough firepower, given half a chance to use it, that we should be able to avoid 'going under' on such a fine day," continued Wallace, as he made two trips and in so doing, placed an extra fully loaded rifle into each of the eight panniers being placed on their packhorses.

Trailing four packhorses out from their campsite that morning, the Barnes Clan headed due south where the best buffalo winter feeding grounds existed out on the open prairie. An hour later after by passing numerous smaller herds of buffalo quietly feeding while looking for just the right herd to sneak, Wallace brought the men to a halt. "Let's take that herd of buffalo over there. We can use that small grove of trees as cover when we pull a sneak on them and if we do it correctly, shooting from that grove we should be able to get them into a "Stand" and kill our four buffalo without any problems of them stampeding off and having to chase any cripples or lose any wounded ones," said Wallace.

By then, the Barnes Clan had learned that when the wisest of the older cows in a herd of buffalo being shot over began smelling fresh blood after the shooting had started, that would send them into a frenzy of behavior and many of them would quickly move away from the hated blood odor. However, the more aggressive bulls many times would just do the opposite. Once they smelled the odor of fresh blood, in their excitement, they also would many times go into a 'frenzy' and end up circling the downed animal, hooking it with their horns as if trying to get it to rise to its feet. That and their inbred urge to attack any of their wounded brethren, coupled with the excitement that came from smelling the odor of blood, caused many healthy animals to remain circling and hooking their wounded while in range of the shooters. With the increasing smell of blood, the herd would continue milling about in aggressive confusion or be in what was later to be called a "Stand" by experienced buffalo hunters. Called a Stand because the remaining healthy animals would just mill about within easy gun range and many times, all would be killed standing or milling about while the shooting was going on until they were no more! Additionally, the Barnes brothers had surmised that the 'booming' sounds of black powder guns shooting did not seem to bother the animals because it sounded like thunder, which was a common and familiar sound out on the Plains.

Quietly moving their horses into the grove of trees which was downwind, the men dismounted and quickly moved through the trunks of the winter barren trees using them as cover until all were within easy gunning range of the small herd of buffalo. Each of the brothers settled down into comfortable sitting positions and with whispers among themselves, advised each other of which buffalo each man was going to shoot when the time came. That was until Otis whispered out so all could hear his words of warning, saying, "Don't shoot. Everybody hold your fire and listen," said Otis, now as serious as if he had a prairie rattlesnake close enough to strike!

Way off in the distance near a small known "Buffalo Jump", the men could hear a wealth of shooting. At first the listening men figured some Indians had run a herd of buffalo off the jump and were down at the bottom of the jump where all the buffalo had fallen and were just shooting all of the crippled beasts. BUT SOMETHING WAS WRONG! OTIS JUST REMEMBERED THAT WHEN THE INDIANS RAN THE BUFFALO OFF THE CLIFF AT THE BUFFALO JUMP SITE, THEY SAVED THEIR POWDER AND JUST KILLED THE CRIPPLED BEASTS AT THE BOTTOM WITH THEIR BOWS AND ARROWS OR SPEARS! However, the more he and the others now listened, the shooting in that direction continued at a fast and furious pace for some unusual reason, like maybe a battle was ongoing!

"Something is damn bad wrong, boys," finally said Wallace. "I damn well knew my sixth sense was not wrong this morning when 'it' was telling me something bad was going to happen this day." Then Wallace abruptly stood up saying, "Otis and Oliver, the two of you go and get our packhorses and tie them off in the middle of this grove of trees so anyone just passing by will not see them. When they do, I want all of you to take those extra gun scabbards in the packhorse's panniers and tie them onto your riding horses. That way, each of you will have two extra rifles along with your own two pistols in case we get jumped by Indians out on the prairie. Now let us get a move on. That shooting we are hearing may very well be coming from a bunch of our fellow trappers cornered by Indians who are trying to fight their ways out of trouble!"

It was just then that the now frightened herd of close at hand buffalo, upon seeing and hearing the men speaking, lumbered off into the distance and out of the way of what they considered was a clear and present danger. As they lumbered out of sight, all were holding their tails straight up into the air as a sign of alarm and agitation for any other nearby buffalo to see and pay heed as to the warnings of danger being flashed.

Minutes later, the Barnes Clan rumbled out of sight into the vast prairie in the direction from whence all of the heard shooting was coming from. After a several mile ride, Wallace held up his hand for all of the men to stop. "Near as I can tell, all of that shooting is coming from where the bottom of that old Buffalo Jump we are aware of is located. There is no way the Indians would be shooting that many crippled buffalo squirming around at the bottom of that cliff and wasting all of that lead and powder," he continued. "Something else is wrong and we need to sneak over and see what the hell is going on, especially if those in trouble might be some of our fellow trappers," continued Wallace. With their rifles at the ready, the men moving line abreast began slowly walking their horses towards the heavy sounds of rifle fire coming from just over the rise near the river. Moving their horses into the river bottom and a grove of aspen off to one side of the bottom of the Buffalo Jump, Wallace all of sudden froze, as did the rest of the brothers following suit. Then they heard him quietly calling for Otis to come forward. After a hurried conversation, Otis dismounted and began stalking ahead on foot towards another nearby grove of aspen in the river bottom. Soon he was out of sight from the rest of the men.

Wallace, then leaving all of their horses tied off in the river bottom out of sight, moved the three of them off into a large jumble of tall sagebrush plants and then all of them knelt down where they could still see but were out of sight and waited. As they did, Wallace turned and filled Oliver and Cedrick in as to what he had just observed before he sent Otis away on an obvious mission. There he explained he had observed a young Indian man in the nearby aspen grove obviously guarding a number of horses. Having learned what the dress of a Blackfoot warrior now looked like after their last run-in with Gray Wolf, Wallace indicated the Indian he had seen was not dressed like a Blackfoot but from some other tribe, like maybe the Arikara they had killed back at Fort Henry. Arikara they had surprised in their sleeping camp and wiped out except for the two who had escaped and slipped off into the Missouri River. That was also the same type of dress on the young man holding all the horses in the aspen grove below. The one and same aspen grove he had just sent Otis into to see if the young Indian watching all the horses was a friend or foe.

About a half-hour later, Otis returned winded and as he knelt down with his brothers, it took a few minutes for him to get his breath back. Then he said, "The Indian I just killed is an Arikara just like those we killed back at Fort Henry last summer. From what I could see from his vantage point, he apparently was left behind by the warriors who now have trapped a small number of Blackfeet and their families at the bottom of the Buffalo Jump. From what I could tell, the Blackfeet just ran a small herd of buffalo off the jump and were down with their women butchering them out when the Arikara surprised and attacked the whole bunch. Our Blackfeet warriors appear to be outnumbered by about two to one near as I could tell. From my vantage point in the trees near their horses, I did count 27 Arikara shooters who have our Blackfeet friends pinned down at the bottom of the cliff face because they are holding the high ground."

For the longest time Wallace just mulled over what he had just heard from his brother about the overwhelming force of deadly Arikara warriors they potentially now faced. Then Wallace asked, "Can the four of us 'back-sneak' that bunch of Arikara and kill a mess of them without being caught in a crossfire with our friends the Blackfeet who do not know we are here?"

For the longest time, Otis thought about what his brother had just asked and then said, "I think so. There are at least 20 of them damn Arikara in a clump behind that mess of boulders at the bottom of the Buffalo Jump. From those positions they hold the high ground over those Blackfeet they have trapped at the base of the Buffalo Jump. If we were to 'back-sneak' that bunch and with our pistols shooting buck and ball kill at least six to eight of them with those weapons and then using all of our rifles, quick kill another eight or so, that would break the back of this attack I would think. Especially in light of them Arikara being surprise attacked from behind by the four of us and with us between them and their only means of escape, namely their horses. I would think the shock and surprise of that kind of attack plus the surprise killings we could inflict with our rifles and pistols upon them should break their will to fight and scatter them to the four winds. If not and the rest of their bunch up the hill gets involved with us four and we get no help from our Blackfeet friends, it's knives and tomahawks 'til death do us part'."

For the longest time, Wallace mulled over what Otis had just said. In this game of sure death if he made the wrong call, he realized he needed to make an "Ace" of a decision! It was then that his 'older brother common sense' kicked in, giving him what he considered the Ace that he so badly needed! Wallace leaned over in order to keep his voice down and whispered something to Otis, who got a big grin on his face and then quietly got up and sneaked back to the Arikara's tied-off horse herd. "Now we wait," said Wallace, as the pinned down and unable to flee Blackfeet, because of having their defenseless families so close at hand, continued fighting back. Twenty minutes later, the brothers could see Otis sneaking his way back through the heavy stands of sagebrush. Moments later he arrived and nodded to Wallace about the success of his mission. A mission that had better produce an Ace in the next few minutes or there would be hell to pay once the four trappers started shooting!

About then, the brothers could see a number of Arikara horses slowly feeding their ways out across the open prairie below their position. It then became apparent that Otis had been sent back to release all of the hated Arikara's horses so their owners would have no means of escape and by feeding their ways out onto the open prairie in plain sight, would alarm the Arikara that all was not well back at the horse herd and their only means of escape.

Moments later, the brothers could see a number of alarmed Arikara who had been holding the high ground above the Buffalo Jump, slinking their way back down the cliff face and over to the group of their compatriots using the boulders below for cover in order to spread the alarm about their escaping horses! Moments later, after the two groups had joined together, all of a sudden there came a long line of Arikara running towards the brothers still hidden in the sagebrush. From their panicked flight, it became obvious that they were running for the aspen grove where they had originally hidden their horses before attacking the Blackfeet at the base of the Buffalo Jump! As they came in a long stream of humanity running back towards their aspen grove, all of a sudden the trappers rose from their positions of hiding and then the surprised Arikara were instantly blanketed with white plumes of black powder smoke! Smoke which enveloped the entire group of fleeing Indians, as the trappers fired buck and ball from their collective pistols, tearing great gaping holes in the line of onrushing Indians trying to make good their escape! In fact, shooting from such close-in ranges at soft targets, many of the speeding buck and ball projectiles not only ripped clear through their first targets but killed or wounded the next Indian in line as well! Almost simultaneously, additional white clouds of black powder smoke then quickly enveloped the ending stream of Arikara warriors as they then now ran headlong into the collective rifle fire of the four trappers from just feet away! When they did, only two shots were fired from the escaping Indians' ranks, as the trappers' buck and ball ripped apart their close-in ranks. However, both of the shots fired by the totally surprised Indians being gutted by such a close-in hail of lead hit their targets! Oliver had a rifle ball cut across his cheek leaving an ugly oozing flesh wound and Otis had a rifle ball fired by a fleeing Indian graze the top of his left hand. Neither wound was fatal and had only been fired by a falling Indian's rifle when he hit the ground after being killed by a trapper's ball or buck fired from just 10-15 feet away!

That was when all hell broke loose! The trappers fresh out of shot and shell, dropped their second empty rifle and with swinging tomahawks, started cutting down the close at hand wounded and now thoroughly confused and milling about surviving Arikara. That was when the killing became even more intense, when the Blackfeet, previously trapped by the Arikara's rifle fire from the higher ground, now realized their foe were being attacked from behind by friendly forces. Upon hearing the supporting gunfire, they rose up en masse and with tomahawks, rifles and spears joined in the battle! Moments later, 21 Blackfeet warriors and the four trappers faced each other in the high emotion of the final killing moments that preceded their fortuitous meeting near the ancient Buffalo Jump!

When those two forces met, Wallace quickly raised his right hand in the universal sign of greeting made by many of the tribes of Plains Indians, as he stood there knee deep in dead and dying Arikara Indians. For a moment, the Blackfoot brave in front of his group of warriors just stood there dumbfounded, staring hard at the four trappers in welcome surprise and amazement. Recognizing those same four trappers who had saved the bathing Blackfeet women and children, the Blackfoot warrior confronting Wallace at the end of the battle with the Arikara slowly raised his hand in the sign of greeting as well... Then with the realization sinking in that his buffalo hunting band had been rescued by the trappers, they had won the fight and were now alive, all hell really broke loose! Every Arikara body was mutilated and scalped by the remaining Blackfeet Indians! All 27 of the Arikara in the final count of bodies, were left in a condition, according to tribal customs, that missing so many body parts would leave them wandering forever in the afterlife. Wandering forever looking for those missing parts and as such, they would not be allowed into The Happy Hunting Grounds...

Then since so many of the Blackfeet had lost their horses when killed or run off by the Arikara in the initial moments of the attack at the Buffalo Jump, the rest of the day was spent by the Blackfeet warriors and trappers in rounding up the Arikara horses that had been turned loose earlier by Otis. This they did as the women, now out of danger, continued butchering out the dead buffalo at the bottom of the jump before the meat began spoiling. That evening, the trappers joined their Blackfeet friends and their busy wives and family members in a celebration dinner. That evening, the trappers were feted to a special dinner in celebration of the huge buffalo meat resources being processed, the great victory in the fight with the hated Arikara, the many coups counted and in the capture of many of the enemy's horses. Noted by the trappers at the special dinner was the fact that they were waited on 'hand and foot' by the four Indian women who had been attacked previously by the Arikara along the Big Muddy, saved from a life of captivity and shame by the more than fortuitous arrival by the Barnes Clan...

After the huge dinner and celebration, the four trappers adjourned to the pile of dead buffalo at the bottom of the Buffalo Jump along with all the Indian women, and by the light of many nearby campfires, butchered out what they had been hunting for earlier in the day. Suffice to say when all was said and done and the trappers' packhorses were retrieved from their distant aspen grove and loaded, the trappers went home the next day with their panniers more than loaded with buffalo meat courtesy of the Blackfeet Indians they had rescued.

(Author's Note: Throughout the buffalo's historic range from Canada to Texas and points east of the Mississippi River, there still to this day exists a number of recognized "Buffalo Jumps", with many more still being discovered annually. The State of Montana alone has over 300 such jump sites identified to date! Archeologists believe Buffalo Jumps have been around and utilized by prehistoric peoples 12,000 years ago up until the introduction of the horse into North America by the Spanish in the 1500's. Upon the arrival of the horse and with the Indians acquiring such animals and becoming 'one' with their horses, much of the hunting of buffalo shifted from using Buffalo Jumps to hunting the buffalo from horseback.

Buffalo Jumps, also called "Pishkuns" by the Blackfeet, which loosely translates into "Deep Blood Kettle", were usually situated at the edge of a good pasture or historical buffalo feeding grounds at one end of the open prairie that sloped gently downward into a shallow draw with a rim or cliff drop-off at the far narrow end. In some places historically utilized by the Native Americans for thousands of years, there are Indian-built rock piles one to two feet high, situated out across the prairie in a wide funnel shape "V" located below one of those historical buffalo feeding areas. Prehistoric Indians on foot discovering a herd of buffalo at or near the head or wide end of one of those "V" funnel-shaped rock pile formations built before the arrival of the horse, would send tribal members to quietly hide behind the rock piles. Then when a herd of buffalo had fed until they were positioned right at the head of one of those laid out in a funnel-shaped arrangement piles of rocks, many times a "Caller" or "Buffalo Runner", usually a young man and fast runner wearing a buffalo skin over his body to give the appearance of a young buffalo calf, would appear in the wide end or mouth of the funnel. There the Caller would move around in such a manner as to arouse the curiosity of the nearby feeding buffalo. Out of that aroused curiosity, the buffalo would then begin moving towards the Caller and once in the area at the head of the funnel, other Indians on the far side of the buffalo herd would spook and head them running into the rock-lined funnel. Then as the spooked buffalo began following the now running Caller down into the narrower end of the funnel, other Indians hidden behind the rock piles would rise up and wave their deer or buffalo hides as the buffalo passed, further spooking the now running animals. As the herd now thoroughly spooked and stampeding downward towards the narrower end of the sloping draw and the cliff beyond, the Caller would then run and hide off to one side or in a crevice and let the herd continue to thunder on by and into the narrow end of the draw outlined by the rock piles which were now getting closer and closer together. Then when the edge of the cliff or precipice appeared to the buffalo at the front of the charging herd and upon seeing the danger, they would try and stop in order to not to be plunged over the cliff. However, the charging animals at the rear of the herd, oblivious to the danger ahead, kept charging and pushing along those buffalo at the head of the herd over the cliff to their waiting deaths below! When they did, the fall either killed those animals or the remaining herd members now being pushed over the cliff by those panicked members behind them, landed on the dead or dying below, crushing them in the process. Any surviving buffalo were then lanced with spears or shot with bows and arrows by tribal members now arriving on the scene once the flood of beasts stopped flowing over the edge of the cliff.

Then with the advent of the horse, the rock piles located in a funnel-shaped Buffalo Jump were no longer needed or used as much because the Indian mounted on his horse was a natural rider and efficient killer with his bow and arrow, lance or rifle when hunting buffalo out on the vast reaches of the prairie. However, when those mounted riders did find a herd of buffalo near one of those old Buffalo Jump areas, the tribe would be notified and then they would stampede those buffalo with their horses over the cliff or Buffalo Jump.

Tribal members, aware of the day of the Buffalo Jump, when the jump was over, would congregate below the top of the cliff and butcher out all they could carry of the now dead and many times crushed buffalo. However, in such buffalo killing events, if the women butchering out the dead buffalo below a jump did not get their work done by the next morning, the buffalo meat was already spoiled and unfit for human consumption. Also, because buffalo do not like the smell of blood or death, they would shy away from such an area, therefore a Buffalo Jump site could only be used maybe twice a year. That was because it took that long for the smell of rotting buffalo that were left behind because of spoilage, to melt into the soil or dissolve away and in so doing, take the smell with it. Today in many archeological digs beneath these old Buffalo Jumps, archeologists have recorded depths of buffalo bones tightly packed sometimes as deep as ten to twelve feet in depth illustrating the size of many kills and the effective manner in which it was used to kill buffalo!)

Two days after the "Buffalo Jump Battle", Cedrick was hauling in firewood in order to make breakfast inside using their fireplace, when he looked up and saw about a dozen Indian riders approaching the cabin from below the meadow. Hustling inside the cabin for the protection it offered, he got his brothers out from their sleeping furs and had them armed in an instant. However, such haste in getting his brothers out from their sleeping furs and arming themselves proved to be a wasted effort. Opening the front door to their cabin, the brothers were greeted with the ever-stoic Gray Wolf sitting in front of the cabin on his horse waiting for the trappers to appear and acknowledge his presence.

When Wallace stepped out from inside the trappers' cabin, he was greeted by Gray Wolf with a smile and an upraised arm of friendship. Wallace handed his rifle back to Otis, walked out front and shook the now extended hand of Gray Wolf saying, "What brings you to our camp, Chief Gray Wolf?"

"I come to once again thank my trapper friends for saving my people at the "Burnt Grass Buffalo Jump" two 'Suns' past. My people tell me that they were surprised by our enemies the Arikara after they had just set up camp to gather in the meat from many buffalo after the jump. It now seems that I owe the 'trespassing' white trappers once again for saving my people from a fate worse than death. Had the Arikara been victorious in battle, they would have taken a large number of our women and children captive and subjected them to a fate worse than death. For saving them from such a life of shame, I find that I am thankful that I did not kill you four the first time we met when I had the chance. It now appears that The Great Spirit has smiled on both of us. So white man trappers, I once again am thankful for your presence on my land," replied Gray Wolf, who was now smiling for a change...

It was then that Wallace invited Gray Wolf in for breakfast and some of the always much-sought after white man's coffee, especially if the cups of coffee were heavily loaded with brown sugar. Hearing Wallace's invite being made to Chief Gray Wolf from inside their cabin, Cedrick put down his rifle and headed for their roaring fireplace to mix up a larger batch of biscuit dough for their guests. He also made plans for making a second pot of coffee because he was sure Gray Wolf's warriors were cold to the bone from the day's weather, swimming the Big Muddy and riding on a horse all the way from the Indians' camp near Medicine Lake to their cabin. However, Cedrick noticed by late morning and when his much-anticipated Dutch oven biscuits were ready to eat, their great aroma could not be appreciated by the all trappers and Indians crowded inside their cabin. It seemed that in the fireplace heat and the heat coming from so many bodies in such a small cabin, the smell of many of those unwashed bodies overrode the great smells of Cedrick's biscuits...

Finally with a surprising early ice-out, the brothers brought in all of their wolf traps as they began making preparations for spring beaver trapping. Because many of the nights still dropped to below zero, the brothers went forth and killed three buffalo. Those buffalo were then quartered out except for their ribs which were left for the wolves and the rest brought back to their meat pole. There the quarters were strung up and daily, Cedrick would remove what meat was needed for each meal or left out to thaw in their cabin when they were out all day on the trap line. Then while Otis and Oliver repaired much of their leather goods and pack saddles for the coming season, Cedrick and Wallace brought down two quarters of buffalo, thawed them out and cut the meat into thin strips. With that, the two men fired up their smoking rack and began making the meat into jerky and days later bagged it up for use out on the trail. The following two days were spent out on the trail riding along the many waterways along the Big Muddy south of their cabin, as the men scouted out the best beaver trapping areas. Once again, the winter kill appeared to not have been much of a factor with the beaver populations as the men observed many heavily furred swimming and dam building rodents each day during their travels.

With some ice still floating in the larger beaver ponds because of the early thaw, Wallace decided it was time to begin their spring beaver trapping. Otis cautioned his older brother that he figured they ought to wait another week or so because there was still so much ice in the area, but Wallace nixed that idea in favor of getting a jump on the trapping season. That and the fact that Wallace had all of the cabin enclosure that he could stand and needed to be out and about doing what he loved doing, namely trapping beaver. The following morning, the four brothers ventured forth and began setting out the first of their traps in an area south of their cabin that had never been trapped by the brothers.

As was their standard procedure, Otis and Oliver being the group's best shooters, remained in their saddles with a watchful eye out for grizzly bears emerging from hibernation or unknown bands of hostile Indians presenting any kind of a threat. Wallace on the other hand, began setting out their beaver traps while Cedrick assisted. After making 11 sets, Wallace found that he was so cold from being immersed up to his waist in the early spring waters, that he had to quit trapping and began stumbling around on the nearby prairie in an attempt to get his legs and feet warmed up and functioning. Cedrick being the brothers' reserve trapper, then began making beaver sets as Wallace continued moving around the nearby prairie albeit somewhat slowly in his efforts to thaw out and warm up his almost frozen feet and legs.

For Cedrick's first five sets, he could hardly set the traps without shaking like a wolf crapping buffalo bones! Cedrick, being the thinnest of the Barnes brothers, soon found his immersions into the earlier than normal icy spring waters, soon had him shaking so badly that he could hardly even depress the springs on the traps! Then Otis saw that Wallace was nowhere to be seen out on the prairie! Taking his horse and riding out where he had last seen Wallace, he soon found his brother. He was lying on the hard and still winter-cold ground shaking like an aspen tree in its last vestiges of being felled by a beaver! Jumping off his horse, Otis discovered his brother was shaking so badly from being immersed in the icy cold waters that he was in the first stages of shock from hypothermia!

Yelling at Oliver, Otis was soon joined by his brother and realizing Wallace was in danger of going even deeper into shock from the cold water immersions experienced earlier, wrapped his brother up in his winter coat as Otis wrapped Wallace's lower ice cold extremities in his winter coat! Then Oliver dashed into the nearby aspen grove and with his fire steel, soon had a small fire going. Then Otis and Oliver carried Wallace over and laid him right next to the fire so he could warm up. Looking back at their new trap line, Otis noticed that Cedrick was staggering around and falling down by another beaver pond like he had drunk too much of their rum! Racing his horse over to his brother, Otis discovered that Cedrick was showing the same hypothermic symptoms like Wallace and was almost blue in his lower extremities from his immersion in the cold water when setting out their traps. Loading his skinny brother into the saddle and holding him in place so he would not fall off, Otis walked his horse over to where Oliver now had a roaring fire going and off-loaded Cedrick into Oliver's arms so he could be placed near the fire to warm up as well.

Two hours later, Wallace and Cedrick appeared to be warming up and with ominous looking storm clouds forming in the northwest, all four men headed for their cabin once Wallace and Cedrick could safely ride without being supported in their saddles. Looking skyward, the brothers could now see rolling blue-black clouds roaring down in their direction from the northwest! Realizing a hard winter blow was coming, the men spurred their horses as fast as Wallace and Cedrick could safely ride but with the distance they had to ride, they were too late getting to the safety their cabin offered. Off in the distance, the men could hear the sounds of a rip-roaring wind coming their way so they headed for the shelter of a nearby row of trees. Within minutes, a 40-50 mile an hour wind was upon them bringing an almost immediate 30 degree drop in temperature! Now the wind chill factor was having an impact on all of the men because none of them had dressed for that kind of weather and soon, snot had frozen beneath each man's nose and frozen tears lined the sides of their faces as they, with their heads leaning into the howling wind, headed for their cabin!

Now realizing the danger at hand and that they were experiencing a "Blue Norther" or violent winter storm from out of the north followed by rapidly dropping temperatures, the men rode with even more urgency towards the safety of their cabin. About half-an-hour later, four damn near frozen men arrived at their cabin. While Oliver unsaddled their horses and pack animals and herded them into the corral for safekeeping, Otis pulled an almost inert and frozen Wallace and Cedrick from their saddles and carried the men inside their cabin. By the time Oliver had taken care of their stock, he was damn near frozen himself since he was also slight of build, poorly dressed and barely staggered through the front door of their cabin as a blanket of wet and heavy snow swirled heavily around him and their cabin. Seating his two near-frozen brothers near their fireplace, Otis lit two candles with a still live coal from their fireplace and then with some straw placed on other coals, soon had a blazing fire going. When he did, he was damn glad his brother Cedrick was such a stickler for keeping a cooking area 'ship shape'. In so doing, before the men had left to begin their spring trapping season, he had shoveled out the ashes from his fireplace into a bucket, set the straw and wood for a new fire when they returned at the end of the day and had even hauled in several armloads of new wood for their next session around their fireplace.

Soon warming coffee laced with a liberal dose of rum began bringing the life back into the half-frozen men. However, for the next eleven days, blizzard after blizzard laced the area, dropping two feet of wind-whipped and drifted snow everywhere. Fortunately, the hilly parts of their meadow remained windblown and clear of snow, allowing the horses to feed between breaks in the rolling blizzards swirling over the land. On the eleventh day, the storms relented but the outside temperature remained at or below zero for the next five days. It was then Wallace realized that his eagerness to get a jump on their spring trapping had been an almost life-ending mistake. It was now obvious that spring had not arrived, just a slight spring warming that still left the land locked in winter's almost icy grip of death!

Weeks later when spring had obviously arrived, it was only then that the brothers ventured forth to continue their spring trapping. Even then wading around in the still icy cold waters had both Wallace and Cedrick on a daily verge of freezing out! But for the next 35 days of spring trapping, the men's traps literally 'rained' Made Beaver and as a result, they soon had trapped 356 beaver along a ten-mile stretch of the river, in addition to the 313 they had trapped in the fall filling their cabin to the rafters! Little did any of the brothers realize, their spring trapping successes in the number of pelts being bundled up daily would save the day in about what was to come ambling down the road in the ways of their life's fortunes.

One late spring morning during breakfast, Wallace returned from where they had stored their bundles of beaver and wolf furs in their cabin saying, "Boys, we are done! We have 669 beaver pelts bundled up along with 20 wolf pelts and that is all that our packhorses, four extra riding and the six Indian horses from our battle on the beach can carry. That is especially so when one considers that we must pack out our remaining provisions, cooking gear and other particulars since we are through trapping on the Big Muddy and must go elsewhere come the fall. With that in mind, we are through beaver trapping this spring and I say even though it is early we head back to the fort so we can get a jump on our next season. Get a jump on our next trapping season by selling our furs and re-provisioning at the same time before everyone else does. Then we can do some scouting around and see where we go next for the coming fall and spring trapping seasons. What do any of you say as to that idea?"

For the longest time, no one said anything to Wallace's 'moving on' suggestion. In typical Barnes Clan fashion, the normally 'quiet as a wet snake moving across the wet grass' when it came to doing a lot of talking brothers, the cabin's interior remained quiet. Then Otis in his typical fashion of not mincing any words replied, "Sounds like it is time to move on. Best we get to making preparations towards getting it done."

For the next two days, the Barnes Clan made ready to move south to Fort Henry with their packs of furs. Little did anyone realize what a fortuitous move that was by leaving earlier than they normally would have left the trapping area come the end of their spring trapping season. By noon on the third day, the cabin had been cleaned out, all the horses packed and loaded and the Barnes Clan caravan of furs and other particulars were heading for the Missouri River where they had left their river-crossing raft. Three days of slow travel found the Barnes's on the banks of the mighty Missouri. There they found that the river was high but passable and after a day's hard work, all the packs, provisions, particulars, horses and men were across. For the next day the men rested as they let their horses graze and rest up for the next phase of their journey.

Arriving at Fort Henry several days later, the Barnes's discovered the fort was a flurry of activity! After meeting with Major Henry, the Barnes's discovered the fort was being abandoned because they had been almost under constant attack by the Blackfeet and Arikara and no longer deemed the presence of the fort in the area to be viable!

Therefore, the fort was in the process of being abandoned and its inhabitants were being moved further south to intercept a supply caravan heading for a place called Malachite's Big Hole, which was located away from the land of the dreaded Arikara Indians! Major Henry further advised that he and General Ashley were abandoning the idea of maintaining forts in the beaver trapping country in favor of initiating a "Rendezvous" system similar to what the French-Canadians had somewhat implemented years earlier. The Rendezvous system being a field supply system whereby supply caravans would come to the trappers versus the trappers having to travel to a vulnerable fort located in the backcountry.

That evening in camp, the Barnes Clan discussed what they were going to do while Cedrick prepared their suppers. Looking at their options, they found them rather limited. As the brothers saw it, they could ride the fort's last keelboat down to St. Louis and sell their furs, but then what? Or they could remain out on the frontier, go west and south to meet General Ashley's supply column by horseback. Once there, they could trade in their furs, re-provision and continue on with their newly chosen profession as trappers in a new area free from the threat of the dreaded Arikara Indians. As the brothers discussed their options, Wallace pointed out that Jed Smith had already taken a contingent of trappers from Fort Wichita according to Major Henry and had started traveling west to meet General Ashley's supply column. Then just as soon as Major Henry had concluded his business at Fort Henry with the remaining company trappers arriving daily from the field, he planned on sending their last keelboat down the Missouri to St. Louis. Then striking out, he too, with a contingent of the remaining men from the fort, were going to travel across country and eventually by July, meet General Ashley in a place he called "The Green River Valley" for the first American fur trappers' rendezvous.

The next day, the Barnes's, after making a collective decision to continue on as trappers, they pitched in with other company employees and helped load the rest of the fort's furs on the last keelboat leaving for St. Louis. In so doing, they bid adieu to their future trapping aspirations up on the Porcupine River for those unknown fortunes lying in the unknowns of the Green River Valley and the long and dangerous trip across country to get there.

CHAPTER SIX

THE "SEEDS–KEE–DEE"

FOUR DAYS LATER in the early summer, Major Henry and the rest of the men from Fort Henry abandoned the fort to the warlike Blackfeet and Arikara Indians who had waged war against the fort and its men ever since its establishment in 1822. As the long caravan of fur trappers, their heavily loaded pack animals and personnel from Fort Henry trooped out from its front gate and headed southwesterly along the Yellowstone, the Barnes's realized how fortunate they had been in deciding to leave for Fort Henry as early in the trapping season as they did. Had they waited until the middle of summer and then headed for Fort Henry with their furs, they would have discovered a destroyed and abandoned fort and trading post! That would have left the brothers not knowing about the coming rendezvous in the Green River Valley, with the only option of traveling all the way down through Arikara and Lakota Indian country to St. Louis in order to sell their furs and re-provision. A trip to St. Louis that would have been very dangerous from those Indian threats and would have more than likely, left the bones of the Barnes brothers scattered across the vast prairie, forever lost to the annals of history and time...

For the next two months, Major Henry and his contingent of company fur trappers and personnel from the fort traveled southwesterly along the Yellowstone until they reached the Powder River. There they turned south and traveled along the Powder until they reached the Platte. Camping along the Platte one evening, the Barnes brothers spent a few minutes along the treacherous shallow and sandy river one evening remembering how quickly a patch of quicksand had swallowed up their unsuspecting younger brother, Sterling, in June of 1822! A body of water they had originally traveled along northward as green fur trappers in order to establish Fort Henry. A fort that was now no more, as was their beloved brother Sterling...

Major Henry continued following the Platte to the Sweetwater River and then turned westerly moving through South Pass, the lowest pass in the Rocky Mountains. From there, there were many more long days in the saddle as his contingent headed southwesterly along the Big Sandy River until they reached the Green River. Then it was down the Green until they reached Malachite's Big Hole in the summer, where Major Henry met General Ashley with the relief supply train and a small herd of replacement horses for trappers who had lost or had previously worn theirs out. With that historic meeting between Major Henry and General Ashley began the fabled and successful Rendezvous system of supplying those fur trappers afield with their annual provisions in exchange for their furs. In short, the supply trains went to a geographic location selected subsequently by the trappers the previous summer (when the beaver were out of their prime) that was beneficial to their lifestyles and the beaver trapping areas in which they lived. Additionally, the rendezvous sites were selected so that they were for the most part surrounded by peaceful Indian tribes also wanting to trade. It was also with the initial establishment of the Rendezvous system that Major Henry separated his relationship from General Ashley and went his own way. Jedidiah Smith then replaced Major Henry as Ashley's new partner in the budding fur trade and rendezvous business.

There after a single day's celebrations fueled with the happiness of surviving difficult trapping seasons and hostile Indians as well as seeing old friends once again safe and sound, the company trappers as per their original contracts with the fur company, gave up one-half of their furs to the American Fur Company. Then their remaining furs were leveraged in purchasing new supplies at Mountain Prices for the coming fall and spring trapping seasons lying ahead.

When it finally came time for the Barnes Clan to trade in their furs, excluding their wolf pelts which were sold separately outside the terms and conditions of the 1822 beaver trapping contract, the Barnes's had managed to catch a massive number of 669 beaver on the Big Muddy! Then to their surprise when the company counters and graders were doing what they did best, discovered they had trapped more beaver than any of the other contract fur company teams! Surprised over the degree of their successes, they found out from the company counters and graders that the average contract beaver trapping team had caught less than 160 beaver in total! As a result, Mountain Prices or not, the Barnes Clan when they had finished with the one-day rendezvous, had more than enough money from the sale of their furs to purchase the needed provisions to last them throughout the coming trapping season. Those trades also generated a Letter of Credit from the fur company buyers for that which they did not spend from the sale of their huge lot of beaver furs amounting to $1,200! A Letter of Credit which Wallace then safely tucked away in his saddlebag to be redeemed in the future from the American Fur Company in St. Louis when the clan had returned to their home state of Missouri and began purchasing land for their new home.

Two days after the first rendezvous fur trading transactions had come and gone, which was no more than a quick fur exchange for new provisions, the Barnes's turn came up for the fur company's lead blacksmith Steve "Cooter" Krentz, to look over their herd of horses for general health and re-shoeing for the upcoming trapping seasons. While that was going on, Cooter Krentz helped the brothers select out the four best pack and riding horses from the herd of horses recovered from the Arikara at the 'Battle of the Beach'. The remaining two horses were then sold to other less fortunate trappers who for whatever reasons had a need for additional horseflesh. Wallace explained to his brothers' questioning eyes as to why they needed four more horses with the comment, "My sixth sense made me do it." Since Wallace had such a good record of his 'sixth sense' being right on the money, there was no further discussion as to his retaining 'four extra horses' reasoning. With the permanent addition of those four horses, that gave the Barnes Clan a total of eight good and four extra riding horses in case some were injured, lost or stolen and twelve packhorses for their coming venture into the fall and following spring trapping seasons.

Once again before heading off into the backcountry, the 'luck of the Irish' held for the Barnes

Clan, coming from a surprising turn of events. While selecting horses and waiting their turn at the company blacksmith area for their horses to be re-shod, the brothers ran into two obviously very hungry and 'disheveled looking' young Shoshoni Indian teenage boys. Two very hungry teenage Shoshoni youngsters who, after 'hanging around the brothers' during the horse shoeing event, were invited to the Barnes Clan's campsite for supper. There during supper, the two young and very hungry Shoshoni teenagers almost ate the Barnes brothers 'out of house and home'! After supper and sitting around their campfire relaxing, the Barnes Clan was surprised over the actions that came next from the young Shoshoni men! It seemed that the young Shoshoni men, out of gratitude for being taken in and fed by total strangers and what the young men considered a newfound friendship, they up and surprised the brothers!

Because of this seemingly newfound friendship, the young Shoshoni men told the brothers of an area they were aware of that was further to the north and full of beaver! An area that because of the fierce winters in that location and troubles with the competing Hudson's Bay Company trappers, was seldom trapped even by anyone in their own band of Shoshoni. Upon hearing that, Wallace's ears perked up and with another cup of coffee apiece, travel directions to this reported haven for beaver was freely provided by the young men. According to their new Indian 'friends', approximately ten days' travel if the weather was good to a place called "Bad Winters" by the Shoshoni or "The Clarks Fork of the Yellowstone" as it was known to the white man, beaver abounded. Beaver abounded in such numbers that they were more numerous than 'the numbers of golden eagle tail feathers on their chief's double train war bonnet' multiplied by the number of days in "One Moon" according to the two young Shoshoni men. Young men who were now enjoying their fourth cup of coffee loaded with brown sugar! As it turned out, a beaver location story told by two Shoshoni men who were so hungry that before they had eaten their fill at supper time, had consumed two full Dutch ovens of Cedrick's biscuits along with a five-pound slab of roasted buffalo meat between the two of them!

Considering the effects their four cups of coffee imbibed by their newfound and likable Shoshoni Indian friends, a huge free supper and the clan's newfound friendship had on the truth, Wallace figured that had to be the place they needed to head to for their coming beaver trapping seasons. After a fifth cup of sugar-loaded coffee, the two young Indian men agreed to show the trappers to this fabled beaver trapping ground if the brothers would give each of them one of the their extra Indian Trade rifles observed in the trappers' campsite and a horse to ride. As it turned out,

Indian Trade rifles the trappers had taken from the Arikara during the Coffee Pot Battle.

(Author's Note: Indian Trade rifles were one of the least expensive rifles used from 1820-1830. They had brass instead of steel fittings, were of a simple Kentucky style with a patch box, single trigger, possessed a straight butt stock instead of one with a drop in it, possessed a 40" barrel, weighed around ten pounds, and were generally caliber .54 in bore size making for easy use with buck and ball.)

Even figuring in the possibility that the Indians would just up and disappear into the mists somewhere along the way after they had received the rifles and horses, Wallace agreed even if it only got the men part-way to this newly described beaver trapping destination in question. Even with just that, he figured from the directions previously given by the two likable young Indian men they could find the rest of the way to those trapping grounds themselves. That evening after the two destitute Shoshoni Indians were sleeping off the effects of a giant meal imbibed earlier around the Barnes's campfire, Otis and Wallace returned to General Ashley's camp and purchased with the credit received from the sale of their wolf pelts, extra bags of flour for biscuit making, two more sacks of green coffee beans, another sack of brown sugar cones, another bag of salt, and extra powder, flints and shot. In so doing, Wallace figured if the two Indian men were going to accompany them all that way to the described beaver trapping grounds, they would have to be fed and fed well, not to mention be provided protection from man and beast. Then as their rewards for showing the trappers to this mystical beaver trapping ground previously discussed, not only would the Indian Trade guns be forthcoming but so would the two horses and some of the extra provisions just purchased if the two young men decided to leave and move on. Little did Wallace realize just how important his latest befriending decisions would become when it came to caring for the two young Indian strangers and his brothers' subsequent survival!

One day later, the Barnes Clan ventured forth from Malachite's Big Hole en route the Clarks Fork of the Yellowstone, alleged outstanding beaver trapping for those who could brave the harsh winters and Hudson's Bay Company competition from some of their trappers. Leading the way en route the Clarks Fork of the Yellowstone were two young Shoshoni Indian men who called themselves "Spotted Feather" and "White Cloud". For the next ten days, the six men headed through the rugged and heavily timbered ups and downs of the "Wind River" and then the "Absaroka" Ranges of mountains. At every turn in the trail, the men witnessed gigantic moose, lone buffalo spotted throughout the timbered meadows, numerous herds of elk around every bend, occasional bighorn sheep, along with grizzly bears, mule deer and wolves. As a result of the area's bounty, the men feasted every night on a different species of big game. This they did with the relish of living in the wilds created only by God's hands and doing what they loved best, namely being part of such magnificence on a daily basis! Come the twelfth day of travel, found the men descending from the beautiful and rugged mountains into the welcome Clarks Fork of the Yellowstone River valley. Sitting on their horses in amazement over what they were seeing, the men continued marveling over the rugged beauty they had just traversed and what was blessing their eyes in front of them! True to Spotted Feather and White Cloud's descriptions of the area, if anything, they had understated the beaver habitat that extensively lay before the trappers! Traveling upstream looking the beaver potential trapping areas over, the men were stunned! There was scant evidence of anyone else trapping or occupying the beaver-rich area! At every turn in the river, the men discovered beaver house after beaver house, numerous dams everywhere and signs at every patch of willows, aspens or cottonwoods of heavy beaver feeding activity! The beaver activity they were observing far exceeded that of what they had seen on the Big Muddy the year before!

Later that night, camped by a small but fast running stream in a dense copse of monster-sized Douglas fir trees, the six men unloaded their horses and made a protective defensive ring in the grove of trees with all of their packs and saddles. As they did, they found that Spotted Feather and White Cloud, contrary to most Indian males in that day and age, pitched right in when it came to any chores needed doing. What was considered women's work in many tribal cultures in that day and age and shunned by Indian males, the two young men routinely did as they were asked or when they found that camp work needed doing. In fact, the Barnes Clan discovered that they had come to enjoy very much the presence of the two young Indian men and they them! That evening after Cedrick had finished with the supper's chores, Wallace approached both young men with their own Indian Trade rifles, powder horns, bags of wads, flints and shot, as was part of the deal to lead the trappers to the land of the beaver. Then he thanked the two young men, who the brothers had discovered during the long days of the trip were poor as church mice and basically homeless outcasts! Basically homeless because both of the young men had been the 'spawn' of Shoshoni women raped by attacking Blackfeet Indians and as a result, when the boys had been born, they became tribal outcasts as unclean just as sure as those who had come from the bad spirits! Looking at their rifles with reverence in their eyes over finally being able to own something of value, the two young men looked at one another in disbelief. Then Spotted

Feather stood up and in his broken English learned from the "Black Robes" (Catholic Priests) who had visited their village years earlier, said, "White Cloud and I thank all of you for treating us with respect. We have both come to respect all of you as well and have come to call all of you our friends. We have also come to love Cedrick's biscuits! We would like to ask of you to allow us to stay and live with the four of you! As all of you have come to know, we have no one else we can call our own because of being a mistake of nature in the eyes of our Wind River tribe. We will both understand if you four choose not to call us your 'brothers' and chase us off like other Shoshoni men have done." With that, Spotted Feather abruptly sat down and with downcast eyes, appeared to be waiting for a refusal from what he and White Cloud had come to call their "White Brothers". Refusals similar to those they had received numerous times before from fellow members of the Wind River Shoshoni tribe when they had asked for any kind of a favor, inclusion or other considerations.

For the longest moments in time, the Barnes brothers just looked at each other not only in shock but surprise over what had been asked of them. Off in a distant stand of trees a great horned owl gave its familiar four-note hooting call and then only the crackling fire blazing away around the group of men disturbed the cooling night air with its familiar sounds. A night's air now heavy with the emotion of the surprising moment that can only come from deep within one's being who had been and was continuing to live in hurt from rejection of their own kind!

After a long period of more 'loud' silence, Otis stood up and looking over at Cedrick said, "Cedrick, would you go over to our packs and bring over one of our remaining kegs of rum. I think all of us need to celebrate and drink to the addition of Spotted Feather and White Cloud as our 'brothers in kind' within the Barnes Clan!"

Without a word and in full support of what his brother Otis had just requested, Cedrick got up and walked over to one of the packs holding a keg of rum. Moments later he had returned and sitting the keg down, began gathering up every-one's coffee cups and without a word of dissent from the rest of the brothers, began filling up the cups with a celebratory drink to their newest family members... When he did, Spotted Feather rose from where he had been sitting on his saddle being used as a chair around the campfire with a questioning look over what had just happened saying, "What does this truly mean?"

"It means," said Wallace, "that you and White Cloud are now members of our family and we are going to celebrate the fact that the two of you wish to become one with us as well. Welcome, boys, to our family!" For some reason after nu-merous cups of the fiery rum had been consumed all around that evening, even a hungry grizzly bear coming into camp that evening would have not awakened anyone... Come the following morning, most everyone was as 'quiet as a mouse pissin' on a ball of cotton', no one spoke very loudly and everyone was walking around a little gingerly so 'their heads would not fall off'. Then on top of that, Cedrick, for the first time in his life, burned the morning's first batch of Dutch oven biscuits come breakfast time...

Having decided that the stand of giant Douglas fir trees next to the stream was a great place to build a cabin out of the way from casual wandering eyes, the men later that afternoon after the effects of the previous evening's rum had worn off set off to the tasks at hand. As usual, Cedrick, the camp cook, selected the location for the placement of their new cabin. With that done, he paced off the steps from where he figured would be the front of their cabin and then grabbing a shovel from one of their packs, began constructing and laying out his outside firepit for the cooking of their meals when the outside weather was reasonable. While those activities were in progress, Otis, Wallace, Spotted Feather and White Cloud headed off into the timber with their two single buck saws and axes. Soon the forest behind where the cabin was to stand rang to the sounds of single buck saws in operation, the crashing of falling trees and the sounds of the axes of Spotted Feather and White Cloud, after being shown what they needed to do when it came to removing the limbs from the logs so they could be used for cabin making. As those activities swirled above the new campsite, Oliver paced off where a new, close at hand horse corral needed to be built and began digging the post-holes outlining its external boundaries.

In the meantime, Cedrick had filled up a bean pot with dried pinto beans, added water from their nearby creek and set the works out into the sun to soak away. Following that, he built up a fire in his new firepit and placed another pot full of water and rice next to the warming end of the fire to also soak away and fluff up. Then the pot-hanging rods and hangers were positioned over the firepit and anchored. Grabbing another ax, off Cedrick went to chop up and gather in several armloads of wood for the days' and eve-nings' fire needs. Then it was over to their last remaining hindquarter of buffalo which was cut into slabs for roasting and chunks for cooking in with the beans once they were ready for cooking. Finally finished with much of his cooking prepa-ration and in between keeping the fire going so he would have plenty of coals for his Dutch oven biscuits, Cedrick assisted Oliver in the digging of the remaining postholes for their new horse's corral.

Then Cedrick went back to his cooking duties as the sun dipped lower in the west. Taking his chunked up buffalo meat, he washed off the fly residue, buffalo hair, packhorse hair and sweat and dirt left on the pieces of meat, drained the bean pot, refilled it with fresh water and meat and set it over the fire on the hanging rods to slow cook. Then into the pot went two handfuls of red pepper flakes, two handfuls of dried onion flakes, salt and black pepper. Finally, into a steel pot went several handfuls of green coffee beans which were set over some coals at the end of the firepit to roast. When they had been sufficiently roasted, Cedrick crushed the coffee beans into smaller granules and set them off to one side. Finally, out came a coffee pot which was filled with creek water and set onto a hanging hook over the fire to boil.

With that, Oliver and Cedrick dragged over to the firepit area all of the men's saddles to be used to sit upon while eating supper. As Oliver dragged out the eating utensils, plates and cups from their camp box, Cedrick began fastening chunks of previously spiced buffalo meat upon the metal skewers in preparation for the fire-roasting that was to come. Then he was off to make up a very generous amount of biscuit dough realizing that the men had not had anything to eat all day and when they came in for supper, they would be as hungry as grizzly bears just prior to hibernation! By now the Heavenly smells of cooking beans loaded with chunks of buffalo meat, dried onions, pepper and red pepper flakes flooded the cooling evening air, all mixed in with the smells of freshly brewing coffee steaming away.

Soon to be added to those smells were the three Dutch ovens in the process of making mounds of biscuits. With that, Oliver went up into the forest and recalled the 'loggers' from their duties. Down the hill came the tired, sweaty and starving men. Over to the creek they went and washed up from all of their heavy duties in the woods and then here they came over to Cedrick's campfire like a herd of hungry buffalo. That was when Cedrick made the last rotation on the chunks and slabs of roasting buffalo meat so it would quickly be done to medium rare as his brothers and the two newest members of his family loved it. Off came the coffee pot as Oliver filled everyone's cups and then out came Cedrick's biscuits to a number of loudly emitted sounds of joy from the brothers seated around the cooking fire! With plates filled with piping hot biscuits, steaming beans and smoking hot chunks of buffalo meat laid over the top of the beans, the camp, with the exception of the crackling fire, went silent as the hungry men rejoiced in their bounty!

After a heavy breakfast of biscuits, beans and coffee the next morning, the entire camp except for Cedrick returned to their log cutting duties. Soon, the forest once again rang with the sounds of single buck saws cutting and falling timber and the ringing of axes. Meanwhile Cedrick took the time to hook up a team of horses and headed into the timber cutting zone where the brothers were sawing the logs to size for their new cabin.

Soon Cedrick was hauling pre-cut logs down to the cabin site for later assemblage into the walls and roof of their new home. Come almost noon-time, Cedrick relinquished the log hauling duties to his brother Otis, while he returned to begin making a lunch for his hardworking brothers.

Otis in the meantime, had assumed a new role, namely that of mentor and teacher. Otis having been more closely associated with the Creek Indians back in Tennessee as a younger man growing up than his brothers, found that he 'took' to Spotted Feather and White Cloud almost like a father. First off, on the hillside where the timber cutting and sawing operations were going on, Otis took the time to instruct the young Indian men that henceforth, he would act as their 'big brother' and teacher when it came to the art and industry of becoming a logger and fur trapper. Both Spotted Feather and White Cloud found the easygoing and quiet man named Otis much to their liking. In fact, he was almost like the real father neither of them ever had but had imagined what he would be like and had hoped for…

Right off the bat as the three men stood there on the hillside talking, Otis informed them that henceforth to make things easier, he was renam-ing them "Feather" and "Cloud" for 'talking's' sake since his family were men of few words! Both young men grinned widely at being given a white man's single name because it 'spoke' even more strongly to the fact that they were now part of the Barnes Brotherhood! Then tying off the team of horses, Otis unharnessed the team and turning to Feather and Cloud began the instruction on how to correctly harness up a team of horses. Following that lesson, taking the team of horses since re-harnessed, Otis began showing the boys the proper care and use of a team of horses hauling heavy and sometimes dangerous loads of logs. Taking Feather and Cloud, Otis had them accompany him and the team down to the cabin site pulling several pre-cut cabin logs to be. These lessons continued for about an hour, especially those lessons on the care and concern for the team when hauling a heavy load and then he had each young Shoshoni man do as he had so instructed. Within the hour both men had fairly well mastered the care and use of a team of horses and when satisfied, Otis turned first Feather and then Cloud, alternating each time, loose in the log hauling part of their operation. Then Otis returned to his single buck saw duties felling even more timber as Feather and then Cloud, once again alternating in hauling logs down to the cabin and then in the limb removal part of the 'logging' operations back up on the hillside.

On one of his log hauling details down to the cabin, Cloud heard a single rifle shot coming from their proposed cabin site and being concerned, hurried his team of horses downhill so he could see who and why someone had just shot. Arriving at the cabin site, Cloud observed Cedrick gutting out a cow elk by the creek near where their new corral was soon to be constructed. As Cloud later discovered from Cedrick, the cow elk had wandered into the men's campsite to get a drink in the creek. Cedrick upon seeing the cow and being short on 'camp meat', shot the elk and now the hardworking men would have all the good eating elk meat they could hold come supper time. Returning to the rest of the men still cutting down and removing the limbs, Cloud let all of them know the shooter was just Cedrick and that there would be fresh elk meat for supper, which brought out smiles on the faces of the hardworking 'logging crew'.

The next several trips down the mountain side with the team of horses brought the pre-cut shorter sitting logs for each of the men, which were then positioned around the campfire. Then it was back up onto the hillside for the serious log hauling of the longer logs for the cabin's walls and roof. Come supper time, Cedrick had fresh elk steak roasting away on the metal skewers, hot coffee and Dutch oven biscuits baking away on a bed of fresh coals. As a special treat for the hardworking men, Cedrick had concocted his rice, raisin, cooked dried apple slices, cinnamon and brown sugar-laced Dutch oven dessert treat. That last item sure brought smiles to the tired 'loggers', especially on the faces of Oliver and Wallace who each had a bad case of the 'sweet tooth' come supper time!

After supper and sitting around on their sitting logs smoking their pipes and drinking a cup of rum, Wallace, who had been somewhat quiet and introspective said, "I have an idea. Since there are now the six of us, that means we are going to have to build a very large cabin in order to comfortably hold all of us, our sleeping sites, provisions and our bundles of furs. That being said, with all the snow that we are looking at come winter time according to Cloud and Feather whose tribal members have trapped in this area in years past, that much snow-weight on a very large roof over our cabin could be a problem because of support issues. If we get that much snow on our roof in addition to the layer of dirt we would have underneath, that may be more weight than our roof timbers can support. I have been thinking about that problem and think I have figured out a workable solution. I would like to propose that we build our cabin large enough to sleep all six of us comfortably and still have a place inside in which to cook our meals in the fireplace and eat when the weather becomes nasty. Then we build a smaller storage cabin in which to store all of our furs, extra provisions, packs and saddle gear. That way all the bulky items can be stored out from our living area and we won't have to build such a large main cabin. Think about that for a minute and also this next idea. Right now we have plenty of grassy areas and nearby meadows in which our rather large horse herd will have enough feed. However, if we get the snows Cloud and Feather talk about, we will also need to build a lean-to or shed of some kind. Into that structure we will need to store some hay that we cut this summer and keep in that third structure as emergency feed for when the snows are too deep for our pack and saddle horses to be able to paw their ways down to the grasses underneath. Now I know I have thrown a lot at the five of you, but I would feel better working harder and longer now during this nicer summer weather building all of those structures than trying to address my very real concerns come the dead of winter when something has collapsed or is too small for our needs," said Wallace finally running down on what he had to say.

Otis, usually one of the quietest brothers of the bunch, spoke up saying, "Guess we all best get to our sleeping blankets because it looks for the next two weeks or so, older brother Wallace is going to drive us like a bunch of black slaves fresh off the boat." With no further words of dissent from anyone, everyone got up, drained their cups of rum and tossed the cups into the wash pans. Then they knocked the ash from the bowls of their pipes, attended to a call of nature so they would not be bothered with having to get up in the middle of the night and stumble upon a hungry grizzly bear, and started heading for their sleeping area over by the corral soon to be constructed once the poles and rails had been cut and hauled down.

"Hey," said Cedrick. "I need some help in hoisting these elk quarters high up into the trees so we don't invite any night visitors like 'Mr. Grizzly' or the like." For the next 20 minutes or so, the men wrestled the now tied-up quarters into several nearby trees out of the reach of any grizzly bears who were not known to be able to climb trees because of their long claws, and then everyone turned in for the night. That was everyone except Cedrick. He still needed to heat up some water and wash all the pots, pans and utensils before he went off to sleep as well.

For the next 13 days, the six men cut timber, hauled logs and built a large cabin, 20 by 24 feet, capable of holding six men inside comfortably. Then when the cabin was roofed with smaller logs and covered over with two feet of soil to prevent seepage during inclement weather as well as prohibiting any attacking Indians from setting the roof afire, the men had a celebratory dinner that night upon completion of those tasks. However, the very next day found all five men back up on the hill cutting and hauling more timber for Wallace's smaller storage shed suggestion. As for Wallace, he now stayed behind being an excellent carpenter, making tables and log chairs to be used inside the cabin during inclement weather, cutting out the door and window openings and was responsible for completing the mammoth job of building a rock, mud and stick fireplace with a high enough chimney that would 'draw' at the end of their cabin.

In between all of those duties, Cedrick continued as the camp's cook since he was the best cook among all of the men. However, when he could, he assisted Wallace in the cabin finishing details which also included drilling holes into the walls of the massive log structure, cutting wooden pegs and driving them into the holes made into the wall's logs onto which to hang clothing to dry, weapons and the like. Up next went a 10 by 15-foot log shed into which upon completion would house most of the men's extra provisions, their leather gear to preclude porcupines from chewing on the sweat-soaked and salty tasting leather, along with other bulky items like their kegs and canisters of powder, kegs of rum and eventually their bundles of beaver fur made ready for travel. Following those endeavors, a lean-to was constructed adjacent the cabin for emergency hay storage for when the winter snows became too deep for the horses to be able to paw their ways down through the layers of snow to the rich, energy producing grasses below. That way, feed would still be available because without a healthy horse in the backcountry, a horseless man was essentially a 'dead man walking'. The next day with Otis and Oliver heading off into the timber to cut corral posts and rails, the rest of the group finished digging postholes for the corral. Two more days of hard work and the corral was finished and their horses had a new home.

Nearing the end of those housekeeping and building duties, the men built several meat smoking racks next to their cabin so they could make jerky from the buffalo and elk they killed in the future. That was followed with the building of two' hell-for-stout' meat poles capable of holding several quarters at a time of elk or buffalo. In between those duties, it was off afield hunting buffalo, moose or elk on a weekly basis to supply the large amounts of fresh meat which was eaten three times daily by the six men or used for smoking the winter's jerky supply for use when out on the trail. One of the seemingly neverending chores was the cutting of firewood for daily use at the campfire, as well as cutting and hauling additional dead trees down from the timbered area behind their cabin and stacked adjacent the cabin for winter use when the snows became too deep to easily cut and haul firewood. Then the men, along with a horde of mosquitoes, cut hay in the nearby meadows to dry and stack inside their emergency hay storage shed for late winter's use. Then as the men smoked their 20 or so beaver traps to rid them of the man smell, they simultaneously used the brain-tanning process to tan deer hides to be made into jerky holding bags, to act as shaved thin window covers and for covering packs of beaver when being transported to the next rendezvous site. Then Cloud and

Feather spent an afternoon searching out and cutting four-foot beaver trap anchor poles from dry willow wood to be used once the fall beaver trapping commenced. (Author's Note: If green wood anchor poles were used, a trapped beaver would chew through it and swim off with the valuable trap to some place safer, whereby it could chew off its foot. By using a dry wood pole, the beaver never tried chewing through the anchor poles to facilitate their escape.) Additionally, the men spent their time in the evenings under candlelight in the cabin casting small mountains of bullets, putting edges on their much-used knives, shovels and axes, and repairing their damaged and wearing out English made clothing. As if the above duties were not time consuming enough, the trappers had to constantly look after and upkeep their weapons and set aside time for meal preparations, followed by the related cooking and cleaning of valuable cast iron cookware. All of that aside, sometime during the daylight hours the men bathed when they could no longer stand themselves or smelled like a bear, shaved (yes, trappers for the most part shaved and cut hair that grew too long to prevent the spread of head lice, a common problem in that day and age), tended to their livestock on a daily basis, scouted out their beaver trapping grounds in preparation for the fall trapping season, treated cuts and scrapes on themselves and their animals, and slept! (Author's Note: After years of research involving the life and times of the Mountain Men, the Author quickly discovered being a trapper in the Old West meant there was a lot more to do than just 'making biscuits and singing cowboy songs'… as illustrated above. AFTER ALL THE ABOVE WORK WAS ACCOMPLISHED, THEN THE REAL WORK BEGAN!)

Wallace, finally satisfied the men were now more or less prepared for the long fall trapping season ahead, headed the group out on a buffalo hunt after a late summer's breakfast. Stalking the first herd of buffalo they encountered feeding near the river's bottoms on the lush grasses, three buffalo were quickly put down. Two of the buffalo killed were by Feather and Cloud, after being trained by Otis on the proper use and shooting techniques required when it came to using their Indian Trade rifles. In fact, since both Feather and Cloud had little or no experience with firearms due to being tribal outcasts without many material things of possession in their lives, Otis quickly discovered that they had developed no bad habits when it came to the use and care of firearms. Under Otis's careful tutelage, both young men soon developed into skillful shooters as evidenced by the killing of their first two buffalo ever killed with only one shot each! That in part, partially validated those skills they had learned under Otis's care with the use of their new firearms. Those skills would someday be proven even more definitively under the most trying of conditions when quick shooting and accuracy became a necessity.

With the next several weeks' worth of meat on the ground, the brothers began butchering out the animals while Cloud and Feather, after reloading, stood guard against any attack from man or beast. Stood guard because many times when someone fired shots in the backcountry, other men or critters, some with evil intent in their hearts, many times would come to investigate such shooting. Many a trapper failed to learn that lesson, soon finding themselves 'going under' after being filled full of arrows, busted up by a speeding lead ball or left as a bear scat out on the prairie or in the timber... Then with heavily loaded packhorses, the trappers headed back to their camp to hoist the quarters high up onto their meat poles in order to allow the meat to glaze over as well as providing for protection against four-footed predators looking for an easy meal. Then it was off to their nearby creek to clean up and rid themselves of the dried blood, fat and bodily juices acquired when gutting and butchering out the buffalo just killed. That evening after a supper replete with buffalo meat, a favorite of the group, the men lit up their clay pipes, including Feather and Cloud who had recently learned to love and enjoy the taste of tobacco in the form of an evening smoke with their 'brothers'. Then they broke out a keg of rum and celebrated a successful year together as a family with their two new 'brothers' and made merry in light of the fact that the beaver were now coming into their prime, the weather had turned colder and tomorrow they would start their first day of the fall beaver trapping season.

The next morning after breakfast, Wallace led the group of trappers out from their camp as he headed for a long line of waterways located up along the northwestern arm of the Clarks Fork of the Yellowstone. Following behind Wallace rode Cloud trailing a packhorse and riding behind him rode Feather trailing another packhorse, both of which were carrying the much-needed trapping gear, wooden anchor poles and accessories in the panniers. Riding behind the two young Shoshoni boys rode their mentor Otis, who was followed by Cedrick and Oliver pulling rear guard duties in case they were ever attacked from the rear. Attacked from the rear, which the trappers had learned over the years was a favorite Indian tactic because of the confusion it always caused among those being attacked from such an unexpected position.

Scouting out the waterways as he went, Wallace's practiced eye noticed all of the fresh beaver sign throughout. Everywhere he looked, he observed many long, well-built and maintained beaver dams, huge beaver houses indicating numerous beaver within and fresh 'cutting' signs along every bank of willows or groves of aspens or cottonwood near the water. With that much beaver evidence in casual sight, Wallace figured he would lead his caravan of trappers even further to the northwest along the Clarks Fork of the Yellowstone. That Wallace did with the intent to eventually trap their ways back down that waterway towards their campsite as the beaver were trapped out above. Then having trapped out that arm of the river come summer-time, head for the next chosen rendezvous site called "Malachite's Big Hole". Following that, Wallace's plan was to return to their same camp-site with their already well-built living and stor-age structures, live there another year and that time, trap out the northeastern arm of the Clarks Fork of the Yellowstone. That way they could trap out all the beaver they could pack out and not have to start all over once again in the build-ing of a cabin and any other structures needed to make a livable camp.

For the next hour or so, Wallace continued traveling to the northwest along the river that he and his brothers had scouted out weeks earlier inventorying the beaver sign. As he did, he led the caravan of trappers in and out of the fingers of timber running down to the river's edge as he proceeded northward enjoying what he was seeing in the tremendous amount of beaver sign and extensive activity along the nearby water-ways and the banks of the Clarks Fork of the Yellowstone River.

It was about then that Wallace smelled the

faint smell of campfire smoke from nearby as he wove his horse in and out of the heavy stands of dark timber growing along the river! Quickly drawing up his horse short in concern over who might be at such a campfire, Wallace found that he was too late in his reaction to his concerns. Wallace had stumbled directly into a small Indian encampment of men who were just arising from their sleeping furs! Upon observing a stream of trappers and their horseflesh emerging from the timber at the edge of their campsite, five Indians immediately jumped up, who as it turned out were just as equally surprised as was Wallace, who was now sitting on his horse staring at the 'exploding' camp in surprise!

ZZIPPP–ZZIPPP–ZZIPPP–ZZIPPP! WENT FOUR HASTILY FIRED ARROWS AT THE FUR TRAPPER SITTING ON HIS HORSE AT THE EDGE OF THE INDIANS' ENCAMPMENT IN STUNNED SURPRISE! Several arrows went over the top of the surprised Wallace but unfortunately not all. **"YEEEHEE!"** neighed Wallace's horse as one of the hastily flung arrows at the trapper found its 'home' as a 'death shot' driven deeply into the side of the horse behind its shoulder! Another arrow simultaneously found itself lodged into the fleshy part of Wallace's left thigh, driving all the way through his muscular leg, with its steel-tipped arrowhead firmly lodging into the ribs of his now stumbling horse! Within moments, Wallace's horse staggered, then stumbled with the arrow firmly lodged into its lungs, then with a death shudder, pitched forward onto the ground on its head carrying Wallace along with it! **ZZIPPP–ZZIPPP!** went two more hastily flung arrows at the trappers' pack string continuing to weave their ways in and out of the heavy timber, unawares of what was occurring to its front, with one arrow lodging into the side of the pannier of Cloud's packhorse! Fortunately, that steel-tipped arrow point smashed itself flat against a shovel being carried in that pannier. However, the second quickly fired arrow found its mark! **PLUNK!** went that arrow point right into the side of Otis's saddle bag clear full of jerky and went no further. However, the impact of that arrow into its flank caused Otis's surprised horse to jump forward a quick step throwing Otis's shot off, just as he fired his rifle at one of his surprised assailants! BOOM! went Otis's rifle just as his horse spooked forward upon feeling the arrow's impact into the saddle bag full of jerky on his hip and in so doing, Otis's shot killed outright one of the Indians' horses picketed nearby with a headshot aimed originally at one of the Indians shooting arrows at the trappers! But his horse's surprising jump forward caused the shot to go high, missing the Indian's head and hitting one of their horses tied nearby right between its eyes!

By now, the surprised trappers had quickly reacted to the danger at hand as the air was filled with white clouds of black powder smoke rolling towards the Indian encampment, along with deadly whistling lead balls! **BOOM!** fired Cloud's Indian Trade rifle, killing outright one Indian running right at him with an upraised tomahawk! **BOOM!** went Feather's Trade rifle as he shot away another Indian's entire lower jaw, dropping him instantly into the Indians' campfire to move no more! **BOOM–BOOM!** went Oliver and Cedrick's rifles simultaneously as their horses moved up into the Indians' encampment and they joined the surprise fracas, dropping two other Indians with back shots as they raced for the safety of their picketed horses to escape! However, one Indian racing for his horse was able to leap onto its back and quickly disappeared into the dense timber before any of the trappers could lethally react! Then other than the acrid smell of black powder smoke hanging heavy in the morning's air and the nervous shuffling of trappers' horses' feet and those from the remaining Indians' picketed horses, the mountain air was quiet once again.

"GET ME TO HELL OFF THIS DEAD SON-OF-A-BITCH!" yelled Wallace, still pinned by an arrow driven clear through the fleshy part of his thigh and into the side of his now dead horse! That he did as he hung onto his saddle horn slumped over his mount, hanging on with both hands to avoid falling off and ripping out the arrow from the muscular tissue of his thigh!

Cloud instantly leapt from his mount, ran over

to Wallace and having seen many arrow wounds among a number of his people in years past, without hesitation whipped out his sheath knife. Grabbing Wallace's thigh where the arrow's shaft had passed through and stuck into the side of his horse, Cloud pulled his leg slightly away from the horse's side, cut through the arrow's shaft next to the horse's side with his razor sharp knife (as Otis had taught him in keeping his knife always sharp enough to shave with) before Wallace knew what was even happening. Then grabbing the feathered end of the shaft, Cloud gave a hard tug, pulling the shaft of the arrow free from the flesh of Wallace's leg! When he did, his shaft pulling was accompanied with a howl of pain when the arrow's shaft was pulled free from Wallace's damaged leg!

When Cloud had jumped from his horse to help Wallace, Feather had reached down and grabbed the reins from his two horses so they would not panic in the ongoing excitement and run off in fright over the action at hand. As for the other three brothers, they had laid their rifles down after leaping off their horses and had run through the Indians' camp with drawn pistols looking for any other like in kind 'problems'. Finding none since the fifth Indian in camp had been able to ride off into the dark timber, the three brothers returned to their rifles and hastily reloaded them in case anyone had heard all the shooting and were now coming their way to investigate. In the meantime, Cloud had walked over to one of the dead Indians, taken out his knife and before Wallace could tell him that there would be no scalping of Indians while he was alive, pulled off the dead man's buckskin shirt, cut off a long slice of the tanned leather free of decorations and walked back to Wallace... Then taking his two hands and without a single word being said to Wallace, who was now sitting on the side of his dead horse holding his madly bleeding wound, took his leg, lifted it up and squeezed hard with his hands on the damaged area. As expected, the blood just flowed and after a short spell, Cloud took the long swatch of buckskin cut from the dead Indian's shirt and wrapped it tightly around Wallace's wounded leg. Cloud then tied it off without a word being said, much to the injured man's amazement!

Feather, still sitting and holding a number of the trappers' horses reins now to prevent escape, after looking down at the dead Indian's clothing quietly said, "Northern Cheyenne! Not good that one was able to run away. He will come back with many others looking for those who killed his brothers!"

"Fortunately, most of the arrows shot at Wallace missed," said a returning Oliver, as he mounted his horse and with his reloaded rifle, rode over to the edge of the stand of timber they were in so he could be on the lookout for any more like in kind, 'Northern Cheyenne'.

Otis and Cedrick dragged the one Indian out from the Indians' campfire which he had fallen into when shot in the jaw by the straight shooting Feather and along with the other bodies, the brothers dragged them into the dark timber and left them for the meat eaters of the forest! Returning from the Indians' picket line of horses, Otis let everyone know that he had discovered one of the Indians horses was shod, more than likely taken from a trapper caught unawares and killed for his lack of awareness in the field. Otis and Cedrick then removed Wallace's saddle from his dead horse and saddled and bridled the Indian horse that was shod, so Wallace would have a good riding horse used to being ridden by a white man. Wallace, not to be outdone by being a problem and being 'Irish' stubborn, insisted on the men proceeding with their original plan and that included setting out their 20 beaver traps before they went back to their camp. That he demanded because Cloud's work on his leg, although sore as hell, had pretty much stopped the bleeding and as long as he did not have to walk around in a muddy beaver pond setting traps on his now bum leg, they would carry on with Cedrick.

Realizing they still had a mountain of work ahead, Otis and Oliver roped up the two remaining Indian horses and trailed them along with the rest of their stock. As it turned out, both horses were of fine stock and would come in handy when the trappers needed extra pack animals so instead of turning them loose, they were added to the trappers' herd of livestock now numbering over 20 head of horses. For the rest of that morning and into the early afternoon, the men set out their traps on their new trap line. However, instead of Wallace being the main trapper as was usual, Cedrick took over those duties.

At their first trap setting site, Cedrick took off his pants, crawled into his pair of leggings and breechclout, waded in and made a set every bit as good as Wallace would have made. Then continuing with Otis as his trapmate and assistant, the two brothers continued setting out their 20 beaver traps much to the satisfaction of Wallace who was watching on. As it turned out that day, Wallace and Oliver from atop their horses provided 'guard duty', Cedrick and Otis set out the trap line and Cloud and Feather, having trapped before with some of their tribal members, did all of the skinning on the seven beaver found hanging in the just set traps upon the trappers' return trip along their newest trap line.

On their return trip back to their campsite, the men stopped along a dense patch of willows and filled their panniers with green 'hooping' limbs (the most flexible) and then continued along their ways back to camp. That evening while Cedrick prepared the men's suppers, Otis showed Cloud and Feather how they were to flesh out and hoop their beaver skins so they would get the best price back at the rendezvous. Then as Feather put into practice what Otis had just taught him regarding the proper fleshing and hooping techniques, Cloud mysteriously saddled his horse and rode off by himself. Right at dark, he returned with a big grin, holding a handful of strange looking plants. Borrowing one of Cedrick's smaller cooking pots, Cloud commenced mashing the plants he had just brought back to camp into a green mush-like looking, evil-smelling substance. Later upon approaching Wallace sitting on his sitting log by the fire with a cup of rum in hand, Cloud asked him to drop his pants...

"WHAT THE HELL FOR?" bellowed Wallace, still in obvious pain and not in any kind of a mood to be 'messed with' as he continued rubbing his sore oozing thigh wound where the Indian's arrow had passed through the meaty part of his thigh and painfully out the other side.

"I have something to put on the wound to make it all better," said Cloud, somewhat intimidated by Wallace's grumpy attitude towards him caused by the throbbing pain he was sharply feeling from the wounded area.

"Do as he tells you, my brother. I am sure Cloud has a reason for what he is asking and wanting to do," counseled Otis, sticking up for what he was now considering one of his 'adoptive sons'.

With a grumpy and impatient look at both Cloud and Otis, Wallace finally stood up, dropped his buckskin pants, revealing a purplish-red looking thigh still wrapped with a bloody piece of a dead Indian's buckskin shirt. Moments later, Cloud had the bloody buckskin rag removed and tossed into the campfire. Then carefully washing off the wound and pouring some rum over the entry and exit holes caused by the arrow, much to Wallace's bellowing out in pain, Cloud continued, knowing Otis would be there to deflect any more grumblings from Wallace. Wiping off the excess rum, Cloud continued massaging the wound to remove any clotted blood in the wound and then rubbed into the entry and exit holes the mashed up evil-smelling poultice he had just made in the bottom of one of Cedrick's cooking pots. As he did, Wallace quit his grumbling realizing that Cloud was just trying to make his wound heal with less pain, so he backed off from his threatening grumbling and just let the young Indian lad do what he figured was the best care for the type of wound he was working with.

Somewhat later and with the wound now wrapped with a clean swatch of the men's gray cloth normally used to repair their clothing, Wallace sat back down on his sitting log just as Cedrick announced that supper was ready. That evening after they had finished eating their supper, the tired and emotionally drained men smoked a pipe bowl full of James River tobacco, brought in their horses from letting them graze and placed them into their corral for safer keeping. Then it was off to their sleeping blankets and furs. However, as they did, the men attended to any calls of nature they had to respond to before bedding down, then it was off to bed for tomorrow would be another busy day with a trap line to run with adjustments to be made in their normally assumed trap line duties.

Right at dawn found Cedrick stoking up the remaining live coals in his cooking fire and making breakfast as the rest of the men attended to their calls of nature, washed up, shaved and then headed for their sitting logs and Cedrick's brand of 'strong as an angry mule's kick' great smelling coffee. When Wallace limped over and sat down on his sitting log and was handed his morning's cup of coffee he said, "Cloud, I don't know what the hell kind of stinking crap you slapped all over my leg last night or what the hell it was called but it sure did the trick. Other than stinking up my sleeping furs all night, it took away a lot of the soreness and my swelling has gone way down. Thank you for what you did."

Cloud just beamed over what he had accomplished and was glad someone had taught him which plants to use when one has an open wound back in his old tribe of Wind River Shoshoni Indians. Then he said, braving Wallace's wrath one more time "Wallace, I need to put some more of that poultice on your wound before we leave today. So if you will allow me, I will do so now."

Without one grumble, Wallace stood up, undid the tie on his buckskin pants and let them slip away so Cloud could once again work his magic on his wound-damaged leg. Once the wound had been cleaned, the smelly mixture of plant material reapplied and rewrapped with a fresh swatch of clean gray cloth, up went Wallace's pants and once again without a single grumble, stinky smell or not, he seemed pleased... Later that morning when the trappers were running their very successful trap line, little did any of them realize that a set of dark eyes was cast upon them from afar within the dark timber watching their every move! Somewhat later, "Dark Eyes" rode off with an even 'darker heart' having seen what he came to see and learn...

For that month of September until the first part of November, the men successfully trapped and hooped 224 beaver, with a majority of them being large in size Made Beaver! By then, Wallace's leg, thanks to Cloud's care, had healed nicely and he was back to being the group's main trapper. Cedrick was also once again back to being Wallace's aide, Otis and Oliver back to being the 'look-outs' for any signs of danger, and Cloud and Feather the group's two main on-site skinners. It was now obvious the new Barnes Clan was operating as an experienced beaver trapping team and the earlier battle with the Northern Cheyenne was almost a forgotten incident. By now, the weather had turned cold and the beaver trapping waters even colder. Many times, Wallace would have to quit setting traps, emptying out the dead beaver and bringing them to shore to be skinned because the waters in which they were trapping were now icy cold! When that cold finally numbed his legs and feet to the point that he was stumbling around in the waterways setting the traps, he would leave the water and begin walking around on dry land in an effort to warm up his legs and feet. When those times occurred, Cedrick would strip off his pants, put on his leggings and breechclout and continue the trap setting as well as removing the trapped beaver for the skinning on-site that followed.

Finally one morning when the two men doing the actual trapping were breaking skim ice every step of the way while checking and re-setting their traps, both men were finding frequent 'walk-abouts' in order to warm up were becoming absolutely necessary. Around noon on one of those kind of November days, found both men doing not only their warm-up 'walk-abouts' but flapping their arms about their torsos to aid in their warm-ups as well. However as they did, a look to the northwest showed gray ominous storm clouds littering the horizon with more threatening and low 'scudding' clouds slowly moving their way. The morning which had been unusually warm back at their camp, had now turned cold and getting colder as the trappers continued doing what had to be done even in the face of an oncoming storm and the icy waters in which they waded. However, Otis, using what he had learned weather-wise while associating and growing up with the Creek Indians back in Tennessee, kept a cocked eye on the developing weather events realizing there could be danger therein if they didn't pay heed to the signs.

Otis, finally realizing that a major winter storm would soon be upon the trappers and when it arrived their fall trapping season for beaver was over, yelled over at Wallace to get his attention and then pointed skyward at the oncoming and threatening cloud formations emanating from where their worst weather came from, namely the northwest. Looking skyward and acknowledging Otis's weather warnings, Wallace yelled over to Cedrick to come ashore and bring the trap he was getting ready to reset. When he did, he too plunged into the near freezing waters at their next trap site, removed a dead beaver and then brought not only his trap but the beaver ashore as well. By now, flecks of snow were spitting through the air and both Cedrick and Wallace felt the urgency to clear the last of the traps in their trap line and head for the safety and comfort of their camp. Removing the last of their traps and beaver at the north end of their trap line, the two men doubled back on the rest of their previously set trap line. When they did, they continued hurriedly removing all of their valuable beaver traps before freeze-up made that almost impossible to do under the soon to be sheets of ice covering all the watered areas. Rounding a finger of Douglas fir trees that ran right to the river's edge, Wallace pulled their last trap as Cedrick put on his wool pants while back on shore, much to his relief for the warmth they would offer after a while of use!

All of a sudden, OUT FROM THE FINGER OF NEARBY TREES PREVIOUSLY HIDDEN BY THE DARK TIMBER, STREAMED A LONG LINE OF HORSEFLESH AND PAINTED NATIVE AMERICAN HUMANITY YELLING LIKE BANSHEES! A HALF-DOZEN QUICK RIFLE SHOTS FROM TEN HARD CHARGING INDIANS AIMED AT OTIS AND OLIVER SITTING LIKE THE SENTINELS THEY WERE AT THE EDGE OF THE GROUP OF TRAPPERS, CLEARED BOTH MEN FROM THEIR SADDLES AND KILLED OUTRIGHT BOTH OF THEIR HORSES AS WELL! **BOOM–BOOM–BOOM– BOOM!** RANG OUT ANOTHER FOUR SHOTS AS THE TRAILING HARD-RIDING INDIANS UNLEASHED THEIR SERIES OF SHOTS AT THE NOW SURPRISED AND BUNCHING UP TRAPPERS! THE SOUNDS OF WHISTLING HOT LEAD "ZIPPED" THROUGH THE CROWDED RANKS OF CLOUD, FEATHER, CEDRICK AND WALLACE, FORTUNATELY NOT TOUCHING A SINGLE MAN…

THEN AS WALLACE AND CEDRICK, THEIR COLD LEGS AND FEET NOW FORGOTTEN, RACED FOR THEIR WEAPONS CARRIED ON THEIR NEARBY HORSES, CLOUD QUIETLY SHOT THE FIRST RACING INDIAN IN LINE

OFF HIS HORSE WHO WAS CLOSEST TO THE GROUP OF TRAPPERS! IN SO DOING, CLOUD CREATED A CHAIN REACTION THAT PROBABLY SAVED ALL OF THE TRAPPERS' LIVES... WHEN THAT INDIAN SHOT BY CLOUD HIT THE GROUND, HIS TUMBLING BODY CAUSED THE FOLLOWING YELLING AND ATTACKING HORSEMEN TO TRY REINING THEIR HORSES OFF TO ONE SIDE TO AVOID HAVING THEIR HORSES STUMBLING OVER THE STILL-ROLLING DEAD INDIAN'S BODY! THAT WAS ALL FEATHER NEEDED, AS HE SHOT THE NEXT CLOSEST INDIAN IN LINE AND IN SO DOING, HIS LEAD BALL PASSED THROUGH THE INDIAN HE HAD JUST GUTSHOT, BLOWING CLEAR THROUGH HIS BODY AND INTO THE FOLLOWING INDIAN'S HORSE'S HEAD, KILLING IT IMMEDIATELY! DOWN WENT THAT TUMBLING HORSE AND IN SO DOING, CAUSED A TREMENDOUS WRECK OF STUMBLING AND FALLING TRAILING HORSES, FLAILING HOOVES AND FLYING INDIAN BODIES, ALONG WITH THEIR CATAPULTING THROUGH THE AIR, RIFLES! HOWEVER, THE LAST TWO INDIANS IN THE HARD-CHARGING LINE OF ATTACKERS MANAGED TO REIN THEIR HORSES OFF TO ONE SIDE FROM THE REST OF THE DEVELOPING WRECK OF HORSES AND MEN AHEAD OF THEM!

HOWEVER, THAT WAS TO NO AVAIL IN THEIR WORLD, AS OLIVER AND OTIS, HAVING RECOVERED FROM HAVING THEIR HORSES SHOT FROM UNDERNEATH THEM, SHOT BOTH REMAINING INDIANS FROM THEIR HORSES! THEN IT WAS FLAILING KNIVES AND TOMAHAWKS AS THE TRAPPERS AND THE REMAINING RANKS OF INDIANS, MANY STILL RECOVERING FROM THEIR HORSE WRECKS, CLOSED IN WITH THE TRAPPERS FOR HAND-TO-HAND COMBAT…

FIRST TO DRAW BLOOD IN THOSE NEXT MOMENTS WAS CLOUD, WHEN HE CLEAVED THE SKULL WITH HIS TOMAHAWK OF AN INDIAN ON THE GROUND TRYING TO RISE UP FROM THE MASS OF WRECKED HORSES AND HUMANITY! CLOUD'S TOMAHAWK BRAINED THAT MAN AND THEN CLOUD REMEMBERED NO MORE AFTER BEING HIT IN THE HEAD FROM BEHIND! FEATHER HOWEVER, WAS LOCKED IN A HAND-TO-HAND BATTLE WITH ANOTHER INDIAN WITH KNIVES FLASHING! ALL OF A SUDDEN, FEATHER FELT A BURNING PAIN ACROSS HIS FACE AS HIS ASSAILANT'S KNIFE BLADE SWIPED ACROSS HIS UPPER CHEEK, NOSE AND FOREHEAD! WHEN FEATHER WENT DOWN IN PAIN, HE HEARD THE ROAR OF CEDRICK'S PISTOL GOING OFF OVER HIS BODY ATTEMPTING TO COVER HIS FALLEN

'BROTHER' AND THEN HE BLACKED OUT FROM THE SHOCK OF HIS BADLY DAMAGED FACE!

WALLACE NEXT FOUND HIMSELF KILLING ONE INDIAN STILL ON THE GROUND TRYING TO RECOVER FROM THE HORSE WRECK WITH A HEAD STOMP AND THEN BRAINING ANOTHER CRIPPLED INDIAN WITH ONE OF THE FIVE-POUND BEAVER TRAPS HE HAD BEEN CARRYING WHEN HE STARTED TO MAKE A RUN FOR HIS HORSE WHICH WAS CARRYING HIS RIFLE! THEN HE FELT A SEARING PAIN ACROSS HIS SHOULDERS FROM BEHIND, INITIATED FROM AN UNSEEN INDIAN, DROPPING HIM TO THE GROUND IN PAIN! LOOKING UP, WALLACE SAW THAT INDIAN NOW RAISING HIS TOMAHAWK OVER HIS HEAD TO SMASH DOWN UPON THE TRAPPER, ONLY TO SEE HIS HEAD EXPLODE BRIGHT CRIMSON RED AND THEN HEARING THE SOUND OF OLIVER'S PISTOL BEING FIRED CLOSE BY. SUFFICE TO SAY, THAT INDIAN DID NOT GET TO USE HIS TOMAHAWK EVER AGAIN IN BATTLE... THEN THE ROARING, CRASHING 'SOUNDS OF BATTLE' AND THOSE NOISES MADE BY INDIAN HORSES IN PAIN SUFFERING FROM BROKEN LIMBS AS A RESULT OF THE MASSIVE HORSE WRECK SUFFERED EARLIER, SOMEWHAT WENT SILENT. THE SHORT BUT VIOLENT

CONFRONTATION, EXCEPT FOR THE CLEAN-UP, WAS NOW OVER...

THAT WAS EXCEPT FOR THE SO NAMED "DARK EYES", THE LONE SURVIVOR FROM THEIR ENCAMPMENT WHICH WALLACE HAD RIDDEN INTO EARLIER BY MISTAKE AND AN INSTANT FIGHT HAD ENSUED. THE ONE AND SAME "DARK EYES" WHO HAD RETURNED TO HIS BAND OF NORTHERN CHEYENNE, ORGANIZED A WAR PARTY AND CAME BACK HUNTING THOSE TRAPPERS WHO HAD EARLIER KILLED HIS FOUR FRIENDS. THE ONE AND SAME "DARK EYES" WHO WAS NOW RUNNING AWAY FROM THE BATTLE JUST ENDED, ONCE AGAIN AS THE LONE SURVIVOR. LEAPING OVER A SMALL BEAVER DAM AND SPRINTING FOR A FINGER OF TREES THAT HAD HIDDEN HIS WAR PARTY EARLIER, HE RACED UP THE BANK FOR THE SAFETY THAT STAND OF TIMBER OFFERED. **WHOOMP!** WENT A .54 CALIBER RIFLE BALL BETWEEN HIS SHOULDER BLADES, TORE THROUGH HIS SPINE AND LODGED INTO HIS MADLY RACING HEART, STILLING IT FOREVER! NEVER AGAIN WOULD "DARK EYES" EVER LEAD A NORTHERN CHEYENNE WAR PARTY AGAINST ANY FUR TRAPPERS, ESPECIALLY WITH SHARP-EYED AND CRACK-SHOOTING OTIS BARNES SHOULDERING A RIFLE AND SHOOTING AT A FLEEING INDIAN

HEADING FOR THE DARK TIMBER... NO MORE WOULD AN INDIAN WITH A TALE OF WOE ORGANIZE A WAR PARTY WITH RETRIBUTION AGAINST THE BARNES CLAN OF TRAPPERS IN MIND...

For the next hour Otis, Cedrick and Oliver tended to the wounded, collected up the Indians' firearms, got control of the Indians' only two surviving uninjured horses, and then killed the war party's survivors, both man and animal... Otis, who had been shot off his horse early on in the fight, nursed a huge black and blue area on his belly where he had been wearing one of his pistols in his sash. As his Irish luck would have it, one of the rifle shots taken at him and Oliver had struck Otis right in his 'pistol', thereby avoiding dying from a stomach wound had the gun not been there to stop the speeding ball. Oliver, other than a badly wrenched back from having his horse shot out from under him and having rolled over on him, would live. As for other injuries, Wallace now sported a badly sliced open 'swipe' mark across his shoulders from being tomahawked from behind by one of their attackers. He too would live but was looking at a rather uncomfortable session of having one of his brothers sewing him up with their large in size leather-sewing needle and binding the wound shut with common twine! Cloud on the other hand, would walk around for about four days with a ringing sore head and a pair of eyes that would not clear or focus. However, by day five after being struck from behind in the back of the head with a stone club, his eyes cleared and if he was careful for the next week in not turning around or bending down too quickly, his headaches disappeared. Shortly thereafter, his headaches finally went away for good as did all of his symptoms from the fight. As for Feather, he too, like Wallace, was looking at a rather uncomfortable session with Otis using a leather sewing needle to sew together the flaps of loose facial meat from across his cheek, nose and forehead caused by a vicious knife swipe before his assailant had been killed by Cedrick.

Slowly heading back to camp led by Otis leading the way with Oliver and Cedrick bringing up the rear of the caravan of the wounded, the men finally made it safely home. However, they had just made it back to camp and as predicted earlier by Feather and Cloud regarding deep snows in the area, the next morning the men awoke to two feet of freshly fallen snow! True as the two Indian boys had spoken, they would have good beaver trapping on the Clarks Fork of the Yellowstone River if they could manage the deep snows that accompanied any trappers living in that northern geographic region of the West come winter time. Now, only time would tell…

That evening back at camp after the battle, Otis took over the leadership of the family as he prepared to be the much-needed 'frontier doctor' for those badly injured in the family. All the injured except Oliver who just suffered his wrenched back in silence, were seated around their table next to their fireplace that evening after the deadly battle with Dark Eyes and his warriors. With the light from the fire in the fireplace and four of their precious beeswax candles lit and set around the men for the best light they offered as well, the all too familiar 'doctoring-up' process began. Opening up another keg of rum, cups were filled and made their ways around into the hands of those most seriously wound-afflicted. After taking some of his precious shaving soap and cleaning out everyone's wounds that were treatable, Otis soaked a rag into the rum and daubed its healing properties onto the wounds as well. Then heating the end of his leather sewing needle over the flame of a candle and after letting it cool, he began his 'doctoring' first on brother Wallace. All work done was done in silence except for the occasional grunt of pain when the needle went too deeply into the viable and now inflamed soft flesh under the wound or into the hardened muscle. Soon Wallace was stitched up and only then was he allowed to partake of his cup of rum as his reward for not raising hell when the needle was 'flashing' and doing its needed work. Next in the line of injured came Cloud, who had a 3" gash on the back of his head cleansed out with shaving-soap water and sewed up. Throughout the procedure, he remained in total stoic silence during the work being performed. Then when his cup of rum was doled out, he drank it down straight away with an all-too-happy gulp, glad he was out from under the 'needle work'! Next in the line of walking wounded came Feather and he would suffer the most, being that it was his very sensitive facial tissue that needed major repairs with needle and thread! However, true to legendary Indian stoicism, only several rapidly blinking eyelids and quiet tears of pain rolling down his damaged cheek were in evidence as the rather large leather sewing needle punched holes in his sensitive facial skin for the extensive sewing-up that was to follow. Then even more pain was suffered as the coarse twine used as a binding material was roughly passed through the needle tears in his sensitive facial flesh! Once again, those pains associated with such a rough sewing job only elicited much blinking of eyelids and a flood of tears of abject pain flowing down Feather's damaged face! After that bit of 'repair work', Feather passed on his cup of rum, headed for his sleeping furs and just laid there all night suffering in silence with a much-burning in pain and lymphatic fluid-oozing face...

Upon finishing his 'frontier doctoring', Otis took a wet rag and made it even wetter as he wiped off his own sweat coated face! He too made sure he got a cup of rum for his efforts in patching up those unlucky enough to run afoul of the swipe of a knife, deadly swing of a tomahawk or the high-speed thudding hammering of a stone club against the back of one's head... Otis found himself later attending to everyone's wounds on a daily basis like it or not! Those duties he found were even more disagreeable than initially sewing everyone up because of the subsequent inflammations now being suffered by those wounded. Otis quickly discovered that swollen and sometimes infected wounds could be even more painful and touchy when the patient had to return to the 'frontier doctor' for further 'medical' assistance... Suffice to say, a pretty serious run was made on the trappers' rapidly dwindling rum supply over the next few days by those men slowly scabbing over.

The next morning, deep snows or not, Otis hobbled the four new Indian horses that they had acquired in the two recent battles with the Northern Cheyenne. That he did because those four horses were unfamiliar with the white men they now served and knew not what was expected of them. That special hobbling accomplished, they were all turned loose in the nearby meadow to feed and fend for themselves in the deep snows along with the rest of the horse herd. Being that the snow was not crusted but just deep, the horses managed to paw away the snow and still pretty easily feed. However, Otis, loosely watching over the horses in case more Northern Cheyenne were in country and might be interested in acquiring extra horseflesh, observed that the big stallion taken in the fight belonging to Dark Eyes seemed to be unable to get along with the rest of the horses in the herd. His aggressive behavior was exhibited throughout the day, as the stallion continued trying to establish dominance among the herd of the trappers' horses. In so doing, that included savagely kicking, biting, outright fighting with the other horses or kicking them in their sides with his powerful hind feet in order to show his dominance! That night, Otis lay awake for most of the night listening to the horses in their corral milling about uneasily and occasionally fighting. The next day when let out to feed, the big stallion continued his aggressive behavior in and among the other gentler horses of the herd. That afternoon when Otis brought the horses back to their corral for their nightly internment, all the horses were corralled except the big, 'meaner than a bug on a hot rock', stallion after an incident at the corral gate.

As Cedrick put the finishing touches on his pot of beans merrily cooking away on a hook over the fire in the fireplace and then upon removing the lid on his cast iron Dutch oven checking the amount of 'brown' on his biscuits, was surprised when he heard a single shot being fired in their compound! Fearing the worst, maybe another attack by Indians, he and the other brothers still recuperating from their wounds, scrambled for their nearby rifles. Running to the door of their cabin with rifles in hand, it was flung open expecting the worst, only to see Otis GUTTING OUT THE 'MEAN AS A SNAKE' STALLION NEXT TO THE HORSE'S CORRAL!

"What the hell happened?" blurted out Cedrick, as he walked out from the cabin and continued looking around their campsite for any other sign of danger or for the person who had just shot one of their horses.

Otis just continued field dressing out the stallion until he had cut through the chest cavity so the serious butchering could begin. Then turning, he quietly replied to Cedrick's question by saying, "I just got tired of this biting son-of-a-bitch and when he bit me when I tried putting him into our corral for the evening, that was the last straw. So I shot the son-of-a-bitch! Now Cedrick, we don't have to go buffalo hunting tomorrow because we have some fresh camp meat and enough for the rest of the week as well. I figure we will have plenty of good eats right here once I get him dressed, skinned and butchered out. What you don't need for our immediate meals tomorrow, I will quarter out and hang from our meat poles so the meat can cool out and glaze right proper like."

Since there was no further conversation between the brothers needed, Otis turned and continued processing the big stallion by roping up and starting to hang its quarters from the meat pole. Half-an-hour later, Otis dragged off the skin holding the horse's pile of guts down to a nearby grove of aspen trees. There he left the entire hide and gut pile and two days later, a pack of wolves discovered the rich find and polished off everything except the hide. In the meantime, Cedrick with a smile over his brother taking things into his own hands regarding the renegade stallion, made sure his biscuits were ready and then called the men over to supper. Opening the front door to the cabin, Cedrick called his brother to supper who was by then hoisting the last quarter of meat up onto their meat pole. Washing up moments later, Otis headed into their cabin for a hot supper served in generous portions and later that night, slept like a baby not having to worry about what kind of horse related troubles were going on outside in the corral.

For the rest of that first winter on the Clarks Fork of the Yellowstone when the snows allowed any kind of movement, the brothers ran their wolf traps, hunted buffalo for their meals when the horsemeat ran out, Otis repaired the pistol that had been struck by a rifle bullet back at the "Dark Eyes Battle" from the spare parts they had acquired at the first rendezvous, and cast bullets for the rest of the clan's rifles and pistols. During those days when it snowed too heavily for any extensive outside activity, the men spent their working hours feeding their horses from their emergency hay pile located under the lean-to, cut and hauled wood from their winter log pile and slept during the long days in their fireplace warmed cabin.

When the first vestiges of spring began show-ing themselves, the men were more than raring to go. With snowstorms reducing almost weekly, much effort was placed in the men's wolf trap-ping, tanning of their skins and fashioning a number of those pelts into heavy winter cloth-ing for the men for the coming winter's trapping season. Then with spring buffalo hunts for meat because six hungry men could really put a dent in any supply of camp meat and with dwindling snows, the horse herd was finally able to be let out for the spring grazing on the rich new grass shoots 'reaching for the sun'.

When that first day of spring trapping arrived, the men stormed out from the confines of their cabin and were more than ready to go. Only the thoughts of wading in the icy cold waters and suffering near frozen feet and legs or sitting long hours every day in the saddle of a horse on cold guard duty, seemed to dim the men's enthusi-asms to be released from the cold grips of winter and being cabin-bound.

Even though the mornings were cold as all get-out, Cedrick had enough of being relegated to cooking inside their cabin on a daily basis. That was why on the first day of their spring trapping season, he was out and about with his outside fire just a-roaring. His Dutch ovens were baking away as fresh buffalo roasted merrily on their metal skewers and the coffee pot burbled hap-pily away as if it was happy for beaver trapping to commence for the family of trappers as well. As it turned out, everyone had healed up from the "Dark Eyes Battle", the remaining captured Indian horse that hadn't been eaten had been broken to pack and be ridden by white men and Feather's face had healed. However in the case of Feather, every time he tried to smile, the damage to his face had been so great and Otis's 'frontier doctoring' had been so primitive, that his easy smile from before had now been replaced with a lop-sided grimace. But in Feather's case, he was still happy to be alive, be part of a family that cared and like his 'brother in kind', Cloud, were now both the proud possessors of two additional Indian Trade rifles. Two Indian Trade rifles since they had counted coups in battle against their sworn enemy the Northern Cheyenne, and then had taken their dead enemy's highly decorated rifles as their rewards.

Leading the trappers that first spring morning was Wallace, once again followed by Cloud and Feather leading two packhorses carrying panniers holding all of the tools and accessories the men would need for the day's trapping adventures. Following Cloud and Feather were Otis, Oliver and Cedrick performing rear guard duties as usual. That day, instead of having to travel far to the northwest up the left section of the Clarks Fork of the Yellowstone as they had done in the previous fall, the men now only had to travel a short distance to their trapping grounds. That had been Wallace's plan from the year before. Namely trap the furthest northwestern reaches of the Clarks Fork of the Yellowstone initially in the fall, then come spring trap the lower reaches of the same river system so they would have less distance to travel back to their cabin in preparation for traveling to the coming summer rendezvous at Malachite's Big Hole in the Green River Valley. Then Wallace's next plan was to return to their same already built cabin for the fall trapping season and trap the remaining northeastern section of the Clarks Fork of the Yellowstone. After that, Wallace was not sure where they would continue trapping in the future, but for now he was not concerned with that matter. Wallace just figured with the six of them as a powerful, well-armed and now very experienced beaver trapping team, they could go just about anywhere they wanted and their horses would carry them there.

Later arriving at the first set of beaver ponds they had planned on trapping, Wallace bailed off his horse and handed its reins to Cloud. Then he stripped off his wool pants and put on his breechclout and leggings. Taking a trap, a four-foot dried wooden pole and a hand ax, Wallace took a deep breath and stepped into the icy pond's waters. **"WHOOOEEE!"** Wallace shouted as the icy waters swirled around his groin area letting him know he was still very much alive! Setting the first trap of the season next to a heavily used beaver slide, he carefully walked the trap's chain out to its end and then drove the four-foot wooden pole into the pond's bottom. Taking a short piece of twine, he made sure the end ring on the trap chain was looped over and down on the pole and then firmly tied to the wood to prevent any trapped beaver from swimming no further than the length of the trap's chain with his foot in the trap. Then until the rodent drowned from trying to swim out into the deeper water to escape, he would remain no further away from the anchor pole than the length the trap's heavy chain allowed. Finished with that chore, Wallace walked back to the previously set trap, 'woofing and chirping' over how cold the pond's waters were on his legs and crotch area. There he bent over and taking his hand, carefully swirled the water over the trap set in about 4" of water until the swirling muddy water concealed the trap with a light film of mud. Handing his hand ax to Cloud, Wallace took the bottle of castoreum handed to him by Cedrick and daubed the evil-smelling liquid on the tip of a freshly cut willow stick. Then Wallace stuck the dry end of the willow stick into the soft mud of the bank so as to allow the end of the stick holding the touch of castoreum to be right over the trap's pan and the jaws of the open trap. Then when the highly territorial beaver swam over to investigate where the strange castoreum odor was emanating from, it hopefully would stand in the shallow water, grab the diagonally placed willow limb smelling of another beaver with its front paws and in so doing, would be standing on the pan of the trap and be immediately caught. Then the beaver in panic would swim off toward the deeper water in an attempt to escape until it hit the end of the trap's chain. There it would continue swimming in its panic with the trap firmly attached to its rear foot or feet until the weight of the five-pound trap would eventually drag the exhausted beaver underwater, causing it to drown. Later when Wallace or Cedrick checked the trap, hopefully they would find the dead beaver hanging in their trap and they would be anywhere from $4-6 richer for every beaver so caught. That kind of success would allow the Barnes Clan to continue living the lifestyle they loved out on the western frontier…

For the rest of that day until the early afternoon, Wallace alternating with Cedrick depending on how cold each man's legs and feet got, set their remaining 20 beaver traps in likely looking places. Then walking ahead a short distance further along the heretofore un-trapped beaver waters, the two men, trailed by the rest of the clan providing guard duty, would scout out potential sites to be trapped in the immediate future. Then after a short break and eating a mess of jerky from their saddlebags, the trappers would travel back down their previously set traps and remove any beaver already caught in those traps. Then they would re-set those traps as long as there was sign that other beaver were still present and bring any dead beaver ashore so either Cloud or Feather could skin out the critter and toss its pelt into a pannier. Reaching the end of their just checked trap line, the trappers would change back into their warmer clothing and all would head home to flesh, defat and hoop out their catch for the day. That was except for Cedrick who would once again begin his supper preparation chores. Such went the men's days since they had already pulled all of their wolf traps for the year. The only change from that daily routine was when they ran out of camp meat and had to take some time to stalk and shoot a buffalo or two and then it was back to the important business of trapping, fleshing, hooping and bundling up beaver skins for transport to the summer rendezvous at Malachite's Big Hole.

By the first of March, the Barnes Clan had amassed 224 beaver pelts bundled up and ready for travel from their fall trapping efforts and to date, had trapped another 343 spring beaver, fleshed and hooped the same! There was much excitement in camp regarding the 567 beaver they had already taken with the prospects of maybe trapping another 100 or so before the beaver went out of prime! With those numbers and with many of them being Made Beaver, the brothers were more than assured of successfully completing another good year and with another such year still facing them come the fall! Another good year facing them when they returned and trapped the northeastern section of the Clarks Fork of the Yellowstone and with similar trapping successes, would be once again assured of being able to continue their lifestyle out on the frontier doing what they loved, plus amassing even more money for their eventual return to Missouri, buying some land and settling down.

CHAPTER SEVEN

MALACHITE'S BIG HOLE – TROUBLE BEGINS!

COME LATE SPRING when the beaver were starting to go out of their prime, the Barnes Clan had trapped an additional 83 beaver. Turned out, that spring was the best beaver trapping spring ever with the Barnes's netting a grand total of 426 beaver with a majority of them being Made Beaver or adults! Come late spring, the Barnes's had caught, fleshed, hooped and eventually bundled a grand total of 650 beaver pelts and 23 wolf pelts ready for travel to the coming rendezvous at Malachite's Big Hole! Wallace's belief in the two young Shoshoni outcast boys discovered at the first rendezvous and their counsel to trap the Clarks Fork of the Yellowstone had certainly paid huge dividends for the clan. Additionally, the two young Shoshoni outcasts had hitched their 'star' to that of the Barnes Clan and through 'thick and thin' were growing into outstanding frontier experienced and highly respected young men. Young men that the Barnes Clan had adopted into the 'Clan' as their own 'Brothers', had no regrets in initiating such actions because they truly were now 'Brothers' in thought, word and deed!

Sitting around their campfire one evening after the end of the spring trapping season with the usual clouds of mosquitoes surrounding each man, Wallace said, "I suspect we ought to be making plans on getting ourselves ready and off to that Malachite's Big Hole for this summer's coming rendezvous. I say that because I don't rightly know what day that rendezvous truly begins and I would hate to arrive there at the rendezvous and find that it is all over and all of our much-needed supplies already divided up among the other trappers."

With those words of frontier wisdom out and into the cooling night air, the rest of the clan just sat there quietly mulling over Wallace's words as they smoked their clay pipes and nursed some of the last of their rum supplies. Then Otis, ever the quiet thinker said, "We have one hell of a load of beaver furs bundled up and ready to go. However, if we take all of them and all the rest of our 'personals' and cooking gear, we don't have enough horses to tote the lot to and from. That is unless a number of us want to walk and

I surely do not favor walking that far to the rendezvous because I didn't plan any better. Best we set to building a cache and stash a mess of our gear that is not needed for this here trip if we are coming back this fall for another season on the Clarks Fork. Don't seem right to pack the same gear both ways if it is not needed out on the trail to keep body and spirit alive and well."

For the longest time once again, the only sound heard in response to what Wallace and Otis had said were the sounds of the ever-present swarms of mosquitoes, regardless of how much nicotine laden tobacco smoke the men put into the air with their pipe smoke or the pinewood smoke from their fire. Then Cloud said, "No matter how we cut it, we are looking at ten to twelve days of travel to get to where we want to go with a heavily loaded pack string. Now Feather and I know the best passes to cross through and that is a help but we can't account for bad weather, a stove-up horse or attacks by hungry grizzly bears. Then too we need to consider we will be crossing several rugged mountain ranges before we arrive onto easier travelling ground further to the west. So, maybe we ought to get an early start as Wallace has suggested and make ready to leave."

Once again, typical of the Barnes Clan and their decided lack of talkativeness, the hum of the clouds of mosquitoes surrounding the six men and the sounds of the crackling wood fire took center stage. Finally Cedrick said, "Sounds good to me. Tomorrow I will start reducing my gear to just that which is necessary to feed all of you 'galoots' while out on the trail to the rendezvous. With some help from the rest of you, we can dig a cache up on the dry hillside behind our cabin and bury what I don't need for out on the trail. Besides, horse travel can be hard on my cast iron cooking gear, especially if there is a rollover or a horse is spooked out on the trail by a 'grizzly' and takes off running through the trees banging and clanging my cookware. Plus to be quite frank, all of my cast iron pots and skillets have been broken in and are well seasoned. As such, I don't favor having to do that all over once again without sufficient bear grease and the time needed to properly season them once again."

With those words and feeling the effects of a hard day just worked, the men as if on cue, dumped out the bowls of their pipes by knocking their contents on the rocks surrounding the firepit, headed off to take care of any calls of nature and then retreated to their sleeping furs. Last to leave the campfire was Cedrick, as he ran through his mind what he would need in the way of cooking gear and utensils for the long trip. A long trip that would lead over and through the Wind River and the Absaroka Mountain Ranges before arriving in the vicinity of Malachite's Big Hole, site for the coming summer rendezvous. Then mentally solving the questions he had in mind, he too headed for the cabin. By the time he arrived to go to sleep, the constant hum of the mosquitoes hovering around the men at the campfire had been replaced with the quiet sounds of five of his brothers sleeping off a hard day's work.

Following breakfast the next morning, while Cedrick cleaned up the camp, the rest of the Clan headed up on the hillside behind their cabin with rifles in one hand and shovels in the other. By noontime a cache had been dug, packed with Douglas fir and pine boughs along with many armfuls of dried grasses to insulate and protect those provisions and equipment soon to be entombed underground. The rest of the day was spent hauling up the hill and packing away those items not needed for the trip to the rendezvous, and then the cache site was cleverly covered over with dirt, grasses, pine cones and the like, so to any casual visitors walking by or over the site would be unaware of what valuables lay beneath their very feet.

Two days later, the Barnes Clan left their campsite and heading in a southwesterly direction led by Cloud and Feather on their trip to the rendezvous at Malachite's Big Hole at the northern end of the Green River Valley. Trailing behind Cloud and Feather rode Wallace, followed by Cedrick, Otis and Oliver. Every horse the trappers possessed was loaded with either bundled furs from the fall and spring trapping seasons, sleeping furs or the minimum required camping and cooking gear needed for the trip. Each man trailed several packhorses and on each packhorse were affixed two additional fully loaded Indian Trade rifles! Trade rifles that were acquired during the "Dark Eyes Battles" and were now being put to good use in protecting the trappers' very valuable pack train from any renegade Indians or overly aggressive grizzly bears.

Following the leads of Cloud and Feather through the heavily forested areas, the men initially stuck to well-traveled game trails in order to avoid unnecessary horse wrecks as they moved through the dense stands of timber. Then it was up and into the rugged Absaroka Range with its heavily timbered slopes and numerous steep grades. As the men with their heavily loaded pack train made their ways across that mountain range, they experienced hundreds of big game animals at just about every turn in the trail -- mule deer, moose, elk, bighorn sheep, mountain goats on the rocky crests, and the occasional lone bull buffalo. The big game bounty was such, like the first time they had traveled through such wondrous and scenic country, that the men treated themselves by feasting on a different species of game animal nightly. Swinging around what Cloud and Feather described as "Eagle Peak", the rest of the clan were led into a meadow ringed by massive fir trees, some of which were ten feet through! There they paused one evening, unpacked all of their animals and let them graze for several hours under the watchful eyes of Otis and Oliver. Come dark, the livestock was brought back into camp, double hobbled, placed on a picket line and then the men found themselves thankfully under their heavy buffalo sleeping skins for a good night's rest. The next morning dawned cold and overcast. Throughout that day's travel and the next, the men were 'dogged' with rainy and cold summer thunderstorms and even some snow at the higher elevations. Two days later found the men still heading southwest in and out of heavy timber, around more rugged mountain peaks and down into deep lush valleys.

Throughout their travels, the brothers marveled over the skillful guidance Cloud and Feather showed as they traversed crosscountry through some of the most rugged and scenic country known to mankind, without having to backtrack even one time! However, wet summer thunderstorms continued until on one day of their travels in the high country, Wallace called an early halt to their travels as the rains came down in torrents and the lightning danced almost continuously across the darkened black and gray skies. 'Holing up' in the deep timber to avoid the worst of the summer's torrents, the men unpacked their livestock and let them out to graze. Cedrick got a fire going and soon was making his signature biscuits along with roasting some bighorn sheep steaks from an animal Otis had shot when they had crossed a nearby meadow faced with a rocky bluff perched with several bands of the great eating critters. After a fast supper to avoid getting any wetter than they were, the men brought in their horses, hobbled them along a picket line and then fled to the warmth and dry of their buffalo sleeping furs under the dense forest canopy. The next morning found the trappers huddling around a roaring campfire in 6" of summer wet snows in July! That day, the men spent most of it cussing the slippery wet snow as their horses stumbled and staggered under their heavy loads with the associated slippery footing as they descended down off the western side of the rugged Absaroka Range. Being such, the men had to dismount numerous times so they could clean out the hard packed snow in the horse's hooves, allowing them better footing when moving through the numerous snow fields.

Now more at home on some of their more familiar stomping grounds, the two Shoshoni guides expertly guided the heavily laden pack train up and into the Wind River Mountain Range of mountains as they continued heading to the southwest. Climbing for most of the day as they wound around and around many dense stands of timber too thick to ride horses through and briskly running streams, the trappers finally crossed through what Feather called the "Togwotee Pass" and then down its backside.

Camping once again by a rushing creek, the men unpacked their horses and let them roll around in the meadow's deep grasses and put on 'the feed bag' until dark. In the meantime, Cedrick spitted chunks of buffalo meat from a lone bull Wallace had shot in a heavily forested thicket. As it turned out, the chunks of backstrap cooked over the fire that evening from that old bull were as tough as the men's buffalo skins covering their bear skin sleeping furs... As was usual among the Barnes Clan when one of their kind 'stumbled' in what he did, he got his ass eaten out! That night, Wallace was told by his brothers that in the future, keep his killing ways directed to a mule deer or bighorn sheep and leave the lone old bull buffalo alone to die a quiet death instead of on the end of one of his speeding lead balls...

Several days later, the men finally hit the north end of the Green River and just followed it down until they arrived at the Malachite's Big Hole Rendezvous site. Riding into the area, the men were greeted with an already gathering crowd of trappers, fur company representatives and hordes of peaceful Indians. Wallace was quick to lead the clan into an unoccupied small stand of cottonwood trees for the shade they offered, unpacked their horses and set them out to graze. As the men set about setting up their campsite, gathering wood and buffalo chips before they were all taken by other arriving trappers and building a firepit for cooking, Wallace took off and found himself on another mission of importance.

Casting about, Wallace finally located company blacksmith and main horse wrangler, Steve "Cooter" Krentz. Making arrangements for the following day, Wallace returned to their campsite for their evening meal. As requested the day before, the next day Wallace and company had their horse herd 'front and center' in front of where Cooter Krentz had set up his company blacksmith operations. Being first in line as Wallace had wanted, he had Cooter pull off all the old and loose shoes from his horses, trim the shoeless hooves of the Indian horses they were using and then shoe the entire bunch. Then as an added precaution because of the rugged country they would be returning into to trap in the fall and spring, Wallace had Cooter and one of his blacksmiths make an extra set of horseshoes specifically for each of their animals. Since Otis was also skilled as a ferrier and had the necessary tools to shoe horses out in the backcountry, Wallace made sure a loose or lost shoe would not be a problem with their horse herd in the future as had been in times past without having replacement shoes to address the problem.

Following the visit to Cooter Krentz and he working his 'magic' on the Barnes Clan's horse herd, the men repacked their horses with all of their bundles of furs and headed for where the fur company had assembled their supply wagons and had laid out the available wares for perusal by the trappers now arriving on an almost daily basis. There with the fur buyers and graders, the Barnes Clan, Cloud and Feather watched the examining process with careful eyes concerning all transactions. Once all 650 of their furs had been graded and counted, the fur company as per the contracts the men had signed years earlier took one half of their furs outright. Then with a large number of other fur trappers looking on enviously at the numbers of Made Beaver the Barnes Clan had trapped in one season, the men were advised they would be averaging $4.10 per remaining pelt, and receiving a company credit for goods and services of $1,332.50.

Pleased with their returns, the Barnes Clan quickly set about purchasing those provisions needed for the coming year back on the Clarks Fork of the Yellowstone. Wallace put Otis in charge of taking Cloud and Feather to that section of the meadow where the wagons and their supplies were arrayed out on the ground on buffalo skins or draped over log tables and banisters. Otis also took Cedrick along because there were things that he cooked with that needed replenishing as well, so those four went shopping for what they figured they might also need for the coming trapping season. When they did, Wallace and Oliver returned to their camp to keep an eye on their camp so things did not 'walk away' in the hands of the friendly Indians milling about at the rendezvous as well.

The first thing that Otis and Cedrick did was trade off the extra Indian Trade rifles they had acquired in battle with the Northern Cheyenne. However, not all rifles were traded off. They made sure Wallace and Oliver had kept the best of the rifles as extras in case their group ran in large numbers of hostile Indians and needed the extra firepower 'to maintain order'... Right off the bat, with Cloud and Feather watching closely at what was being purchased and why, Otis and Cedrick headed for the latest in firearms section of the fur company's displays. There they passed on purchasing any more rifles or pistols because what was offered for sale was 'a kit and a kin' to what they already possessed. However, they did purchase with their fur and Indian Trade rifle credits, two kegs of powder, 50 one-pound tins of FFg black powder for their rifles and pistols (they still had plenty of DuPont FFFFg priming powder), and 100 pounds of lead pigs for making bullets. Seeing that was all they needed in that category since they still had some of those items cached back at their campsite, they had the company Clerk and his assistants stack those goods off to one side where they could be watched to avoid any of those supplies 'walking off' in the hands of the milling numbers of Indians about and proceeded on with their shopping. Soon extra knives, sewing needles, awls, two mirrors, three straight razors, shaving soap, fire steels, gun wadding, two extra ramrods, two hand axes, one shovel, two files, four whetstones, four beaver traps, a spool of twine, a 100' spool of cotton lead rope, extra leather patching and strapping, six new heavy capotes, 18 pairs of socks, 12 pairs of gloves, six pairs of heavy wool pants to fit each man, and six wide-brimmed felt hats to replace their old and worn out ones.

As the Clerk's assistants ran back and forth with the goods being selected and piled off to one side, Otis and Cedrick 'ticked' off in their minds as to what else was needed for another trapping season. As they did, Cloud and Feather's heads just swirled over the 'white man's fancies' being selected for purchase. Then it was off to the food provision section of the fur company's displays and there Cedrick took over as he selected sacks of green coffee beans, pinto beans, rice, dried raisins and dried apple slices. Then without missing a beat and remembering how big eaters his group was, selected a number of sacks of brown sugar, sugar cones and flour, along with several jugs of honey and bear grease. Then off Cedrick went to the spice section of the fur company's offerings where he selected sacks of salt, black pepper, red pepper flakes, cinnamon, nutmeg and white pepper.

Following those selections, Otis and Cedrick walked over to the kegs of rum on display and with a happy grin, accepted cups of free company offered rum for their 'shopping' trappers. Then the company man dispensing the cups of rum looked over at obvious Indians Cloud and Feather, and turning said to Otis, "Do those Indians belong to the two of you and if they do, do you want them damn Indians served some of this here rum?"

Otis's face never changed in its looks one wit upon hearing those uncalled for and sharp words coming from the fur company's rum dispenser but the tone and tenor of his voice certainly changed… "Those two young men are part of our party and yes, since they are our equals, they are to be served a cup of rum just the same as me and my brother here," said Otis quietly.

About then, 'trouble' reared its ugly head from an unexpected quarter. Six other trappers walked up to the fur company's designated rum dispenser and one very large in size trapper with a heavy beard that had grown so long that it extended over the man's rotund belly, said, "Step aside, you damn 'War-hoop', and let a real man through." With those words, the huge man reached out and bodily shoved Cloud and Feather aside, barged right up to the company man dispensing the free cups of rum and reached out with a filthy hand for his cup of the 'devil's brew' saying, "Fill her up and don't spare the rum unless you desire to be shaken like a rat."

"Hold your horses there, fella!" said Otis. "Those two young men you just shoved aside are my partners and were there before you waiting for their cup of rum being that they are trappers and all," continued Otis, in a very level but meaningful tone of voice carrying an edge of warning for anyone who cared to listen to how he had just said what he said...

"Mister, you all need to mind your manners. I don't cotton to any damn stinking, bug ridden Indian standing afore me taking what is rightly mine ahead of me," said the huge bearded man, much to the laughter of his five compatriots standing behind him enjoying their friend's bout of rude manners and behavior when it came to others like the two Indian men he had just shoved off to one side of the rum keg.

WHOOOMP! went Otis's cast iron hard fist into the face of "Big Beard" with the same energy of an angry mule's kick on the end of it! **PLUFFMP!** went Big Beard's blubbery ass as he hit the ground like a 'lung shot' cow buffalo! Big Beard never moved one wit once he hit the ground after being knocked out cold with Otis's one punch! However, his five partners seeing their leader being decked with just one punch from a smaller man, started to go for their rifles and pistols.

The first two fur trappers going for their weapons found Cloud and Feather quickly standing alongside the two men with a sheath knife pressed firmly against their throats by two very determined looking young men! However, that didn't stop the remaining three trappers at the back of the bunch in going for their weapons only to be faced by Otis and Cedrick covering them with four hastily drawn from their sashes, .54 caliber horse pistols loaded with the ever-deadly at close range, buck and ball!

"Hold her right there!" shouted Jedidiah Smith, who upon seeing Big Beard hit the ground with a great amount of velocity and flying dust, came running up to the altercation. "You men drop your weapons or I swear, I will shoot the lot of you and if I can't get that done by myself, I have 80 fur company men around me who can and happily will!" he bellowed.

Otis and Cedrick slowly lowered their pistols but not without really closely watching those who had caused them to unlimber their 'street howitzers' in the first place, for any further actions on the parts of the rude trappers. However, Cloud and Feather did not remove their knives from the throats of the two trappers they had held at bay until Otis told the two men to lower their weapons and walk over to where he stood.

"Now what the hell brought all of this crap about?" demanded Jedidiah Smith.

"Ask your own company man," replied Otis. "But if he lies to you, he can expect to have his ass mashed into the dirt the same as the bearded one still lying there if I have my druthers," said Otis quietly with a cold stare that would have stopped a bull buffalo in a full charge...

With that, Jedidiah Smith looked over at his company man designated as the rum dispenser, with a knowing and disgusted look that would have also wilted a bull buffalo in a full charge, looking for answers. "Jed, this here bearded trapper started it by pushing these two young Indian men aside so he could get to the free rum first," truthfully reported a near panicked company man not wanting to cross his boss or the hard fisted Otis for that matter.

"Well then, serve these two Indian boys. I suspect these two other trappers from the Barnes Clan have good reason in backing them up and I suggest you do as they say!" quietly replied Jedidiah Smith.

With those words, it was amazing just how fast Cloud and Feather were served, and 'their cups runneth over'… Then as if nothing out of the ordinary had occurred, Otis ordered that six kegs of Fourth Proof rum be set aside to be paid for from the $1,332.50 credit they had earned and been granted by the fur company's buyers and by trading in the Indian Trade rifles. Then with that and Otis's wink over at Cedrick, the Barnes Clan walked off with a cup of rum in hand to look over the rest of what the fur company had to offer in the ways of wares. However, the bearded one remained as still as death locked in his own world until he was finally brought around by his friends. But as Otis walked away from the kegs of sweet smelling rum, he had a nagging feeling that 'trouble' would soon be one of their bedfellows if that bunch of six trappers led by the bearded one had their way and discovered the location of where the Barnes Clan would be trapping in the fall...

Later that afternoon the Barnes Clan brought over their packhorses, loaded up their recently purchased supplies and returned them to their camp. There they loaded and adjusted the packs full of those supplies in readiness for the start of their return trip to their cabin come the end of the week. The rest of that week the Barnes Clan mingled with their old friends like Jim Bridger, Jed Smith, Jim Beckwourth, "Bear Scat" Sutta, William Jackson, Tom "Iron Hand" Warren, and the like, and watched with amusement the antics of a number of the trapping fraternity gathered at the rendezvous. A trapping fraternity that had wandered the frontier for the last year hardly seeing any other life like their own kind and now being gathered all together, found that they could really cut loose! Trappers at the rendezvous who in their joy of the moment, would cut loose with wild celebrations, bouts of heavy drinking, wrestling matches, shooting events, wife swapping, horse trading, horse racing, story-telling, fighting, and just plain old simple hell-raising in general. Then they like the Barnes Clan, their numbers just drifted off back into the wilds of the frontier at the end of the rendezvous, many of them broke, once again to partake of the life of loneliness, isolation, danger and the like. Trappers who drifted off back into the wilds of the frontier, only to leave their bones many times where no one would ever find them, or care...

However another thing came out of the rendezvous that year that was so subtle, most of the trapping fraternity friends with the Barnes Clan did not see or experience. Spotted Feather and White Cloud had gained even greater respect and love for a white man named Otis Barnes. A white man named Otis Barnes who had stood up for them in their time of need and danger and had treated them as his equals. That was something the two young Shoshoni men had never experienced during their entire tribal times and would discuss among themselves many times in the coming months. In so doing, they would find that those feelings of respect and love were going to be with them and for Otis forever since they now considered him their adoptive father...

A day after the rendezvous at Malachite's Big Hole had seemingly 'blown over', the Barnes Clan drifted off back into the wilds of the frontier just like everyone else who had attended the historic event. It took the Barnes men the better part of that morning of departure to get all of their animals packed with their provisions and harnessing correctly adjusted to make sure their animals were not 'sored up' by the weight or ill adjustment of their loads. Then once again with Cloud and Feather in the lead and the rest of the Barnes Clan bringing up the rear with their heavily packed animals, the men turned their eyes and animals towards the northeast and a place called the Clarks Fork of the Yellowstone.

Reversing their previous route taken through the Wind River Range, the Barnes Clan soon found they were once again thankfully deeply buried in the natural beauty of what was early America. Once again, the men found themselves traveling through pristine forests where some species of trees were twelve feet through, seven- and sometimes eight-point elk still in velvet were discovered to be commonplace, majestic moose with six-foot-wide antlers with a body weight weighing around 1,500 pounds were in abundance, all shadowed by numerous 40" mule deer bucks and bighorn sheep with 40+" curls! Creeks and streams ran crystal clear and when one walked along their banks, silver flashes of movement could be seen beneath the frothing waters, darting underneath the stream's banks. Ponds and lakes that dotted the trappers' travels harbored ducks and Canada geese and beaver ponds abounded with America's most colorful waterfowl, namely the wood duck. Unlike their trip to the rendezvous, the weather was so balmy that no summer thundershowers dogged the travelers and not a single grizzly bear crossed their paths. Although the evidence of the great bear was everywhere, many times leaving a hind footprint that was 12-14" in width for the travelers to experience! Lastly and surprisingly, not a single horse wreck occurred throughout the entire return trip to the men's cabin just south of the Clarks Fork of the Yellowstone. Also as luck would have it, the only Indians who crossed the trails with the trappers were the friendly Shoshoni, and a number of those travelers knew Spotted Feather and White Cloud when they were younger and living as outcasts within the Wind River Band.

On day seven of their return travels, Otis noticed Feather and Cloud several times quietly conferring together and 'eye-balling' along their back trail more often than not. He too had been occasionally checking their back trail as if expecting someone trailing them to make his appearance. But every time he checked when his sixth sense 'demanded' that he do so, his normally sharp eyes detected nothing of suspicion. Finally riding over to Cloud, Otis stopped him and asked, "Who is tailing us?"

For a long moment Cloud said nothing and then spoke up saying, "Feather and I think there is someone following us. But every time we look, we see nothing. But The Great Spirit has been talking to us and reminding us to watch our back trail in case there is someone there and if there is, do what is necessary."

"I too have had a suspicion that someone is tailing us. I suspect maybe it is another trapper or group of trappers who saw all the beaver furs we brought to the rendezvous, want to be just as successful as we were and is now following us to see where we are trapping so he or they too can be as successful. Because we have such a large horse herd, none of us can be spared to go back on our trail and just sit and watch to see if we really are being tailed. However, you and Feather be sure and keep a sharp eye on our back trail as we double back on some of our switchback climbs over these mountains ahead just in case someone shows himself from far below. If you see someone or anything suspicious, let me or the brothers know right away," said Otis.

With a nod of his head, the two men separated once again as a rather steep and narrow portion of the trail required their full attention making sure a heavily loaded horse did not slip and fall over the rim into the canyon below. Traveling once again back over the Togwotee Pass and while stopping and letting the horses have a breather up on top, Otis handed his packhorse's reins to Wallace and then rode his horse back down the mountain grade just climbed. Picking a good observational spot, Otis then sat there for a short while watching their back trail for any signs of trappers following them. Nothing moved or suspicious caught his eyes so once again he rejoined the rest of the clan up on top of the rugged pass and they then continued on towards their still several days' distant cabin.

Chapter Eight

RETURN TO THE CLARKS FORK OF THE YELLOWSTONE

SEVERAL DAYS LATER, the trappers' caravan of pack and riding horses rounded the finger of trees just below their cabin and turned into their meadow. As soon as they did, the tired riding and packhorses recognized their familiar meadow and a rider could sense under him their quickened pace knowing they would soon be turned loose to water, feed and be free of their confining saddles and heavy itchy packs. Riding up to their corrals, the horses suddenly began acting all quirky and nervous like. Sensing the nervousness under them, the men began looking all around for any signs of suspicious animal activity or Indians close at hand that might be the reason for 'setting' their horses off.

Figuring maybe his sixth sense had been right

all along back on the trail, Otis turned in his saddle to once again examine his back trail below the finger of trees to see if they had been followed by other competing trappers or Indians. It was at that very moment that he was exploded out from his saddle and flung to the ground under his horse's hooves in an instant! **"URRRGHHH!"** roared a sow grizzly as she, being rudely awakened from her 'day bed' inside the trappers' cabin by the sounds of nearby arriving horses and men talking, made her presence and attitude known! Scant seconds later, she blasted forth through the cabin's front door opening and into the front yard! All of a sudden, the quiet approach of the string of horses and trappers turned into a rodeo of supreme proportions! Horses terrified over the close at hand and mad as hell charging grizzly bear coming their way caused the horses to do what they did best during such trying times. The first thing they did was 'unload' what they were carrying by bucking and 'sun fishing' and then running for their lives as if their tails were on fire! Every trapper was unhorsed except Feather and Cloud who were bringing up the distant rear of the caravan. Being last in line, they were able to lightly step from their horses with rifles in hand and shoot. Cloud's shot hit the fast moving grizzly bear too far back to do anything other than further enrage the bear over the now felt pain in its side by what the sow bear figured was caused by the humans to its front! Feather's shot missed clean as a whistle in his haste to fire and he immediately began reloading. In the meantime, the enraged bear, NOW BEING FOLLOWED BY TWO SEVERAL-YEAR-OLD 250-POUND CUBS, slammed into the unhorsed trappers and terrified group of 'going out of their minds' stampeding horses! Otis, lying stunned on the ground was the first to feel the wrath of the much-surprised sow when she grabbed him up off the ground by his left shoulder with her mouth and flung him clear over the corral fence with a toss of her powerful neck and shoulder muscles! When she did, Otis's rifle went one way and he went the other! Wallace on the other hand, forced from his saddle with rifle in hand, drew down on the now charging sow showing signs of frothy blood coming from its mouth from Cloud's earlier gut-shot and fired! **BOOM!** went Wallace's shot into the chest area of the attacking sow with little or no visible effect! When hit with Wallace's shot, the impact only physically swayed the adrenalin maddened bear for an instant and then she was upon the trapper and began mauling him! **BOOM–BOOM–BOOM!** went three quick pistol shots into the shoulder and head of the bear now savaging Wallace from Cedrick and Feather! The impact from those bullets dropped the sow over the top of Wallace with him still in the clutches of her jaws, as her dying body began twitching its last…

With the sounds of those pistols being fired,

one of the charging cubs turned from following its mother and charged Oliver, who very calmly shot it dead with a headshot from his pistol! With that, the second cub, following his sibling, turned and bowled Oliver 'head over hat pins'! By now, if the bear attacks were not causing enough misery, all of the trappers were also being stomped and run over by frantic pack and saddle horses still trying to get away from the area of the corral and the remaining savagely attacking bear! The second cub, confused by an inert mother bear not providing any kind of a lead and all of the confusion caused by panicking nearby horses, stood up on its hind legs to fight off a nearby running horse. Then **BOOM!** it was shot dead by Otis who had managed to retrieve his rifle and unable to use his left arm or shoulder, had shot the bear with just the use of his still functioning right hand, arm and shoulder! Then other than several nearby packhorses still bucking and trying to throw off their heavy packs that were now leaning sideways on the animals' bodies so they could escape from the area smelling of human terror and the smell of fresh blood, quiet reigned in the trappers' compound...

Then the clean-up and recovery from the surprise savagery of the female grizzly bear and her two cubs' sudden attack slowly began. First Wallace was dragged out from under the now dead sow and Otis was helped from out of the horse corral. Moments later, both men were assisted as they walked over to their sitting logs by the firepit and were seated on a sitting log. Other than being badly shaken from being bowled over by one of the yearling bears and footsore after being stomped on by an escaping packhorse, Oliver would live. Feather and Cloud, both being stomped and bumped by escaping horses, were only bruised and foot sore. Cedrick was the only trapper physically unharmed but in the panic of being physically and surprisingly attacked by one of the most vicious animals on the frontier, he had messed in his buckskins...

However, the next order of business after seeing that Otis and Wallace would live was to round up their scattered all over the meadow horse herd, and remove their packs of foodstuffs and saddles before any more damage was done to the trappers' provisions or their horses. For the next hour, Cloud, Feather, Oliver and Cedrick rounded up the scattered horses and returned them to the firepit area. There they were tied off because to take them to their corral would court another disastrous rodeo because of the presence of the three dead bears still in that immediate area. As the horses were unpacked so there would be no more damage to their lifeline of provisions, Otis and Wallace sat there on their sitting logs in dried blood, bear spittle, gathering flies and misery from all of their now throbbing and stiffening wounds.

Finally while Oliver, Feather and Cloud

tended to the removal and butchering of the two 250-pound bear cubs before they bloated (the sow was determined to be to rangy and thin to be of any use as food), Cedrick, after he had tended to his embarrassing soiled buckskins, tended to his two wounded brothers. Taking Wallace first because of all of the blood he was still oozing, Cedrick removed his shirt to find a mass of rips, tears and puncture wounds from the sow's teeth all across his chest and throughout the area of his right shoulder. Half-an-hour later after washing out the wounds with soap and water and binding them with gray cloth recovered from one of their packs, Cedrick had done all he could do for Wallace. Otis, ever the stoic one of the brothers, just sat on his sitting log in painful silence until Cedrick could turn his attention to that brother. Upon examination, Cedrick discovered Otis was suffering from several deep puncture wounds on his shoulder which was badly sprained from being jerked up off the ground and bodily tossed over the corral fence with a violent shake of the bear's head. Once again, washing the wounds out with soap and water and leaving them open so they could drain, was about all that Cedrick could do to alleviate his brother's type of wounds and deep shoulder pain at that moment in time.

By then, Cloud, Oliver and Feather had skinned out the two cubs and gutted the same since they were now to be used as a source of camp meat. As for their skins, gut piles and the dead sow's carcass, they were dragged down below their cabin and left in a grove of aspen trees for the critters to find and eat. Then upon their return, the now cooling cub carcasses were hoisted up onto their meat poles so they could continue cooling out and glazing.

With the evidence of an oncoming summer thunderstorm brewing from the northwest, the four basically uninjured trappers unpacked all of their provisions and stored them in their storage shed and cabin. Shortly thereafter all of their saddles and packs were also transported to and stored in the storage shed as well to preclude a soaking from the oncoming storm. Soon cooling breezes began blowing ahead of the storm and finally the rains began softly falling as the four trappers finally got the last of their horse herd into their corral for safekeeping. With that, Wallace and Otis, along with the last of the trappers' personal gear, were moved inside their cabin, only to find that it stunk to high Heaven due to the three grizzly bears living in it for the previous month while the men were at the rendezvous. So as the rains quietly drummed on the top of their roof and the lightning danced and sizzled high overhead, the trappers left their front door wide open in an effort to do what they could to reduce the stink caused by three grizzly bears living in their cabin. Their only fear when they went to bed that night was that another grizzly looking for a place to get out from the storm, would choose their still airing out cabin and make himself right at home by coming through the still open and welcoming front door. The next morning after breakfast, the men cleaned out the offal and scat from within the cabin trying to make it smell better. As for Otis and Wallace, both were too sore and sick to be of much help and stayed in bed resting up after their close call with an enraged female grizzly.

As for the remaining four 'brothers' come the next day, they had a 'world' of work lying ahead of them before they could set one beaver trap come the approaching fall trapping season. First and foremost, outside firepit wood had to be hauled, cut and stacked, and then cut a ready to use pile of wood for the indoor fireplace which had to be stacked inside their cabin as well. Then it was back onto their hillside and the cutting of dead lightning struck pine and fir trees into sections to be hauled down by horse teams and stacked near their cabin for later use as a winter woodpile. Putting off the next chore as long as they could because the men did not like doing it, they finally caved to the pressure of time, need and just getting it done. Down alongside the grassy marshes near the Yellowstone River went the four uninjured men. There they cut and laid out on a nearby hillside to dry a small mountain of hay to be used to feed their livestock during the coldest months of winter when the snows were too deep for the horses to paw down to the ground in order to reach the much-needed feed. That chore they hated because the local mosquitoes were not in the haying business but sure as hell were in the mood and business of 'mining' the shallow blood vessels of the trappers as they sweated, cut and hauled the hay.

Following that disdainful chore, Oliver and Cloud spent several days cutting mountain mahogany smoking wood from thickets high up on the nearby mountains and hauled that special hardwood down to their smoking racks. As that was being done, Cedrick and Feather spent part of a day digging up their old cache and hauling what had been left behind back into the camp for everyday use. Then out to the nearest herd of buffalo and three dead buffalo later, the men found themselves butchering out the beasts, hauling the meat back to their campsite, cutting the meat into inch-wide thin strips and slow smoking the same under a low-heat fire those many hundreds of pounds of the rich and great tasting meat soon to be made into that wholesome trapper's standby, jerky. Then as that meat was sufficiently dried and smoked, it was bagged up into their tanned deerskin bags and hung from pegs high on the walls of their cabin for use during the winter months when afield. Following that welcome chore, it was back to the sides of the marshes where the previously cut, laid out on the ground and now dried hay was gathered up and hauled by the pannier full back to the campsite and stacked under the lean-to for use during the bitterest of winter months when horse feed was scarce or the snows too deep. Once again, the hordes of mosquitoes 'thanked' the trappers in the only way they knew how for their 'liquid' considerations while the downed and dry hay was gathered up for the hauling back to the cabin's storage lean-to.

All the while the other three uninjured brothers were doing the above work, Cedrick was tending to his cooking duties and checking the healing progress of his two grizzly bear-mauled brothers. A chore Cedrick soon found distasteful when he had to heat-sterilize the tip of his knife and lance the numerous pus pockets that developed in the flesh of the two men as they slowly healed up. However, the worst of his 'doctoring' duties were when he had to take the inflamed and damaged tissue around such pockets of pus and squeeze them until the blood ran in order to further cleanse the puncture wounds so they would heal.

After three weeks of hard work getting their camp ready for the fall trapping season and the healing up of Wallace and Otis so they could ride once again, the clan found themselves riding a number of miles along the northeastern section of the Clarks Fork of the Yellowstone checking out the beaver trapping potential. To a man, they could hardly believe what they were seeing during those inspection rides. It seemed that just about every slack inch of water was already ponded up, there were many long and active mud and stick dams in place, large conical beaver houses dotted every body of ponded water, and swimming beaver carrying freshly cut sticks or paws carrying more dam building or repairing mud were much in evidence! Additionally, there was much evidence of beaver activity all along both banks of the Yellowstone just as far north as the men when they rode into what they figured had to be Canada before turning back! There the men turned back because they didn't want to be competing with the Hudson's Bay men on their turf and sure as hell didn't want them competing with them on their turf in the United States.

By early fall, Wallace had totally healed up from his mauling and now sported a chest and shoulder full of long scars as mute testimony as to the ordeal he had suffered through under the jaws of an enraged female grizzly bear. On a daily basis, Wallace was reminded of his grizzly bear encounter and often wondered if any such encounters with the bears and Indians of late as they had been encountering as trappers, was any kind of a sixth sense premonition of what was coming in the Barnes Clan's future... Otis on the other hand, still sported a much-scarred and somewhat stiffened shoulder from his 'bout' with the grizzly. However, both men could now shoot just as good as they ever could but their tomahawk accuracy and throwing abilities had suffered somewhat. Lastly, Cloud and Feather noticed that when Otis and the brothers got into playful wrestling matches, Otis was still the stronger of all of the brothers, grizzly bear scars or not...

As the days shortened and the morning's temperatures grew colder, the men hurried through their mule deer killing activities so they would have enough brain-tanned skins to cover the packs of beaver fur being transported to the coming summer's rendezvous. As they did, they ate deer meat in every form and presentation possible until Cedrick, tired of cooking deer meat for every meal, called it quits and told the brothers to go out and kill a buffalo for a change in their meat diets! That they were all too happy to do and soon, quarters of buffalo swung slowly from their hanging ropes under the meat poles and the gray jays celebrated on a daily basis by visiting their newfound meat supply slowly swinging in the soft breezes! As far as the gray jays and Northern chickadees went, they preferred their buffalo meat anyway it came...

One morning when Wallace exited the cabin and headed out back to take care of a call of nature, he yelled over his shoulder to Cedrick in order to get his attention. When he saw Cedrick looking up from his cooking duties around the campfire he said, "Today we need to get out our wolf and beaver traps from the storage shed and smoke the hell out of them." Then Wallace hurried up his walking so he could get to his favorite 'dump log' and 'rid himself' of the rich rice, brown sugar and raisin dessert Cedrick had made the evening before, much to the men's great delight.

That evening while sitting around the campfire after a heavy supper of skewered buffalo meat, pinto beans heavily loaded with red pepper flakes (eliminated constipation caused from such a high meat diet), coffee and Dutch oven biscuits, Wallace said, "I think we need to get our beaver trapping gear all set for the fall beaver trapping to come. Tomorrow we need to cut at least 24 four-foot dry wooden poles for our deep water anchors on the beaver sets. We also need to get four panniers ready and load them with our beaver traps including the four new ones we purchased at the last rendezvous. Cloud and Feather, make sure you load two shovels, two hand axes, that spool of wire so we can tie our trap chains to the anchor pole, and a couple bottles of that castoreum we purchased while at the rendezvous as well. Otis, we need to have all of our saddle bags stuffed with some of that mahogany smoked jerky and Oliver, I suggest you refill all of our powder horns full of that new powder we purchased so that we don't have any misfires should shooting be called for. I also think we need to throw a couple of those one-pound tins of DuPont powder into each pannier just in case we get into some kind of 'hoo-rah' and run low in our powder horns. Cedrick, the two of us need to set down and cast a mess of new balls for our rifles and pistols. Lastly, I think since we are trapping in a new territory and are going to be getting closer to those Hudson's Bay trappers to the north, I suggest each of us carry an extra rifle in our panniers just in case things get hot between us and them mean-assed French-Canadian trappers if we happen to 'cross swords' with any of them."

Then running down on his mental list of instructions for the fall beaver trapping season, Wallace took another deep drag on his much-loved clay pipe full of tobacco and then said, "I would also suggest that each of you load buck and ball in your pistols in case we run into a mess of Indians and need some help in the close-in work department if they try rushing and overwhelming us, as Indians are wont to do when they attack."

Then taking another deep pull on the stem of his pipe, Wallace recommenced saying, "I would also like to suggest we start trapping on that northeastern section of the Yellowstone kind of like we did last trapping season on the northwestern leg of that river. I say we go far to the north and trap our ways back down the river towards our cabin and away from the Hudson's Bay men's territory. That way if we trap out that northern portion of the river, there won't be any reason for the Hudson's Bay men to trap down the river into our territory and country if it's all trapped out. Then come the spring trapping season, we trap out the remaining lower section of that northeastern arm of the river, load up our stock and head down to next summer's rendezvous, leaving us with just a short pull into that neck of the woods. Then there and having trapped out this portion of the country, figure where we will be going next and continue doing what we enjoy. What say, you men, as to those suggestions?"

Once again, Otis was the first of the brothers to speak his piece by saying, "Me, Cloud and Feather will go down to the willows tomorrow and cut those four-foot anchor poles from the dry wood that we can find. I like your suggestion about carrying our extra firepower. I don't worry so much about those cowardly French-Canadians but by going that far to the north, we are getting deeper into the territory of those murdering devils the Blackfeet, who are not aware of our peace with our local band of Blackfeet. If we tangle with that horde, they will come at us and do to us like General Jackson did to them damn British at the Battle of New Orleans if we ain't careful. I am of the opinion that the only thing them Blackfeet respect is the front end of a rifle and the more we can point in their direction, the more respect we are going to get!"

Then Feather spoke up by saying, "Otis is right. We will be right next to the Blackfeet Nation's territory and they have a tendency to send war parties far and wide to season their young men in order to make them warriors and count coups. It would be wise to carry as much in the ways of our rifles and pistols as possible just in case." With his friend's words out and around the campfire, Cloud nodded his head in such a fashion the rest of the clan could see he much respected the wisdom and foresight of the words of his friend Feather.

Cedrick was the next to speak up saying, "Seeing we soon will be up to our eyes in beaver ponds and hooping those skins late into the evening, I am going to prepare a big pot of beans so we can have them with our buffalo meat for the next couple of suppers." With those words, he walked over to the storage shed carrying a big kettle and was soon back at the campfire picking out the rocks, clumps of dirt and twigs normally found in the sack of pinto beans by the firelight.

Hearing no further brotherly dissent, Wallace rose, tapped out the ash from his pipe saying, "We have a full day ahead of us tomorrow. I am going to bed." With those words he rose from his sitting log and headed for the cabin. Shortly thereafter, only the dying campfire remained, and *six sets of eyes intently looking on at the Barnes Clan gathered around their campfire from a safe distance away at the edge of the meadow...*

The next day, Cedrick as usual was up before dawn with a campfire going, the coffee pot merrily bubbling away and Dutch oven biscuits baking over a mess of coals. Taking a wash pan and with a small tree limb, Cedrick began banging on the pan in order to wake up the rest of the crew for breakfast. Soon out from the cabin staggered the rest of the clan rubbing the sleep from their eyes. Then it was a trip up behind the cabin to take care of their individual calls of nature and then over to the spring box at the head of the horse corral. There the men washed up, did the best they could do with their long hair and then headed for their individual sitting logs stationed around the campfire. Soon the men were quietly partaking of their first cup of coffee and awaiting the arrival of their plates full of piping hot biscuits from the three Dutch ovens now being carefully tended to by Cedrick. When the plates full of biscuits arrived followed by the men's second cup of coffee, quiet reigned around the campfire, except for the hum of the ever-present mosquitoes and the crackling of the fire.

Streaming out from their camp somewhat later, Wallace led the fur trappers' caravan up to the Clarks Fork of the Yellowstone and then turned his group towards the northeast. There the men rode along the Yellowstone in that direction for about two-and-a-half hours surveying their new trapping grounds. Bringing the group to a stop along a heavily watered area sectioned off by a number of active beaver dams, beaver houses and numerous well used 'slides', Wallace sat quietly on his horse surveying the scene before him. Satisfied over what he was seeing, Wallace easily stepped off his horse, walked back to the two packhorses being led by Cloud and Feather saying, "You three might as well as dismount. This is as good an area as I have seen this morning in which to start our fall beaver trapping season."

Without any further words, Cloud, Feather and Cedrick dismounted and moved to the two packhorses carrying all of their needed traps and trapping gear. As they began removing the needed trapping essentials, Wallace stripped down and removed his warm Linsey-woolsy pants purchased at the last rendezvous and stepped into his breechclout and leggings like those most Indians of the era wore, for his work in the water. Leaving his rifle and pistols with Otis and Oliver who remained seated on their horses acting as lookouts, Wallace took a beaver trap, a length of twine in his teeth, a hand ax and one of their four-foot dry wood anchor poles (dry so the beaver would not chew on them when trying to escape after being trapped), and began walking upstream looking for a fresh and well used beaver slide that caught his eye. Twenty minutes later, the first trap had been set and the ring on the trap's chain had been fastened to the wooden anchor pole driven into the pond's bottom precluding escape by any beaver so trapped. By late afternoon, all 24 of the clan's traps had been set downstream from their first set, and now found the men in an aspen grove quietly sitting on the ground by their horses eating jerky that had been carried in their saddle bags. Since they had only eaten biscuits for breakfast that morning so they could begin their trapping season, their 'growling' inside welcomed the great tasting jerky. Soon the men began drifting off to sleep one by one in the quiet and shade of the aspen grove until all were asleep. They had gotten up early, eaten a light breakfast in order to get afield, ridden 15 miles or so along the northeastern section of the Clarks Fork of the Yellowstone and then had begun their trap setting. Now their bodies were 'saying' time to rest and the men did so in the cool and quiet of the aspen grove.

An hour or so later, Cloud was the first to awake with a start! In his world of sleep, he had heard a horse neigh off in a distance. Ten thousand years of genetics had honed his Indian skills to such a level that it seemed even when asleep, his senses were always somewhat awake and tuned into his surroundings. The cave bears of pre-historic times had seen to it that only those Indians whose senses were tuned into their surroundings were the ones who avoided becoming cave bear 'bear scat' out on the frozen wastes of yesteryear...

Slowly rising up on his elbows so as not to alert any close at hand enemies who might be looking on as to his movement, a life skill he had learned in his days of youth, Cloud peered all around within the aspen grove looking for any signs of danger. Seeing nothing other than a robin scratching around in the leaves beneath a nearby aspen, Cloud expanded his looking around to now include the area outside the grove of aspens in which the tired trappers were still resting. THEN HE SAW IT! Across the prairie and alongside the beaver pond area where they had just set their last beaver trap, Cloud observed five mounted trappers on horses and another one on the ground next to that beaver pond. There that man on the ground was removing the last beaver trap Wallace had set earlier in the afternoon!

Slowly reaching over to the sleeping Feather, Cloud woke him up, all the while not letting his eyes leave that of the trap-stealing trapper! Awakening and seeing Cloud intently staring at something, Feather woke up Otis, who just as quietly woke the rest of the clan from their afternoon sleep. Soon, all of the men were watching the series of events taking place over at the beaver pond where they had set their last trap in their new trap line earlier in the afternoon. Tying the latest stolen trap to a number of other freshly stolen traps hanging on the side of a packhorse apparently taken from the rest of the Barnes brothers' new trap line, a huge bearded man, the one and same who had rudely confronted Cloud and Feather at the rum keg at the rendezvous, mounted his horse. Then with a long look all around to see if they had been observed stealing traps, the six trappers continued heading northeasterly along the Yellowstone and then slowly rode out of sight like they were heading for Canada.

"Ain't no use in taking them on in broad daylight out on the open prairie," said Wallace quietly. "If we do, a number of us may never see another sunset if we take them on in an open and out in front of God and everybody shootout! We will wait until dusk and then have Cloud and Feather track them while the rest of us provide them protection from a possible ambush," he continued with a coldness seldom heard in Wallace's voice. "Then we will use darkness and surprise on our side to lessen the chances of any of us getting hurt or killed," he continued.

"Wallace, stealing a man's traps and livelihood out here on the frontier justifies a killing! Same as if they were to steal a man's horse out here and leave him afoot," quietly said Otis.

Wallace said nothing in reply to Otis's statement but Cloud and Feather could read in the man's eyes that 'certain death was in the wind' for what had just occurred! When Wallace was sure the six trap robbers were out of sight, he sent Otis and Oliver back along their previously set trap line to check on the rest of their traps. When those two brothers returned somewhat later, it was with the news that the trap robbers likely from hidden positions had followed the Barnes Clan to each and every trap set and had stolen every valuable and hard to replace while out on the frontier, trap! Later in the afternoon found Cloud and Feather 'cold-tracking' the shod hoofprints of six riding and nine packhorses slowly walking up alongside the south side of the Clarks Fork of the Yellowstone. Long about dark, Cloud and Feather stopped walking ahead of the Barnes Clan as they 'cold-tracked' the six trap-stealing thieves led by the bearded one, when they had smelled smoke from a nearby campfire somewhere ahead of them!

By now, the Barnes Clan knew the trap robbers, led by the large bearded man, was the same 'bearded one' who had caused a problem back at the rendezvous over Cloud or Feather drinking ahead of him at the rum keg set aside for company trappers. The same bearded man of huge proportions who had been knocked out cold by Otis for his physical abuse of Cloud and Feather! The same bearded trapper and his five henchmen who had apparently trailed the Barnes Clan to their successful beaver trapping grounds and had stolen their traps on their newest just set trap line along the Clarks Fork in order to rid themselves of any local competition. The same trappers who Otis, Feather and Cloud had sensed were following them earlier on their ride into the backcountry. The same trappers were now unaware that 'death was coming' and 'he' was riding the 'black horse of death' if they were caught with the Barnes Clan's stolen traps...

Come dark and following their noses and ears, the Barnes Clan quietly fanned out and were slowly approaching a blazing campfire illuminating six unawares trappers preparing their evening meal and laying out their sleeping furs near the fire. Fortunately, there was a hard wind now blowing through the trees from out of the northwest which covered any sounds the men might be making as they approached the trap robber's campfire. Off to one side were picketed on a long rope the trap robbers' 15 riding and packhorses. Prior to the men sneaking up on the bearded one's campsite so they could be confronted and see to it that justice was done and their 24 traps recovered, Wallace had the men load their weapons with buck and ball. He figured that if any shooting were to occur, it would be at close range and his party would be better served with buck and ball heading in the direction of the six outlaw trappers instead of single balls.

Once the Barnes Clan was within striking distance but still outside the light of the six trappers' campfire, Wallace, with hand signals, held everyone lined out in place. Earlier he had discussed that their plan would be to wait until the men had bedded down and then approach and try to get the drop on them before any shooting occurred. Then from there, they would take care of the business at hand. It was then that the fabled Irish luck of the Barnes Clan ran out! **CRAAASSSH!** went a long dead with rotting roots lodgepole pine tree as it dropped among the Barnes men in the strong wind blowing through the treetops! As luck would have it, the pine, wavering for some time, was influenced by the evening's strong wind blowing through the trees, toppled over and came crashing down among the waiting Barnes brothers, Cloud and Feather!

With that loud crash occurring in and among the Barnes brothers and next to the animals' picket line, the horses reacted in fright, creating an even louder ruckus! Instantly the six previously sleeping trappers were awake, armed and standing up in their sleeping furs trying to figure out what the hell had just happened! Then spotting the Barnes's emerging into the firelight in a line abreast, the six trap-stealing trappers unleashed a wall of flame, shot and 'shell' into the line of advancing Barnes without warning! **BOOM–BOOM–BOOM–BOOM–BOOM–POOOFF!** ROARED THE SIX NOW FEELING TRAPPED TRAPPERS' RIFLES ALMOST IN UNISON (one rifle misfired)! In that unexpected fusillade of shooting, Wallace had the two little fingers on his left hand shot away, Otis had his wide-brimmed hat shot off his head and the inside of Cedrick's thigh suffered a grazing wound! Other than that, all those five shots fired in haste at the Barnes Clan did no further damage other than scaring the hell out of the line of advancing men!

However, that roar of fire and flame was replied to instantly by the Barnes Clan, Cloud and Feather. Simultaneously triggers were squeezed causing flints to snap forward striking the striker pans on the Barnes Clan's rifles. There was a slight pause and then the sparks from the flints igniting the powders in their rifles and death was on its way... **BOOM–BOOM–BOOM–BOOM– BOOM!** went five shots fired in deadly reply and they did considerably more damage than that first round of shooting by the six trap thieves! Five of the trap robbing trappers, illuminated by the light from their campfire, staggered and fell under the accurate fire from Wallace and his brothers who were now standing just a few scant yards away from their targets! The sixth trap robbing trapper surprisingly not hit in the Barnes Clan's initial return rifle fire, turned to run and then quickly fell under the buck and ball fired from two hastily fired pistol shots from Otis and Cedrick! Then other than the trap-thieves' horses' nervous stomping and milling around on their short leashes on their picket line smell- ing death and the acrid smell of black powder smoke, all was quiet until Otis yelled out in hor- ror, **"OLIVER!"**

With Otis's yell, everyone turned and looked back in his direction only to see him running in the light of the trap robbers' campfire light back to where they had come from before the shooting started. Then everyone saw what Otis was yell- ing about. Beneath the pine tree that had toppled over from root rot and fallen among them that had initially alerted the sleeping trap thieves laid Oliver, crushed under the weight of the tree! When everyone got to the fallen tree and lifted it up off Oliver, they could plainly see the vast amount of gray matter oozing from the man's skull! In seconds it was apparent that Oliver had been killed by a fluke falling pine tree in an overly mature forest just as he had moved under its deadly flight to earth moments earlier...

Forgetting the now recently killed trap robbing trappers, the grief among the brothers was instant and inconsolable! Cloud and Feather, shocked over what had happened, were not prepared for the open grief and feelings they were now seeing being exhibited by the remaining Barnes brothers who were normally stoic and very quiet in life! All three remaining brothers were kneeling over Oliver's crushed body openly crying like babies! All Cloud and Feather could do was stand there and feel deeply for their friends' loss of one of their own blood...

(Author's Note: While on fall hunting season horseback patrols as a Special Agent with the U.S. Fish and Wildlife Service in the Yellowstone and Absaroka backcountry protecting the grizzly bear, an animal species then protected by the Endangered Species Act, the Author was surprised at seeing a chain saw being packed on one of our pack animals prior to any backcountry patrol. Not wanting to show my stupidity being unfamiliar at the time over what those patrols entailed, I just kept my mouth shut and eyes open as to why the need for such equipment. EVERY TIME at the end of those long horseback patrols in the backcountry checking big game sportsmen and sportswomen, riding back over our previous route of travel on established horse or game trails, we had to stop, unlimber the chain saw from our pack animal and cut through overly mature trees that had fallen across the trail after we had ridden through just hours earlier! I later discovered that 'tree falling episodes' were a common and sometimes deadly occurrence in overly mature pine and fir forests in much of the pristine backcountry traveled while protecting the grizzly bear against the illegal take by hunters during the big game hunting seasons. Also, twice on my patrols with other officers, I heard the crashing of other nearby falling trees in the overly mature coniferous forest in which we were traveling! Those trips became even more deadly if a strong wind was blowing or a storm was brewing in the area. When those events occurred, one could hear the constant crashing of the overly mature trees hitting the ground all around as we moved through the forests on horseback!)

Somewhat later, Otis and Cedrick after finding a shovel in the now dead trap-stealing trappers' packs, a grave was dug and Oliver's body was placed gently therein. The next morning, all of the men gathered the largest rocks they could carry and laid those over Oliver's gravesite. This they did to prevent the wolves and grizzly bears from smelling and then digging up the body and eating it. Then after Oliver had been laid to rest, each brother in his own way while Cloud and Feather stood off to one side looking on, said their final good-byes to their brother. Then with mist filled eyes and heavy hearts, the remaining brothers turned away and in their own way of handling such heartfelt grief, began another day in their lives as fur trappers out on the unforgiving frontier.

After that, no more was said over the loss of their brother. Wallace with a now patched up left hand where he had lost his two little fingers from the trap thieves initial rifle fire, directed the rounding up of the entire riding horse and pack string, had the same re-loaded with the dead trappers' packs of supplies and then everyone walked those horses and their packs back to where the Barnes's had hidden their horses early on when they began their deadly approach. Those horses were then mounted and the entire train moved back along their previous trap line that had been picked clean, and Cedrick reset their 24 beaver traps in their original locations. Then the trappers quietly rode their horses and trailed those they had now acquired from the trap-stealing trappers, back to their cabin for safekeeping.

Once back at their camp, all the horses were unpacked and the packs and the trap-stealing trappers' provisions were inventoried and then stored in their storage shed. In so doing, the Barnes Clan found themselves the proud possessors of a year's supplies upon examining the packs' contents once belonging to the six trap thieves, who had since been relegated to the dustbins of history! Following that, all of their horses were let out to water and feed while Otis and Cedrick took a saw and ax into the timber behind their cabin and began falling lodgepole pine trees and cutting them into additional posts and rails. That night all the horses were brought back to camp and those that fit were placed into their corral and the remainder were hobbled and picketed until the corral could be enlarged to hold the Barnes's original horse herd and those 15 animals recently acquired from the now dead six trap-stealing trappers. For the next two days, the men's traps were run and trapped beaver retrieved were skinned on-site by Cloud, Feather and Cedrick. Cedrick ran the trap line as Cloud and Feather skinned out their catches until Wallace's hand could heal, as Otis now stood as the lone guardian over the trap setting trappers. Finally several days later the corral had been enlarged so that it could hold all of the men's horses and things began slowly getting back to normal.

Once Wallace's hand had healed sufficiently whereby he could set the traps and resume his role as the clan's main trapper, he returned to those duties. With that, Cedrick once again became Wallace's assistant, Feather did all of the skinning while on-site and now Cloud and Otis formed the two members of the group providing guard duty oversight from horseback. Once again, the beaver began rolling in and many nights found the men were up late fleshing, de-fatting and hooping the day's beaver pelts. In between those duties associated with the beaver trapping, the men made time to hunt buffalo for their camp meat and cut additional hay for their now expanded and extremely valuable horse herd.

Come the end of the fall beaver trapping sea-son, one could almost see the relief on the men's faces which were now showing the strain and stress of trapping, caring for the pelts, caring for an expanded horse herd, providing camp meat and then finding some time to just relax around the campfire with their pipes and a cup of rum. The good thing the men now had going for them was that they were not going to run out of sup-plies. Especially in light of all the year's provi-sions they had acquired from the six now dead trap-stealing trappers in addition to their own, which thankfully now included those supplies of rum from both camps…

CHAPTER NINE

THE "BUFFALO", "WOLVERINE" AND "BLACKFEET"

WHEN THE BARNES'S FIGURED they had trapped out the beaver on the northeastern upper reaches of the Clarks Fork of the Yellowstone as per Wallace's plan, they would establish newer trap lines by working closer and closer back towards their cabin site lying to the southwest. That they figured they would continue doing until they had trapped out that entire 15-mile section of the Yellowstone and then they would abandon their cabin for good and head for the upcoming rendezvous come early summer. To date, the Barnes's, Cloud and Feather had trapped and pelted out a total of 273 Made Beaver during that fall trapping season!

Then the winter's cold descended upon the men and with the early vestiges of freeze-up just around the corner, they pulled their beaver traps thereby ending their latest fall beaver trapping season on the northeastern arm of the Clarks Fork of the Yellowstone. Then it was off to pay a visit to the closest buffalo herd to their cabin and three dead buffalo later, found the men quartering out the animals and later hanging them from their meat poles back at camp right at dusk as their future camp meat supplies. After the buffalo meat had been cared for and the men had washed up at their spring box, they headed for their campfire and their individual sitting logs. As Cedrick was making a hearty supper of beans, biscuits, coffee and freshly skewered buffalo meat, a keg of rum was brought forth from the storage shed so the men could celebrate the end of another successful fall beaver trapping season. However, the men soon discovered that their end of the fall trapping season celebration was dampened somewhat without one of their 'own' present to also enjoy and participate in the event. As that realization of the deep loss of a brother slowly began sinking in among the men once again, along with the night's deepening shadows and after several cups of rum, a thoughtful silence soon descended upon the men. As it did, within moments, each of the men found themselves recalling happier memories of Oliver among themselves. That evening eventually found all of the men eating their supper in silence and then quietly heading for their cabin and sleeping furs in a somber mood over the open and raw memories that came from the recent loss of one of their own... It was obvious because of the lack of discussion around their outside cooking fire that evening, that the easy smile and usually quiet presence of Oliver was now being deeply felt. But true to the Barnes Clan temperament, not a word was said about the absence of one of their kind that evening but their thoughts were one and the same regarding the unusual loss of their brother, as all of them ambled off to bed on a somber note...

Somewhat later after the first snowfall, found the men killing buffalo in different locations around their campsite and then setting their wolf traps around those carcasses after the men had opened them up so their odor of death would carry in the wind to the noses of nearby and always hungry wolves. A week later upon riding up to their most recent buffalo kill site for wolf trap setting, the men stumbled upon a rolling fat grizzly bear not yet in hibernation feasting on the recently killed buffalo's carcass! A rodeo of sorts then ensued when the horses realized there was a 'bear in camp' and after five shots into the great beast and a short chase of the much-wounded animal, they managed to down the critter. Cedrick happy as all get-out over the fortunate kill, commenced gutting out the bear while Otis and Cloud rode back to the last buffalo carcass where they had originally jumped the feeding grizzly before it had run off wounded. There they sprung the remaining wolf traps they had set around that carcass that the bear had not inadvertently sprung when it was feeding upon the carcass. That they did so one of their own feet didn't 'stray' into one of the toothed traps and suffer the consequences. Then with their feet 'safe' they skinned out that buffalo. Removing its hide, they then dragged the buffalo's hide over to where the rest of the clan was finishing up butchering out the bear. Rolling out the buffalo's skin with the fur side down upon the fresh snow, the men carefully placed the bear's front- and hindquarters upon the skin, along with about 20 pounds or so of fine "leaf lard" that Cedrick had carefully excised from the pre-hibernation fat grizzly bear's intestines. Then tying a rope to the buffalo's hide and tying it behind "Molly" their always dependable packhorse, they slowly dragged the buffalo hide carrying the bear's quarters and precious for cooking leaf lard across the freshly fallen snow, like the meat quarters and leaf lard were upon a 'skin sled'. Arriving back at camp, the bear's quarters were hoisted up onto their meat pole to cool out and glaze, minus a number of steaks removed by Cedrick for the men's supper that evening.

Then Cedrick took one of his Dutch ovens and set it alongside his outdoor fire to heat up. Into that Dutch oven went several large handfuls of the bear's leaf lard, and soon its light oil was beginning to melt down and render out in the Dutch. As it did, Cedrick would spoon off the light tasting and excellent cooking oil into one of his steel pots where it was allowed to congeal in the cold winter's air. By day's end, Cedrick had over two gallons of the rendered grizzly bear's leaf lard which made for use as a sweet tasting and light Dutch oven baking oil base, especially when he made up his flaky Dutch oven pie dough or special biscuits covered with brown sugar.

The remainder of that winter found the men trapping wolves, cutting wood, casting bullets, caring for their livestock, killing buffalo for their weekly camp meat needs which was pretty great considering there were five hungry men to feed, repairing their clothing, making new clothing and packing their beaver skins into tanned deer-skin covered, 90-pound bundles (about 60 beaver skins to a 90-pound bundle) ready for transport to the next rendezvous. One winter morning Otis found himself with nothing to do. He had repaired all of their firearms, put an edge to everyone's knife and tomahawk blades and had made himself a pest by trying to help Cedrick out with the cooking duties.

Finally Wallace had enough of his younger brother's antics and told him, "Otis, why don't you and the boys get into your heavy winter gear, fasten on your snowshoes and check those remaining two wolf traps that were set next to camp by the last buffalo we killed and quartered out? That way you will have something to do because we can't leave those traps there any longer due to the increasing depth of the snows. So, why don't you go and remove them? That way if we do happen to have a wolf in the trap, we don't have to worry about other wolves or any grizzly bears not yet in hibernation eating them out of our traps and destroying the pelt."

It didn't take Otis very long to get dressed, gather up his 'Possibles' and build a fire under Cloud and Feather to hurry up, get ready and accompany him. Later that morning, the three men left the confines of their cabin on their snowshoes en route to check two of their wolf traps set next to the remains of the last buffalo the men had killed and butchered out for camp meat. The morning was clear and cold and the men found themselves making good time snowshoeing across the country to the wolf traps set around the old buffalo's now frozen carcass. An hour later the men arrived at the carcass and found their two wolf traps buried under three feet of snow. However, in one trap lying under the snow was a pure black wolf with an excellent pelt. Otis dug out and hefted up the 140-pound, frozen hard as a brick, black wolf's carcass and with the boys carrying the rest of the just pulled toothed wolf traps, started back to the cabin. They hadn't been slow traveling long because of the weight Otis was carrying, when off in the distance they could hear a pack of wolves hot on the trail of some unfortunate nearby game. Stopping to get his wind back and listen, Otis finally said, "Let us go, boys. I got my wind back and from the sounds of it, that is one large pack of wolves and they are hot on the trail of their supper."

Ten minutes later, the men observed black looking and ominous clouds rolling in from the northwest portending of another oncoming snowstorm. With an eye on the rolling ominous black clouds, Otis redoubled his efforts in carrying the frozen solid black wolf carcass and soon both he and the boys were sweating heavily in an attempt to get back to their cabin and outrun the oncoming and possibly dangerous winter storm.

Shortly thereafter Cloud said, "Otis, I think we may have a problem. I noticed that those wolves have quit howling and one time when I looked back, I could see a number of gray and black shapes darting here and there in and out of the timber. I think they are on our trail and not that of a snowbound deer, buffalo or elk!"

Stopping one more time for a breather, Otis turned and sure as hell, spotted what he quick counted 20 or more wolves now out in the open speeding across the top of the snow hot on THEIR trail! Otis, realizing the winter had been hard and the snows deep, figured that many of the big game animals had moved to lower elevations where food was easier to get. He also quickly concluded that the wolves hard on their trail may have had evil thoughts on what they intended to do with the trappers once they caught them since there was no other reason for them to be following the men so closely unless the wolves were hungry with killing on their minds!

"Boys, let's head for that stand of aspen and 'hole' up there for defense until we see what the intentions are of those wolves trailing us," said Otis, as he shifted the weight of the wolf he was carrying and then began his shuffling walk on his snowshoes in a quickened pace as he headed towards the protective stand of aspen trees in which the three of them could turn and face the oncoming pack.

Soon the men were in the protective cover of the aspens, had dropped their wolf traps and the black wolf's carcass and stood there watching the oncoming pack of wolves determinedly heading their way with their noses down and hot on their trail! "Boys, set your rifles. I think those wolves mean to have us for their supper unless we can change their minds with a good dose of hot lead!" said a grim-faced Otis as he cocked his rifle.

What happened behavior-wise next was totally unlike any pack of wolves Otis, Cloud or Feather had ever seen. Instead of warily circling the men cautiously checking things out, the wolves continued tracking down the trail the men had left with their snowshoes and did not slow down! It was now obvious the hungry wolves meant to attack the three trappers for the food source they represented! As it turned out, the first three wolves died within yards of the three trappers when shot by Otis, Cloud and Feather! Then the men dropped their rifles, quickly drew their tomahawks and prepared to defend themselves! That they had to do because wanting to travel light that morning in the deep snows, none of the men had brought along any of their pistols.

The next attacking wolf in line went airborne in his attack mode and smashed right into Otis snarling and slashing with his teeth all the way! But when it did, it had its head split wide open with Otis's recently sharpened tomahawk! However, the collision between the flying through the air adult 100-pound wolf and the stout trapper, resulted in both flying and tumbling into the brush in the aspen grove in a cloud of flying snow, blood and wolf slobber! Cloud fared somewhat better because the attacking wolf he tomahawked dropped like a stone at his feet, violently shaking his life away with a split braincase. Feather fared the worst of the lot when the pack of wolves had violently attacked! When he had swung his tomahawk at the onrushing wolf coming at him, he missed its head and struck it between his shoulders! Down they both went with the wolf biting and slashing with its teeth into the upraised arm of Feather! Springing back to his feet after he had killed his attacking wolf, Otis grabbed his dropped rifle and swung it as hard as he could at the next in line attacking wolf, busting its wooden stock over that flying through the air wolf's head! That finished that wolf as well and the rifle as any kind of a shooting piece until the broken stock could be mended...

Then for some reason, the rest of the pack of wolves hesitated in their headlong attacks. That gave Cloud the time he needed to reload and in so doing, he managed to get a quick shot off at a nearby circling wolf. When he did, the injured wolf let out a howl of what had to be anguish and two other wolves from the pack instantly attacked and began tearing at the crippled wolf in hunger! Meanwhile, Cloud now seeing Feather still struggling with his biting wolf, turned and brought the barrel of his rifle down hard on the back of the wolf attacking Feather, breaking its back! With a howl of pain, that wolf died midhowl as Feather's tomahawk struck the wolf true that second time, splitting its head wide open! Then it appeared to be over as the remainder of the wolves warily circled the embattled trappers until two more shots rang out and two of their kind, under the dual firing of a reloaded Cloud and Feather, dropped dead in their tracks! Then it was over as the wolves in a skulking manner, moved off and disappeared in the direction from whence they had come.

Three hours later Otis, Cloud and Feather dragged themselves back into the trappers' camp slightly worse for wear from their wolf trap removal detail. Otis was still carrying on his shoulder the frozen black wolf they had found in the trap by the buffalo's carcass so it could be thawed and skinned in camp, and his stock-broken rifle in his hand. As for Cloud and Feather, between the two of them they carried nine freshly skinned out and valuable wolf pelts! After Feather's arm wounds had been cleaned out, washed with soapy water and bound, the men spent the next two days fleshing and stretching the now ten valuable wolf pelts. Wolf trapping continued as long as the bitter winter weather allowed and by the end of wolf trapping season, the clan had 33 wolf skins or one of their better years ever, pelted out, dried and hanging in their storage shed!

Finally after many long cold days, "Old Man Winter" began losing his grip and "Mother Nature" began blessing the land with longer days and warmer nights, until the snows started receding and the spring grasses began poking their nutritious sprouts above the now partially thawed ground. Once that change occurred, the horse herd happily fed on the green sprouts until they almost foundered! As they did, one could see the winter thin horses beginning to round out once again into their healthy selves. However, being the last few trappers in line with a caravan of horses feeding upon the rich new shoots of grass was not the place to be. In fact by the third horse in line, the air was 'blue in color' and the smell of putrid horse methane gas was so 'rich' and powerful it would have sent a hungry grizzly bear running for the next hillside holding its nose... It was alright for a hungry grizzly bear to eat guts from a rotten gut pile, but to smell fresh spring grass methane coming from the 'last part over the fence' of a horse was certainly a 'smell and experience of another kind and color'...

Such was the unlucky lot of any trapper in a caravan of horses, as the Barnes Clan began the spring trapping season on the northeastern arm of the Clarks Fork of the Yellowstone. However as they did, they discovered themselves buried in herds of buffalo which had moved south from the northern reaches because of the lingering winter cold and deeper snows found in that region. Every day the trappers were afield along the Yellowstone that spring after 'ice-out', they found their movements hindered by the many herds of buffalo numbering in the hundreds of thousands! Buffalo herds that were so thick and numerous, that any kind of movement by the trappers among them trying to set their traps or check the same along the watered areas, became dangerously problematic because of the possibility of the cantankerous nature of the beasts, especially the short-tempered bulls and stampede issues. Especially when the hungry packs of prairie wolves or the dreaded grizzly bears, fresh out from hibernation and starving, chose to run down and kill a cow or calf buffalo in among the numerous herds and in so doing, causing a stampede of the rest of the near at hand alarmed beasts out across the lands in a panic!

However, the trapping of beaver continued no matter the nearby and sometimes dangerous herds of buffalo. Little by little, the horde of beaver pelts continued stacking up in the storage shed as a finished product or as a pelted out and hooped skin stood up along the wall drying in the trappers' cabin. Soon the 273 beaver pelts trapped during the previous fall season now stored in the storage shed, were joined by another 198 beaver trapped during the spring season and the trapping was not yet over because the beaver were still in their prime and the catching was good!

One morning early when the Barnes Clan were on the upper reaches of their trap line, they noticed and heard many herds of nearby buffalo nervously moving about. Typical of buffalo herd behavior, when one herd stampeded for some reason, other nearby herds upon hearing or seeing a nearby stampede, would stampede as well. Throughout that morning, the men continued hearing herd after herd of buffalo stampeding here and there just because another herd did so. Soon, the constant rumbling sounds of stampeding buffalo's hooves began sounding somewhat like the faraway sounds of thunder during a summer thunderstorm. It now seemed as if the entire countryside in the direction of their cabin holding any herds of buffalo, found them on the move if the sounds of thundering hooves indicated anything unusual going on…

Finished with their daily trap setting, the clan rode back down their previously set trap line checking for any trapped beaver which had swum into the traps after they had been recently set. In so doing, Wallace had to wade out in the icy spring waters and retrieve eight of the highly territorial and curious beaver just freshly caught. However in so doing, twice the men and horses were forced into the water and marshes to escape panicked herds of buffalo 'thundering' nearby and around them! Finished and at the southern end of their newly established trap line, Wallace called it quits and told the men to make ready to head further south to their cabin and call it a day. Besides, they had eight new beaver pelts in one of their packhorse's panniers and they needed to defat, de-flesh and hoop out the same so they would not spoil and could begin the drying process.

With that, Wallace slipped out from his wet breechclout and leggings and back into his much-warmer Linsey-woolsy pants, cinched them up and put both of his pistols back behind his sash just in case their use was called for. Then after walking around out on the now empty prairie for about a half-hour in order to warm up and get some feeling back into his feet and legs after spending his morning in the icy spring waters setting beaver traps, Wallace mounted up with the rest of the men. But as he did, that old nagging 'sixth sense' began bringing feelings of concern into his being. Figuring it was just all of the nearby buffalo activity swirling around him, he dismissed his inner feelings. Soon the men were strung out in a caravan working their ways carefully through the numerous buffalo herds nervously moving into their area as they headed for their cabin and the rest of the work needed when it came to tending to their fresh pelts.

Rounding the last finger of trees a half-mile before the trappers entered their own tree lined meadow leading up to their cabin, Wallace all of a sudden jerked his horse's reins hard right and galloped off into the timber with a wave of his hand indicating the rest of the men were to quickly follow! As he did, his dependable old 'sixth sense' was now flooding back! When all of the clan was safely hidden in the tree line, Wallace pointed out towards the prairie below their cabin with a grim look on his face. With the wondering as to what the hell had just happened, the trappers saw the prairie below their cabin littered with a number of freshly killed buffalo! There were at least eight dead buffalo suspiciously littering the prairie just below the opening in the trees leading up into their meadow and cabin! Now the men realized why the buffalo had been so nervous all morning long with that amount of killing below their cabin and the much-hated smell of blood occurring nearby.

Apparently in the men's absence from their cabin running their trap line, someone or a number of unidentified individuals had entered their home area and initiated a buffalo hunt! In so doing, they had killed a number of buffalo and a combination of the shooting and the intense smell of blood had panicked the herds of buffalo in the area, causing all the other buffalo to react accordingly. Since that morning, the men had worked most of the day under a strong wind coming out from the northern reaches and blowing southward. So it was no wonder the sounds of shooting had been carried further south instead of alerting the men as to the presence of humans shooting near their home area. But where were the shooters since no one was around the buffalo carcasses scattered across the prairie just below the meadow leading to their cabin? That was really strange because buffalo needed little time to bloat and spoil when left un-gutted out in the sun's rays as their shooters had obviously purposely done. When that realization hit all of the men almost at the same time, one could hear the very distinctive sounds of five rifles being cocked among the trappers and made ready for action if such a response was called for.

"Otis, I suspect the shooters of all of those buffalo after killing them, somehow discovered our cabin up at the head of the meadow and instead of caring for all of that meat, rode up to investigate. Then whatever struck their fancy up at our cabin was so good that they just abandoned all those dead buffalo for what they found and no longer interested in them, left them to lie and rot! If that is the case, we have a corral full of valuable horses just waiting to be stolen, a shed full of bundled beaver furs worth several thousand dollars if there is any kind of a beaver market this year and a whole host of other valuable provisions, including a huge rum supply just waiting to be filched. You take Cloud and Feather with you and quietly go up and see what the hell is going on up at our cabin. If my senses are correct, whoever shot all those buffalo below our cabin are now at our cabin taking what does not belong to them. If my suspicions are correct, you need to find out just how many of them are there and who they are. We will wait here out of sight with the horses in the dark timber until your return. Now all of you be careful because I have a 'sixth sense' bad feeling we may have run into a nest of Northern Cheyenne or Blackfeet from the north of us and from all of the dead buffalo scattered about, a passel of them killing sons-a-bitches at that!"

Without a word, Otis slipped from his saddle, hefted his now repaired rifle from his episode with the wolves and beckoned for Cloud and Feather to follow. Soon they had quietly slipped off into the timber with their rifles and disappeared. With that, Wallace and Cedrick led all the rest of their horses deeper into the timber to avoid any casual chance discovery by whoever was possibly at their cabin and then quietly waited for the men's return. About an hour later Otis, Cloud and Feather could be seen working their ways through the trees with grim looks spelled clear across their faces. Wallace and Cedrick dismounted as Otis, Cloud and Feather continued approaching on foot and then waited for what they had to say once they arrived.

"Well, we have very bad news!" said Otis as he placed the butt of his rifle stock down on the dirt and leaned against its barrel with both of his hands clasped around it for support. "We have a camp full of Blackfeet Indians, 13 in number, as identified by Cloud and Feather. We also have what appears to be four French-Canadians from listening to them speak in their broken English and lastly, three unknown and unfortunate fur trappers who are tied up to the fence rails at our horse corral! Obviously the three fur trappers have been captured, taken prisoner and are being held for some damn reason. That camp full of Indians and "Frenchies" have discovered our storage shed and have unloaded all of our bundles of furs and our packhorses' packs and appear to be inclined to steal everything they can get their hands on! Additionally, they have discovered our rum supplies and every one of them are drinking it like it belonged to them. In fact, most of the Indians are already about two-thirds drunk and are staggering around and raising hell like they own the place. Also from all appearances, the Frenchies don't appear to be far behind the Indians in their drunkenness either. It is my guess that the huge supplies of rum that we had are what has taken that group's mind off all the buffalo they killed earlier and the butchering at hand in exchange for "Lady Rum". As for the three unknown trappers, it appears they are in bad shape from all of the beatings they have taken prior to being tied up at our corrals! In fact, the Blackfeet in their drunkenness are beating those three men every time they happen to pass by them celebrating as they are with our rum supplies! There doesn't appear to be anyone left on guard duty and on the lookout for the return of the cabin's owners. I would say once the rum started flowing, everyone got involved in the drinking and no one was left to watch out to make sure the place is secure from our return. Now I don't speak French and don't understand what they are saying very well either. But, all three of us after we sneaked in on them, we swear that the tall skinny one is the leader of the group and several times we heard others off and on calling him The Wolverine! If that is the case, I would bet on a stack of bibles that is the French-Canadian that Vasquez spoke and wrote about in his field reports and the same one who Major Henry told us to be on the lookout for, that evil, Hudson's Bay Company fur stealing son-of-a-bitch when we trapped The Big Muddy some time back. Also, he may be the one and same that escaped in his nightshirt when we got into that shootout some time back when a bunch of those Hudson's Bay Company trappers raided our furs and provisions that first time and made off with them. That being the case, I plan on shooting that son-of-a-bitch square between the eyes so we never have to worry about him in the future," said Otis with a grim look that did not foretell of good things to come for the tall and skinny French-speaking Canadian being called The Wolverine by some of his French-Canadian compatriots...

"I don't know what the hell it is, either Cedrick's cooking or your ugly looks, Otis, but it seems like ever since we have come into this country to trap, we have had a string of bad luck following us every step of the way. First we lost Sterling back on the Platte to the quicksand, then Oliver to that damn tree that had to fall on him just as we were taking care of business with that bunch of six American trappers who made the mistake of stealing all of our traps. Then, there were all those other damn 'wrecks' with the Indians, grizzly bears and French-Canadians that we have had to put up with in between. It just doesn't seem right that all we want to do is trap beaver for a living and instead we find ourselves facing every kind of danger and advisory in between. Now, here we are again, in between a rock and a hard place. Well, this time, 'the good Lord a-willing and the creeks don't get any higher', we are going to finish this mess off once and for all!" said Wallace with more than a determined and 'tired of it all' look on his face.

"The way I see it, we are outnumbered all to hell and facing some personal 'hellfire and brimstone' afore this is all settled and done with no matter how lucky we get. But we Barnes's have never been a clan to run from that which is not right. I say, let them have our rum and drink it until they drop like a log upon the ground in a drunken stupor. That should even up our odds when we show up if that were to happen. In the meantime, we need to free those three trappers tied up at our corral and get them onto our side afore we begin "rendering unto Caesar that which is Caesars" as the Good Book says we are to do. With those three captured trappers, providing they can shoot straight and armed with our extra Indian Trade rifles shooting buck and ball carried in our panniers, that ought to count for something positive happening in our corner 'when push comes to shove'. Then between our eight rifles, ten pistols and tomahawks, even though we are outnumbered, that should carry the day. Especially if the Blackfeet Indians and the French-Canadians are still feeling the effects of drinking our rum, that ought to give us the edge," said Wallace, as he got more 'fired up' over the deadly events now facing the Barnes Clan.

"Alright, here is what we are going to do and if any of you think differently, 'chirp' up now so we all can hear what you have to say. I say we wait until dark then we strike. We load every piece of 'artillery' that we have with buck and ball. That way if we are shooting by firelight, we will have a better chance of dragging all of these bastards down in the first volley. Then we free those three trappers, arm them and let them in on our plan before we begin attacking. We then kill the rest of those sons-a-bitches and we can sell their horses at the next rendezvous. If we were to do that, that should pay us back for all of that damn expensive rum those bastards drank without our say so," said Wallace. Then he looked at the men for any other thoughts they might be harboring regarding what was coming and soon to be upon them, 'come hell or high water'…

Then Otis spoke up in a calm and quiet tone of voice saying, "Don't any of you bastards shoot that Frenchie called The Wolverine. He is mine and if I catch any of you shooting at him, when this is all settled and done and I am still alive, you will have to answer to me."

It was at that very moment in time that the luck of the Irish held for the Barnes Clan. A cold breath of wind rustled through the timber and with it, a single wet snowflake prophetically landed on Otis's nose! Looking up, the clan could see that in all of the intensity of the moment at hand, every one of them had failed to earlier look skyward so they could read the spring weather and any turns it might take. Had they done so, they would have seen the oncoming dark clouds of a spring snowstorm of heavy wet snow coming their way. A heavy and wet spring snow that would more than cover their sneaking around, releasing the three captured trappers and executing their battle plan under the cover of darkness and now falling snows...

That night, as the happy-sounding noises coming from the trappers' cabin told anyone listening nearby that the rum-soaked party was still going on inside while the spring snowstorm was on going outside, three silent figures sneaked up behind the three trappers left outside to die from exposure still tied to the corral. Simultaneously, the hands of Otis, Cloud and Feather wrapped around the three trappers' mouths from out of the darkness precluding any of them from yelling out in surprise or fear and warning the 'party' going on inside their cabin. Then with whispered voices in each tied up trappers' ear letting them know that the hands covering their faces belonged to friends, the men were then cut down and quietly led away and out of sight. Twenty minutes later the three still amazed trappers found themselves alongside the rest of the Barnes Clan by a small fire in the dark timber eating strips of jerky and getting some warmth back into their bodies and their physical and mental strength back for what was soon to come.

Once the three just released trappers had recovered somewhat and had their wits about them, Wallace made the introductions all around and explained why they were there and ready to strike at those living it up in their warm cabin and drinking stolen rum. Then the three trappers, who remembered the Barnes Clan members from the last rendezvous, told their sad story of being ambushed while out running their trap line in the distant Wind River Mountain Range and being captured by the horde of Blackfeet Indians and four French-Canadians. They also explained that their group of trappers once numbered six men but the Indians had killed the other three trappers outright in cold blood when they had been initially captured. It didn't take long to see that those three remaining trappers 'thirsted' for revenge over what had happened to them and their lifelong friends and trapping partners...

Later that night as the wet spring snows continued falling heavily, the several inches of freshly fallen snows hid any sounds the group of eight trappers were making as they warily circled the cabin still resounding to the sounds of many men having a drunken good time. That was when circumstances put Wallace's attack plan into deadly motion. About then three Indians exited the cabin, staggered out into the front yard and began urinating and happily talking in their tongue all at once. All three Indians died silently from being 'tomahawked' in the middle of their "Ti-Pee"... With that, the odds against the eight determined trappers from the 'new' Barnes Clan had been reduced by three Indians with more to come. The 'more to come' was soon in the offing, as three more Indians and one French-Canadian exited the front door of the cabin, laughing and talking all at once. All of them died when Otis, Cloud and Feather, with slashing tomahawks, did to them what they had done earlier when attacked by wolves...

It was then that the decision was made before the now seven dead men would be missed, that the party inside the cabin would be terminated along with the remaining celebrants! Bunching up quietly at the front door and led by Wallace, Otis, Cedrick, Cloud and Feather, the men threw open the front door to their cabin and to the total surprise of the remaining eight men left inside standing (two Indians were laid out on the floor having passed out from the rum), quickly streamed into the cabin! Then before the drunken celebrants could react and go for their weapons, ten leveled pistols loaded with buck and ball at distances less than twelve feet belched clouds of white smoke, flame, hot lead and timely death, felling the eight drunken men like a 'swath of hay in front of a sickle'! In an instant, the cabin which initially smelled of body odor mixed with the sweet smell of rum when the Barnes Clan had barged in and begun shooting, was now transfixed to the rafters with a dense cloud of white black powder smoke so thick one could hardly see! Thereupon according to Wallace's plan, the five men quickly exited the cabin leaving the front door wide open and then they waited outside to see if any survivors came spilling out through the clouds of black powder smoke. Moments later two more drunken Indians with rifles in hand, staggered out the door's opening, only to be cut down with so much buck and ball, that the air was filled with flying chunks of tissue from the humans and wood chips blown off from the outside walls of the cabin! Suffice to say, the two drunken Indians were dead before they hit the ground and when they joined their 'Cloud People', even their mothers would not have recognized their shot all to hell bodies caused by eight rapidly firing rifles shooting deadly buck and ball from just ten feet away into just two Indians...

Then once quickly reloaded, the Barnes Clan entered the still black powder smoke-filled cabin one more time and began dragging out the bodies one by one into the front yard. There they were laid into a gruesome blown all to hell pile until the cabin had been cleared of such bloodied 'trash'. As for the French-Canadian called The Wolverine by his outlaw compatriots, his badly shot up body was dragged out last with at least seven bullet holes in his head and torso from the wall of buck and ball that had come his and the others way during the initial fusillade! Never again would The Wolverine roam the frontier preying on those unsuspecting trappers encountered around him. According to Vasquez's earlier field notes, The Wolverine was the best and most deadly shooter in all of Canada. However, that would be something that was pretty hard for him to do in the future in his present shot all to hell physical condition...

That night after the acrid black powder smoke had finally sufficiently cleared from the men's cabin, they went inside where coffee was made and Cedrick made his Dutch oven biscuits in their fireplace for the men since they hadn't eaten in many hours. Then aside from the stink of death, heavy smell of sweat, black powder, blood and urine spilled from some of the men who had so violently died earlier in the evening that their bladders had let loose, the men curled up in their warm cabin and found some welcome sleep out from the snowstorm after a long day afield that had ended in nothing short of extreme emotion...

The next morning as Cedrick made the men's breakfast, the remaining group of trappers fleshed out and hooped the beaver pelts trapped by the Barnes Clan from the day before. Then the men were treated to hot coffee and Cedrick's special Dutch oven biscuits made with ample helpings of raisins, brown sugar and cinnamon throughout. Later that morning, the three remaining trappers each taking two Indian horses apiece loaded with their previously stolen provisions, mounted up and began their return to their cabin and trap line located in the distant Wind River Mountain Range. However, before they left, they agreed to meet at the rendezvous coming up and tip a few cups of rum in celebration of those trappers from the Barnes Clan who had rescued them from sure death at the hands of the Blackfeet, The Wolverine and his fellow French-Canadians. With a wave of their hands, those three trappers left the scene of death as the Barnes Clan then dragged the dead Blackfeet Indians and French-Canadians off and away down by the beaver ponds where all the dead buffalo, now bloated, lay and left them for the critters of the land and air to enjoy…

Following the disposal of the bodies, the Barnes Clan made for their trap line, removed the dead beaver and reset their traps in the beaver rich area like nothing out of the ordinary had just occurred. On the way back, Otis shot a cow buffalo and it was butchered on the spot. Later when the men arrived back at their camp, Cedrick headed for his beloved firepit to begin supper preparations. As it was, snow on the ground or not, the men had decided to eat outside that evening because their cabin still smelled heavily of sweat, blood, urine, black powder and the lingering odor of the smell of death created by the human body when it realizes its death is close at hand and exudes its own personal and unique smell of death…

After hanging the buffalo's quarters from their meat poles, the men took their wash pans, filled them with heated water and headed for their cabin. There they spent the remainder of the day fleshing out their pelts from the day's catch on their trap line and washing the blood splatters off the walls and floor of their cabin. They also took time to scrub the still pungent smelling urine stains off their dirt floor with scrubbing hands full of ashes removed from their outside firepit and brought into the cabin in their wash pans. Then that ash and waste dirt from the cabin's floor was scooped up, taken outside and sprinkled in the snow off to one side of their cabin to let nature and the sunlight do its cleansing work. That evening after eating their supper outside in the cold night air, the men retreated to their cabin whereupon everyone had a pipe full of their pungent James River smoking tobacco. By the time the men slipped into their sleeping furs that evening, the pungent smell of smoking tobacco heavily permeated the air in the cabin overriding the remaining man smells of blood, urine and the stench of death. With that, the Barnes Clan found they were 'home' once again…

CHAPTER TEN

FREE TRAPPERS!

FOR THE REST OF THAT SPRING trapping season until the beaver went out of prime, the Barnes Clan hard-trapped the northeastern section of the Clarks Fork of the Yellowstone without any further problems from 'man nor beast'. About the time the beaver went out of their prime, the Barnes Clan found that they had thoroughly trapped out the beaver from that section of the Clarks Fork and had added another 35 beaver to their spring trappings. With that in mind and like Wallace had planned earlier, it was now time to abandon their cabin and move on to new beaver trapping grounds since they had trapped out that portion of the Clarks Fork of the Yellowstone. Then while attending the upcoming rendezvous at Malachite's Big Hole in the Green River Valley and discussing new beaver trapping areas with the likes of Jim Bridger, the clan would decide where they were heading for next, come the fall beaver trapping season.

Come the first few days of June found the Barnes Clan in a flurry of activity around their cabin. The first order of business for the Barnes Clan was the very important job of packing and bundling the remainder of their beaver and wolf furs for travel to the upcoming rendezvous. That in mind, the men finished bundling up the 273 furs taken during the fall trapping season and the 198 and last 35 beaver pelts taken last in the spring trapping season, for a total of 506 beaver taken! In a word, the men figured they now had a small fortune in beaver skins! Secondly, they had trapped a total of 33 wolves in the fall and winter months and an additional 11 animals in the late spring for a grand total of 44 wolves, or the most the Barnes Clan had ever trapped to date! Those pelts they bundled and made ready for the packhorses to carry back to the upcoming rendezvous as well.

Then they had 15 additional riding and packhorses they had acquired in the fatal shootout with the six trap-robbing trappers. Additionally, they had those six trappers' annual provisions purchased at the rendezvous that the Barnes Clan had acquired after the shootout. As additional 'riches', the Barnes Clan were now the possessors of 20 horses and mules acquired from the 13

Blackfeet Indians and four French-Canadians, six of which were given back to the three trappers the Indians and French-Canadians had captured earlier. So as it now stood, the Barnes Clan in addition to their own horse herd of 20 animals, counting Cloud and Feather's, between the dead six trap-robbing trappers and the 13 Blackfeet Indians and four French-Canadian trappers and outlaws, they were the proud possessors of an additional 29 valuable horses and mules! Twenty-nine horses and mules not needed by the Barnes Clan and would be sold as replacement livestock to other less fortunate trappers once at the rendezvous in the Green River Valley. *Wallace figured the amount of money collected from selling their extra horses, mules, riding saddles, pack saddles and firearms would more than cover paying for all of their needed provisions for the coming fall and spring trapping season and then some! Then any monies generated from the sale of their beaver and wolf hides would be pure profit to be held and used someday when all of the brothers returned home to Missouri to purchase their new farm, livestock and needed farming implements! That was if the good Lord was willing for such an event to ever take place...*

Last but certainly not least, the Barnes Clan was the proud possessor of all the saddles, pack saddles, rifles and pistols taken from the six now dead trap-robbing trappers and from the 17 now dead Blackfeet and French-Canadians! No matter how one looked at that stockpile of goods, they would move fast once offered at the upcoming rendezvous to less fortunate trappers in need of replacement weapons or tack. Additionally, there would be those buyers from the usual numbers of peaceful Indians surrounding any given rendezvous who also had need for weapons and riding gear of any kind...

In all the preparations for leaving their cabin one last time, Cedrick made sure all of his cooking equipment was carefully packed, as well as all of the cooking implements they had acquired from the six trap robbing trappers dispatched earlier. That way there would be no need to purchase any additional cooking implements for future use which were sold by their weights and very expensive to procure at any trading post or rendezvous.

By the end of that first week in June, the Barnes Clan was in the final process of making ready to leave. They had been up way before daylight in order to get all of their goods and provisions packed on their packhorses. Finally, all that remained to be packed was Cedrick's small amount of cooking gear after being used in making all the men a huge breakfast of coffee, biscuits and staked buffalo meat because no one knew when the next meal would be out along the trail. Additionally, every man would be needed to maintain order in their long heavily loaded pack string not to mention their herd of loose horses and mules to be herded along with the rest of the Barnes Clan's extra horses. Finally breakfast was done, the cooking equipment cleaned up and packed and after one last look around to make sure nothing of value was left behind, Wallace propped open the door to their cabin. *That way he figured if a grizzly bear wanted to make the cabin his new home, he wouldn't have to rip off the front door in order to enter. Also, if another group of trappers happened on the scene, they would have a good cabin in which to live or use in order to get out from under the effects of a nasty storm. So, the cabin was left habitable for either man or beast, depending upon who got there 'firstest with the mostest'.*

Then with one last look around at what had been their home for several fur trapping seasons and some rather rough, deadly and surprising times, Wallace mounted his horse and adjusted the rifle lying across his lap for its quick use should the need arise. Then Wallace nodded to Cloud and Feather to once again lead the way across the soon to be traveled Absaroka Range, the Wind River Range and down into the upper reaches of the Green River Valley en route Malachite's Big Hole located on the Henry's Fork of the Green River between the confluences of Burnt Fork and Birch Creek. The site's location of the coming rendezvous as had been determined by all of the trappers at the previous rendezvous to be held sometime during the summer months when the beaver were out of 'prime' and the supply train carrying all of the much-needed provisions for the coming trapping seasons arrived from its month's long trip from St. Louis.

Throughout a number of the following days of June, the Barnes Clan was safely led by Spotted Feather and White Cloud who in their earlier days had lived in those areas, up, over and through the Absaroka and Wind River Ranges and into the upper reaches of the fabled Green River Valley. Throughout their rugged and sometimes dangerous trip, the trappers were once again amazed at not only the geographic beauty surrounding them upon crossing over the two stunning mountain ranges but the absolute wealth of natural resources such mountainous areas possessed! Every stream crossed was crystal clear, cold and full of darting piscatorial 'silver streaks' when one approached their streambanks and cast their shadows across the waters. As for the timbered areas, they were full of blue grouse at almost every turn in the trail, living up to their name "Fool Grouse" for letting man get so dangerously close at times before they flew. Then there was the magnificent, huge bodied moose, the largest member of the deer family, numerous grand elk, dainty mule deer, black bear by the score, and uncomfortable numbers of grizzly bears, the most ferocious predator in the area, all of which were never far from daily view! Every marshy area crossed was full of molting ducks and geese, not to mention river otter, mink and beaver dotting the area. Truly, that portion of America that the Barnes Clan, Spotted Feather and White Cloud were traversing through had been especially made by the Hands of God for all of those who took the time to see and enjoy!

Into the upper reaches of the Green River Valley rode the men only to be confronted by vast herds of peacefully grazing buffalo, small groups of the speedsters of the Plains, namely the dainty prong-horn antelope, mule deer spotted throughout the brushy draws and sagebrush covered rims, and the occasional roaming and always hungry grizzly bear. Additionally, while traveling across numerous sagebrush flats, the Barnes Clan were confronted with numerous flocks of greater sage grouse, with some flocks numbering 200 or more when they rose up into the air in alarm over the arriving trappers and their large caravan of hors-es and mules! Also dotted throughout the valley were strings of other just arriving trappers and groups of friendly Indians heading in the same direction as the Barnes Clan, namely Malachite's Big Hole, site of the 1826 Rendezvous, located in the Green River Valley.

Finally arriving at the rendezvous location, the Barnes Clan observed scores of milling about and setting up their campsites trappers and Indians as they settled in for the big event soon to come. Eager to find a good campsite, Wallace led his group to the river's side and under a densely wooded grove of cottonwoods. There as Cedrick began establishing the men's campsite, the rest gathered in their horses and mules and began hobbling and picketing all of them before they could wander off and mix in with other loose herds of livestock owned by other trappers and the still flocking into the area friendly Indians' herds of horses as well. Once their campsite had been established, the men collectively gathered up every nearby stick of driftwood they could find along the high water mark of the river and every handy dry buffalo 'chip' they could find as well for fuel for their campfire. Those articles were then stacked alongside Cedrick's newly established firepit and then the men pitched their 'Possibles' and sleeping furs under the cottonwoods, as other trappers and Indians continued streaming into the area on a daily basis looking for campsites as well. However, the men stacked their bundles of furs close in to their campsite where they could be closely watched and then all the saddles and pack saddles were stacked under their stand of cottonwoods in order to remain dry in case of a surprise summer afternoon thunderstorm. Stacking their cooking and eating provisions near their firepit, the men then laid all of the firearms they had seized in their battles with the six trappers and the Blackfeet and French-Canadians under their sleeping furs where they would be out of sight from any nearby wandering Indian or trapper who lacked such firepower and possibly possessed a set of 'light' fingers, a bad heart and greedy eyes...

Within a few days the immediate area around their campsite was soon crowded with other trappers who were friends of the Barnes Clan, as well as the three trappers they had rescued earlier from capture by the murdering devils from the Blackfeet Nation and their four French-Canadian outlaw counterparts. Fortunately, the Barnes Clan still had three unopened kegs of rum. Rum that they had purchased at an earlier rendezvous and the remaining two unopened kegs of rum from the six trap-stealing trappers they had so handily dispatched the night Oliver was killed by a 'happenstance' falling tree just as they were 'settling up their score'. Other than that, all the rest of their rum had been swilled down by the Barnes Clan earlier in the year and the 13 Blackfeet Indians and the four French-Canadians the evening they had discovered the open Barnes Clan's cabin and had 'made themselves right at home'... However, realizing with the horses, bundles of beaver pelts and extra firearms 'wealth' they now possessed, they could buy all the rum they wanted, one of their remaining kegs of rum was opened for their closest of friends and happily shared among their many, less well-off fellow trapper friends who were low on such supplies of the much-favored rum.

Several days later on July the 1st, General Ashley arrived with a long mule pack train full of supplies and being all business because he was still facing an 80-plus-day return trip back to St. Louis before 'the snows flew', the selling of pelts and the purchasing of the coming year's provisions began almost immediately! Once General Ashley's pack strings were unloaded and he was set up for business around their wagons and horses, there was a hurried rush to sell their hard won furs by the trappers and friendly Indians gathered around the rendezvous campsite... Loading up all of their horses with their furs and leaving Cedrick back at camp to watch over their extra horse and mule herd as well as their hidden cache of firearms, the rest of the Barnes Clan stood in line waiting their turn to sell their furs and re-provision for the coming fall and spring trapping seasons.

It was then that Wallace realized what a 'crush of men' were gathered to sell their furs and re-provision for the coming trapping seasons. Standing there in line waiting his turn to trade, Wallace soon learned there was almost 100 company contract trappers gathered there to settle up with General Ashley. Additionally, there were almost 30 deserters from the Hudson's Bay Company ready to trade with anyone who had some provisions for trade. Next in line were 13 men with Etienne Provost, a trapper from further to the west looking for supplies as well. Then there were seven men with Jed Smith wanting to trade, about 25 men with a man named John

Weber needing to trade and reprovision, and a large number of friendly Indians desiring to trade and pick up their share of the white man's provisions as well! All in all, a gaily happy crowd of trappers and traders ready to sell everything they had spent a year working on to accumulate. And in so doing, intending to 'blow the lot' over a few days of wild celebration over another successful year afield. A successful year afield 'remaining above the ground' with a full head of hair and not being part of a grizzly bear scat somewhere in the forest or out on the prairie…

Suffice to say, the trading of furs and re-provisioning rush was nothing short of a mad scramble! A mad scramble especially when the trappers learned that General Ashley had failed to bring along any rum or whiskey, and WAS ONLY GOING TO BE THERE ONE DAY SELLING HIS GOODS BROUGHT IN FROM ST. LOUIS! ALL OF THAT GOING ON WHILE THE FREE TRAPPERS WERE GIVEN $5 PER POUND FOR THEIR BEAVER PELTS WHILE THE CONTRACT TRAPPERS WORKING FOR GENERAL ASHLEY AND THE AMERICAN FUR COMPANY, AS REQUIRED BY THE CONTRACTS SUCH MEN HAD SIGNED IN 1822, ONLY RECEIVED $3 PER POUND FOR THEIR BEAVER! Suffice to say, the 'Irish' was up in Otis and Wallace over the inherently unfair trading practices and treatment given the company men! Otis, the fighter of the bunch, upon hearing how disadvantaged they were, was ready to go to 'war'! However, Wallace settled Otis down and told him to begin acquiring the few provisions they would need for the coming trapping seasons and take Feather and Cloud with him so they could get their needed share as quickly as possible since Ashley was only going to be there for one day! However, Wallace cautioned Otis to buy their needed supplies with the fact in mind they still had many provisions left over from the year before, as well as the lot of provisions from the six trappers they had run to ground for stealing all of their traps.

Then looking at his older brother more closely, Otis realized that Wallace had a sly plan 'up his sleeve' that would soon rectify the unfair trading practices put into play by the greedy General Ashley! With that plan in the back of his mind, Wallace sold their half-contract share of their 506 beaver at $3 per pound or for $1,518, and their 44 wolf furs at $20 each for a total of $880, for a grand total of $2,398 in trade, without a word of dissent over the prices paid. Then as the Barnes Clan soon discovered, they had to pay a very steep price for everything they needed to purchase at Mountain Prices! As Otis, Feather and Cloud carefully looked over the goods they planned on purchasing, they quickly discovered that General Ashley was charging the company trappers prices that were at least 1,000% over what the same goods cost the general earlier in

St. Louis! With that in mind, the Barnes Clan only purchased about $350 worth of powder, flints, lead pigs, flour, beans, rice, jugs of honey, bear grease and the like. With that, they accepted a Letter of Credit from General Ashley to be redeemed at the American Fur Company's house of business in St. Louis for $2,048, which was slipped into Wallace's saddle bag for later redemption, when they were through with the risky and many times dangerous business of fur trapping and were in the mood to buy some land and settle down.

Then while Otis, Feather and Cloud were quickly gathering up their needed supplies, Wallace, now knowing that the rendezvous would be over by the next day, rode back to their campsite. Then he had Cedrick quickly go about the Indian and trappers' camps making it known that they had horses and mules for sale, as well as a number of Lancaster flintlocks, Indian Trade rifles and pistols. Riding back to camp somewhat later, Cedrick saw that Wallace was almost overwhelmed by anxious extra horse and mule buyers, not to mention associated tack for those animals! Hurrying into camp, he was soon assisting his older brother with the horse and mule sales along with the selling of their extra riding and packing gear needed to accompany those horse and mule sales.

About then, Otis, Feather and Cloud rode back into camp with their pack animals loaded with

provisions and seeing the crowd of eager buyers, tied off their livestock out of the way in their
grove of cottonwood trees and joined right in the
selling frenzy of horses, mules, rifles, pistols, riding and packing gear! By early afternoon, a fraz-
zled group of Barnes men were arrayed around
their campfire talking over the results of their
firearms, tack and livestock sales. As it turned
out, they had sold all the extra livestock, rifles
and pistols that they did not need for a carefully
selected mound of Made Beaver pelts!

Then leaving Cedrick to guard their camp
once again, Wallace, Otis, Cloud and Feather
mounted their horses and leading their loaded
pack animals with those furs just traded for the
horses and weapons, they headed once again
for the company's trading site. After standing in
line once again, it was finally their turn to trade
in their recently acquired from other trappers
Made Beaver to the Company Clerks and graders. When the main Company Clerk attempted to
reduce the value of that number of those pelts by
half, recognizing Wallace and clan as Company
Trappers, Wallace stepped in and advised that
load of beaver pelts was not part of what they
had trapped but what they had just traded their
extra horses, mules and guns for. Ignoring what
Wallace had advised, the Company Clerk still
recognizing the Barnes Clan as part of their
company's trappers from the earlier 1822 day
of sign-up, stubbornly shook his head and once

again began sorting out half of the pelts into the company's pile as per the Barnes's earlier signed contracts with the American Fur Company! That was when the Company Clerk found himself facing four cocked rifles leveled at his belly by the Barnes Clan!

"Whoa, hold her right there!" said General Ashley who was overseeing the fur exchanges and sales. "There is no need for that kind of behavior," he continued, as he came running over to get a handle on things before any shooting started over a disagreement over the furs being presented for sale and the prices to be paid.

Confronting the 'hoo-rah' between the Barnes Clan and the company fur buyer, General Ashley said, "What the hell is the matter with you Barnes's? Long as I am around, there will be no need for gunplay!"

"There is when your company man attempts to steal our furs," said Wallace quietly and in a cold tone of voice not to be misunderstood...

"What the hell do you mean? You boys full well know whatever you trap, the company gets half and you get to keep the other half," said General Ashley.

"Not half of these particular furs," uttered a now tight-jawed Wallace staring back at the General with icy cold eyes. "Those particular furs we rightly came by in trading our extra horses, mules, rifles, pistols, saddles and pack gear to other than company trappers from these other groups of attendees at this rendezvous. Free Trappers and other groups of independent trappers who had a need for such things in return for the equal value of their furs at the Free Trapper's prices of $5 per pound that you are offering."

"That don't make it right," said General Ashley. "The furs they traded you for those items you mentioned rightly belong to the company by virtue of the fact that we are the only buyer here. Therefore you Barnes's being company trappers, owe one-half of such furs to us as per the contracts you all signed way back in the early spring of '22 with Major Henry and the fact that we are the only fur buyers at the rendezvous."

"They traded fair and square for our goods at the prices we quoted for what they purchased and as it now stands, those furs are rightly ours! I am here this afternoon to sell these furs at the same prices you are providing the Free Trappers, namely $5 per pound for their beaver," said Wallace like a man on a mission, **and truth be known, he was!**

"As I said earlier, if that is the way you are going to be, we will buy them alright but at only $3 per pound for your beaver skins, same as before when you sold your first batch of furs to us earlier in the day," said General Ashley firmly.

"No, I don't think so. Those earlier furs sold to the American Fur Company were to honor our original contract just in case there was some disagreement over what constituted a three-year contract period of time. But since these latest furs came from Free Trappers and the other attending trappers from different groups that we know who are here today, we want Free Trapper prices," quietly said Wallace, "and that is $5 per pound or we will not be interested in selling them. If we have to, we will just trap further north this next trapping season and then take all of our furs to Canada and trade them to the Hudson's Bay Company!"

About then Jed Smith, Jim Bridger, the three trappers that the Barnes Clan had rescued from the Blackfeet and the Frenchies, and another dozen men overhearing the entire somewhat heated conversation between the Company Clerks, General Ashley and Wallace Barnes, began walking forward. As they did, they made it plain they supported the Barnes Clan with their voices and their argument for higher prices for their unusually acquired stocks of valuable Made Beaver!

"You Barnes's being company trappers and all, I can't support any higher prices than what was offered to you boys earlier," stubbornly continued General Ashley. "To do otherwise would cause an uprising among all the rest of the trappers wanting to be paid higher prices for their furs as well, and that is not something I can support in light of all the risks I take in getting provisions to you men all the way here from St. Louis and my furs safely back to our fur house."

"Then you are now looking at Free Trappers

this afternoon, as God is my witness," said a steely voiced Wallace, who among the Barnes Clan was known as being as stubborn as a blacksmith's anvil was 'heavy and hard'...

"The group of you minus them two damn 'Injuns' signed a contract with me saying you would be company trappers and abide by our rules," said a getting more and more frustrated General Ashley, as he faced off with what he considered a minor revolt in the making and a loss of money and face if he relented in the face of Wallace's argument! Little did General Ashley realize that Wallace was quietly holding a hand of "Aces and Eights"!

"This is the frontier where a man is only as good as his word, handshake and where fair is fair. My brothers and I have slaved under your rules for three years now and you have unfairly profited for that period of time over our hard work and risk to our way of thinking. There will be no more of that kind of unfair treatment. Either you pay us as the Free Trappers we have now just become or you cannot have any of our furs," said Wallace firmly, and the tone and tenor of his voice made it clear that he was through arguing over the sale of the furs unless things were set right at the $5 a pound level for all the beaver furs now being offered for sale...

About then General Ashley seeing a major altercation in the making, stepped forward, took the Company Clerk by his shoulders and moved him back away from the confrontation growing uglier by the minute. Then for the longest time he just glowered at the Barnes Clan members standing defiantly before him, like they were spoiled children and needed to be treated as such!

That was when Wallace quietly said something to Otis and he immediately left. Minutes later Otis returned after retrieving several crumpled pieces of worn papers from Wallace's saddlebag and handed those pieces of paper to Wallace. Taking those papers, unfolding and handing them to the general, Wallace quietly but firmly said, "The terms and conditions of your contract calls for one, two or three-year obligations. My brothers and I signed up for three years and those three years have more than passed. Far as I am concerned, you can now take these contracts that all of us signed and use it for 'ass-wipe'!" quietly said Wallace. With those words, Wallace let the papers fall to the ground since he was correct and for the last three-plus years, he and his brothers had obligingly slaved under the terms and conditions of those contracts, had met their obligations and now they were done as American Fur Company, Company Contract Trappers... Like Wallace had known earlier, he held a hand full of 'Aces and Eights'...

Without picking up the contracts and reading them, figuring most Mountain Men were illiterate and could not read what they had signed anyway, the general quickly came to the realization that

Wallace was an educated man who could read and was probably more than right regarding his contract's three-year terms of conditions. Having his bluff called, General Ashley said, "Clerk, pay this here "Free Trapper" what he has coming based on the count and grade of the furs he has for sale at the $5 per pound rate. Not a dollar more or less mind you when it comes to settling up with these men over their furs! I also suggest these furs be graded more than fairly unless you want to be confronted once again with their four rifles..." With those words, the general whirled and left the confrontation to go away and settle itself based on his orders given to the American Fur Company's Company Clerk.

"Well, you heard the general. Grade these furs and be on with it," said Wallace to the Company Clerk standing there with his mouth agape over the decision the general had just made on the spot without even looking at the contracts still lying on the ground! With that, a fuming general, more interested in making money to further his future political career than doing what was right at the rendezvous, left the front of the line and headed for another confrontation igniting between a group of mad fur trappers and another Company fur grader...

One hour later after the counting and grading of the Barnes's furs was done, Wallace was handed an American Fur Company Letter of Credit for $2,140! That coupled with his previous

Letter of Credit and the sales of firearms, tack and extra horses for an additional amount meant the Barnes Clan had amassed a small fortune for that day and age of a total of $4,188! That second Letter of Credit went into Wallace's saddlebags as well, making their ultimate dream of becoming gentlemen farmers back in the State of Missouri when they were through with the fur trapping business just one step closer to fruition!

(Author's Note: Most current-day historians through their research of trappers' journals and other historical documents, have estimated that the majority of fur trappers on the frontier from around 1807-1840, only remained in the fur trapping business for a period of approximately of 2.7 years. After that most trappers quit the business, went broke, disappeared never to be heard from again, or had 'gone under' from a horse wreck, speeding lead ball, a stone or steel-tipped arrow point, drowning, freezing to death, or died in the jaws of a critter like a grizzly bear...)

The very next day, General Ashley and his long and heavily loaded mule train and company traders began their almost 80-day trek back to St. Louis and their company fur house with about $60,000 in furs. That was also the second day the Barnes Clan celebrated with a special supper of roasted buffalo meat, beans, coffee and Cedrick's special biscuits filled with raisins, chopped apples (dried and soaked) covered with brown sugar and cinnamon as Free Trappers!

July 2nd was also the last day of the one-day 1826 Rendezvous, as many of the trappers began heading back into the 'wilds' and another lonely year roaming the frontier's waterways looking for the riches offered by a rapidly diminishing in numbers furry rodent called a beaver...

(Author's Note: To this day, some 200-plus years later as these words are committed to print, beaver numbers have never returned to their days of greatness when it came to their overall population numbers. As an indication of some of the numbers of beaver taken, earlier historical research discovered that several steamboats during the fur trade era leaving the Bismarck, North Dakota, area, upon striking floating logs or unseen sandbars, sank while transporting over 900,000 beaver pelts in each instance when they went to the bottom of the river! Like the buffalo, the beaver never came back to their former greatness in numbers...)

CHAPTER ELEVEN

JIM BRIDGER AND TRAPPING THE "HAMS"

SEVERAL OLD FRIENDS like Jim Bridger and Jedidiah Smith hung back at the last rendezvous site with the Barnes Clan in order to give their livestock a couple more days of grazing before they hit the trail once again on the way to their next trapping ground selections. As a means of protection and the fact that Cedrick was such a good cook, several groups of trappers banded together and camped with the Barnes Clan in their grove of cottonwood trees. Being that through an oversight, General Ashley forgot to bring any whiskey or rum to the rendezvous, the Barnes Clan and an unfinished keg of rum once again quickly became a favorite gathering spot for the likes of Bridger, Smith, Sublette, Jackson, Harlan Waugh, and "Bear Scat" Sutta.

One evening around the campfire after a supper of antelope steaks, pinto beans with rice, wild onions and some of Cedrick's special biscuits slathered with honey from a jug purchased at the rendezvous, Bridger spoke up. "Say, you Barnes's, where you be a-going next?"

"Don't rightly know as of yet," said Wallace, "but somewhere to our south and west so we be closer to the site of the trapper designated 1827 Rendezvous near Bear Lake and a mess of beaver if we had our druthers. That way we won't have to travel so far to the next rendezvous. But fact of the matter is, we had hoped some of our friends would have some suggestions where there would be good beaver trapping away from Indians on the prod and away from those damn Frenchies running with the Hudson's Bay Fur Company. Seems like we have stumbled upon way more than our fair share of bad luck these last few years between mean-assed grizzly bears, thieving trap robbers and Indians upset over our presence in their neck of the woods. By now, it is our wish to avoid any more such encounters in the future if that is at all possible."

"Sounds like me. I be a-going to the west to trap over on the Salt River Range for this next go around. There be one hell of a good spot just south where I will be a-trapping called the Hams River, if you boys be interested. I traveled over that country way back in '23 and always thought of a-going back there to try my luck someday.

However, my insides are a-telling me to go west this time so I will be also closer to the next rendezvous and can catch a mess of them beaver all at the same time in the Salt River country," said Bridger, as he refilled his pipe once more and lit it with a live coal taken from the fire. Taking a few deep puffs on his pipe, Bridger continued saying, "Say, 'how's' about your bunch following me when I head west from here and when it be time for me to turn and head north to the Salt River country where I want to trap come this fall, you boys can split off and head south to the Hams River country? Then come next summer, me and my boys can head south to the Hams country, hook up with you lads and the two groups of us can travel to the rendezvous over at Bear Lake. I know where that spot is and by doing it that-a-way, we can have the extra protection all of our guns will have when going through some of that dangerous Indian country. Having been there afore, I can draw you fellows a map that would take you right to them Hams River trapping grounds so close that you kin spit in it. What do you boys have to say about 'them apples'?"

For the longest time, Wallace and Otis had been talking about trapping further to the southwest in order to be closer to the previously decided upon 1827 Rendezvous site at a place near what was called "Bear Lake." They also both knew Bridger's reputation for his extensive wandering all through the frontier and his remarkable memory when it came to the lay of the land, its overall geography and his uncanny ability to find his way back into places previously visited. With that in mind and having watched his brother's facial expressions and those from Cloud and Feather showing looks of extreme interest in what Bridger was suggesting Wallace figured he already had his group's answer. Knowing his brothers that well and feeling that they were now showing an interest in what Bridger was suggesting albeit not really saying so, Wallace replied, "I think what you have just suggested is of interest to me, my brothers, Cloud and Feather. What say tomorrow after supper we sit down and discuss the traveling particulars, especially the suggestion that when you turn north to your trapping grounds, you draw us a map on how to get to the Hams River so we don't go up and get ourselves lost out in the middle of nowhere in this big country of ours."

The following evening after supper, Jim Bridger and his trapping partners got together with the Barnes Clan for discussions on their upcoming trips to their fall trapping grounds. Lengthy discussions followed and by the time of their parting later that evening, a traveling together decision had been made, a date of departure decided upon and the route of travel planned out. Two days later found a long caravan of trappers heading to the southwest led by the venerable Jim Bridger, Mountain Man and "Man of the Mountains".

Several days later of slow traveling brought the travelers deep within the Salt River Range. Their last evening together as friends, fellow travelers and fur trappers, found the men gathered around the campfire as Cedrick prepared supper for the entire group of men. There Jim Bridger sat down on a log and drew Wallace a map showing his next route of travel that would take him from their current location to the Hams River country and the site of the Barnes Clan's fall trapping enterprise. In celebration of that moment in time, the group of trappers drained the remaining rum from one of their wooden kegs.

The following morning with a wave of fare-well by both parties and an understanding they would meet later in the spring, the trappers parted company with Jim Bridger's party heading north into the Salt River country for a season of beaver trapping and the Barnes Clan heading to the south to the Hams River country and for what fortune, good or bad, awaited them as fur trappers in that neck of the woods. Traveling south along the Hams River, Wallace stopped the clan almost due east of where he figured from Bridger's map sat Bear Lake further to the west. There he quietly sat on his horse surveying the surrounding area. All along the Hams River were numerous signs of extensive beaver activity. Conical shaped beaver houses abounded in the ponded areas, stick and mud dams stitched across the various waterways, and along the watered banks were signs of much beaver activity in felled trees and trees partially felled. Sitting there in the afternoon's cool, Wallace thought, *Bridger had been right in his assessments of the country they now inhabited. The country was indeed full of much beaver sign, Indian sign had been lacking, there was horse feed a-plenty, that area was shielded by many small mountain ranges from the worst of the weather that came predominantly from out of the northwest, and the land and timber lent itself to making a good home for the fall and spring beaver trapping seasons. Yes, Bridger sure knew about the land he had extensively traveled and seemed to forget no details related to what he had seen!*

Turning in his saddle and facing the rest of the group quietly sitting on their horses, Wallace said, "I suggest we make our camp over in that stand of timber under that low ridge to our west. From the looks of that wet meadow up at the head of that long draw, I can see that the area is well watered and there is good sized timber close at hand for building our cabin. The way I see it, we can place our cabin just under that ridgeline, place our horse corral over there in that small grove of sagebrush and pines, and that leaves enough good ground for Cedrick to build our outside firepit. What do the rest of you have to say? Hopefully all of you have had enough saddle-time today to last you for a while and if so, let us get to doing what needs to be done in building up our new home site."

There was little dissent from the clan as they turned their riding and packhorses towards the head of the long draw leading to an abrupt ridgeline. Once there, the men tiredly dismounted, walked around to get the soreness out from their knees from the long horse ride. However, shortly thereafter the work began of setting up their temporary campsite. In numerous practiced moves, the men immediately began unpacking their packhorses and taking their packs, arranged them in a circle under the small grove of pines as a means of protection should they be attacked by Indians found in the area. Then their packhorses were all hobbled and turned loose in the adjoining meadow so they could roll around and scratch their backs stiff from carrying the heavy packs for so many miles as well as graze and water. However, the men kept their riding horses saddled just in case of any surprise attack by local Indians at least for the afternoon.

Cedrick on the other hand, grabbed a shovel from one of the packs and walked over to the area he figured where a cabin would be built, paced off a rough area upon which their cabin would stand and then paced off another area next to the soon to be built cabin for an outside firepit, cooking and lounging area. While Cedrick began establishing his cooking site and made ready for the work to follow, Cloud and Feather strode over to the grove of pines and began scraping out sleeping areas for all of the men under the shade of the trees. Once the understory had been cleared away, they brought forth the individual men's sleeping furs and began arranging their sleeping sites. While that activity was going on, Wallace and Otis with rifles in hand began walking the immediate area to ascertain what timber would be available in the future for the cabin making to follow. Finished with their sleeping site preparations, Cloud and Feather then grabbed their bows and arrows and walked back into the sagebrush and timber looking for a deer to kill so Cedrick could have a supply of meat for the men's supper later come nightfall.

For the next three weeks, found the men hard at work building their new cabin. Following those labors, they constructed a storage shed, a horse corral for their now expanded horse herd and cut their winter wood supply. Then with a team of horses, brought down from the hillside the logs cut for their winter wood supply and placed them near their cabin for easy access. Then the men built several long meat smoking racks, assembled two meat poles next to their cabin in the trees and began hunting the herds of nearby deer, elk and buffalo so they could lay up a winter's supply of energy jerky, have meat for their daily meals and a supply of hides to tan so their beaver pelts could be covered during transit to the coming year's rendezvous.

With their campsite finally completed and almost ready for the fall beaver trapping season and the oncoming winter months, the men allowed themselves an afternoon of buffalo hunting and butchering. There they found the herds of buffalo nowhere near as extensive as they had been or as numerous further to the east. In fact, buffalo that far west were scarce, causing the men to rely more on elk, mule deer, beaver and antelope for the major sources of their meat supplies. However, true to his second calling, Cedrick always managed to provide excellent meals for the men no matter what kinds of meat they managed to bring home. Before long, elk meat quickly supplanted buffalo as the favorite meat of the men and soon at least one elk, many time two, hung from the camp's meat poles. Subsequently, when the smoking racks were in operation, they were covered with the meat from an elk instead of that from a buffalo. In fact, if the men got hungry for the taste of a buffalo, they found themselves almost every time heading to the grasslands further to the east for their favorite source of meat.

One fall morning after the men had shaved, cleaned up as best as they could and were sitting around the outside campfire having their morning coffee while Cedrick put the finishing touches on their breakfasts, Wallace said, "I think we best be checking out the beaver trapping areas and come up with a trapping plan that suits our tastes." Typical of the Barnes Clan, no one said anything for a while relative to the subject just broached as they quietly nursed and enjoyed their cups of coffee. However, seeing that he had their attention, Wallace continued saying, "I say when we are done with eating this morning, we saddle up and begin checking out not only the many marshlands around the Hams River Valley but the actual river itself to see where we want to start our fall trapping which I feel is fast approaching." Once again, no one said anything relative to what Wallace had just suggested as they mulled his suggestion over and continued enjoying their coffee in the quiet of the morning's cool. But Wallace knew his brothers. He knew that by broaching the beaver trapping subject, his brothers were already making plans to follow through on his suggestions.

Once breakfast was finished, as Cedrick attended to the care of his beloved cast iron cooking pots and implements, the rest of the men headed for the corral and began saddling up their riding and packhorses for the work that lay ahead. Later that afternoon found the men slowly riding along the many adjacent river marshes and along the Hams specifically checking out their future trapping opportunities. As they did, once again Wallace thought, *Bridger was sure right about the beaver in this area. Everywhere we look we are seeing beaver, lots of them and many appear to be Made Beaver as well! Once again, the clan has made a good choice when it came to the beaver trapping country chosen, thanks to their friend, Jim Bridger...*

Finally the men drew up into a group and began discussing their trapping options after scoping out the plentiful beaver trapping opportunities lying before them. To a man, they all wanted to start their fall trapping season by trapping the many smaller waterways and marshes and save the river areas for when they had trapped out the marshes' beaver. All of the men felt that the river had less beaver along its shores and inlets so they wanted to trap those areas where they could easily catch the most beaver. With that decision made the men headed back to their campsite, killing a large eight-point bull elk for camp meat while en route. As Wallace and Otis dismounted in the brushy kill-site and began butchering out the elk, Cloud, Cedrick and Feather stayed saddled and on the watch for any sign of danger. This the three men did realizing that while out on the frontier, anytime anyone fired a rifle, many times those sounds 'invited' curious unwanted guests to come looking, be they man or beast! They didn't have long to wait when Cloud spotted a large boar grizzly bear ambling along the river banks and its related brushy areas looking for his next meal after hearing the sound of shooting. Then it quickly became obvious from his actions that the bear had also winded the smell of blood and death emanating from the bull elk butchering-site! Rising up to his full nine feet in height on his hind legs in order to smell that delightful dinner smell better, the nearsighted bear following his nose looked right at the men just a few short yards distant busily butchering out the large elk. Dropping down onto all fours and fearing no man or his smell, here the great bear came towards the kill site at a typical hungry bear loping run!

"We have a grizzly bear who has winded the dead elk and is now coming our way at a fast run," yelled Cloud, as his horse upon seeing the bear busting his way through the sagebrush and coming his way at a dead run began 'crow-hopping' around in fear!

With those words of warning, the two men quit butchering the elk and ran for their horses. That they did not a minute too soon as their riding horses now seeing and hearing the brush-busting oncoming bear, began showing signs of extreme nervousness as well. Within moments, the bear, ignoring the gathering of men and 'crow-hopping' horses, ran right up to the dead animal, lunged at its carcass and bit down on its head like it was in the act of killing a live elk. **BOOM-BOOM-BOOM-BOOM!** simultaneously went the rifles of Cloud, Feather, Wallace and Otis, with little effect on the bear other than rolling him off the elk's carcass and extremely pissing him off with just painful but not mortal wounds from hastily fired rifles from off nervous moving around horses, spoiling most everyone's aim!

In an instant, the bear was almost upon the shooters and their now bucking and terrified horses! **BOOM!** went Cedrick's rifle after he had quickly dismounted his bucking horse and taking careful aim, dropped the charging bear with one shot, sending its heavy lead slug into the bear's neck! With the impact of the heavy lead slug striking the bear's neck, its rolling and still thrashing carcass slopped right under the nearby crowd of milling horses causing a major panic among the terrified animals! Instantly, Otis found himself slung off his bucking horse and into the nearby marsh with a loud **KER-PLUSH!** Wallace on the other hand, found himself in a dense patch of chokecherry brush, having lost his rifle in the process of being bucked high into the air and into the berries! As for Cloud, he found himself bucked off and under the numerous stomping hooves of the men's horses as they tried running away from the still thrashing and foul smelling dying grizzly bear! Feather turned out to be the lucky one when it came to the grizzly bear caused "Frontier Rodeo". He too was bucked off and landed onto the back of another now fleeing and now riderless horse! That riderless horse objected to the surprising arrival of another rider upon its back and saw to it that the newly arriving 'rider' was quickly bucked off by the terrified horse as well! With that, that horse too was now heading for the safety of the nearest mountainside and away from the perceived danger!

Cedrick, upon realizing the immediate danger

was past with the killing of the grizzly, began laughing at the consternation and Frontier Rodeo created when the bear had made his inopportune appearance. In his mirth, took two steps forward to get clear of the brush so he could more easily reload his rifle. When he did and still laughing over what had just happened to the rest of the clan, instantly had his mouth filled full of an aroused cloud of stinging "yellow jackets"! Yelling, gagging and puking up a mouthful of the stinging and biting insects, Cedrick staggered two steps forward and when he did, he removed his foot which had partially obstructed the full emergence of the disturbed stinging insects from their nest located underground under his feet. By removing his foot and allowing the full horde of insects to leave their nest and attack their agitator, he was quickly enveloped by a cloud of the stinging and biting insects! Soon, anything that moved was seen by the now furious insects as a threat which included all of the trappers and their remaining close at hand horses. When that happened, 'everyone' received the full and unwanted attention from the horde of thoroughly pissed off 'winged stingers and biters'! Moments later found the scene around the dead elk abandoned by fleeing horses and equally 'high-stepping' trappers, as they all headed post haste for the nearest beaver pond to rid their bare heads, hands, faces and necks of the winged attackers! Soon, everyone was up to his neck in muddy beaver pond waters swatting at those few remaining yellow jackets pursuing the fleeing trappers into the comforting waters...

For the next 20 minutes or so, the Barnes Clan swatted at the few remaining yellow jackets hovering around the trappers up to their necks in the calming muddy beaver pond waters. As for their horses, they were now long gone and heading for the safety of their familiar horse corral and away from the stinging insects that bit or stung anything that moved above ground! However, the meat loving yellow jackets quickly lost interest in the trappers in the pond and turned their interest to the partially gutted elk just lying feet away from their nest and hungry larvae in their nest lodged deep underground. With that, the horde of insects now descended upon the hapless elk carcass and began biting off chunks of meat and carrying it back to their underground nest. As they did, it quickly became apparent that woe would befall anyone trying to take the elk carcass back from the hungry horde of insects...

Realizing they were more or less safe for the moment, the Barnes Clan slowly emerged from the beaver pond, picked up their rifles carelessly discarded upon the bank when they were under attack earlier from the yellow jackets, and quickly made their way out from the area of the insects' nest and dead elk now covered with hundreds of winged critters. However, the joy of being out of the 'stinging zone' of the yellow jackets by the

Barnes Clan as they hurried for their cabin and horse corral quickly turned to consternation. Otis was the first to notice that the exposed neck and arms of his brother Wallace, was covered with ugly, wiggly dark worm-like critters attached to any bare skin they could find! He then realized that not only was his brother covered with ugly black leeches, but he was as well! Moments later found the entire Barnes Clan stripped naked out in the sagebrush trying to rid their bodies of hundreds of black leeches attached to every part of their bodies including those body parts originally covered with loose fitting buckskins! Leeches that they had unknowingly picked up while being immersed up to their necks in the 'safety' of the beaver pond trying to avoid the stinging yellow jackets! Then their consternation turned to disgust when all of the naked men realized the leeches were EVERYWHERE, including heavily gathered around their 'man parts' as well as any crevice found on their 'last part over the fence'! Then that consternation turned to disgust as the trappers soon found most of the getting fatter and fatter by the moment leeches, were not easily removed with one's fingers but for the most part, the blades of their sheath knives were required!

Soon the nearby critters of the 'sage' observed five naked trappers, now being graced with the attention of numerous mosquitoes from the nearby watered areas, as they were forced into using their knives to scrape off the leeches that had attached themselves to the trappers' bodies! Those knife scraping actions only led to the appearance of five naked men being covered with their own blood when they had to scrape off the many becoming more and more engorged leeches... Then their consternation quickly turned to widespread embarrassment when they had to help each other in removing those leeches found in the most sensitive of areas of their bodies with the point of the remover's knife blade!

That evening the Barnes Clan feasted on coffee, biscuits and beans for their supper. Missing were the skewers of fresh bull elk meat which now from the distant sounds of it, was being appreciated by the local wolf pack frequenting the kill-site area below their cabin as well. The next morning, careful to avoid the area of the yellow jackets' nest, the men discovered that all that remained of their big bull elk killed from the afternoon before were the hide, hooves, antlers and picked clean skull. In comparison, as for the trappers, they did not present any evidence of being future beauty queens either! Each man was a mess of welts from the numerous yellow jacket bites and stings all over their exposed parts. Then there were all the mosquito welts gathered when the men had stripped down naked in order to remove the 'dad-burn' leeches. Lastly, every place of bare skin showed dramatic swelling evidence as having been visited by hungry, blood sucking leeches. Suffice to say each man rode 'heavily in his stirrups' that fine day, taking the weight off their collective bottoms due to their rather sensitive, tissue damaged areas throughout their 'last parts over the fence' from the hordes of leeches found in the beaver ponds and the subsequent and sometimes clumsy 'knife work' in removing said leeches!

By early the following morning after 'the lost battle at the yellow jacket site', Wallace had selected a concentration of beaver ponds in which to begin the Barnes Clan fall trapping season. Slipping back into his trapping routine, Wallace, now aware of the leech menace lurking in the trapping waters, tightly wrapped his groin area with a leech impervious heavy gray cloth wrapping. Then stripping totally naked from the waist on down except for his protective wrapping, a breechclout and leggings, he located a fresh beaver slide area and quickly set his trap. Then upon seeing the hordes of leeches swimming his way in the clear waters, he moved rapidly out into the deeper waters of the pond and quickly drove the anchor stake into the bottom of the pond before the hordes of swimming leeches arrived. Stopping to brush off the leeches attempting to fasten onto his skin, he tied off the trap chain ring to the anchor pole and then quickly moved on as Cedrick baited the area over the trap with a castoreum treated twig stuck into the ground and hanging over the pan at an angle. As Cedrick did that, Wallace hustled out from the leech infested waters, knocked off the few leeches still trying to attach themselves and then moved off to the next trap site. In the meantime, Otis and Cloud formed the mounted pair of sentries standing guard over the trappers in and around the ponded areas. Feather on the other hand, tended to the riding horses of Wallace and Cedrick as well as led the trailing packhorses as the men moved along their trap line. By mid-morning all of their 24 beaver traps had been set and the men then entered a small aspen grove in order to remain out of sight from any hostile Indians who might be in the immediate vicinity, ate some jerky and allowed Wallace to warm up. Several hours later, the Barnes Clan re-visited their newly set line of traps and retrieved six of the highly territorial beaver just recently caught after the traps had been set. Once Wallace had retrieved those recently caught beaver, Cedrick and Feather took turns in skinning out their heavily fatted catches. Then as they had done since they had started trapping beaver years earlier, the animal's carcasses were cast off into the brush for the critters to eat and the fresh pelts tossed into a pannier on the packhorse for return to their cabin for de-fatting and hooping so they could dry and be made ready for transport to the coming summer's rendezvous. Thus began the Barnes Clan's regimen for the fall beaver trapping season in 1827 until just prior to freeze-up. In between their trapping activities, found the Barnes Clan quietly tending to their 254 recently fall-caught pelts, casting bullets for their firearms, hunting elk for their camp meat supplies, cutting more firewood and tending to the safety and care of their life giving horse herd.

One morning early with a nip of "Old Man Winter" in the air, Cedrick was putting the finishing touches on his breakfast meal. Making a final check on his Dutch oven biscuits, all of a sudden he had a 'sixth sense' feeling of dread come over him that was almost physical in nature. Turning and looking across the meadow where he had released their horses earlier that morning so they could feed, he saw nothing out of the ordinary that caused him any concern. Shuffling that unusual feeling that he was being watched to the back alleys of his mind after another careful check all around, Cedrick let the rest of his group know that breakfast was ready. Moments later, the rest of his trappers tumbled out from the cabin or arrived from the spring box near the horse corrals where they had been washing up and shaving. Soon the clanking of metal coffee cups being retrieved out from the camp box and being filled with steaming hot coffee took his mind off his earlier unusual feelings. Handing out skewers of sizzling elk meat to the men seated on their sitting logs around the fire, Cedrick turned and began filling each man's plate with heaping serving spoonfuls of heavily spiced with red pepper flakes cooked pinto beans and fresh hot biscuits just retrieved from his two active Dutch ovens. Then as he began filling his own plate with food, the blast of unusual feelings of dread once again swept over him like a morning chill. Turning around once again, Cedrick took another look over at their valuable and quietly feeding horse herd again and saw nothing that aroused his concerns. Looking over at his hungrily eating group of men to see if any of them had also sensed anything out of place, he saw nothing of suspicion on any of their faces as they hungrily dove into their breakfast meal. Then something made him take a second look at his brother Otis. Otis, usually the one who was almost Indian like in his many personal and inner ways, especially when it came to being very alert when it came to his surroundings, had paused and was now looking over at their horse herd as well. Then shaking his head like he would do to rid it of a thought not wanted or one to be ignored, Otis returned to 'worrying' one of Cedrick's hot biscuits. Cedrick, feeling if Otis had not sensed anything out of the ordinary, he should do the same, returned to finishing his own now rapidly cooling in the morning's air, breakfast.

Twenty minutes later found the men saddling their riding stock and moving the remainder of their horses from the meadow back into the corral for safer keeping. Somewhat later with Wallace in the lead followed by Cloud and Feather trailing the packhorses, the Barnes Clan moved out from their cabin site with Otis and Cedrick bringing up the rear of their caravan. Once on-site of their trap line, Wallace whooped and hollered over the cold air as he stripped down to once again resume his duties as the clan's lead trapper. Without any further ado, Wallace tightly fastened his gray cloth wrapping over his private parts and backside in order to discourage any easy entry by hungry leeches found in the beaver pond's waters. Then when he entered the icy cold waters of the beaver pond for the first time that morning, one would have thought a bull buffalo had just been gored, as Wallace bellowed loudly when the cold waters closed over his 'man parts'... Once again moving quickly because of the now observed oncoming swimming leeches wiggling their ways through the water towards him and now the near winter's icy waters, Wallace efficiently checked and re-set his 24 beaver traps like the skilled trapper he was. In the interim, Otis and Cloud grinned over Wallace's unpleasant and loudly uttered verbal utterances over the cold waters striking his sensitive body areas! However, that in no way reflected a reduction of their watchfulness over their trappers on the ground or the seriousness of their sentry guard duties at hand.

However, as Cedrick retrieved a new bottle of castoreum from a pack animal's pannier, that same cold feeling he had felt earlier that morning while making breakfast for the men 'belted' through his being once again, only that time with an almost felt physical presence! Stopping what he was doing and looking back towards from whence they had just come, HE CAUGHT A QUICK GLIMPSE OF UNUSUAL MOVEMENT IN THE DARK TIMBER THEY HAD JUST TRAVELED THROUGH! Then Cedrick saw Otis standing up in his stirrups and looking back in the same direction they had just traveled as well…

"Cedrick, get Wallace out of the water quickly and get him to warming up. I think we may have company," said Otis, as he slowly lowered himself back down into his saddle and readjusted his rifle across his saddle to a more ready for action position.

Moments later, Wallace was out of the water and stomping around trying to get some life back into his feet and legs, as his eyes questioned those warning actions of Cedrick and Otis's. As he did, Otis and Cloud moved their horses over to the group of men doing the trapping and as they did, their eyes never quit examining their back trail. Then Otis leaned over in his saddle and quietly said to Cedrick, Feather and Wallace, "I saw some movement on our back trail that was not just that of any kind of an animal moving through the timber. The movement I saw did a lot of starting and stopping like it was someone looking on at what we were doing and trying hard not to be seen. I think we need to move back to our cabin from the north instead of returning back the way we came and take a 'gander' to see if our horse herd left back in the corral is safe."

Without a word, Wallace took off his wet cloth wrappings covering his groin and buttocks area to keep the leeches off his 'man-parts', removed his wet leggings and breechclout, then stiffly crawled back into his warmer Linsey-woolsy pants, wool shirt and heavier and warmer winter moccasins. Then he once again stomped about as if that stomping would help speed up the feeling returning to his feet and legs after being immersed in the icy waters so long. Moments later with sharp-eyed Otis in the lead and Cloud and Feather trailing him, the remainder of the Barnes Clan began moving from out in the open by the beaver ponds into the brush along the Hams River and were soon out of sight. Keeping to the brush and heavily wooded areas, Otis quietly led the group back into the heavy timber below the ridgeline leading directly back to their cabin. Once along the ridgeline, he turned in a southerly direction and slowly headed back towards the cabin. Stopping about 50 yards from their cabin, the men tied off their horses in the heavy timber, checked their weapons one more time to make sure they were primed and ready and then began slowly moving through the dense timber towards their cabin. Finally stopping everyone else where they stood, Otis quietly sneaked on alone as the same cold feelings once again came back to Cedrick as he watched his brother move on out of sight, moving as stealthily as a snake across a wet grass field...

About 15 minutes later, Otis reappeared almost ghost-like from out of the limited light found in the dense stand of timber into which the rest of the trappers were quietly standing awaiting his return. Then he gathered the clan around him quietly saying, "There are about ten who appear to be Blackfeet Indians looting our cabin and pack-saddling up our horses! They have all of our horses tied on a long picket line and from the looks of it they mean to steal what they can get their hands on from in the cabin and take livestock as well. I thought I saw something moving stealthily back there in the timber earlier. I would bet it was one of those Indians trailing us to make sure we were out of the area before they looted our cabin in the process of stealing much of our provisions. That is just like what we have learned about the Indians since we have been trapping in their country. They have a low birth rate and with the men being killed off in battle all of the time, they are reluctant to get out into the open and in battle unless they have the numbers on whoever they are attacking. Well, we may be outnumbered but they will find that they have messed with the wrong group of trappers! Here is what I propose we do since we are outnumbered from what I could see and count. There appears to be about ten of those red devils moving in and out and around our cabin, helping themselves to our provisions and horses as well. I say we approach our cabin from behind using it as our cover. That way they should not see us coming and we can set up a crossfire when they discover we are on-site and they make a run for their horses or want to stand and fight. I suggest we put our best shooters on the corral side of the cabin. That is also the side where they have placed their horses. That being said, I would bet that is the direction in which they will choose to run in order to escape if they do not want to stand and fight. Therefore, Cloud, Feather and I will take our two Trade rifles from the panniers and our own firearms and set up on the northeastern side of our cabin. Then when they discover we are back and onto them, that is when they should make a run for their horses. If that happens and when they do, Cloud, Feather and I should be able to kill at least five of them before they know it between the firepower of our rifles and the Trade rifles from the panniers. As for you, Wallace and Cedrick, you two sneak in from behind the winter woodpile on the southwestern side of our cabin when they are not looking. That way you will have the cover of our woodpile for the safety it offers and you will be the closest to those who bolt from our cabin front door and make a run for our horses or theirs. Being that close, the two of you can make the best use of your pistols at such a close range after you have shot your rifles dry. After that, it will be our pistols from our side of the cabin, knives and tomahawks from yours. Need I say more, we need to kill all of them as quickly as possible! To do otherwise will allow anyone who escapes to run back to their camp and then bring in more of their kind to clean out whoever is left alive among us after we take care of the business here."

"Seems like we had to do something like this a few years earlier with other Indians or a mess of them damn Frenchies," said Wallace quietly, full well realizing the deadly odds the five of them faced and the likelihood that all of their group would not survive what they were about to try and do…

Following Wallace's statement, there were no other words spoken because none were necessary in light of the deadly life and death situation facing them. Otis had a good plan and in the men's following silence, it was obvious that the men concurred in what he had suggested. It was plain that all of the Indians had to be killed and hopefully none of their own clan would suffer the same fate. Moments later with Otis saying that he would start the shooting and the others should follow his lead, so when he did the Indians would be the most vulnerable and out in the open. Then the group quietly shook hands. With those words, the group broke up and made their ways towards their positions near the cabin for what was soon to follow…

About 20 minutes later, Otis, Cloud and Feather

were in position and had not been discovered as they made their approach through the timber and hid in behind the corral full of horses. Laying the two Indian Trade rifles filled with buck and ball alongside for quick retrieval when the time was right, Otis laid down behind the horse corral in ambush! Meanwhile, Cloud and Feather changed positions, slinked in behind the cabin's northern wall and the storage shed and then laid silently there hidden in ambush waiting for Otis's opening shot. There the three men waited in stony silence for the deadly violence to come. There they waited because Wallace and Cedrick had the furthest to go in order to get safely into position behind their winter woodpile of logs. In the meantime, they watched the Indians running back and forth from the cabin quickly removing everything of value they could lay their hands upon that they could use back at their own encampment. Once outside, they stacked the stolen items next to the corral for quick packing onto the packhorses once they were ready to leave. Somewhat later, it appeared that all of the Indians were out from the cabin and six of their number made for the corrals to ready the horses for transport. As they did, four of their kind ran for the trappers' storage shed to procure the needed pack saddles so the goods to be stolen could be transported more easily back to their winter encampment some miles away.

That was when the 'wheels came off the trappers' wagon' and their plan of attack! It appeared one Indian was heading for his horse so he could ride out from the trappers' camp and make sure the trappers were still in the field running their trap line and not close at hand. That meant he had to be killed before he rode off, otherwise he could return at a later date with more warriors and kill off the remaining trappers. Realizing the implications of his escape, Otis rose up from his hidden position and with one shot from his rifle, cleared that Indian from his saddle with a head-shot! With the **BOOMING** sound from Otis's rifle being fired within the campsite, the entire group of Indians streaming back and forth in front of the cabin was almost instantly engulfed with streams of white black powder smoke, as Indian and trapper alike discovered targets and began shooting at each other!

Cloud and Feather rose up from their hiding place by the cabin and storage shed and killed two of their targets coming to the shed to get several more pack saddles! Following their shooting, Indian bullets fired back at the two young men tore great splinters from the walls of the cabin and storage shed where the two had been hiding! Meanwhile, Otis's second shot with the Indian Trade rifle cleared two Indians off their horses who had just fired their rifles and then jumped into their saddles on their horses near the corral and made ready to escape! Otis's shot from just 20 feet away killed one Indian outright and the other was blown from his saddle with buckshot in his side. Upon hitting the ground, that wounded Indian crawled off a few feet away and began attempting to reload his rifle so he could continue doing battle. Meanwhile, Cedrick and Wallace, who was now more than warmed up from his earlier immersion in the cold waters of the beaver ponds, began pouring round after round from their rifles and pistols into the remaining huddled mass of Indians attempting to reload their rifles after firing their first shots, poorly aimed as they were, at the trappers shooting at the Indians from both sides of the cabin!

That was when Wallace was shot a grazing blow alongside his cheek with a non-lethal strike! Down he went in pain and shock as the Indian who had shot him threw down his rifle, drew his tomahawk and charged the downed trapper. That was when Cedrick shot the attacking Indian dead in the face with his last pistol shot full of buck and ball! Then total pandemonium reigned as trappers shot their rifles and pistols dry and then those few Indians remaining, most of whom were carrying buck and ball in their bodies, attempted to fight or flee. Moments later, it was all over as quickly as it had all started and The Great Spirit shed a tear over the loss of his children who were, with the last tomahawk chops to their heads by Cloud, Feather and Otis, now on their ways to joining their Cloud People ancestors...

That was when Otis felt an impact of a bullet

striking him a grazing blow across his muscular chest, knocking him down! However, just before he had been shot, he saw another mounted Indian riding 'hellbent for leather' into the meadow below their cabin, then drawing up his horse in flying dust and dirt, pull his rifle to his shoulder and shoot. Otis clearly saw the white cloud of black powder smoke from the close at hand Indian rider just about the time he felt the bullet's impact! Fortunately when the Indian had shot, his horse had flinched and the bullet only tore a strip of muscular tissue from Otis's chest area and did not break any bones. However, the impact of the bullet knocked the sturdy Irishman flat on his behind and left him gasping for air! Then the remaining Barnes Clan saw the Indian who had just shot Otis turn his horse abruptly around and flee the area as if the devil was on his tail! However as he fled, Cedrick got a clear look at Otis's assailant. The Indian who had just shot his brother was clearly a 'marked man'! Cedrick clearly saw that the Indian was clearly disfigured. In the place where the Indian's nose should have been were only two holes in his face! It was apparent that the man had been in a fight and someone had taken his knife or tomahawk and cut off the Indian's nose, leaving only the two nostril holes in his face! It was a face Cedrick would clearly remember and see again... It was then that Cedrick understood more clearly the meanings of his earlier 'sixth sense' warnings...

Standing there helplessly with every rifle and pistol shot dry, the Barnes Clan could only watch the eleventh Indian who had been sent out previously to scout the trappers' location in the field, flee the scene of battle. When that Indian fled the scene, every standing member of the Barnes Clan realized with that Indian's escape, they knew they would have to face him once again someday and when they did, he more than likely would be accompanied with more of his kind and with a killing vengeance in his heart!

Realizing there was nothing they could do about the escaping Indian, Wallace, bleeding like a stuck hog from his facial wound, ran over to his brother Otis, to see how badly he had been hit. Seeing his brother still crawling around on the ground trying to get the air back into his lungs after being hit a glancing blow in his chest area and seeing only a badly bleeding superficial chest wound, Wallace felt his heart starting up once again. Then Otis was immediately surrounded by Cloud and Feather and bodily lifted up to his feet, as the two Indian men showed great relief on their faces over the fact that Otis, who was like a father to them, with just only a painful chest wound, would live!

After everyone had reloaded all of their rifles and pistols, Cedrick sat Wallace and Otis down around his outside cooking firepit and began washing out the two brothers' wounds. In the meantime, Cloud and Feather began carrying back into the cabin all of their scattered about provisions that the raiding Blackfeet Indians had removed in preparation for their flight after the theft. When they did, they found the inside of their cabin had been trashed by the Indians in their haste and hurry to steal everything of value that they could and then leave before the cabin's owners returned and the unexpected deadly confrontation occurred! By late afternoon, Cloud and Feather had all of the previously bundled beaver furs back inside their storage shed and all of their provisions back inside their cabin. Then they gathered together all ten of the Indians' valuable horses and placed them inside their corral for safer keeping. In the meantime, after washing out the facial and chest wounds of his two brothers, Cedrick, along with a great deal of hollering on the part of the injured, began sewing shut Wallace's facial wound and Otis's chest wound. Otis's wound was the worst to repair because the bullet had torn off a massive chunk of muscle from clear across his hairy chest. In order to properly close the wound and sew it shut, Cedrick had to take one of his razors and shave all of Otis's hair from the area around the wound along the jagged flaps of torn skin! That caused even more bleeding and soon Otis had blood running clear down inside the front of his pants as the wound kept bleeding profusely while Cedrick kept carefully shaving away all of his chest hair! With that effort finally accomplished,

Otis with a cup of rum finally sat still and in stoic silence as Cedrick finally painfully sewed the individual torn flaps of skin together as best as he could.

Then later after all of that frontier 'doctoring', with Otis and Wallace on their horses, the ten dead Blackfeet Indians' bodies were tied behind their horses one at a time by Cloud and Feather and dragged down to the Hams River and tossed into its currents. This they did, but not before stripping the dead of any identifying clothing or jewelry so if ever retrieved by Indians of their band or tribe, identification would be most difficult, especially after the bodies had been in a watery grave for a few days and their skin began falling off. Five trips later and with Otis and Wallace's wounds still bleeding over the men's exertions from riding their horses and rolling the Indians' bodies into the river, the men sat around the firepit with another cup of rum, all the while holding a cloth rag on their wounds to try and stop the still seeping lymph fluids. As they did, Cedrick put together a supper of only coffee and biscuits because he had not had the time to prepare anything else. Then as Otis and Wallace cleaned all of the seized Indians' firearms, Cloud and Feather flopped down in their sleeping furs and were soon fast asleep...

However, Cedrick's day was not yet done as he still had to clean the facial and chest wounds of his two brothers one more time before all three could head for their sleeping furs as well. But not before the men had placed two bundles of bulky furs inside the door to their cabin in case any Indians came back looking for the trappers that evening. Following that, the men made sure every one of their loaded rifles and pistols were placed within easy reach in case their use was called for during the night. Then with only the glow from a dying fire inside the trappers' fireplace for light, the rest of the men thankfully retired to their sleeping furs for the evening. However, the three Barnes brothers found sleep hard to come by that evening, several cups of imbibed rum and all. The brothers found sleep hard to come by because of the specter of the eleventh Indian, his escape and what the future consequences of that escape foretold for the Barnes Clan. Those dark thoughts dogged all three men mentally until sleep and emotional exhaustion finally overcame them, releasing them into a gentler world...

For the next two weeks, the Barnes Clan rather slowly but doggedly ran their trap line. Ran their trap line rather slowly because they were not only on extra alert for any returning hostile Indians but also because of wounds that refused to heal up more quickly than they did. The soreness of unhealed wounds and the constant dripping blood and lymph fluids made for uncomfortable bending and leaning over in the beaver trapping and processing activities or even the mounting and riding of horses. It was then one evening around their outside campfire during supper that Otis remembered something from his days while running with his Creek Indian friends back in Tennessee. Spreading honey on one of his biscuits, Otis paused and thought back to his earlier times with the Creeks. Several times he remembered back when his Creek Indian friends had suffered wounds that stubbornly refused to heal, honey was the treatment they had used to address such issues. Without saying a word, Otis rose and removed his buckskin shirt revealing an ugly yellow and purplish swollen chest wound. Taking up his just used jug of honey, he poured some honey into his hand and then smeared it liberally all over the wound! When he did so with much winching, he took his finger tips and made sure he pushed some of the honey deeply into the major oozing wounds as well. Then he walked over to Wallace and without a word to the men all looking at him like he had gone daft, he poured some more honey into his hand and tenderly rubbed it onto his brother's swollen and infected facial wound as well. Finished with those tasks and after cleaning off his hands, Otis sat down on his sitting log and explained what and why he had just done what he did. For the next three days of trap line running labors, Otis put up with a shirt that kept sticking to his honey coated chest and Wallace kept busy swatting all kinds of flies attracted to the sticky mess smeared all over the wounds on his face. But heal up quickly after that they did, just in time for the season's freeze-up and the needed change-up in the men's activities in making preparations for the winter season. (Author's Note: Little did the men understand the age-old healing properties of honey, especially how the sticky liquid blunted the deleterious bacterial effects commonly associated with many open and poorly treated wounds in the days of old when good hygiene and wound care was questionable.)

With the ice becoming thicker and thicker every day making the running of a trap line more and more difficult, the men finally pulled all of their beaver traps and retired to their cabin, ending their fall beaver trapping season. The following day, the men saddled up their riding horses and trailing six additional packhorses, went forth on a combined elk and deer hunt. Two days later with three elk and four mule deer hanging from their meat poles and their smoking fires going day and night, the men ate well because of Cedrick's expertise as a cook, plus were able to set aside four large bags of excellent tasting venison jerky to be eaten while out wolf trapping in the coming days while on the winter trail as well.

Finally the work began that had been largely ignored during the fall trapping season because of the long hours of associated work processing the pelts daily. Leather gear was repaired, pack saddle straps were re-leathered, a small mountain of bullets was cast for their rifles and pistols, edges were set to their knives, axes and shovels, and firewood cut daily for use in their outdoor firepit. Then when the weather became too adverse for general outside activity around their campfire other than caring for their now expanded horse herd, the men adjourned to their cabin where numerous clothing repairs were made as well as new clothing, gloves, fur hats and moccasins made from their tanned leather supplies. Following those activities weather permitting, the men spent their days running their wolf trap lines and in the processing of their catches' furs. Soon, 23 wolf pelts hung from their inside cabin walls in the various stages of being stretched and drying for later transport to the upcoming rendezvous in the Bear Lake area of what is today the modern-day State of Utah.

CHAPTER TWELVE

<hr>

SPRING TRAPPING AND NO MORE SPECIAL BISCUITS...

ONE MORNING AS THE LAST vestiges of what had been a long and hard winter began releasing its icy grip on the Hams River country, Otis stepped from the cabin and looked skyward to check the day's weather signs. Rays drifting through the conifers from a warming spring sun greeted his eyes and a cloudless azure blue sky made him smile over the day's weather prospects lying ahead. About then his older brother Wallace, pushed by him and made quick tracks for his 'special sitting log' behind their cabin so he could take care of an urgent call of nature. Otis just smiled as his brother slipped and slid in the remaining patches of snow left behind. This he did as he hurried along bent over like a scuttling land crab because of his urgency to get to his 'special sitting log' and rid himself of what he was 'carrying' now of 'primary importance'!

A few yards away standing by his cooking fire was Cedrick, with a big knowing grin watching his older brother on the run for his 'special sitting log' behind their cabin so he could take care of an urgent call of nature. Cedrick's 'knowing grin' was based on the fact that the evening before, he had served the men in part a mess of beans heavily spiced with red pepper flakes because most of the clan had been grumbling about being constipated. Cedrick realizing a diet heavy on the meaty side of the menu had that kind of an effect on many people, had purposely heavily hot-spiced his previous supper's pot of beans. That he did with the thought in mind of helping his clan along with their constipation problems by 'firing' things up a bit. Must have worked like a charm, thought Cedrick, as he saw the obvious instant relief on his brother's face while sitting on his 'special sitting log' off to one side and behind their cabin...

Realizing that day would be the very first day of their spring beaver trapping, Cedrick put the finishing touches on his special kind of biscuits as an act of celebration of the coming day's spring beaver trapping events. Into his biscuit mixing dough went several handfuls of previously plumped-up in hot water raisins, copious amounts of brown sugar, topped off with a generous helping of cinnamon mixed throughout the dough. Then into his previously heated three Dutch ovens sitting on a bed of coals went biscuit sized gobs of the dough just mixed. Finally on went the Dutch ovens' flanged lids with several small shovelfuls of coals heaped on top to aid in the biscuit browning process. Within minutes the Heavenly smell of Cedrick's special biscuits wafting through the morning air could be smelled, especially after they had been laid out minutes later in a wooden bowl for cooling. Then with a shout that 'breakfast was ready', Cedrick began removing the men's steel plates from their warming rocks laid alongside the fire and ladled each plate full of another helping of his made to order spicy beans, steaming chunks of fire roasted elk backstrap and several of his camp's famous special biscuits.

About then, the rest of the Barnes Clan, including Wallace now tightening up the tie on his buckskin pants, tumbled onto their sitting logs around the campfire. This they did as Otis began pouring hot coffee into each man's cup held at the end of an eagerly extended hand. Soon, the only sounds coming from the Barnes Clan was the clanking of their spoons and forks against their metal plates and much lip smacking over Cedrick's special celebratory first day of spring beaver trapping biscuits slathered in honey from a nearby jug. A stone crockware jug that had been previously placed alongside the warming fire so the warmed honey would be less viscous and pour more easily over the men's biscuits. That Cedrick did because the Barnes Clan to a 'lad' had a sweet tooth for having the warm honey poured over their biscuits that would have matched the desires of that of a 'she' grizzly bear in the middle of a mess of bee hives…

Half-an-hour later, Wallace led the Barnes Clan's caravan of horses and men from their cabin site down to the Hams River. Arriving about 30 minutes later along a set of open water beaver ponds, Wallace held up his hand to stop, dismounted and walked back to a packhorse being led by Cloud. There he stripped down to his bare nothings from the waist on down and tied his gray cloth wrapping tightly around his groin area and buttocks to keep the leeches off his private parts. Over that went his breechclout and leggings and he was almost set to begin his beaver trapping. Then Wallace grabbed a five-pound beaver trap from a pannier, a four-foot dried wooden pole from another pannier, a hand ax, and began 'woofing and chirping' out loud as his warm naked body began entering the beaver pond's icy waters at the end of a well-used slide. That 'woofing and chirping' became even louder and more profound when the pond's icy waters closed around his 'man parts' seconds later! Moving quickly to avoid the masses of now swimming his way leeches sensing a warm blooded creature near at hand, Wallace quickly made his trap set in about 4" of water near a well-used beaver slide dotted with fresh beaver tracks in the soft mud. Then swirling his hand in the water close to the trap stirring up the muddy bottom, he covered the lethal instrument with just a slight film of mud from the pond's bottom. That he did so any arriving beaver would not see the trap when it arrived, stood up and grabbed the end of a willow stick stuck in the nearby bank previously dipped in castoreum in order to see what new beaver was in his territorial area. When the beaver did that, he hopefully would step in the nearby hidden beaver trap and would soon be on his way to a rendezvous and later made into some gentleman's beaver hat in the eastern United States or Europe. Then careful not to jerk the trap from its set position near the slide, Wallace carefully walked out the length of the trap's chain into deeper water and at its end, slipped the trap's chain ring over the wooden pole and then with his hand ax, hammered the stout pole into the bottom of the beaver pond. That way any beaver so trapped, in panic would swim off into deeper water trying to escape. When it did, the animal could only swim the distance of the trap's heavy chain and then be stopped in its escape efforts because of the wooden pole anchor tied to the end of the trap's chain. There the beaver would swim until exhausted and then the five-pound trap would drag the critter underwater where it would drown. Taking a piece of twine, he reached underwater and tied the trap chain's ring to the pole so if the beaver managed to uproot the pole and swim off, the trapper could later recover the floating wooden pole with the valuable and hard to replace trap still attached. Then Wallace moved off quickly before the oncoming horde of swimming leeches could get to him and find a place to attach onto his bare skin. Then still 'woofing and chirping' over the icy cold water and mud he found himself walking around in, he exited the beaver pond into the warmer air temperature on the land surrounding the beaver pond with much 'woofing and blowing 'relief. Six hours later, 23 other freshly used beaver slides had been located along the numerous waterways adjoining the Hams River and each now had a freshly set trap laid alongside where it stood the best chance of catching an unsuspecting beaver.

After all the trap setting was accomplished, Wallace then changed into his warmer clothing, mounted his horse after walking around on the dry ground to warm up and began looking for new trap sites along the river once they had trapped out the beaver along their current trap line. After that, it was back to his almost-nakedness and into the icy waters once again to pull from any of the previously set traps beaver just freshly caught that morning. For the next two months the Barnes Clan continued running their trap line on a daily basis, with predictable results common among the better Mountain Men of the day when the beaver numbers were great which resulted in lots of catching. "Catching" that required many subsequent long evening hours of defatting and hooping those numerous beaver pelts so they could dry out. That area of the Hams was rich with the furry rodent and soon hooped and drying beaver skins adorned the cabin's walls or were laid alongside the outside of the cabin's walls and on top of its and the storage shed's roofs in order to aid in the critical drying process.

By the end of that spring's trapping season when the beaver went out of their prime, the Barnes Clan had amassed 271 beaver, most of which were adult or Made Beaver. 'Made Beaver', which were worth anywhere from $3 to $6 a pound once they were sold at the upcoming rendezvous. And with beaver pelts running around 1½ pounds each, that meant anywhere from $4.50 to $9 per pelt in return to the trapper! That was providing the trappers of such furs made it through the lands of the murderous Blackfeet Nation, did a proper job skinning and hooping the pelt, and safely got to the coming rendezvous to be held in the vicinity of Bear Lake...

Sitting around their outdoor campfire one evening in and among the hundreds of hovering mosquitoes, Wallace, after thoughtfully 'pulling' on the stem of his pipe and then pleasurably emitting a large smoky cloud of James River tobacco smoke into the air said, "Near as I can figure, we have 525 beaver pelts, most of which are Made Beaver and 23 fine wolf pelts to take to the upcoming rendezvous. Even if we only get $3 per pound for our beaver skins, that represents a small fortune for us. But being Free Trappers as we now are, I would bet we will get at least $4-5 per pound and that is an even bigger fortune. That being the case, we should be able to walk away with a substantial Letter of Credit in addition to paying for and meeting all of our needs for another year of trapping. That said, maybe with another good year of beaver and wolf trapping behind us, we can amass enough money through all of our previous Letters of Credit to quit this trade and buy a sizeable spread of land back home. With that, we can once again become farmers and maybe even make a little Shine for the city folks and the extra coin it will bring into our coffers as well."

"Well, brother, we have got to get to the upcoming rendezvous first, sell our furs for what you think they are worth, and then hang onto our money and not drink it all up like most of the other trappers are wont to do at the rendezvous," said Cedrick, as he served up his special celebratory biscuits once again to the clan as they sat around the campfire eating and drinking in celebration of another successful year of trapping. Then Cedrick brought around the jug of warmed honey for the men to pour over their piping hot Dutch oven biscuits as they all favored doing.

However when he did, wood smoke or pipe smoke hanging heavy in the air or not, numerous mosquitoes always seemed to 'find' themselves stuck in the sticky honey gobbed biscuits, causing the men numerous times to pick the pesky insects out from the honey and toss them off to one side. However as the evening wore on and the cups of rum consumed during the end of the spring trapping season celebration continued, many mosquitoes ended up being stuck in the sticky honeyed biscuits, which were now overlooked and just eaten straight away...

The next morning after celebrating the end of another successful beaver and wolf trapping season the evening before, the Barnes Clan was not concerned about urgent calls of nature over at their designated 'special sitting logs' behind the cabin over constipation issues. It seemed that morning to a man, they all were moving about very slowly and not speaking very loudly to each other because of the after effects of imbibing so many cups of their rum the evening before... However, Cedrick was still the cook and found he was not very hungry, carrying what felt like a lead weight in the pit of his stomach and walking around with a head about to explode! Yet being the camp's cook, he still had to roast greasy elk ribs, mush with his hands a mound of slimy biscuit dough and stir a pot of pinto beans full of beaver fat chunks so they would not burn in order for his clan to have something to eat for their breakfast... Somewhat later, it seemed that Cedrick's brand of "trapper's coffee" was the only breakfast 'hit' of the morning!

An hour later of sitting very still on his sitting log by the fire so his head would not fall off his shoulders as a result of too many cups of rum drunk the evening before, Otis said, "Say, Wallace, isn't Bridger supposed to work his way down sometime soon from his trapping grounds up on the Salt River Range to our camp and then the two of our outfits travel together for the extra protection that offers over to the rendezvous?"

"That was the plan," said Wallace quietly, "Providing he and his fellow trappers have not 'gone under'. The last thing he told me before we separated company was that he planned on by late spring to head south from his trapping grounds on the Salt River Range, hook up with us and then our two groups would head west over to the new rendezvous site near Bear Lake. He figured that by so doing, the two groups of us would represent a sizeable force and with all of our rifles, hopefully be able to keep any curious or hostile Indians at bay. Plus he figured that in our travels west, we would run into other groups of trappers going to the rendezvous as well and by joining in with us, would present an even greater risk to any Indians who would want to take us on in order to kill and rob us of our furs and valuable horses."

"That being the case, we had best be ready

to ride if and when Bridger and his men arrive. You know Jim. All the other times we have seen him at a rendezvous, he can't wait to get there to meet his old buddies, see who still has his hair, celebrate and once into his 'rum cups', is a real "Stem-Winder", said Otis with a grin.

With that in mind, the next morning the men saw to it that their horse herd spent every day putting on the 'feed bag' for the much-anticipated long hard ride ahead to the coming rendezvous grounds. Additionally, the men using their remaining leather reserves made several more pack saddles for some of the now captured ten Indians' horses to carry their extra bundles of furs, remaining provisions, sleeping and cooking gear while en route the much-anticipated rendezvous.

As it just so turned out, two days later with a shout and yell, the Barnes Clan greeted their fellow arriving trappers in Jim Bridger's party fresh in from their travels down from their trapping grounds in the Salt River Range. For the next two days, the two groups of men celebrated each others' successful year of trapping as they let their horses and mules continue 'taking on the feed bag' in anticipation of the rugged crosscountry trip ahead to the Bear Lake country further to their west.

Come the morning before the group's planned departure en route the rendezvous, which according to Jim Bridger was somewhere in what he called Willow Valley near the south end of Bear Lake, Cedrick was up early. Instead of just having to feed the five men from the Barnes Clan, he was also cooking for Jim Bridger's three-man party as well. However, he had prepared for just such increased duties and with the help of Cloud, had chunks of skewered elk backstraps roasting away, his two-gallon coffee pot boiling up many spurts of aromatic coffee smelling steam, a fresh pot of his regular spiced with black pepper and not red pepper flakes pinto beans and lastly, his special biscuit mix ready to go into his three Dutch ovens warming over beds of coals.

Scurrying around his outdoor firepit watching over his cooking, Cedrick suddenly felt that almost physical 'sixth sense' feeling come over him that he had when the Barnes Clan had tangled with the group of Blackfeet caught stealing their provisions and furs from their cabin months earlier... Pausing and looking all around for any sign of danger, Cedrick saw nothing out of the ordinary. Then he stood there for a few more minutes examining the trappers' two combined horse and mule herds feeding in the nearby meadow to see if they were in any kind of danger from Indian horse thieves or a hungry bear. Then Cedrick heard Cloud say, "What is the matter, Cedrick? Why are you looking around like something is the matter?"

Catching himself and shaking off the eerie feeling he was getting, Cedrick turned and replied,

"Oh, it's nothing, Cloud. I just thought for a moment that something was not right but after looking around I see that our livestock are alright, our breakfast is almost ready, the biscuits will soon be baking and look at the beautiful day the good Lord has given us." With that, Cedrick returned to his cooking duties and buried within his soul his eerie concerns as maybe 'they' were just a bad case of indigestion from eating too much of his heavy cooking from the night before.

The following morning of their planned departure, the eight trappers were up around four in the morning because of all the work that lay ahead. As seven of their number began saddling their riding horses and packing all of their things onto the pack animals, Cedrick, ever the loyal cook, was hard at it making a hearty breakfast that would 'keep' the men going during a long and hard day of travel. A hard day of travel, herding along two long pack trains of heavily loaded animals still getting adjusted to the heavy loads they would be carrying and each other.

Cedrick began his 'breakfast morning' with his metal skewers heavily loaded with chunks of the last of his elk meat roasting over his firepit. Those efforts were followed with his careful tending of a pot full of the last of his group's rice, which was cooking away after being heavily laced with raisins, brown sugar and liberal doses of cinnamon. Collateral with those duties, he kept a 'cocked' eye on his starting to boil, two-gallon coffee pot and his three Dutch ovens 'huffing' small jets of steam out from under their lids letting him know his special biscuits were almost done. Biscuits baking away in the Dutch ovens that were especially made with previously soaked, small slices of dried apple, lots of raisins, brown sugar and cinnamon. No one made better 'special' biscuits like Cedrick and that morning, every man's sweet tooth would be more than satisfied with what he was serving up for breakfast.

"Breakfast is ready," yelled Cedrick as he placed more sticks of wood on his cooking fire so the arriving men would be well warmed. Then as the men scrambled for any place on the sitting logs arranged around the campfire, Cedrick and Cloud began serving the hungry men previously warmed metal plates loaded with chunks of elk meat that was still sizzling, piping hot specially made biscuits and gobs of a hot rice dish the men soon found more than pleasing to their palates! Then as Cloud served the men their morning coffee, Cedrick loaded his and Cloud's plates full of the morning meal as well. Soon the only sounds heard around the campfire that morning were the clanking of forks and spoons against the men's metal eating plates, the crackling of the morning fire, the incessant hum of the ever-present mosquitoes, and the nervous shuffling of the feet of the now packed and loaded horses and mules eager to once again be on the trail…

Later that morning found Jim Bridger in the

lead of a long caravan of fully loaded horses and mules, with Cloud, Feather and Cedrick as outriders providing extra watching eyes and protection as the trappers began their travels to a much-anticipated rendezvous to be held somewhere at the south end of Bear Lake in Willow Valley. Come noontime, the men paused along a stream in the high mountain west and let their animals take long drinks for the long and dry trail lying across the sage, rabbit brush and salt flats still lying ahead. Instead of a hot meal fixed by Cedrick that afternoon, the men feasted on sticks of jerky and deep draughts of the cool water from the same stream the men's horses and mules were drinking from.

That evening the men feasted upon the whole roasted carcass of a fat doe antelope that Jim Bridger had surprised feeding and subsequently shot in a small draw, along with cool water from a nearby stream. Once again the next morning, the trappers were up early way before daylight and by noon had finally loaded all of their mules and horses with the caravan's supplies and bundles of furs. Then with only jerky for breakfast and none of Cedrick's 'special' biscuits because every cooking utensil had been carefully packed away for the trip, the men continued their westward movement to the site of the upcoming rendezvous.

Later when moving through a dense stand of scrubby pine trees and tall stands of big sage,

Cedrick, last man in the long line of trappers' horses and mules, was surprised to all of sudden see a previously hidden Indian abruptly stand up in the stand of big sagebrush to his front! Hardly believing his eyes at the closeness of the Indian previously unseen, Cedrick all of a sudden realized the Indian he was looking at WAS THE SAME ONE WHO HAD GOTTEN AWAY IN THEIR EARLIER BATTLE WITH THE BLACKFEET BACK AT THEIR OLD CABIN! THIS HE KNEW BECAUSE THE INDIAN HE WAS LOOKING AT FROM JUST A FEW FEET AWAY WAS THE ONE WITH ONLY TWO HOLES IN THE FRONT OF HIS FACE FROM WHICH TO BREATHE AND TOTALLY LACKING A NOSE THAT SOMEHOW HAD BEEN CHOPPED OFF THE MAN'S FACE BY A KNIFE OR TOMAHAWK! THEN ALL OF A SUDDEN, THE EERIE ALMOST PHYSICAL 'SIXTH SENSE' FEELINGS OF DREAD HE HAD FELT SEVERAL DAYS EARLIER, CAME ROARING BACK AT HIM WITH A RUSH!

THEN WITH A BLOOD-CURDLING YELL, THE INDIAN WITH THE DEFORMED FACE WHO HAD ABRUPTLY STOOD UP IN THE SAGEBRUSH IN FRONT OF CEDRICK LOOSED AN ARROW RIGHT AT HIM! STILL STUNNED OVER THE SURPRISE ATTACK BY THE INDIAN WITH NO NOSE, SOON SUPPORTED BY A DOZEN OTHERS SUDDENLY RISING UP OUT FROM THE DENSE STAND OF SAGEBRUSH,

CEDRICK WATCHED IN HORROR AS THE JUST LOOSED ARROW WAS COMING RIGHT AT HIM AS IF IN SLOW MOTION!

ZZIPPP-THUMP! WENT THE ARROW RIGHT INTO CEDRICK'S CHEST AREA, ENTERING JUST BELOW HIS BREAST BONE! IN A MICRO-SECOND, CEDRICK FELT THE STEEL-TIPPED ARROW PLUNGING DEEPLY INTO HIS VITALS, SEVERING THE ARTERY LEADING INTO HIS LIVER! INSTANTLY, A TREMENDOUS BURNING FIRE WAS FELT INSIDE HIS CHEST, AS THE SLICED ARTERY RELEASED ITS FLOW OF HOT BLOOD WITH A RUSH INTO CEDRICK'S BODY CAVITY! DROPPING HIS RIFLE, CEDRICK GRABBED THE ARROW'S SHAFT WITH BOTH HANDS IN UTTER PAIN AND JUST HUNG ON AS IF THAT WOULD HELP. IN HIS EYES HE COULD SEE THE REST OF THE TRAPPERS SHOOTING BACK INTO THE GROUP OF AMBUSHING INDIANS, AS WHITE CLOUDS OF BLACK POWDER SMOKE ROARED ACROSS THE TOPS OF THE SAGEBRUSH, MOMENTARILY HIDING THE ATTACKING INDIANS AS WELL AS THE TRAPPERS! THEN HE SAW THROUGH DIMMING EYES INDIANS DROPPING, HORSES AND MULES BUCKING IN TERROR, INDIANS CONTINUING TO SHOOT THEIR RIFLES AND ARROWS AT THE LINE OF TRAPPERS, AND THEN CHARGING THE HORSEMEN WITH UPRAISED TOMAHAWKS,

ALL AMID THE SOUNDS OF WOUNDED AND DYING MEN AND HORSES!

THEN CEDRICK LOOKED DOWN AT THE FRONT OF HIS CHEST AT THE ARROW STICKING INTO HIS VITALS AND THE FRESH BLOOD STREAMING OUT FROM BELOW THE ARROW SHAFT'S ENTRY POINT INTO HIS CHEST AND SPILLING ACROSS THE FRONT OF HIS BUCKSKIN SHIRT. THE 'BURNING FIRE FEELING' IN HIS GUTS BECAME SO INTENSE THAT HE LOOKED UP TO SEE IF ANY OF HIS BROTHERS COULD HELP HIM... WHEN HE DID, THE BATTLE TO HIS FRONT WAS NOW SWIMMING IN A HAZY DARKNESS AND HALOS OF LIGHT WERE FLASHING ACROSS THE TOP OF HIS EYES MAKING ANYTHING HE WAS NOW DIZZILY LOOKING AT BEGIN TO FADE... THE ROARING IN HIS EARS BEGAN GETTING QUIETER AND THEN HIS LAST THOUGHTS WERE TRYING TO REACH OUT AND SOFTEN HIS FALL FROM HIS HORSE...

Otis, upon seeing the first Indian rise out from the sagebrush and shoot an arrow at Cedrick from just feet away, quickly swung his rifle which had been lying across his saddle and without raising it to his shoulder, leveled it and shot that close at hand Indian dead! Then all hell broke loose as other Indians lying hidden in the sagebrush rose from both sides of the line of trappers and their animals moving through the sagebrush field and began firing their rifles and shooting their arrows! It was just then that Otis lost sight of his brother when he had his horse shot out from under him and as his horse dropped, he deftly stepped out from his stirrups, swung his rifle barrel at the Indian who had just shot at him and had killed his horse instead. That rifle barrel met the Indian's head with such force, that it crushed into the man's skull and remained stuck there no matter how hard Otis tried to pull it away! Then leaving his rifle stuck in the Indian's skull, Otis drew both of his pistols from his sash and shot two Indians rushing at him from just mere feet away with upraised tomahawks, shooting and killing both men!

Jim Reed and Peter Softer, Jim Bridger's two trapping companions, both died in the initial fusillade of shots fired into the caravan of trappers as they were passing through the sagebrush 'ambush' field, as did both of their riding horses!

Wallace, finding himself surrounded on two sides by Indians rising up out from the dense sagebrush field with aimed rifles in hand, quickly spurred his horse and both Indians firing at him simultaneously, ended up shooting each other... Another Indian rose up about the same time in front of Wallace and his bolting horse and was run over and killed by the trapper's horse's hooves! Whirling his horse around from the front of the line of trappers and their packhorses where he had been riding and talking with Jim Bridger,

Wallace stormed back through the ambush of Indians behind him yelling like a banshee, shooting his rifle then dropping it, drawing both pistols from his sash and shooting two Indians at point-blank range with deadly accurate results! In his split seconds of rifle and pistol shooting, Wallace and his horse had killed three Indians in the process!

Jim Bridger, also riding at the head of the pack string leading the way since he knew where he needed to go, instantly sensing their danger when ambushed, went 'frontier crazy'! Whirling his horse around, he rode down one Indian, killed another with his rifle and another with his pistol, whom he shot down through the top of his head as he rode by the man trying to hastily reload his Indian Trade rifle! Then Jim jumped off his horse and ran screaming like a banshee through the sagebrush and killed two more Indians with his tomahawk in the process of also hurriedly reloading their rifles!

Cloud was 'blown' off his horse when an Indian rose up from the sagebrush right alongside him as he rode by and tried to 'snap-shoot' him off his horse! In so doing, all the Indian did was miss hitting Cloud but his stream of black powder smoke and flame from the near headshot miss, blew him off his horse! When Cloud hit the ground, he found himself lying stunned on the ground, seeing nothing but bright lights from the force of the Indian's rifle exploding right in his face and hearing nothing but a loud ringing noise in his head from the close-in shot! Feather, seeing what had happened since he had been riding alongside Cloud, quickly drew his tomahawk, reached over the side of his horse, grabbed the Indian shooter's buckskin shirt, jerked him forward and split open the head of his friend's shooter! In so doing, Feather broke off the head of his tomahawk in his adversary's skull because he had struck the man so forcefully because of the intense emotion of the moment!

Then other than the heavy breathing from all of the living trappers because of the emotion of the deadly moment now past, with the killing of the ambushing Indians and a number of frightened horses and mules milling around in the sagebrush, ALL WAS QUIET ONCE AGAIN IN THE SAGEBRUSH FIELD! The surprise ambush by a number of Blackfeet Indians, who were later identified by Bridger by their dress and the markings on their horses later discovered hidden away in a nearby stand of pines, apparently had been led by the Indian with no nose! The same 'no nose' Indian who had escaped from an earlier fight with the Barnes Clan when they had raided the trappers' cabin, leaving 16 dead Blackfeet Indians in their wake after that battle had ended! Additionally, three trappers died in the initial ambush, as well as having three trappers' horses shot out from under them!

Then Otis and Wallace, looking around to see

who was still standing, noticed Cedrick's horse standing off in the sagebrush by itself! Fearing the worst, Wallace rode and Otis ran over to Cedrick's horse and expecting the worst, had their suspicions confirmed! Lying there in a large pool of blood now slowly sinking into the sandy soil laid Cedrick! On his face he wore a surprised look! In both of his hands were the feathers on the shaft end of an arrow that when he had fallen off his horse, he had inadvertently landed directly upon the arrow sticking out from his belly area. The impact of landing upon that arrow and the weight of his falling body had driven the arrow almost clear through his body! That was the second time that Cloud and Feather had seen the two Barnes brothers, both normally very stoic, strong and reserved men, break down and cry like babies over the death of their youngest brother and the third member to do so from their dwindling blood family now reduced from five to just two!

That afternoon, the remaining men dug a deep grave and quietly placed all three trappers killed in the battle together in death as they had been in their recent lives. After burying the men, all of the dead Indians were then dragged over on top of the gravesite, along with the three horses killed during the ambush which were placed over the site of the grave as well. Then the men cut and dragged a number of pine logs and armloads of sagebrush and placed all of those materials on top of the pile of dead Indians and horses. This was done at the behest of Jim Bridger who figured when they left the next day, they would set the brush and logs afire so the bodies of the Indians and horses would begin to burn up. That way he figured no grizzly bear would dig up the three dead trappers buried underneath, since the smell of their decaying bodies would no longer be an issue with all the smells of the burned dead Indians and horses atop the gravesite. Neither would digging up the gravesite become an issue with the local Indians since they would be spooked off by all of the bones and artifacts from their dead tribal members.

Realizing that life must go on, Bridger and Wallace left the killing field looking for the valuable horses of the Indians who had just ambushed them. A short time later those horses were discovered tied off in some distant trees and all of them were brought back to the killing field where the trappers had been ambushed. However in so doing, Bridger and company discovered a welcome surprise to what had started out being a very bad day. There among the number of Indians' horses stood five other horses. It was soon discovered that the five other horses had at one time belonged to other recently ambushed trappers who had also been en route the upcoming rendezvous! There on three of the five horses were bundles of beaver pelts from those trappers' trapping successes as well as their riding saddles! These spoils of the recent fight were gladly taken as well, but in no way compensated the Barnes Clan or Jim Bridger for the loss of their three friends and family. Shortly afterwards, the men removed all telltale riding equipment from the Indians' horses and placed those items on the pile of dead horses and Indians to be burned the following day as well. Then all visible markings on the Indians' horses like painted symbols on the animals' bodies, and manes and tails cropped in a certain manner by the previous owners by washing and re-cutting, were removed as well in case other Indians discovered such marked horses in among the trappers. That they did because if the trappers were subsequently captured by other like in kind Indians who discovered familiar tribal or band marking on the extra horses, their deaths would have been forthcoming and painfully slow in the process, if history was any teacher...

Following that, the men moved the remainder of their fur caravan off a few hundred yards from the ambush site where a small spring existed and made their camp for the evening. All of their horses were then unpacked and the equipment stacked in a defensive circle around their sleeping furs in case any other Indians came calling that evening or the next morning after hearing all of the earlier shooting during the ambush. Then the horses and mules were hobbled and let out to graze under the watchful eyes of Cloud and Feather. That night instead of feasting upon Cedrick's 'special' biscuits for their evening meal, the remaining five men ate cold jerky from their saddlebags in silence and then quietly and emotionally drained, retreated to their sleeping furs. The next morning, there were no 'special' biscuits for breakfast, just jerky once again. Then after loading all the pack animals and saddling up their riding horses and another riding horse for Otis taken from the captured trappers' stock since his had been killed in the battle with the Blackfeet, the men rode in silence back to the pile of dead Indians and horses placed over the burial site of the three dead trappers. With his flint and steel, Otis started the dry sagebrush afire gathered for the funeral pyre from the day before and soon a roaring fire was blazing, beginning the process of consuming the bodies of the 16 Blackfeet Indians, all of their riding gear and the three horses also killed in the battle. Then realizing that the funeral pyre smoke might attract unwanted attention, the trappers continued their travels towards the rendezvous site in a heightened state of awareness just in case there were more hostile Indians in the area who crossed their path and elected to do battle.

As they rode on, Wallace, Otis, Cloud and Feather looked back several times at the roiling clouds of black smoke being emitted from the distant grove of trees generated from the fat being consumed on all of the burning bodies. As they did in their own ways, the Barnes Clan remembered the quiet cook and much-loved brother from their camp named Cedrick. A much-loved brother and man who through his meals and cheerful demeanor, always seemed to make their day... He had been a much-loved man, who in his time had discovered the mystery of being and of nature. No longer would Cedrick have to wonder about the eerie feelings he had received prior to the occurrence of any deadly events. They had come and gone and so had he, just like his two other brothers, Sterling and Oliver. Gone as a consequence of living out on the beautiful but many times fraught with danger, frontier...

Two days of uneventful travel later, the recently ambushed trappers and their now larger horse and mule herd rode into the upper reaches of Willow Valley near the southeastern corner of Bear Lake. When they did, they discovered the campsites of around 50 other trappers and friendly Indians who had already gathered at the proposed rendezvous site. Moving in among the other trappers and Indians for the protection the larger group offered, Bridger and the Barnes Clan made camp near a small, barely flowing stream. While Otis began scrounging around their new campsite looking for firewood, the rest of the men unloaded all of their horses and mules and after being hobbled, let them out to graze nearby away from other herds of already grazing livestock belonging to other trappers and friendly Indians.

As the rest of the men laid out their sleeping furs under several nearby cottonwood trees, Otis, now the designated camp cook, began assembling the cooking gear he figured he would need for the men during their stay at the rendezvous. He then began unpacking the packs holding their remaining provisions, dug into their bag of pinto beans and filled a cooking kettle full of beans and water and set it aside to soak. Then as Cloud and Feather mounted up and left the area to see what they could kill in the way of camp meat, Otis, Jim Bridger and Wallace found their campsite soon surrounded by old friends who had previously arrived for the rendezvous. That evening after a supper of antelope steaks and slightly burned Dutch oven biscuits, Bridger and company broke out their last keg of rum and celebrated another successful trapping season with a handful of old friends like Jed Smith, "Bear Scat" Sutta, Tom Jackson, William Sublette and Tom "Iron Hand" Warren. However, as the men discovered among themselves, provisions were in short order and almost everyone subsisted on just venison, beans and biscuits until the much-anticipated supply train would arrive from faraway St. Louis.

For the next five days in late May, the men slept in, visited and watched for the arrival of General Ashley and his caravan so they could start the rendezvous off with a bang. In the meantime, additional streams of trappers and friendly Indians poured into the previously designated rendezvous site until over several hundred men waited around for the arrival of General Ashley. In the meantime, Cloud and Feather kept their camp supplied with antelope and mule deer as camp meat since no buffalo as a meat supply were in evidence so far west. Then one afternoon, Cloud came riding into camp in a cloud of dust waving his arms and speaking excitedly in his native Shoshoni tongue! "Settle down!" said Otis, as Cloud's horse sprayed dust and flying pieces of horse crap into the air when hastily reined in next to the firepit, as well as all over a wooden bowl full of Otis's rising biscuit dough! "What the hell ails you, boy?" grumbled Otis as he scooped up his bowl of biscuit dough and turned away from the cloud of flying dust and bits and pieces of horse crap stirred up by Cloud's fast-arriving horse.

"Feather got a moose! Feather got a moose and a big one at that!" yelled an excited Cloud as he bailed off his horse with a huge grin on his face, and then fell flat on his face from all of his forward motion and a stubbed toe that had dug itself in against an exposed cottonwood tree root!

"Well, I'll be damned! No more mule deer for this camp. By Gum, we eat some damn good moose meat tonight!" said a normally much-reserved Otis in an excited tone of voice.

"Where he be, boy?" asked Bridger.

"About a mile to our north near the lake in a big patch of willows," said a still excited Cloud.

"Otis, you get them beans a-cooking and me and Cloud here are going to saddle up a couple packhorses and see what we can do about bringing back to our camp some of that great tasting moose meat," said Bridger, whose tone and tenor of voice was starting to show some excitement in it as well over the prospects of some excellent tasting moose meat soon to come!

Then Wallace just returning from taking care of a call of nature and overhearing the excited talking about some fresh moose meat soon to be in camp and realizing how much that could be in poundage, yelled over at Jed Smith's nearby camp. "Jed, we have a passel of moose meat soon coming into this camp. If you and the boys want some, be sure and send over your camp cook when Cloud, Feather and Bridger return." Upon hearing those words, Jed Smith waved his arm back in happy acknowledgement.

Two hours later found Cloud, Feather and Jim Bridger coming back into camp leading three heavily loaded packhorses carrying the front shoulders, two hindquarters and two sides of moose ribs. Within moments, there were many eager hands from other nearby trappers lending help in unloading and beginning the process of boning out about 500 pounds of moose meat! Soon the three trappers' campsites nearest that of the Barnes Clan rang with much excitement around their campfires as the skilled Mountain Men cooks began rendering a frontier supper beyond compare. Well, that was in light of the fact that there was no buffalo meat in camp, which was still most trappers' favorite and preferred kind of meat. Well, that was if bighorn sheep meat wasn't available, then if it was, 'meat preference' was a 'cat of another color' when it came to eating the meat from that of a succulent bighorn...

The next day on May the 25th, several shouts from the edge of the trappers' camps announced the happy arrival of General Ashley with the rendezvous annual supply train! Then to the trappers' excitement and amazement, General Ashley rode into the encampment at the head of 300 fully loaded mules being herded along by his company traders and mule skinners! With Ashley's arrival, a murmur of excitement and new life now rippled through the rendezvous site. For the next four hours as Ashley's men began setting up their immediate campsite and trading center of activity, several hundred trappers and Indians gathered all around that camp set-up activity with great expectation and excitement. Now the trappers and Indians would have their much-needed annual supplies, there would soon be much celebrating, wrestling contests, shooting events, Indian wife swapping, fur trading, purchasing of much-needed supplies, and drinking rum and whiskey until one could not stand of his own accord...

General Ashley's days of hard and oftentimes dangerous travel from St. Louis, up along the

Platte which had claimed the life of Sterling Barnes in a pit of quicksand, through South Pass, across the Green River Valley and into the Bear Lake area took 78 days, and the General was more than ready for the trading and celebrations to begin. For the next two days, General Ashley's 30 or so men prepared their trading sites and then the long awaited day of expectation arrived! With the sound of a shot heard around the entire rendezvous fired from a small cannon Ashley had trailed all the way from St. Louis, streams of more than ready trappers began arriving at the trading sites trailing their loaded pack animals. There after much pushing, shoving and near horse and mule wrecks, organization and sanity finally settled in. It was then that the serious trading began. Trappers stood in long lines with their loaded horses and mules, patiently awaiting their turns at Ashley's Company fur graders and counters for the processing of their furs. Then after their sales figures had been decided, the rush was on with Letters of Credit in hand for the much-needed re-provisioning before all of the vital goods like liquor, powder, pigs of lead, clothing, cooking implements, the newest types of firearms, heavy wool capotes, new wide-brimmed hats and the like were gone until the following year's supply train had once again arrived at the designated rendezvous site.

For the next eight weeks as more and more trappers streamed into the rendezvous site, the trading and celebrating throughout the camp continued with the traditional and reckless abandon commonly found at all rendezvous. There were horse races, fights, foot races to see who was the fastest trapper in camp which Feather won, squaw trading, gambling with their hard won profits from a year's trapping, and every night much carousing, fighting and drinking until the wee hours when physical exhaustion or one ran out of money overcame the many celebrants. Before this drunken celebration was over and the trappers headed back into their choice of beaver trapping country for the coming trapping seasons, many would go back with just the clothes on their back, a rifle across the saddle, several horses or mules, a year's provisions in tow, and little or nothing else to show for a previous year of fur trapping once the rendezvous was over...

When it finally came time for the Barnes Clan and Jim Bridger to stand in line and trade their furs, they did so separately. Jim went first and traded in all of his beaver pelts trapped up on the Salt River Range with his two now dead partners, receiving $5 on the average per pound per pelt. When the Barnes Clan moved forward with their 525 beaver pelts, they also received $5/pound for their beaver furs, being that they were Free Trappers and all (American Fur Company's company trappers only received $3/pound for their furs that year). With each Made Beaver pelt weighing about 1½ pounds, the Barnes Clan received $3,937.50 for all of their trapped furs! They then traded in their half-share of beaver pelts (the other half share went to Bridger) discovered along with the herd of Indian horses that had been taken from other trappers, after the 'Sagebrush ambush battle' had been 'settled'. Those beaver pelts brought an additional $5/pound or $562.50 for a grand total of $4,500! Then the Barnes Clan sold off their share of the Blackfeet Indians' and trappers' horses for an additional $400 in pelts. Lastly, they received another $370 in pelts for the Blackfeet Indians' horses who had been caught raiding their last cabin. Altogether, they now had a total of $5,270 in a Letter of Credit from the American Fur Company!

Having decided that the Barnes Clan and Jim Bridger, since they had lost trapping partners, would trap the coming fall and the spring together for the extra protection their numbers would bring, they shared the cost of another year's provisions. That came to $900 for Bridger and the Barnes Clan to each 'pony up' for the $1,800 spent at Mountain Prices for their next year's provisions. Since both groups still had all of their essential gear, all they needed were just the basic provisions and not the expensive cooking, trapping or firearms equipment. With that decided, the Barnes Clan received a Letter of Credit to be drawn on the company's fur house in St. Louis for $4,370, or a small fortune! Wallace, with General Ashley's Letter of Credit for $4,370, walked over to his horse and removing his other Letters of Credit from previous years of beaver trapping, tied the bundle of letters into one packet and then placed them back into his saddle bag. But for now, the Barnes Clan had decided at least one more year trapping out on the frontier, especially with famed Mountain Man Jim Bridger, was in the cards for the men.

CHAPTER THIRTEEN

TRAPPING THE "BEAR" WITH BRIDGER

BY THE MIDDLE OF JUNE, both Bridger and the Barnes Clan were getting tired of all the noisy and sometimes lethal and drunken hell-raising at many of the different rendezvous events taking place. In fact, four late arriving trappers had just moved in right next to the Bridger and Barnes Clan's campsite and proved to be bad neighbors! Two of the newly arriving trappers were French-Canadian deserters from the Hudson's Bay Company and their two partners turned out to be 'renegade' and mean spirited Gros Ventre Indians. Aside from nightly noisy drunken celebrations at their new neighbors' camp, Cloud and Feather soon discovered that the Gros Ventre considered themselves bitter enemies of the Shoshoni! Soon many sarcastic looks were being directed at Cloud and Feather by the Gros Ventre arrivals as they worked around their adjacent campsites. That was not to mention, many snide and tribally degrading remarks being verbally hurled their ways as well. Fortunately for the Gros Ventre, Cloud and Feather just ignored the degrading remarks being hurled their way on a daily basis. Additionally since they had decided to team up after having lost three of their partners and trap as a group for the added protection it offered, the men began realizing what work now lay ahead for all of them before they could set one beaver or wolf trap. They also realized just how fast time could fly, especially when one had to travel to new beaver trapping grounds, build a place to live, construct horse corrals in order to more safely protect one's primary means of travel, locate good beaver producing grounds and prepare for the harsh northern winters lying ahead.

With those thoughts of what lay ahead, the five trappers quietly sat around their rendezvous campfire one evening after a supper of heavily spiced with fresh red pepper flakes, pinto beans, biscuits, antelope steaks (antelope because all of the huge moose had since been eaten), and coffee. As they did, one could almost tell from their quiet behavior around the campfire that all were 'hankering' for the peace and quiet found on a new trapping site. After a long quiet spell, the men lit up their pipes, sat back with a cup of rum apiece and just enjoyed their fire and own camp-site's clouds of mosquitoes. Finally Jim Bridger spoke up saying, "Boys, I think I would like to trap the Bear River just south and east of us here during this fall and spring's trapping seasons. Last time I was in that neck of the woods, there were beaver a-plenty and good graze just about everywhere I looked for our horses, even come the winter months because of the almost constant winds blowing the pastures and meadows clear of snow. Plus, the area I have in mind is not too far from next year's rendezvous which is to be back in this same country. Last time I was there traveling through, I did not 'seed hide nor hair' of any other kind of human varmint, the beaver ponds near the Bear River were full of fresh bea-ver houses and they was eating every tree, bush and willow patch they could fix their 'chompers' onto. I figure if we can get there without getting our hair lifted or 'a-goin' under', we ought to do right fair come this time next year with more than our share of pelts to show for a year's hard work."

"Well, Jim, since you know the way, me and the boys have already talked over the fact that we would be trapping with you come this fall and next spring, so I guess we are going with you come 'hell or high water'. The only thing left is when do we leave this here rendezvous for that

Bear River country that you are talking about? I ask because most of our horses need new shoes. I suggest we set to getting that done in the next day or so before everyone else has that same idea and jams up the few blacksmiths that Ashley brought along with him. But other than that, with all the provisions we have, we are ready to 'give her another whirl' if that be to your way of thinking and satisfaction somewhere along that Bear River you are always talking about," said Wallace.

"Now that I come to think of it, my horses could use some new shoes as well. What say we all head over to the blacksmiths' area tomorrow, get our horses shoed and then come back for one more supper with some of our friends. After that, we can get hell out of here before any undue trouble comes our way," said Bridger nodding towards the adjacent camp of bad neighbors. "Asides, I ain't getting any younger and I just as soon get there on the beaver trapping grounds afore anyone else does. Them damn beaver ain't a-going to stay there forever in the numbers I 'seed' the last time I was there the way they are being trapped out from this country in general," said Bridger as he finished off his cup of rum and laid the cup down by his place at the fire. Then without another word, Bridger ambled off in a shuffling style of walking like many trappers of the day wearing moccasins exhibited towards his sleeping furs like he knew where he was a-going and damn glad to get there. Moments later, the Barnes Clan finished off their cups of rum and then ambled off towards their sleeping furs as well, followed by small clouds of still hopeful mosquitoes. Soon the only sounds heard around the trappers' camp were the heavy sounds of men snoring and the constant humming of the ever-present mosquitoes over each man's head lying exposed outside his sleeping furs.

The next morning found the Barnes Clan and Bridger taking their entire riding and pack string over to the place that had been set up as a 'blacksmith shop' under the shade of a mess of cottonwood trees. Arriving just before daylight in order to be first in line with so many animals needing attention, the group of trappers had to get the blacksmiths out from their beds and get them up so they could fire up their forges for the shoeing work at hand needing to be done. Then while three "Smithies" began removing the shoes from the men's horses and mules, two other Smithies began shoeing the animals from the company's barrels of "Store Bought" horseshoes brought along for just such occasions. However, fitting the men's mules to the correct fitting shoes took some doing and hot-forge adjusting in order to get the correct shoe sizes by individual animal. Six hours later the shoeing work was finally accomplished, several animals had their problem teeth floated and a number of bridles had been readjusted for the most cantankerous mules whose old bridles did not fit correctly. Bridger saw to it that his Letter of Credit was adjusted downward to pay for all of the shoeing and adjustment work that was needed for the group's string of animals since he did not have to be the camp's cook, leaving that to Otis.

Additionally, the Smithies lanced and removed several boils off Feather's backside that had been bothering him for some time. As a result of such minor boil surgery leaving him with a sore hind end, Feather walked his horse back to their camp and once there, Otis treated his sore behind with a liberal application of bag balm to help salve the soreness and ensure faster healing. Come the next day, Feather was up and moving around like nothing had been painfully lanced and drained from his hind end other than some of his pride...

For the rest of that day, the men packed all of their gear onto the pack saddles and made ready for the following day's departure for the Bear River country, which according to Jim was just 'a short piece' to their south and then a little 'crow-hop' to the east. Before daylight the next morning, the men were up early and while Otis fixed the men's breakfast of biscuits, beans and coffee, the arduous job of carefully saddling and adjusting the packs on all of their packhorses and mules began. After a quick breakfast and while Otis cleaned up his cooking gear and saw to it that it was properly packed away to avoid breakage in case of a horse wreck, the rest of the packing labors were finally successfully completed by the rest of the trappers.

By noon, the trappers' first long heavily loaded pack string led by Jim Bridger, trailed by Cloud and Feather each leading another long pack string, further trailed by Wallace leading a fourth long pack string, was finally brought up by Otis who was just a lone, heavily armed rider protecting the caravan's rear. There were lots of waves and shouts of encouragement and "see you next year and keep your hair" salutations as the much-recognized Mountain Men made their ways through the rendezvous camp and headed almost due south to their new trapping grounds on the Bear River. Even their four distasteful neighbors camping next to the Bridger and Barnes Clan's camp seemed to be very interested in the leaving party of trappers... As such, there were no friendly waves of good-bye from that distasteful group, as Bridger's and the Barnes Clan's friends had done when the caravan of leaving trappers had passed. As it turned out, the Hudson's Bay deserters and their two renegade Gros Ventre Indian friends just watched the famous Mountain Man and his group ride off and the direction of travel they were taking.

Four days later the heavily loaded pack strings found their leaders quietly overlooking the slowly flowing Bear River lying below them. To their south lay several long meadows and to their north and east lay several long and heavily timbered ridges interspersed with grassy meadows. Without a word, Bridger pointed with his right hand and arm towards the long timbered ridges lying to their north and east, and then carefully headed the men and heavily loaded pack animals down to the edge of the river. Riding northward along the river's edge, Bridger finally located a shallow ford and took the pack string across the river and then led them up into the low foothills leading to the timbered ridges lying just beyond.

There once in the comforting reaches of the timber and out of sight from any wandering eyes of hostile Indians, Bridger led the men into a large grassy depression bordered by trees on all sides with a meadow enveloping the entire secluded area within the pines. Stopping he looked around and then headed the pack string towards the end of the shallow depression and up into the timber lying at the northern most end of the meadow. There he stopped alongside a fast moving stream, dismounted and rubbed his sore knees from the day's long ride into the area. Turning, he motioned for the rest of the trappers to dismount as he continued looking all around just in case some form of danger from man or beast lay close at hand.

"This is it, boys. This can be the site for our new home for the rest of the year and beyond. We have plenty of water for drinking and our livestock, lots of good graze for our animals, all the timber we will need is close at hand in order to build a cabin and fuel our fires, and we are out of the north wind and out of sight from anyone looking for a mess of trappers to overrun or steal our valuable livestock," said Bridger quietly as his frontier experienced eyes still roamed the area as if looking for any flaws in the living area just chosen.

As the rest of the men dismounted and continued looking around at their new home site, not Otis. When he dismounted, he walked over to a small stand of Douglas fir trees and began mentally figuring and looking just where their new cabin would be built. With that potential location in mind, he walked off a few paces and dragged an "X" in the dirt with his boot marking the location of his new outdoor cooking firepit and sitting area. Then without another word as the rest of the men began unsaddling all of their horses, Otis retrieved a shovel from one of the packs on a packhorse and walked back to the "X" just marked in the soil. Laying his rifle down but still near at hand in case any danger reared its head, Otis began digging his cooking fire and general firepit. As he did, the rest of the men now began removing the pack saddles from their beasts of burden and as a standard frontier practice, began arranging them in a defensive circle under a small stand of pine trees for the protection they would offer in the event they were suddenly attacked by Indians. However, those packs holding a number of their needed provisions and all of their cooking implements were removed and placed near the firepit being built in order to facilitate Otis when he needed to cook the trappers' daily meals.

Then as Otis continued work on his firepit, the rest of the men brought over a number of large stones from the nearby creek so he could line the firepit. Then as Otis lined the firepit the way he wanted, the rest of the men hobbled all of their horses and mules and led them into the meadow so they could graze and become familiar with their new surroundings. With Feather sitting off to one side of the now quietly grazing herd of mules and horses making sure no one had observed their arrival and came looking for some valuable horseflesh, the rest of the men laid out their sleeping furs and began gathering up old pine cones and limb wood for Otis's soon to be cooking fire. As they did, Otis using a small hand ax, drove the hanging and cooking steels in place into the ground so they would be ready when called upon to hang their ever-present coffee or bean pot. Then with his fire steel, Otis set ablaze his recently laid fire so come nightfall, he would have the required amount of coals in order to bake his soon to be made Dutch oven biscuits. Soon, he had a pot of rice and another pot of pinto beans soaking away and placed close to the firepit, the coffee pot filled with water from their nearby creek, a Dutch oven roasting their green coffee beans and beginning to make up his biscuit dough. Additionally, Otis had a treat in mind for all of the men for their coming supper. Into another steel pot with water went several large handfuls of dried raisins and then that pot was set alongside the fire in order to warm up so the raisins would plump up faster but not boil away.

Meanwhile, Jim Bridger gathered up his newest Lancaster reserve rifle purchased at the last rendezvous that he had named "Old Meat in the Pot" and headed off into the timbered hills behind the men's campsite with procuring some camp meat in mind. About 40 minutes later, the men back at camp heard the unmistakable sound of a single rifle shot and then nothing further. Not hearing any more shooting, the Barnes Clan relaxed, figuring Bridger had connected with some camp meat as they continued on with their chores in setting up their camp. About 20 minutes later, Bridger came trotting back to camp with the news that he had a cow elk down and needed some help in getting its carcass back to camp before it began to bloat or some critter decided to make an early supper stop. Minutes later, Cloud and Feather began following Bridger back into the timber, trailing two hastily retrieved from the meadow pack mules carrying their pack saddles once again. An hour later, a nearby shout heralded the arrival of Bridger, Cloud and Feather leading two heavily loaded pack mules carrying quarters of the cow elk as they walked back into their new campsite with smiles of success splashed across their faces.

When the happy hunting crew arrived back into camp, they were greeted with a freshly assembled meat pole set-up that Wallace and Otis had just finished constructing by the creek in anticipation of its immediate use when Bridger and the boys arrived back in camp. Soon, the elk's quarters were skinned out and hanging from several ropes attached to the new meat pole so they could cool out and the meat could form a protective glaze. That evening the men feasted on freshly roasted elk spitted over the fire, their usual strong "trapper's coffee" which was so thick it could stand up a horseshoe inside the cup without falling against the sides, and their usual but welcome fare of Dutch oven biscuits. However, that evening when the men bit into their biscuits, there were several gasps of surprise, followed by smiles and then after a short pause, memorable appreciation. That evening, the men discovered that their Dutch oven biscuits contained raisins and brown sugar! Shades of Cedrick, thought the men simultaneously when their teeth crunched down on the slightly over done biscuits and their tongues tasted the generous helpings of brown sugar, cinnamon and plumped-up raisins that awaited their tongue and taste buds...

Then all the men's appreciative eyes went to their new cook Otis, who just looked back at the surprised men and grinned his signature grin acknowledging the 'memories' they were 'tasting' back in time as well... The rest of the supper that evening was eaten in silence as the men remembered back in time to the loss of one of their own and the hope that when the time came, they would be once again eating such biscuits in the presence of their first cook, brother and friend in the place where all beaver trappers finally ended up...

The next morning the men were up early and while Otis was making their breakfasts, the dirt fairly flew as the men began digging postholes for the posts to come when their new horse and mule corral was finally constructed. This they did with the vigor of men possessed realizing that without their horse and mule transport while on the grizzly bear and hostile Indian-riddled frontier, they were 'dead men walking'... After breakfast and by early afternoon, the postholes had been dug and by nightfall, the posts were up and set. The next day the rails were cut and spiked into place on the posts. By day three come nightfall, the trappers' horses and mules were safely ensconced behind a hell-for-stout corral.

After that the real work began as the men cut and dragged the needed green logs for the construction of a cabin needed to house the men during the worst the environment had to offer in the way of the winter weather found in that part of the country. By the end of August, the cabin was up, roofed over with logs and dirt, and an adjoining storage shed had been constructed to eventually protect from the weather their soon to be bundles of furs, extra provisions and pack saddles not being used. Collaterally, Wallace had made bedframes for each man during the evening hours. Wallace made bedframes that were intertwined with stretched rope netting for laying sleeping hides and furs upon so the men would not be lying upon the damp soil 'flooring' of their cabin. Wallace, a natural when it came to his carpentering abilities, also constructed from a number of smaller logs a table and chairs for when the winter weather confined the men to the cabin. Lastly, Otis and Cloud constructed meat smoking racks near their cabin for the making of jerky.

With the mornings getting colder and colder, the men redoubled their efforts in getting ready for the fall trapping season and winter months to come. Numerous mule deer were harvested and turned into jerky, and later their skins were 'brain-tanned' to be used in wrapping up the bundles of valuable beaver and wolf furs prior to the often hazardous transport to the upcoming rendezvous. Then the men went back up onto the ridges behind their cabin and began sawing down a number of the old and dead lightning struck trees, whose dry wood was cut and stacked near their cabin to be used later during the worst of the winter weather.

Then with even more increased urgency, wolf

and beaver traps were smoked under a pine-wood fire to kill the man and blood smells from previous catches. Additionally, knives were sharpened, a small mountain of bullets were cast from the pigs of lead purchased at the last rendezvous for their rifles and pistols, powder horns were filled with courser grained rifle and finer grained flash pan powders, 'Possibles bags' refilled with balls and greased patches, and all weapons thoroughly cleaned so accuracy at distance could be maintained unhindered by black powder fouling. With those necessary chores out of the way, there was nothing more the men could do until the beaver came into their prime except kill more elk, butcher them out and make jerky on the new smoking racks for use on the trail trapping beaver and winter wolves.

One morning when Otis was putting the finishing touches on the men's breakfast, Wallace and Bridger sat around the campfire discussing the day's events to come. Between the two men, they had decided to have their group mount up right after breakfast and begin scouting out the most heavily beaver populated areas to determine the location where they wanted to begin their fall trapping season. Shortly after breakfast, the five men streamed out from their campsite and headed south along the Bear River. This they did figuring they would trap out the southern portion of the "Bear" near their cabin site during the coming fall season. Then in the spring, trap out the northern portion of the river near their cabin as well. That way, they would be closer to the coming year's previously determined rendez-vous site upon completion of their spring trap-ping activities or when the beaver were trapped out, whichever came first.

Moving southward along the Bear, the men discovered many signs of heavy beaver use. Everywhere they looked were ponded up wa-tered areas with extensive signs of mud and stick dams, numerous freshly made beaver lodges, evidence of fresh tree cuttings and well used bea-ver slides in abundance, along with swimming beaver observed throughout in large numbers. After several hours of traveling along the river looking, the men finally decided where they would begin running their fall trap lines. With that decision made, the men adjoined to a rather large patch of willows and began harvesting wil-low limbs to be used in hooping the fresh beaver skins once beaver had been caught and defatted. For the next hour the men loaded the panniers on their two packhorses with fresh willow limbs and fought off hordes of hungry mosquitoes attracted to the heavily perspiring men in the process. Additionally, Otis and Wallace scouted out the willow patch and managed to cut 40 dead and dry willow poles that were about four feet in length which were to be used as anchor poles once the traps had been set.

As they did, the men were surprised when a

small herd of buffalo came down from the nearby foothills to the river to drink. Minutes later, two cow buffalo breathed their last due to the excellent shooting by Otis and Bridger! As the men approached the two dead cow buffalo, the rest of the small herd, instead of standing around their fallen brethren like they usually did trying to get them to stand up, ran off. It was then that Bridger gave out a loud appreciative yell, bailed off his horse and ran up to one of the dead cows. Taking out his sheath knife, he opened up the cow's side below the last rib, fished around inside the cow's belly area and then cut off a lobe of fresh and still bleeding liver. Holding up the chunk of liver in exultation, he bit off a large chunk and began chewing it with obvious relish! In seconds, the whole of his chin was covered with blood from the still draining liver as the Barnes Clan, still seated upon their horses looked at their fur trapper friend in amazement over what they considered his crazy in the head actions!

"Light down, you men, and join me!" shouted Bridger through his mouth still partially full of raw and bloody partially chewed cow buffalo's liver!

For the longest time, not one of the still mounted men moved a muscle as they sat there in disbelief over their friend Bridger, having apparently gone crazy as he continued eating with relish a chunk of raw buffalo liver in front of God and everybody!

In the meantime, Bridger, finishing his first chunk of raw liver, turned back towards the dead cow, took his knife and cut off another chunk of the animal's still quivering liver. Turning, he once again took a huge bite from the chunk of bleeding liver and began chewing like a man starved. Then realizing something was wrong, he swallowed the chewed portion of the just removed liver and said, "What the "Sam Hell" is the matter with the four of you? Ain't the four of you hungry for some of this fresh buffalo liver?"

Once again, it was like his words had fallen on deaf ears as the Barnes Clan moved not a muscle in response to Jim's questions. Then finally Wallace spoke up saying, "None of us have ever eaten raw liver. We have always fried it up back home with onions and then we have eaten it. But we have never eaten raw liver like you are doing."

"Jesus, Man! Where have the four of you been? You have been trappers for years, eaten buffalo before and none of you have ever eaten fresh liver from the side of a dead buffalo right after killing the animal?" asked an incredulous-looking Jim Bridger.

"Hell, Man! We have never even seen it done before today until you bailed off your horse like a mad man, cut open that cow, cut off a chunk of liver and then like a damn hungry bear, began eating still warm and raw liver," said Wallace, almost gagging as he responded!

"Well, I'll be damned!" exclaimed Bridger, as he stood there in as much amazement as were his four friends were over what was being done by one of their own at the side of a dead buffalo. "Well, come on then. You might as well learn about what is some of the best eating around in these here parts. Get off them damn horses, come on over here and learn yourselves about what is good for what ails a body out here on the frontier," said Bridger with a big bloody faced grin, still hardly believing the abject looks of disbelief that he was seeing spread across the faces of his four friends and fellow trappers!

For the longest time, still not one of the Barnes Clan moved and then finally Otis bailed off his horse, walked over to where Jim Bridger stood saying, "I figure if that is something you are a-doing, then I damn sure as hell can do it as well," mumbled Otis as he fumbled for his sheath knife. Then looking at Bridger one more time to make sure he was seeing what he was seeing, Otis stepped forward, reached inside the cow's body cavity, cut off a small chunk of liver and popped it into his mouth and began chewing it with a look upon his face like he was eating up a mess of pissed-off hornets! Then all of a sudden the looks on Otis's face changed from like he was in the process of eating a mess of live hornets to one of extreme surprise! "Hell, that ain't half bad. In fact, that is downright pretty damn good tasting once one gets it past the end of his nose, across his gums and begins a-gumming it without thinking about what he is doing."

Bridger just stood there looking at Otis with a big grin like a hog in a patch of fresh melons. Then he said, "See, I told you it ain't half bad. In fact, you live out here very long and you will learn that to eat such meat ain't half bad and in fact, turns out that it is damn good for what ails a body living out here on the frontier like we are a-doing."

Seeing his younger brother gagging down the fresh buffalo liver and not about to be outdone, Wallace stepped off his horse, walked over to Otis, borrowed his knife and followed suit as his brother had done when it came to cutting off a small chunk of fresh liver and eating the same. "Damn. If that ain't half-bad," said an obviously amazed and now pleased Wallace with what he had just learned and done.

Well that was too much for Feather and Cloud who were soon at the side of the dead buffalo, cutting out several chunks and eating the same as their friends had done. Since both Cloud and Feather had been outcasts in their Wind River Tribe of Shoshoni early on, they had never been allowed to go on a tribal buffalo hunt. Therefore, they had never experienced eating fresh liver from the side of a freshly killed buffalo like many of their kind had done for centuries for the specialized nutrition it offered. That was when Bridger learned from Wallace that none of them had ever seen that done before, much less having participated in doing so themselves in all the years they had lived out on the frontier as trappers. As it turned out, those five hungry trappers, after a long day in the saddle, managed to eat the entire raw liver from that first buffalo...

After eating the rest of that liver, Cloud and Feather took their two fully loaded packhorses carrying panniers full of fresh willow limbs to be used for hooping of skins from soon to be caught beaver and the 30 four-foot wooden trap anchor poles and headed back to camp. In the meantime, Bridger, Wallace and Otis skinned out one buffalo and laid its skin hair side down upon the ground. They then quartered out both animals, laying the fresh meat out on the skin side of the fresh hide just removed from the first animal. By the time both animals had been quartered out, Cloud and Feather had returned with the two packhorses carrying empty panniers. Those animals were loaded with the front and hindquarters and sets of hump ribs for return back to their camp and hanging on the meat poles to cool and glaze. With that chore out of the way, the five men returned to their camp, exhausted but full of spirit from a day having gone so well and with a valuable lesson learned by four of the trappers when it came to the value of eating some meats without cooking...

(Author's Note: In 1975, the Author, a Senior Resident Agent for the U.S. Fish and Wildlife

Service's Division of Law Enforcement over the States of North and South Dakota, participated in an Agency buffalo culling operation on the Sully's Hill National Game Preserve. The Author, being a history buff and aware that the mountain men and a number of Plains Indian tribes ate raw liver from freshly killed buffalo, decided to do the same. The Author found the eating of raw liver from a freshly killed buffalo was not a bad experience. The liver was somewhat gamey and tasting of minerals but was not found to be distasteful. However, the methane gas generated within the Author's system shortly thereafter was such that he was glad he was out on the open and windy prairie of North Dakota while working and not in a crowded shopping mall...)

Two weeks later the men decided the Bear River beaver were coming into their prime and decided to start their fall trapping season along the river's system and into its many adjacent waterways. Come the first morning of setting and running a fall trap line as Otis prepared the men's breakfast, the rest of the group prepared the riding and the loading of the packhorses for the day's labors lying ahead. After breakfast, the men streamed out from their campsite and into the adjacent Bear River country. Arriving shortly thereafter at the spot chosen earlier to begin their fall trapping ventures, Wallace and Jim Bridger dismounted and prepared themselves for the trapping activities lying ahead. Both men had decided they would do the trap setting for the group. It had also been decided that they would combine their trap numbers and run 30 traps a day. In so doing, Wallace would set one trap while Bridger would forge ahead on foot along the waterway and set the second trap. Then Wallace would pass where Bridger was setting the second trap, find a suitable location for the next set and set the third trap. Then Bridger would pass Wallace and set trap number four and so on. When they did, Cloud would act as one trapper's assistant and Feather would act as the other trapper's assistant. As assistants, Cloud and Feather would do all the skinning on-site and provide the supplies as each trapper requested. As for Otis, being as fine a shooter as was Bridger, he would remain 'horsed' and on guard in order to face down any dangers or emergencies, be they from man or beast.

True to form for the wet and cold activity to follow, both men stripped down from their warmer clothing and slipped into a pair of leather breechclouts and leggings, retrieved a five-pound beaver trap and trailed by an assistant carrying the four-foot anchor pole, hand ax, trap twine and castoreum, off the men went. When they did, Otis trailed the two trappers' riding horses in case a quick mount was required in the face of danger, and Cloud and Feather trailed their own riding and packhorses as the trappers moved along the waterways setting their traps.

At the end of setting all 30 of their traps, the two trappers moved about on the open ground adjacent the just trapped waterways trying to get the feelings back into their feet and legs after being immersed in the cold fall waters. When they thusly moved about getting warm life back into their feet and legs, the other three men remained close at hand, horsed and heavily armed just in case. Then after the two trappers had warmed back up, they would walk over to rest in any handy grove of trees where they would be out of sight from any prying eyes, the cold fall winds, eat some jerky and relax. Shortly thereafter, the two trappers would once again run their trap line in the reverse order, removing any of the highly territorial beaver who had already discovered the strong smelling castoreum lure and its immediately adjacent trap and had been trapped. When that occurred, Cloud or Feather would quickly take the dead beaver from the hands of the trapper, carefully skin out the animal, toss the carcass aside for any of the numerous quadruped local predators to eat and placed the fresh pelt into one of their packhorse's panniers for transport back to their cabin. Finally back at the trap line's starting point, the two trappers would dress out from their wet leather breechclouts and leggings into their warmer wool pants and then head for home for the fresh pelt care that was required daily. Then as the 'pelting crew' worked their 'magic' on the fresh pelts, Otis would be working his 'magic' when it came to preparing the men's evening meals. This regimen went on like clockwork by the experienced trapping crew for the first ten days of that fall's trapping season on the "Bear".

Come day eleven of the fall trapping season, the men arrived at the starting point on their new trap line. There the men dismounted, partially disrobed, climbed into their breechclouts and leggings and headed for the locations of their first traps. Not seeing any dead beaver floating in the water, Bridger called to his assistant for the twig stuck into the bank and angled over the pan of the trap to be replenished with castoreum. Walking up to the trap's location and looking down, HE THEN DISCOVERED TO HIS SURPRISE THAT THE BEAVER TRAP AND CHAIN WERE LONG GONE! Looking down at the pond's muddy bottom, Bridger could see from all the marks in the disturbed bottom that the trap had been forcefully removed! Kneeling and looking down, Bridger discovered a slight footprint near where the trap had originally been set! Looking further out into the beaver pond for the anchor pole, Bridger could see that the entire pole had also disappeared...

About that same moment in time, Bridger heard Wallace who was checking the next trap on their trap line say, "JIM, SOME SON-OF-A-BITCH STOLE MY TRAP! I CAN SEE WHERE HE KNELT HERE TO REMOVE MY TRAP AND

MY ANCHOR POLE IS NOWHERE TO BE SEEN AS WELL..."

Without saying a word, Bridger trotted past Wallace in order to check trap number three and when he did, HE DISCOVERED THAT SOMEONE HAD REMOVED THAT VALUABLE TRAP AS WELL! Before the morning was out, the two trap setters had discovered that someone had stolen all 30 of their valuable beaver traps and they and the traps had disappeared! It was plain in the minds of the men that whoever had stolen the traps was an experienced Mountain Man, or were a number of such individuals based on the clever way they had concealed most of their tracks and knew how to find each and every trap based on the original trap setter's footprints and trailing horse's hoofprints! Not only that but the disturbing fact that neither 'hide nor hair' had been seen by the trappers of anyone else in the area watching the trappers setting their traps or removing the same was more than worrying!

Immediately Otis was called in from his sentry position and the men gathered together to discuss the disastrous theft and loss of all of their beaver traps! True, they still had ten reserve beaver traps back at their campsite, but to lose all 30 of their field traps was truly a disaster in the making! First of all, the traps were very valuable and second of all, they could not be replaced until the following summer at the next rendezvous! Lastly, whoever stole the traps was seriously messing with the trappers' livelihood and their very existence! That morning, standing around their empty trap line and missing 30 valuable traps, the men decided whoever had ever done such a thing, if ever caught, was going to pay the ultimate price for such an evil and deadly deed that ultimately not only threatened Bridger and the Barnes Clan's livelihood but their lives!

Realizing what was now at stake and further realizing that no one man could pack off 30 five-pound beaver traps and their chains without leaving just a few footprints, Otis began walking along the outside edge of their trap line looking for any clues of accomplices related to the theft of their traps. Twenty minutes later, Otis discovered off to one side ten sets of trap line paralleling horse tracks and THEY WERE FROM SHOD HORSES, NOT FROM UNSHOD INDIAN HORSES! Additionally, three of the horses from the depths of their tracks in the rain softened ground, showed they were being ridden. The other seven sets of horse tracks were shallower in nature in the softened ground showing that they more than likely were pack animals.

By now, the rest of the group of trappers had finished dressing out and had ridden up to where Otis was tracking the ten sets of horse hoofprints and bringing his riding horse along, so the trail could be more quickly followed by mounted men. Mounting up and checking their rifles to make sure they were primed and ready, with Cloud and Feather far out in the lead since they were excellent trackers, the men set off after the tracks left behind by the trap thieves. But in so doing, they did not ride 'hellbent-for-election' but at a steady, cautious and controlled pace, with Cloud and Feather way out in front looking for any kind of an ambush of sorts in case they were detected. Looking out for an ambush because it was obvious whoever took the traps did not want to be followed and if they were, surely did not want to be caught by the aggrieved party knowing what would be lethally coming next!

For the next two days without let-up, the Barnes Clan and Jim Bridger relentlessly 'cold-tracked' the trap thieves' sets of horse tracks, including the tracks of a fourth horse now obviously all of a sudden being ridden. It now became apparent to the trackers that in order for the trap thieves to keep all tracks at a minimum, only one man had stolen all of the traps and then as he had, he walked the stolen traps over to the riders riding off to one side of the trap line who were cleverly doing so to avoid leaving a readily easy trail to follow. That way all the thieves' tracks were kept to a minimum, hence one of the horses appearing to be riderless early on when their shod tracks had initially been discovered by Otis. Additionally, it became obvious to the pursuers that the trap thieves must have been watching the activities of the Barnes Clan and Jim Bridger for some time. In so doing, they had determined that the best time to steal the beaver traps was late in the afternoon after the original trap setters had checked their trap line and had gone back to their cabin for the day. However, now that all of the traps would have been discovered stolen, the thief had rejoined the thieves' pack string and now all of them were heading further south in a hurry in order to get out of the country to avoid being caught and punished for their most grievous act.

Bridger was now sure they were following four mounted horsemen because of the depth of the horses' hoofprints along with their pack string of six horses, and from all indications only shod horseshoe prints at that. From that physical evidence, Bridger deduced that they had to be trappers of some sort from the recent rendezvous just attended because for the most part, Indians rode unshod horses so they weren't from some local band! Besides, if a local band of Indians had discovered the trappers and their trap line, they would have at some point in time attacked in order to kill all of the offending trappers or at least drive them from the Indians' territory.

After several days of methodical yet relentless pursuit of the trap thieves, the Barnes Clan and Bridger were in heavy timber and based on the trail being followed, the thieves had to be thinking that any kind of pursuit was now not forth coming. This the pursuing trappers surmised because the four trap thieves were now making little or no effort to hide their tracks or the location of each evening's campsite. Come day three of the pursuit, the trap thieves were observed from a distance away riding into a larger camp of men, both white men and Indians alike, like they had somehow planned such a get-together out on the trail all along!

Seeing the above get-together, Bridger and the Barnes Clan holed up in a dense stand of timber to avoid detection that evening. Later from his point of observation overlooking the now enlarged camp of trappers and Indians, Bridger could see something that he did not like. Right off the bat from his concealed position of hiding, Bridger could see the four disagreeable trappers who had moved right next to their campsite back at the rendezvous! Those trappers being the two loud and obnoxious French-Canadians that they had later learned from word of mouth at the rendezvous, had just deserted the Hudson's Bay Company and became Free Trappers. That and their two trouble-making Gros Ventre Indian partners who had taken a very real disliking to Cloud and Feather because they were Shoshoni, historically lifelong enemies of the Gros Ventre! As for the other six trappers in this new group of men just joined by their trap thieves, they all spoke the French language as well. With that, Bridger surmised from his close-in place of hiding and observation, that they too were deserters from the Hudson's Bay Company making it on their own as Free Trappers.

Slipping out from his place of concealment, Bridger made a hasty retreat back to where he left the Barnes Clan hidden in the deep timber. There they got together once again and Bridger filled them in on what he had observed. When he did, he warned the clan that their four trap thieves had now swelled into a group of ten instead of just four possible adversaries! Then Bridger looked all of the clan in their eyes saying, "If we take on that number of men, sure as God made little green apples, some of us are going to die right along with a number of them before all of the black powder smoke clears away!"

Letting those words of dire warning sink into those serious onlooking men from the Barnes Clan, Bridger continued saying, "However, I have a plan that might work just as well, allowing us to get our traps back, we don't have to fire a shot and they won't be able to pursue us once we 'pull the trigger' on my plan."

"Let us hear the plan, Jim. Because if it is not a good one, I am for going in there shooting when they are all asleep and killing every trap-stealing son-of-a-bitch that gets in my way," said Otis, the one family member who was not afraid of anything other than his blessed mother's wooden spoon and getting whacked with it when he was younger for getting out of line. Well, that and the wrath of God, both of equal consequence to his way of thinking!

Bridger just smiled over Otis's showing of grit

saying, "Here is what I propose. Come dark when all of them bastards are sleeping, we send Cloud and Feather into their camp. Send in those two because they are the smallest of the bunch of us, are damn fine shooters if the occasion arises, and they can quietly slink around like a mink on a creek bank looking for a frog or a fish. That way, they can look for our traps and if they can find them, gather them up and quietly slink back out from them bastards' camp like a snake crawling across a wet and grassy field. In the meantime, we load up everything we have in the way of our 'smoke poles' with buck and ball and like Cloud and Feather, slither into these Frenchie camps and lay in wait in case Cloud and Feather are discovered recovering our traps. If they are discovered, we will lay down a load of buck and ball across their bows and those left standing, it is tomahawk time as I 'seed' it!"

Looking around at the grim looking faces surrounding him, Bridger said, "Good, then it is done. Come the 'deep of dark', we send in Cloud and Feather and the rest of us laying off to one side prepared to lay down a flurry of buck and ball if they are discovered. By the way, if Cloud and Feather make it out with our traps, Otis and I have a little chore to attend to as well. With Wallace, Cloud and Feather then providing cover for Otis and me, we will slip back into their camp and see to it that even if they want to, there will be no horseback pursuit as we fade back into the countryside and head back to our camp. Now I didn't say we run off their horses and leave them afoot. If we were to do that, it is akin to a death sentence for each and every one of them out here on the frontier, and then we are no different than they. Besides, I don't know the guilt of the men our trap thieves have joined up with and don't favor killing those who don't deserve it. However, if they do find some way to come after us after Otis and I fix 'their wagons', then a killing it shall be and may the good Lord forgive the lot of us for what we will be doing to our own kind."

Around midnight, after the camp of Hudson's Bay Company deserters had drunken themselves into a stupor with a keg of Fourth Proof rum, Bridger and the Barnes Clan put their plan into motion. First Cloud and Feather, stripped down to their breechclouts and tomahawks and in the remaining dim light from the trappers' dying campfires, slinked into the thieves' camp looking for their traps. The 30 stolen traps were quickly discovered hidden under a buffalo skin and quietly retrieved by Cloud and Feather. That they did with a slight degree of difficulty because of their weights and their penchant for their chains making 'clinking' noises as one walked off with them. Then after placing the traps into the two hidden packhorse's panniers, Cloud and Feather returned so they could provide cover against discovery by the camp of Frenchies and their Indian allies so Otis and Bridger could pull off the daring second part of Bridger's plan. Moments later, Otis and Jim Bridger slipped into the now almost darkened camp because the original campfires had now burned so low. Slipping over to where the men had piled all of their horses' riding saddles and gear, Otis and Jim began silently working their 'magic'! Shortly thereafter, the two trappers slipped back out from the Frenchies' camp unobserved and then the five men made their ways back into the night-darkened deep timber. There they quietly retrieved their riding and trap-loaded packhorses and began leading their horses as they walked away from the nearby still sleeping camp full of the Hudson's Bay men and their Indian allies in order to keep all noises at a minimum. Once sufficiently far enough away from the camp just raided to be unheard, the men mounted up and letting their horses pick the trail in the darkness, rode all night back towards their campsite far to the north.

Four days later and without any signs of pursuit, the five tired men rode back into their campsite, hobbled their horses so they could feed in the nearby meadow and then tended to their starving horses still in the corral. Fortunately, the men had channeled a small portion of their nearby stream so that it flowed through the corral. Being that they were gone so long after the trap thieves, the remainder of their stock in the corral had been unable to feed! However, with the flow of water through their corral, the animals were able to at least drink even though they had nothing to eat except the bark off the corral's railings, which the starving animals did a number on! Otis hurriedly hobbled the remaining stock animals in the corral and then all he saw were horses' hind ends as the starving animals made for their meadow to feed like a pack of hungry wolves on a buffalo's carcass! Following that, Otis headed for the cabin and some much-needed sleep as the rest of his clan had done earlier. Entering the cabin, the first thing he heard were the sounds of deep snoring from exhausted men. Otis soon joined in with that chorus of snoring without even undressing. He just flopped down on his bed and was soon lost to his dream world as well...

Daylight the next morning, Otis was up early, had an outside fire going and in the process of making breakfast. As he did, the rest of the crew washed up, took care of any calls of nature they might have, shaved and then adjoined to their outside firepit for the warmth that blazing fire represented. When they did, they were met with fresh cups of coffee and a breakfast of only biscuits. That was because the men had not had the time to kill any camp meat on their ways back to their camp, so 'it was trapper's coffee, biscuits and cowboy songs'...

Mounting up after breakfast and making sure each man was fully armed with two pistols and an extra rifle in each pack animal's pannier, mindful of the French-Canadian trappers they had 'more or less' ambushed when they had retrieved their stolen traps, off they went to establish a new trap line. As for the French-Canadian trappers and their Indian allies the Barnes Clan and Jim Bridger had 'more or less ambushed', they were 'no shows' over the next two months. They were 'no shows' because it is hard to ride one's horse when all of them sometime during the night had all of their cinches cut clean off from their saddles and the reins had been cut clean off from the men's horses' bridles with all those parts being dropped quietly into the Frenchies' dying campfires...

Soon the men were back in their regular trapping 'form' when it came to running a trap line for beaver, defatting and hooping the same. True to Jim Bridger's predictions and his great mind for the geographic area and that of the natural world, there were beaver aplenty along the lower Bear River and in its many adjacent waterways. Come the fall beaver trapping season's freeze-up, the men had amassed 293 beaver by running 30 traps by two very skilled beaver trappers in Wallace and Jim Bridger in a beaver rich area!

Come freeze-up and removal of all of their beaver traps before they were hidden under the thick ice of winter, the men found the time for hunting. Being that buffalo were scarce in their area, the men had to travel one day to the east in order to run into enough buffalo to kill a mess of the critters for the making of jerky and meeting their daily needs for camp meat. However, the men were successful and soon their two meat poles hung heavy with buffalo meat hindquarters along with the many little birds like Northern chickadees, pigmy nuthatches and Steller's jays picking at the scraps of fat left on the exposed hanging meat quarters. Then those meat supplies were augmented as needed with meat quarters from elk and mule deer common to the area when the need for more fresh meat arose.

When the heavy winter snows began blanketing the area, the men were relegated to staying closer to their camp and using those times to cast more bullets for their rifles and pistols, hunting yarded up deer when they could from snowshoes, sharpening their knives and shovels used to shovel snow, putting edges onto their axes used in cutting firewood from their winter wood caches, mending the horses' leather gear, tending to their horse herd, and the bundling of their beaver furs for the travel to the coming summer's rendezvous. Then once the deep of winter arrived when the wolves were in their prime, out the trappers went in order to set up the bait stations and then run their wolf trap lines as well when the snows allowed travel by horseback.

There they would kill mule deer or elk, open up the animals so the smell of 'death' would be apparent and then set their wolf traps around the carcasses in the snow in the hope the wolf packs who being 'winter hungry', would lower their cautions because of their hungers and 'find' their ways into the men's toothed traps. Finding that a very successful way to trap wolves, the trappers were soon amassing a number of prime wolf pelts back at their cabin and in their storage shed. On one particular day, the men discovered that they had successfully trapped 13 wolves on one of their trapping runs and by the time they had removed the dead wolves from their traps, re-set the traps and had skinned out their catches, that caused the men to arrive late back at their cabin in the evening's darkness.

Turning into their secluded cabin area and now braving a steadily falling snow, the men did not notice right away that the gate to their corral was ajar and every animal left inside the corral earlier that morning was missing, until they rode up and got right alongside the corral's rails! Because of the falling snow and onset of darkness, the men had also failed to see the depressions of many horses' hooves in the snow leading from their corral and away from their campsite! At first there was much consternation and the air was turned 'blue' with much swearing and then the 'calm before the storm' set in among the now very determined men! That 'calm before the storm' was made even more so when after checking, the men realized that who had taken all of their extra riding and packhorses had also made off with all of their bundled up beaver furs from their storage shed as well! Unable to track the stolen extra riding and pack animals because of the falling snows and darkness, the men decided to wait until morning and then pursue whoever had chanced upon their campsite, spotted the valuable stock and furs and had stolen the same! In so doing, they figured the darkness and heavily falling snows would slow down the horse thieves that evening trying to make their escape successful, yet make the following morning's pursuit when it came to tracking easier. With those thoughts in mind, that calmed the men down somewhat but did nothing to smooth out the killing urges over what had been done.

Realizing what lay ahead the following day, the men made ready once back inside their cabin under the light of their beeswax candles. There they refilled all of their powder horns, reamed and cleaned all of their rifles of their black powder fouling for greater accuracy, refilled their 'Possibles bags' with greased wads, additional balls and the like, and then readied their heaviest winter clothing for whatever challenges lay ahead in pursuing those who had stolen their horses and valuable furs from their fall trappings. Horses without which the men would not be able to carry their bundles of furs to the coming rendezvous or pack their camp's essentials to the next spot chosen to trap beaver in the coming fall trapping season! In short, failure in retrieving all of their stock and furs was not an option because their livelihood was on the line...

Sleep was fleeting that night among the men, realizing that if they failed to retrieve their live-stock and furs, they more than likely would fail that year in making enough money to cover all of their expenses, especially those expenses needed in the purchasing of more horses if they wished to continue as successful trappers. The thought also crossed the men's minds that such horse thieves once caught would not release the stolen horses without some sort of stiff and deadly re-sistance if given just half a chance. To the men's way of thinking, that meant meeting such stiff resistance could also mean some of them might not live to see another sunrise once the shooting started in the horse and fur recovery process either! As Wallace lay in his sleeping furs that evening he found sleep to be a 'fleeting friend'. Once again, they had become victims of horse and fur thefts! Here all any of them ever wanted was to trap beaver and amass enough money to return to Missouri, buy some land and settle down. However, ever since they had begun this 'trapping' thing out on the frontier, the brothers had had to fight their ways through every kind of 'thick and thin' with Indians, grizzly bears, French fur trappers and every kind of trap thief imaginable! Thefts that if not adjudicated once and for all could easily spell doom for the Barnes Clan. And once again, the worrisome realization kept manifesting itself over the fact that his family had gone west to trap beaver and seemed to always be targeted by the evil wills of his fellow man and the primitives living in the area... Before sleep overtook Wallace, he finally had to ask himself, "Would the family's bad luck and constant trials ever end?" Finally sleep overtook his worries and became his friend... Little did Wallace realize that evening that his family's overworked Irish 'guardian angel' had also drifted off to sleep...

Before daylight the following morning, the men dressed heavily in their warmest winter gear and with saddlebags filled with jerky for a long journey on a cold trail, saddled up their remaining horses and headed out following the slight horse hoofprint indentations left in the snow after the previous day's snowstorm. A snowstorm that had thankfully now ceased covering the land, making pursuit and tracking one hell of a lot easier for the aggrieved trappers. With Cloud and Feather in the lead following the faint snow filled hoof indentations, Bridger, Wallace and Otis rode guard duty over their trackers in case of the possibility of a deadly ambush being laid down by the horse thieves for any pursuers who might now be hot on their trails.

For two long, cold and hard days, the men followed the trail of their stolen horses and those of their fast moving thieves from daylight until dark. At night, all of the men huddled together for the shared body warmth under a tree without the benefit of a warm fire in order not to give their presence away in case their thieves were watching their back trail. By daylight the next morning, the strongly determined and cold men were once again hot on the trail, which by now was getting easier to follow because it was getting fresher. Fresher because the horse thieves' mistakenly figuring the recent snowstorm had covered all of their tracks, made their escape from any kind of pursuit a success. As such, they were now taking their time so as not to physically stress all of their heavily loaded horses due to the lack of good grazing opportunities and time to do so in the deep snows. However, as the Barnes Clan pursued the horse thieves and partially froze during the mid-winter days and nights in the process, their resolve to settle the score and get back their livestock and valuable furs grew more and more determined and deadly of mind…

By the evening of the third day, Feather far out in front of the trailing Barnes Clan and Jim Bridger, spotted a faint flicker of light from a small campfire in a distant grove of fir trees! Drawing up his horse abruptly, he waited until the rest of the group of frost covered trappers drew up alongside. Without a word, Feather pointed in the direction of the faint flickering light from a distant campfire. Without a word among the men, they quietly dismounted and tied their horses off into some nearby sagebrush in a draw so they would be out of sight. This they did so their horses smelling other horses once they got closer, would not 'nicker or neigh' to the other horses in recognition, thereby alerting the camp of horse and fur thieves of the possibility of the approaching danger.

Checking their rifles and making sure their pistols being carried behind their belt sashes were readily available for quick action if it became necessary, the men began quietly sneaking on foot in the snow towards the distant light from which they suspected was that of the horse and fur thieves' campsite. Twenty minutes later, the men had cautiously sneaked unseen right up to the edge of the campsite backlit by a now built-up and roaring fire. That was when the Barnes Clan and Bridger realized the camp was occupied by the same two disagreeable French-Canadians who had camped next to their campsite back at the rendezvous! The same evil folks they should have killed for stealing their traps earlier but had let that issue pass with a 'cinch and bridle cutting' as a less than deadly warning! Additionally, the camp contained the same two disagreeable Gros Ventre Indians who had made life tribally miserable for Cloud and Feather at the last rendezvous as well!

Then the men suddenly realized there were two other Indians in camp! As it turned out, the two other Indians appeared to be from first glance, sitting terrified off to one side under a horse blanket, in their late teens or early twenty's, women! The two women were huddled together under one blanket and were holding onto each other like their lives depended on it and the looks on their faces read of nothing but terror and deep despair! What happened next angered the men, especially and unusually, the normally reserved and quiet Cloud and Feather! One of the Gros Ventre men ambled over to the terrified looking women, grabbed up one by her long black hair, jerked her to her feet, whipped her body around in his arms and pulled her buckskin dress up over her head exposing her naked body! Then to the woman's terrified screams and the raucous laughter from the two French-Canadians, the Gros Ventre attempted to viciously rape the now squirming and fighting back young woman from behind. That was when the remaining woman jumped to her feet and taking up a nearby piece of limb wood from the fire, attacked the Gros Ventre attempting to rape the other woman, who was now totally undressed and bent over in front of her Gros Ventre assailant! When she hit the Gros Ventre attempting to rape the other Indian female, he viciously turned and struck her forcefully in her face, knocking her out! Then the now leering Gros Ventre turned his attention back to the Indian woman forcefully held in his hands, dropped his buckskin pants and to the **BOOMING!** sound of a nearby fired rifle, had his head's contents exploded all over the hapless

Indian woman bent over in front of him! That shot dropped the Gros Ventre from off the backside of the Indian woman and left him quivering his last on the hard and cold ground…

In a sudden and surprising move, Cloud blowing up in violent indignation, had raised up his rifle at that very moment the Gros Ventre was attempting to penetrate the terrified woman held in his hands and had shot him in the head! When he fired, as expected, all hell broke loose in the thieves' campsite! **BOOM!** went Feather's rifle almost simultaneously and the other Gros Ventre, now in the process of scrambling for his rifle upon hearing Cloud shooting and seeing his fellow Indian partner's head exploding, never knew what hit him either! Feather very calmly had shot the remaining Gros Ventre in the back of his head as he was scrambling for his near at hand rifle! **BOOM–BOOM–BOOM!** immediately went the rifles of Wallace, Bridger and Otis and none missed… One French-Canadian died with a look of extreme surprise after first hearing a shot fired from out of the dark when Cloud had shot the Indian attempting to rape the young woman! Just a mere second later, Bridger's bullet hit him in his neck and he hit the ground like a buffalo that had been headshot! The remaining French-Canadian who had been holding his rifle in his arms and looking on at the rape with a carnal interest, died immediately trying to swing his weapon in the direction from whence had come that first shot fired by Cloud! That was when he was shot in the head and heart by Otis and Wallace, simultaneously, stopping all further living and defensive actions on his part! NOW that group's bad behavior at the rendezvous, prior trap stealing, latest horse and fur stealing episodes along with their vicious treatment of two defenseless women, had been 'frontier-squared' away… Then aside from a drifting white cloud of black powder smoke hanging heavily throughout much of the thieves' campsite, other than their crackling campfire, all was quiet. As for the two Indian women, they were now once again in each other's arms holding onto one another in an obvious new terror over what had just violently occurred just moments earlier!

With that 'business' taken care of, the men from the Barnes Clan and Jim Bridger slowly stepped into the light of the French-Canadians' campfire and just stood there at the ready with drawn pistols in hand in case there were other previously unseen horse thieves in camp. Seeing no other signs of danger, Cloud and Feather walked over to the two terrified Indian women and began calmly speaking to them in the Blackfeet tongue, much to the amazement of their white compatriots! Soon the women had calmed down somewhat but terror still was registered in their eyes realizing they had now gone from the physical and sexual abuse problems from just four rough frontier men to five equally rough looking men.

Especially after those very rough looking men had spent a number of hard and cold winter days out on the trail with little or no sleep!

As Bridger and Otis walked over to the horse herd to make sure everything was alright with their and the thieves' stock animals, Wallace walked over to the two Indian women and said to Cloud, "You speak their tongue? Why is that, Cloud?" he asked.

"Wallace, Feather and I are the spawn of Blackfeet men raping two Shoshoni women who were out picking berries one afternoon many years ago. As a result, both Feather and I are part Blackfeet and part Shoshoni. As such when younger, we both learned to speak in the Blackfeet tongue from several captured Blackfeet slaves of the Shoshoni. Near as I can understand from these two young women, they were captured last year by two trappers while out bathing in a creek. Those two trappers took them away from their people and 'kept' them as their wives. However, at the last rendezvous, these four men we just killed purchased the two Blackfeet women who are sisters and kept them as what they called 'Play-Pretties' in order to satisfy themselves whenever they felt the urge. Tonight we stopped their evening of 'terror' and now, they are ours to do with as we please," continued Cloud, with a curious look on his face over the words he had just spoken as to what might be their actions involving the two terrified women…

"Hell, Cloud, what are we going to do with them? We are in the country of the Blackfeet and if we are caught with them, their tribe will skin us alive and that is the least they would do to us for disrespecting their women," said Bridger, who after living on the frontier, more than knew the ways of the Blackfeet! "Asides, I ain't never took an Indian or any other woman for that matter and don't intend to do so now or never, unless I be married to them as the Good Book commands," continued Bridger with a deadly serious look on his face.

"Well, we can't leave them here all alone and in the dead of winter just to starve or have the critters kill them off and eat them," said Cloud in a concerned tone and tenor sounding voice that was very unusual for him... A look over at Feather showed the same kind of concern spelled clear across his face as well, over the upcoming welfare of the two young, still looking dazed and terrified over the recent turn of events, women...

About then Otis quietly spoke up saying, "We can't leave these two young women out here in the wilds in the dead of winter all alone and, we aren't! We will just have to take them back with us and if any of their kind happens along and are friendly, we can give them back to their own people. Asides, Wallace and me are both born and bred of the Catholic faith. Even though we are not 'practicing' with our Church-going way out here on the frontier, our dear mother made sure we understood what was right from wrong according to the Good Book. And that included not 'bedding' any woman unless we have been married right and proper like in the Catholic Church. So with that in mind, Wallace or I have no carnal designs on these two poor young women and that is final."

"That we cannot do, namely leaving them out here all alone just to die or returning them back to their people either!" said Feather somewhat forcefully. "They have been taken by the white man and in so doing they would now be considered unclean and made outcasts by their own people if returned. In the event that happened, that culturally would require those two women to live on just what other members of their tribe cared to share with them. By turning them back to their tribe, we would be committing them to a life of shame, misery and without a man to care for them, a life of near starvation."

"What Feather just said is true. My first wife was a Blackfoot and they don't treat kindly to anyone they consider 'unclean'," said Bridger. "I would say we have just added two new members to our group, for better or for worse. But we could do worse. Blackfoot women are usually good natured and damn hardworking and if I do say so myself, we could use a woman's hand around our cabin from time to time," he continued with a big grin. Then more important considerations came to the forefront as the rest of that evening was spent with the men staying up most of the night enjoying their first warm campfire in days, discussing the day's events and eating the food that had been originally prepared for the French-Canadians and Gros Ventre, who were no longer in any kind of a condition to eat anything...

The next morning found Cloud and Feather closely following Bridger as they began trailing all of the dead trappers and Indians' now heavily loaded livestock back to their campsite. Horses heavily loaded in that they were not only carrying all of their previously stolen furs from the Barnes Clan and Bridger's camp, but all of the living essentials and annual supplies from the now dead Frenchies and two Gros Ventre as well. Trailing Cloud and Feather were the two young Blackfeet women riding and leading the four dead men's horse herd with concerning looks as to what was going to happen to them in the hands of the new trappers. Riding on either side of the long caravan of horses and men rode Wallace and Otis as outlying protectors against unprovoked attacks by either 'man or beast'. Four days later, the group finally rode back into their own campsite. There they unloaded all of their livestock, hobbled them and turned them loose in their windswept meadow for some much-needed time to graze. Then the men returned their numerous bundles of wolf and beaver furs to their storage shed along with all the extra pack saddles, riding gear and annual provisions removed from their herd and from those of the pack and riding horses from the now dead Frenchies and Gros Ventre.

Then the two Blackfeet women standing near the cabin with looks of worry on their faces and still holding onto and comforting each other wondering what was coming next in their lives, got surprised... It was about then that Wallace and Otis appeared from their storage shed carrying heavy armloads of sleeping furs and two tanned buffalo hides. Walking back to their cabin, Otis and Wallace stopped at the cabin's front door, turned and hailed the two women over to them with hand gestures since they did not speak the Blackfoot language. When they did with all of those sleeping furs in their arms, the two women came hesitantly with terrified looks of dread spread across their faces obviously figuring in their minds there was soon more carnal shame coming their ways! Seeing those looks of dread associated with the sleeping furs, Otis handed each woman an armload of furs and then beckoned for the women to follow him inside. He then disappeared into the darkened interior of the cabin carrying the two heavy buffalo hides followed by the two still hesitant women. When they did, the looks on Cloud and Feather's faces not knowing what Otis and Wallace had in mind with those sleeping furs and tanned buffalo hides, showed the same worry and concern for the virtues of the young Blackfeet women as well...

Once inside the cabin, Wallace and Otis lit their beeswax candles and then began removing rum kegs, extra powder kegs and the like from their cabin. Those they stacked just outside the front door of their cabin for subsequent transport and storage in their adjacent storage shed. In so doing, they were able to make available sleeping space in the northwestern corner of their cabin. Then with Wallace holding up one end of the largest tanned buffalo hide, Otis nailed the edges of the tanned hide to one of the rafters of their cabin. Then when one side of the hide was all nailed up and the bottom side of the hide let down, it had formed a hide wall creating a small but livable space in the back of their cabin for the women. A small space being created in which the Blackfoot women could live and have some privacy away from the men's beds and other activities being carried on inside the cabin. Then laying down the armloads of sleeping furs behind the buffalo hide 'wall' on top of the remaining hide, Otis beckoned for the women to bed down and rest. With looks of surprise and still some concerns, the two women slipped in behind the buffalo skin 'wall' and sat down on their comfortable furs. Soon, the two physically and emotionally drained women found themselves fast asleep on their sleeping furs in their little 'buffalo hide corner' of the cabin. As Otis and Wallace had indicated, they were from good Catholic stock, their mother had taught them well and the two

Blackfoot women were safe from any further physical abuses or man caused depredations... Outside, two young Shoshoni men found themselves terribly relieved over what they had just witnessed with the tender care being tendered to the two young and very beautiful Blackfeet Indian women by Otis and Wallace... Now Cloud and Feather found they could relax and once again, their hearts swelled with pride over what they had just witnessed in the treatment of the two women by their personally adopted and much-loved adoptive father, Otis.

Then without another thought over what had just been done, the men set to work once again. Cloud and Feather quickly gathered in more dry firewood for their inside fireplace as Bridger walked the meadow keeping careful watch over the grazing and now increased in size herd of valuable livestock. Otis in the meantime set a pot of beans off to one side of the inside fireplace hearth to soak, got a fire going in the fireplace so he could have some coals for biscuit making and began mixing up and making a large batch of dough since they now had two more mouths to feed in their little family of fur trappers. Then Cloud and Feather, with surprising newfound energies, scurried over to their camp's meat pole and cut off two backstraps from one of the elk hanging there and carried them into Otis as per his request. As darkness continued falling, Bridger, Cloud and Feather brought in their increased in size horse herd and safely placed them inside their corral. That they did after the animals had a chance to water in the nearby creek for the night after being allowed to graze in the nearby meadow for several hours. Then the two men grinned over the valuable addition of six riding and the same number of good looking packhorses taken from the Frenchies and Gros Ventre. All had gone well when it came to the recovery of their stolen stock animals and their furs, and Cloud and Feather found the time to quietly thank among themselves The Great Spirit for giving them another day and...

With that the men retreated into their cabin as darkness fell in earnest and so did the outside winter temperatures to below zero! Once inside, the warmth of the cabin caused the men to take off all of their heavy winter gear down to their buckskin shirts and pants. Then as Wallace, Cloud, Feather and Bridger sat in their log chairs around their table and visited, Otis continued with his duties as camp cook bringing forth a supper. Then all of a sudden, Otis surprisingly found himself quietly surrounded by the two Blackfoot women indicating through their hand gestures their willingness to help with the making of their suppers! Looking around at the rest of the men in surprise, all Otis could see were smiles, ESPECIALLY on the faces of Cloud and Feather! Soon the two women were hand-making biscuit sized lumps of dough and handing them to Otis for placement into the heated Dutch ovens sitting in the hearth's bed of coals. Then when shown where the eating ware was kept in a camp box, the women set the table like they had seen it done in their previous lives living with the other trappers earlier in their existence of capture, sexual abuse and essentially slavery...

That was when Cloud began quietly talking with the two women in their native tongue. As the other men just listened and looked on, Cloud spoke at length with both of the women and then after a short period of time, turned saying to the men, "These two women are sisters and are 19 and 20 years old. The younger sister wearing the beaded necklace is named "Kanti", which in the language of the Blackfeet means "Sings". The older sister with the blue beading on her shirt is named "Nuttah", which in the language of the Blackfeet means, "My Heart". Nuttah tells me eight moons ago that she and Kanti were bathing and washing their hair in a creek near where their band was encamped nearby. That was when they were surprised by two trappers, knocked in the head so they could not scream and carried off on horseback a long distance away from their people into the trappers' tipi located by a river. There the two trappers did bad things to them, hurting them in the process since neither of the sisters had ever been with a man before. Then the trappers made them into slaves during the day skinning and processing the river otter, beaver and muskrat hides brought in by the two trappers. Then again once it got dark, the two trappers did many bad things to the two sisters! Then they were brought down to the white man's big camp with all the other white men at the rendezvous and sold to the four Hudson's Bay Company men we killed several nights ago. There they both say they were used by all of the men who spoke in a funny language and their deadly enemy, the Gros Ventre. Kanti says she hopes the white trappers and Shoshoni Indian men who have now captured them will not hurt them. Nuttah also wants to know if they can have some food since both are still very hungry because the 'dead ones' did not feed them very well." With those words of translation, Cloud finally stopped and for the longest moment in time no one said anything regarding what they had just learned. But in so learning, there were lots of smiles of better understanding among the trappers regarding who the two women were and what they had endured before being recently freed by Bridger and the Barnes Clan.

That was when Otis quietly stood up from the fireplace's hearth with a plate full of biscuits, walked over to their table and quietly bade with hand gestures that Kanti and Nuttah sit at the table. Looking at Otis in amazement over his warm gestures, the two women hesitantly sat down at the table still not truly understanding what was happening. Then Otis cut off several chunks of roasted elk backstrap and laid the steaming and great smelling meat on each of the two lady's plates. That they understood and in an instant, both women were eating like they had not been fed for weeks on end! Then when Otis poured each woman a steaming cup of coffee, they just looked up at him and then down at their cups of coffee in wonder over being treated so kindly. Otis then spooned into each woman's cup of coffee several spoonfuls of brown sugar and then he could see the women were once again amazed over their gentle kind treatment. But once they had tasted the sweetened drink, they were hooked and before the night was over, each had consumed several cups of the strong tasting and yet sweetened brew, soon to become one of their favorites…

In the meantime, the rest of the trappers just sat there watching Otis's treatment of their new guests with approval, ESPECIALLY Cloud and Feather… Then the rest of the men, hungry as well, seated themselves around the women or in their chairs and began eating the fare Otis had prepared in such short order. Later that night, it was obvious the coffee had 'gone through' the ladies' systems and that they needed to go outside and tend to a call of nature. Sensing their needs and embarrassment over that fact, Feather walked over to their front door, opened it and told the ladies they could go outside and tend to themselves in the Blackfoot language. Both Kanti and Nuttah showed great relief and soon disappeared into the night. Then the men, not saying a word, wondered to a man if they would indeed return now that they were free. Moments later, both women returned shivering from the outside cold and then asked Cloud if they could now go to bed. Cloud nodded and in an instant, both sisters disappeared behind the buffalo skin curtain that had been hung for them near their sleeping furs so they could have some privacy. Moments later, not a sound could be heard coming from their corner of the cabin.

After the disappearance of the two sisters, Wallace and Bridger broke out a keg of rum from the storage shed now more than full of supplies that they had purchased at the rendezvous and with those taken from the Frenchies' camp. That was also followed with the searching for and retrieval of a 'carrot' of James River smoking tobacco. With that and moments later, the men lost in their thoughts, sat quietly in the haze of their pipe smoke and sweet tasting but powerful drinks of rum, wondering what was coming next with their two newest additions to their cabin. Later, knocking the ash from their pipes and putting their cups into the wash pan, the men bade each other good night. Moments later the now semi-darkened cabin lit only by the dying fire in the fireplace, smelling richly of Virginia tobacco smoke and sweet smelling rum, rumbled to the sounds of five exhausted men deeply sleeping after another more than surprising day out on the unpredictable frontier. In fact, if one looked carefully, they could see that some of Wallace's concerns about their frequent plights with the previous occurring violent elements out on the frontier may have ended for the moment. In fact, it now appeared that the Barnes Clan's Irish 'guardian angel' was awake once again...

The next morning right at daylight, found Otis up, scraping out the ash and building another fire in the cabin's fireplace. Then he began spitting the remainder of the elk backstraps over the open fire and roasting green coffee beans in a Dutch oven so he could later make some coffee for the men and women. Then all of a sudden he was physically reminded that they now had two new members of the Bridger and Barnes Clan. That reminder was further reinforced upon hearing the faint rustling of two women's deerskin dresses as they neared where he was working and then kneeling alongside him on the fireplace's hearth. Looking, Otis was surprised to see Kanti and Nuttah kneeling there as if expecting to be told what they needed to do in order to help with breakfast. Not understanding the Blackfoot women's language, Otis heard Jim Bridger saying from his nearby sleeping area, "Otis, they are asking you if they can go outside to the bathroom and then if you need some help or want them to do something in the making of breakfast."

With the booming of Bridger's voice, within minutes the rest of the clan was awake and getting ready to meet their day. Bridger then said something to Kanti since he fluently spoke the Blackfoot language having been married to a Blackfoot woman at one time and out the door the two women went. Moments later they returned after going to the bathroom outside, stomping their moccasins and slapping their arms around their sides trying to warm up. Otis seeing that, made a hand gesture for the two ladies to come over by the fireplace so they could warm up which they did in an instant. Then realizing the women only had the clothing they were wearing, called Cloud over to where he was kneeling stirring a cooking pot of previously soaked pinto beans.

"You and Feather need to get your tail ends out to our storage shed and bring me back four of our tanned river otter skins, two bear skin robes, two wolf skins, several tanned deerskins, and a buffalo robe for these women. They are freezing to death and need to make some decent winter clothing if they are going to run with us," said Otis. "Then when you have finished with that, bring me my sewing and mending kit that we use to repair our clothing or patch each other up when we have been injured or have injured ourselves," continued Otis. "With those items in hand, maybe one of you can tell them they are to be used in making themselves some warmer clothing," continued Otis, as he stirred the pot of cooking beans one more time.

Otis was surprised at just how fast Cloud and Feather responded to his request to go out into the winter's cold morning, rummage around in the unheated storage shed and bring back the requested furs. But in a flash, they were out the door and a few long minutes later they returned with armloads of the requested furs. Then the two young men retrieved the trappers' clothing repair kits and brought forth leather and sewing needles, a sharp cutting knife, twine and leather ties so the women could fashion some better winter clothing and replace the flimsy buckskin apparel they were wearing. Seeing what Cloud and Feather had just done and realizing what for, the two women relayed their appreciation with smiles easily meant to be clearly understood by both young men... The rest of that day and into the next within the cabin, the two women cut and sewed the tanned skins and warm robes into winter clothing that they could each wear around the cabin or upon horseback when out in the winter weather. This they did with huge smiles of appreciation over being warm once again.

After breakfast several days later, the men sat around their table with cups of coffee in hand discussing the continuance of their wolf trapping activities. Of most concern was what to do with the two women when the men were on foot or on horseback out in the outback running wolf trap lines. It soon became apparent that the men were now facing a dilemma regarding the women. Collectively they felt they could not leave the defenseless women at their cabin while they were out wolf trapping. If they did and someone else came in and stole their horses, that meant the women would be captured as well and once again possibly subjected to captivity and further abuses. Secondly, they couldn't just leave the women by themselves because they might take the trappers' horses and ride off with them as well back to their own people. It was then decided that the trappers would take the women with them on all trapping ventures now that they had some great and warm winter clothing to wear, including some very warm wolf skin hoods and warmer winter moccasins. Two strong proponents for the latter choice of options among the men were not surprisingly, Cloud and Feather…

The following morning, Wallace instructed Cloud and Feather to each select one of the women that they would be responsible for in everything that they did, including teaching them to speak English because both of those young men spoke the ladies' 'lingo' and could make their requests understood. That both men quickly acceded to, with Cloud verbally picking Kanti as the woman he would be responsible for, and Feather verbalizing that he would be proud to be responsible for the teaching and actions of Nuttah henceforth.

Upon hearing what had been planned for the sisters, Feather and Cloud smiled deeply. Turning, Otis could see that both men appeared to be more than excited over the prospects of treating Kanti and Nuttah like the ladies they were and as part of the group of men, as well as being allowed to participate in the trappers' outside activities…

After breakfast the next morning, the men and women dressed for the cold weather they would be facing that day while riding in the backcountry and in the process, setting out new wolf trap lines. Both of the ladies seemed very excited to be going along as were Cloud and Feather for some reason… With Wallace and Bridger leading the way in locating a good wolf trap line location, Cloud and Feather led two packhorses carrying all the needed trapping gear in their panniers with Kanti and Nuttah at their sides. As usual, Otis brought up the rear making sure there would be no surprise Indian attacks from the back of their little caravan. With those arrangements in place, the group headed off into likely looking wolf country on the ridges behind their cabin. Simultaneously, Cloud and Feather looked knowingly at each other as they rode along with the two young Blackfoot Indian women and thanked The Great Spirit for the 'special blessings' He had brought into their lives as well…

The group of trappers had only traveled about a mile when they jumped a small herd of elk and killed two fat cows. One of the cows was opened up immediately and had her intestines spilled forth upon the ground for the smells they emitted. Then as Wallace and Bridger set out cleverly concealed wolf traps, Cloud and Feather explained to Kanti and Nuttah what was being done and why. As they did, Otis kept a sharp eye peeled for any sign of danger as Wallace and Bridger set out their respective wolf traps. Then with Cloud and Feather tying ropes to the smaller yearling cow elk, they dragged that dead animal about a mile in the snow until Bridger and Wallace had decided on setting more wolf traps in another likely looking location. Once again, that elk was opened up and had its intestines spilled forth onto the open ground for the smells it would generate. Once again, Wallace and Bridger cleverly set their wolf traps hoping to catch one or more of the historically savvy and trap-wise wolves. Wolves whose valuable tanned winter pelts would bring a princely sum once sold at the next rendezvous. Then the men scouted for a last site in which to set their traps after killing a 'trap-bait' mule deer buck while en route. Once again the cavity opening process was repeated with the deer, so the smell of death might overcome a wolf's normal extreme caution because of the good smells and its hunger and lead him or her into being trapped.

Upon completion of their wolf trap setting duties, the group of trappers rode their horses off a ways from their last trap set and sat quietly out from the wind on their horses feasting upon several sticks of rich tasting elk jerky, all the while watching their back trail for any sign of discovery. Signs of discovery from either the shots they had fired in killing the elk and deer or being observed by Indians setting out their own wolf traps for the excellent winter furs that would generate. That was when the sharp-eyed Otis spotted six Indian riders moving along on their horses on another ridgeline about a half-a-mile away! Being deep in the country of the dreaded Blackfeet Indians, seeing them in country was to be expected and not unusual. Without a word, the trappers slipped off their ridgeline and down into a leafless grove of cottonwood trees where they could continue watching their back trail and yet not be readily observed by the Indians. When they did, Cloud and Feather noticed that their female charges both appeared alarmed upon seeing the distant Indian riders riding along another ridgeline and what they represented if they were to capture the young Indian women. There the men waited atop their horses hidden in the stand of timber for about an hour in the winter cold air making certain the Indian riders had not observed the trappers running a wolf trap line or heard them shoot and it was now safe to move on. Upon Bridger's command, the trappers rode up out from the grove of trees, took another careful look all around for the Indian riders and then headed back towards their cabin for the warmth and comfort it offered.

Riding back to their cabin a different way than they had left, the men and women dismounted, hobbled their horses just ridden and then opened the corral gate. There the men hobbled all of the rest of their horses and the entire herd was first led to water in the nearby creek since the little ditch of water in their corral had long frozen over. There Otis and Cloud had broken the ice so they could water and then they were led out into the big and wind-swept meadow where they could feed. After they were turned loose, Otis, Kanti and Nuttah headed for the cabin to build up a fire, warm up and begin the supper's preparations. Meanwhile, Bridger and Feather headed for the frozen elk carcass hanging on their meat pole, running off the gray jays and chickadees picking at the meat in the process and removed the remains of a hindquarter. Then the two men hauled the hindquarter into the cabin and laid it onto the table so Otis could remove the cuts of meat he needed for his supper meal that evening and the next morning's hearty breakfast.

Once Otis had removed what cuts of elk meat he wanted, Cloud bodily picked up the remaining elk quarter with little difficulty and headed out the cabin's door so he could rehang the remaining unused elk hindquarter back onto their meat pole. When he lifted up the remaining elk hindquarter, Kanti picked up the leg bone portion and with a smile at Cloud, the two of them headed out the cabin door en route the meat hanging pole near the horse corral.

ZZIPPP-THUNK! went an arrow right past Cloud's face, missed Kanti's face by mere inches, drove through her wolf skin parka's hood and impaled itself into the cabin's log wall right next to the front door! Dropping the elk's bony leg portion of the hindquarter, Kanti screamed as she tried to run only finding that her parka's hood was stuck to the cabin's wall by the arrow just shot at Cloud! **BOOM!** went Cloud's pistol shot at a Blackfoot warrior's head standing by the side of the trappers' cabin as he was trying to nock another arrow and finish off the man he had just surprised with a near miss. However, that was not to be, as Cloud's bullet, although hastily fired, hit the Indian getting ready to shoot another arrow at the trapper square in his chest, dropping him instantly to the ground! A combination of Cloud's shooting and Kanti's scream brought instant reaction from the surprised men inside the cabin! First out the door in order to meet whatever threat was now present was Feather, who instantly took a rifle ball through his open mouth and out the side of his right cheek! Fortunately, the bullet entered his open mouth, missed hitting any teeth and exited out his cheek without breaking his jaw or cheek bone! However, the impact of that bullet hitting Feather in the cheek spun him to the ground where he lay in a stunned clump of humanity and a spreading pool of blood! Next coming out the door right behind Feather was Otis, who upon seeing an Indian shoot at Feather, instinctively ducked off to one side, then straightened up and quickly 'snap-shot' the Indian who had just shot Feather through the mouth! Otis's shot, although hastily taken, was true in flight right into the Indian shooter's stomach, dropping him instantly to the snowy ground! Dropping his now empty rifle, Otis quickly drew his pistol from his sash and face-shot another Indian running right at him from the near corner of their cabin with an upraised tomahawk! Then Otis was instantly bowled over from behind by another Indian who had been hidden at the opposite corner of the trappers' cabin! Slamming to the ground, Otis turned and looked up in surprise at what had just violently collided with him. There he saw a large Indian with a pot belly starting to smash down upon him with his upraised tomahawk! Instinctively, Otis slammed the barrel of his now empty pistol savagely down upon the Indian's foot from just a foot or so away causing the man to drop his upraised tomahawk in extreme pain, bend over and grab his badly smashed foot with both hands! That was when Otis drew his sheath knife while lying on his back and thrust its razor sharp blade into the top of the Indian's now bent over head still howling in pain over his smashed toes! When violently head-stabbed with the knife, the Indian immediately dropped forward right on top of Otis! When he fell, Otis was instantly covered with the Indian's rush of blood from the stab wound through the top of his skull, making the trapper lying on the ground look like he himself had been the one who had been mortally wounded!

Next out the door was Wallace, who upon seeing an Indian trying to hastily mount his now skittish and rearing horse, back shot him, killing him instantly! Dropping his now empty Lancaster rifle, Wallace grabbed his .54 caliber pistol from his sash and tried shooting another mounted Indian, who upon seeing all of his comrades dropping like flies, had mounted up and was trying to ride away from the unexpected death erupting from the trappers' cabin. Wallace missed the Indian and instead hit his horse in the right hindquarter with a loud "SLAPPING" sound, as the heavy bullet blew through its thick hide, mushroomed into the horse's muscle and shattered its hip! Staggering in pain, the crippled horse began hobbling around with its broken hip just as Bridger emerged from the cabin. That Indian trying to spur his crippled horse away from the fury erupting from the trappers' cabin found himself instantly headshot by the quick and accurate shooting Jim Bridger! Then the trappers' campsite was quiet except for the groaning coming from face-shot Feather and the whimpering of a badly crippled Indian's horse trying to move away from the pain in his hip, all to no avail…

Then Bridger seeing the danger was past, took

out his knife and cut out the arrow still impaling Kanti's parka hood to the cabin's wall. Kanti, having shucked herself out from her impaled wolf skin parka, seeing Otis trying to crawl out from under the still madly bleeding Indian on top of him, and remembering Otis's kindness to her and her sister, jumped over to see if she could help save the gentle man from 'bleeding to death'.

As she did, Bridger hurriedly reloaded his rifle and then stood ready to defend the men around him if the need arose. Quickly counting the Indian bodies lying in their yard, Bridger realized that there were now six dead Blackfeet Indians strewn around their cabin! He then remembered back to their recent wolf-trapping trip when they had spotted six Indians way off in a distance. Indians that the men thought had not seen them or had heard them shoot the elk. Jim figured in fact they had been seen and as such, the Indians had backtracked the trappers and not realizing just how many trappers there were, had foolishly tried a surprise attack. Now all of the attackers lay dead around the campsite, turning the snow on the ground bright red with their pools of steaming blood in the cold winter's air...

About then Nuttah ran out from the cabin, dropped to her knees and began crying over the badly bleeding Feather thinking his wound was mortal. Moments later, Wallace had Feather back inside the cabin and was holding a rag against the side of his face and inside his mouth in an attempt to stem the flow of blood from the hole in his cheek with compression. In the meantime, blood-spattered Otis, realizing he was alright after stabbing his assailant in the top of his head, along with Cloud, rounded up the five valuable and uninjured Indians' horses and herded them into their corral along with the rest of the trappers' horses. Kanti, upon seeing that Feather was wounded, worked with Wallace attempting to stem the flow of blood from an ugly but not mortal facial wound! As those actions were occurring, Otis reloaded his rifle and then slowly walked the crippled horse out from their campsite and down to the edge of the Bear River. There he shot the horse and put it out of his misery. That he did figuring the horse was crippled for life in its present condition and it did not make good sense to keep such an injured critter alive and around their campsite as an open invite for any hungry grizzly bear upon which to easily chase down and upon which to dine...

Meanwhile back in the cabin, Kanti and Nuttah, using their Indian know-how, managed to finally get the blood flow from Feather's cheek stemmed. Then after washing out the wound with rum, and all to complete stoic silence from Feather, Wallace began sewing up Feather's facial wound. Fortunately for Feather, being shot from such close range, the super-heated lead bullet had cauterized his wound as it passed through

the side of his cheek, making his eventual healing, aside from the pain when eating or drinking for the next two weeks or so, livable. Otis
on the other hand, after walking back to their
compound from his horse shooting detail, had to
spend about half-an-hour stripping down to bare
naked in the cold winter's air, washing off all the
now sticky blood from the Indian that had fallen
onto him after being stabbed down through the
top of his head! Suffice to say, when he entered
the cabin with just his still bloodied shorts and
socks on in the dead of winter and soaked all to
hell from washing in the creek's freezing waters,
brought the rest of the group to smiles. Brought
to smiles over the man's shivering discomfort
over being almost half-frozen having to wash
the blood off with such icy creek waters, looking
funny in what he was wearing, but happy that he
was uninjured! In reality, there was much happiness in the cabin that evening knowing everyone
would heal up and be alright...

Later that evening, a newly dressed in dry
clothing Otis, along with Cloud, Wallace and
Bridger, saddled up their horses and dragged the
six dead Indians down to the still flowing and
not completely frozen over Bear River and tossed
their bodies into an open spot in its icy waters.
The next morning, Wallace and Bridger rode their
horses back down to the Bear River to see if the
bodies needed to be moved elsewhere in order to
keep any other Indians guessing as to the demise

of the missing warriors and not blame the nearby trappers for their disappearance. There they were unable to find any of the bodies since all six had drifted downstream and then further down, had drifted up under an ice jam and were forever lost to the ages, much to the two men's satisfactions. As for the Indian's crippled horse that Otis put out of its misery down by the river, all that was left was part of its skull, pelvis and several long leg bones. From all of the tracks around where the carcass had laid were numbers of wolf tracks and one set of very large tracks from a grizzly bear that had not gone into hibernation as of yet. All the critters had apparently feasted, leaving little trace of what had happened to one of the Blackfeet Indian attackers' horses.

As for the remaining five horses in the trappers' corral, the very next day they had all of their markings and tribal symbols washed off from their bodies and their manes and tails recut so they could not be identified as horses once belonging to the Blackfeet warriors who had tangled with the trappers and lost. That Jim Bridger demanded of the men, realizing how much marked horses meant to the Blackfeet and the importance of the identifying marks upon them. Marks previously made by its owner upon a horse that could get one in trouble if discovered by another knowing Blackfoot warrior upon recognizing a friend's traditional markings on a horse now in the hands of a white man trapper!

Until the wolves went out of their 'prime', Bridger and the Barnes Clan made life miserable for the four-legged predators. By the end of spring that year, the trappers had caught 48 wolves in their prime and had stretched the same! Wolf pelts that would command the highest prices come sale day at the upcoming rendezvous to once again be held in the vicinity of Bear Lake. However, that wasn't the only great event taking place that year with the group of trappers trapping in the Bear River country. Kanti and Nuttah were learning the English language from Cloud and Feather, and Feather's facial wound had healed up beautifully leaving only a small jagged scar on his right cheek. Additionally, Kanti and Nuttah had fallen in love with Cloud and Feather and those two young men were deeply in love with the two ladies as well! To the rest of the men in the group and Kanti and Nuttah, all in a few short months of relationships, they had grown to love and respect one another as if they were brothers, sisters AND MORE! By the advent of the spring beaver trapping season, Cloud and Feather no longer harbored lonely thoughts about being social outcasts in the Wind River Band of the Shoshoni. Now they thought of themselves as warriors, trappers and someday to be husband and wife with Kanti and Nuttah respectively! That was just as soon as the Catholic Church would allow such in accordance with the religious beliefs strongly held by Otis and

Wallace. Beliefs held by Otis and Wallace who were now considered 'family members' to be listened to in such serious and lifelong matters such as baptism and marriage when it came to Cloud and Feather. With that in mind, Cloud and Feather held off physically consummating their relationships with the two women they were in love with until they could be married in the eyes of the Catholic Church back in Missouri and in the eyes of Otis and Wallace!

Come the start of the spring beaver trapping season with the beaver in their prime after living under the ice and in the icy cold waters for the last several months, the Barnes Clan and Jim Bridger headed out. Headed out that was, after a celebratory breakfast of Dutch oven biscuits, hot coffee, skewered moose meat and beans. In the lead of the trappers' caravan of horses rode Jim Bridger and Wallace. They were closely followed by Cloud and Feather. Trailing those two men were Kanti and Nuttah leading their two packhorses with panniers full of the needed trapping equipment and anchor poles for the traps. Bringing up the rear of the trappers' caravan rode sharp-eyed Otis Barnes and crack rifle shot as always, constantly on the lookout for any kind of unexpected danger.

As planned the year before by Bridger, this would be the year the trappers would trap out the northern reaches of the Bear River close to the area in which the trappers lived. After a short ride that morning, Bridger and Wallace finally stopped near a vast stretch of likely look- ing, beaver trapping watered areas and heavily utilized beaver ponds. Sitting there quietly on their horses, the two trappers quietly surveyed the beaver waters to their front and side. The entire watered areas the trappers had chosen that morning were heavily dotted with conical beaver houses, dammed up by numerous, well maintained stick and mud dams and showing extensive evidence of heavy willow and cotton- wood tree cutting activities. Additionally, there were several freshly cut and felled cottonwoods lying in several ponded up waters.

To Wallace Barnes and Jim Bridger, the area looked heaven-sent for any beaver trapper look- ing to ply his trade. Dismounting and asking Kanti and Nuttah to ride off a short distance away so Bridger and Wallace could change into their buckskin leggings and breechclouts for the water immersion beaver trapping work, the two trappers partially disrobed and dressed into their working clothing. Then with the faith- ful Otis remaining in his saddle as the group's guardian watching out for any signs of danger, Wallace and Bridger walked along the edges of the chosen watered area looking for the freshest beaver slide and usage areas. Those two men were closely followed by Cloud and Feather carrying the heavy beaver traps, four-foot-long dried wooden anchor poles, hand axes, trap anchor twine and bottles of castoreum. As the two experienced trappers began setting their 30 beaver traps, Cloud and Feather were kept busy running back and forth hauling the needed traps and anchor poles to the two experienced Mountain Men doing the trapping. About the same time, Kanti and Nuttah arrived back with the rest of the trappers, after having attended to a call of nature while being absent that period of time when Wallace and Bridger were stripping down and changing into their trapping gear. Come around two o'clock in the now warming up afternoon sun's rays, found the trappers resting alongside their horses in a grove of budding out aspens, discussing the morning's trapping activity and eating elk jerky. As the early afternoon sun and air continued warming the trappers, soon with the exception of Otis, the men and women laid back on the warm prairie soil under the trees and quickly drifted off fast asleep.

Their sleep was shortly thereafter disturbed by Otis, who softly called for the men to wake up. When everyone was awakened, Otis pointed out to a small herd of buffalo that had ventured into their area and were now watering not far from where Wallace and Bridger had set their last beaver traps. The trappers, not seeing any buffalo for most of the previous winter in their area, hastily mounted their horses and after a short stalk, had shot and killed three cow buffalo. Riding up to the first dead cow, Bridger excitedly jumped off his horse and handed its reins to Otis. Bridger then commenced opening up the cow's side below its last rib and extracted an entire lobe of its still warm and bleeding liver. Turning with a big smile on his face, Jim called Kanti and Nuttah to dismount and soon the three of them were eagerly eating chunks of the raw and still quivering buffalo liver as the rest of the men began dismounting. Soon every one of the group of trappers were eagerly eating chunks of raw buffalo liver.

Then all of a sudden, Otis tossed his uneaten chunk of buffalo liver away and made a quick move for his nearby horse and rifle! But his hurried move was in vain and too late! Quickly surrounding the small band of trappers gathered around the dead cow buffalo rode two long lines of Blackfeet Indians until they had entirely encircled the Barnes Clan and Jim Bridger! Then the Indians just quietly sat there on their horses looking on at the now surrounded group of what appeared to be soon to be dead trappers...

"Don't anyone make any hostile moves," said Bridger. "They have us outnumbered at least four or five to one and if we make any kind of an offensive move, we will all be cut down and killed as fast as a meadowlark can sing one note of his morning's song!"

It was then about another dozen Blackfeet Indians rode up to the long line of Indians surrounding the trappers. This time it was evident from their long single and double train eagle feather war bonnets and how part of the line of surrounding Indians separated so the newcomers could enter the circle of Indians, that they were the ones in command of what was about to happen next to the outnumbered trappers!

"Hold your fire, boys! The Blackfeet respect bravery and if we show only respect for them and not fear, we may have a chance to view the next sunrise," said Bridger as he just cradled his rifle lightly in his right arm but not in an offensive manner.

"WHAT THE HELL...," said Bridger, as one of the Indians trailing a long double train war bonnet, broke away from the small group of obvious chiefs and sub-chiefs quietly sitting on their horses looking down at the group of trappers, and rapidly rode right at the surrounded men and women with his beautiful golden eagle war bonnet's feathers streaming impressively out behind him!

"FATHER!" screamed Kanti and Nuttah simultaneously, as they broke away from the trappers and ran crying across the prairie towards the Indian riding 'hellbent for leather' towards the two running and crying women! Seconds later, the impressive Indian chief had bailed off his horse, gathered both young women up in his arms in an obvious great show of surprise and extreme happiness!

For the longest time, the confused group of

trappers trying to figure out what the hell was happening just remained in a huddle expecting the worst at any moment. Then Bridger said, "HELLFIRE AND DAMNATION! I THINK THEM TWO WOMEN ARE THAT INDIAN CHIEF'S TWO LONG-LOST DAUGHTERS! THOSE TWO GIRLS MUST BE HIS KIDS THOSE TWO RENEGADE TRAPPERS CAUGHT BATHING SOMETIME BACK NEAR THE INDIANS' ENCAMPMENT, KNOCKED THEM IN THE HEAD SO THEY WOULD NOT SOUND THE ALARM AND RAN OFF WITH THEM," said Bridger slowly...

"Lower all of the barrels of your rifles way down, boys," uttered Bridger, so as not to ruffle any feathers of all the mean and sullen looking Indians still surrounding the small group of trappers. "We best let them two girls have the time to sort this all out with their father. I don't want him a-thinkin' we are the ones who ran off with his daughters. He may still be mad as hell at all trappers for capturing and 'spoiling' his two daughters as most trappers usually do." But as he spoke those words to the rest of the men, it was obvious if things turned out for the worst, he had his eyes set on killing at least that Indian chief closest to the two women before he was overrun, killed and then mutilated in true Indian fashion. True to form, Old Jim Bridger wasn't a-goin' under without putting up a damn good fight and if any Indian wanted his 'top-knot', he was welcome to try and come and get it!

Then all of a sudden, Kanti on one arm and

Nuttah on the other led the chief with the double train war bonnet down the side hill and directly at the group of still very concerned trappers not having any idea over what might be coming next. Then at the last moment, Kanti and Nuttah broke away from the Indian chief they had been leading towards the group of trappers and ran the rest of the way downhill to the trappers still gathered around the carcass of the dead buffalo.

Without a word, both Kanti and Nuttah ran to White Cloud and Spotted Feather, then taking them by their arms, escorted them back towards the Indian chief still slowly walking towards the trappers. Escorted White Cloud and Spotted Feather like two little kids would do when they had something to proudly show off to a parent. Then after meeting the impressive looking chief, the five Indians quietly out of earshot talked among themselves for many long minutes and heartbeats taking place within the small group of trappers…

"Boys, we may have caught a break. Them two girls I imagine are telling their father that we have rescued them from the two evil trappers that purchased them some time back. I sure as hell hope they are also telling that man that we have been treating them very well and 'fine as frog hair' ever since. Damn, I am sure glad none of you fellas were so inclined to take them girls off and bed them against their wills. Had any of you done so, we would be cooling off as coyote bait on these here prairie hills right about now had any of you done so," said Bridger slowly as he kept his 'shooting eye' on the chief just in case... "However, we still ain't got much of a chance if that there Blackfoot chief don't buy them two girls' stories," continued Bridger with just the lilt of a sound of worry rising up in his voice. Not that he minded dying, mind you, but what was pissing him off was that he would only get off one shot once the shooting started and then they would be quickly overwhelmed and butchered!

Then the group surrounding the chief parted and he began proudly once again walking down towards the trappers. Moments later, the chief impassively walked right up to Bridger saying in clipped English, obviously having been taught to him by the Spanish "Black Robes" when he was a younger man, " "Man of the Mountains", I am proud to meet you! You are famous among my people because of your trapping, tracking and shooting abilities. I am also aware that one time in the past, you were married to one of my people from a different band. My name is Black Wolf, Chief of the Southern Bear River Band of Blackfeet. My lost to me many moons ago daughters tell me you and yours have kept them warm, fed, and safe from harm. They also tell me that you and your kind standing here today have killed off the evil trappers who 'took them against their will' and did so many times. When you killed them, you then took my daughters away from them and that was good! They also tell me that none of you have bedded them against their wills like all of the other trappers have done. That is also good because if any of you had, then all of you would have died where you now stand! My daughters also tell me that they have since their time of rescue, fallen in love with White Cloud and Spotted Feather and wish my blessings so they can live together as man and wife. That I will allow because they cannot come back to my band to live since they have been previously shamed by the evil white trappers, and are no longer pure in the eyes of my people as is required by our culture. None of my young men will marry them now being that they are that way, so they have my blessing and can go and choose who they want to marry. As I have been told here today by my two daughters, they have chosen to be with White Cloud and Spotted Feather for as long as there are buffalo. Since you and yours, Man of the Mountains, have been so honorable, you will live this day. You may also trap and hunt in the land of the Southern Bear River Band of the Blackfeet as our Brothers without any fear of death or disturbance from my people. That is my wish as their chief and my People will honor those wishes. Now, I am tired of such talk. I now know that my daughters are safe and happy. That makes me happy as well and their mother will be happy with my words about our daughters when she hears my words.

Take care of them, Man of the Mountains, and if you and yours do, then my People will take care of you as our brothers as well, as long as you roam our sacred lands."

"Now, let us talk of other things," said Black Wolf. "My young men are hungry and you have just killed three buffalo. Would you and your trappers share some of your buffalo meat with us? I ask because we have ridden long and hard this day after some bad Indians from another band who killed some of my people. We have been chasing these 'rabbit eating people' (Paiutes) for two days now and they still live further towards the land of the setting sun. We did not figure they would move so fast after killing a number of our people or take so many days to capture and kill those 'bad Indians' and now we are out of food," continued Black Wolf.

"Black Wolf, I am glad that me and my men are now called 'Brothers' by the great Blackfeet Nation. We would be glad to share our three buffalo with you and your men. Our camp is not far from here. Let us butcher out some of these buffalo and take the meat back to our camp. There your men and horses can rest and me and my men will fix food for all of you," said Bridger in the tongue of the Blackfeet. With those words from Bridger, Black Wolf smiled, turned and made a 'come-hither 'gesture to his warriors still surrounding the group of trappers and his two daughters. Soon, the trappers and a dozen

Indians had butchered out the buffalo, hungrily eating all of the raw livers from the three animals in the process and then with the trappers' pack-horses' panniers fully loaded with fresh, boned-out buffalo meat, the entire group in a long line headed towards the trappers' cabin.

Once back at their cabin while the 28 Blackfoot warriors unsaddled their horses and let them out to graze and water, the trappers hurriedly set to work putting together a meal for their new 'Brothers'. Otis had Cloud and Feather break out their three Dutch ovens and the two like in kind ovens retrieved from the Frenchies' camp after they had been killed and no longer had any need for them. As the two men retrieved the five Dutch ovens, Otis built up his outside cooking fire in order to generate a huge bed of coals for the Dutch ovens. Then as Bridger and Wallace spitted huge chunks of buffalo on their skewers and placed them over the fire to cook, Otis went to their creek for a pail of water. Soon Otis was making up a small mountain of biscuit dough while Wallace and Bridger tended to the roasting buffalo meat. About then, Cloud and Feather had liberally greased up the five Dutch ovens with bear grease and prepared them for the biscuit baking to come. Then Otis had the two boys fill up their two two-gallon coffee pots and set them over the fire on the hanging irons to boil. As they did, Kanti and Nuttah dug out all of the trappers' coffee cups and bowls that could also be used to drink coffee from because they had so many 'guests' for the soon to be coming meal.

Twenty minutes later, the trappers were serving the hungry Indians half-raw cooked buffalo meat (as they liked it), hot coffee and Dutch oven biscuits from the five now baking ovens. As Otis turned out biscuits about every three minutes now that the ovens were hot, they were eagerly gobbled up by the more than hungry Indian 'guests'! Working up his second mountain of biscuit dough, Otis quietly said to Bridger, "Damn, I am sure glad we not only have our provisions but those we took from the Frenchies' camp after we killed them off as well! Otherwise, the way these biscuits are disappearing down the maws of these hungry Indians, we would be out of biscuit making flour before we can replenish our stores at the next rendezvous!"

After an hour of cooking, baking and eating, the 28 Indians were finally filled up. With that and still many miles of remaining pursuit after the Paiutes who had killed some of their people, the Blackfeet warriors mounted up and were ready to leave and continue their chase. When they were ready to depart, Black Wolf gathered his two daughters around him and there was much hugging and some tears from the ladies as their father prepared to continue leading his war party. Then Black Wolf suddenly turned to White Cloud and Spotted Feather who were standing nearby and in the tongue of the Blackfeet, made sure those two young men knew they had better take care of his daughters or else! Then turning to Bridger, Black Wolf said, "I hope that Man of the Mountains is an honorable man when it comes to watching out for my daughters when they are in his camp as well. Then in a surprising move, Black Wolf turned to Otis who was standing quietly off to one side watching, by saying, "It is you that the young people have come to love as one of their own and respect most highly from what I hear and can see. Please see to it that The Great Spirit always walks with these young people and their young to come." With those words out and before Bridger or Otis could reply, Black Wolf had vaulted back up into his saddle and with a wave of his hand and a look down at Bridger and Otis that only a loving and concerned father could give, led his stream of horseflesh and humanity out from the trappers' campsite and was soon gone in a cloud of silently drifting on the wind, dust…

Behind the exiting Indians remained five exhausted and relieved trappers and two tired and still misty-eyed Indian women. Misty-eyed Indian women realizing because of the nature and the strict cultural mores of the Blackfeet, that was probably the last time they would ever see their father. That and because of the fighting nature of the Blackfeet and their sworn word that they would fight against the sacred ground trespassing white man until the stars left the night sky... Scattered around camp were many over-turned kettles, dishes and the like and little fresh buffalo meat! The hungry Indians had consumed almost every bit of the fresh buffalo meat brought into camp and over 100 Dutch oven biscuits, not to mention consuming five gallons of the trapper's style of coffee laced heavily with lumps of much-loved by the Indians, brown sugar! Yes, as Black Wolf had so advised, "his young men were hungry"... Then the next day when the sun was high and with the warming air around the trappers' camp, the odiferous smells from over 20 Indians attending to a call of nature and doing so as they did around their own village, right next to their living area, became readily apparent that the trappers recently had a number of Indians at their campsite for company...

For the next couple of months until the beaver went out of prime, the family of trappers ran their trap lines, skinned, defatted and stretched 313 mostly Made Beaver! In fact, the trappers pretty well had eliminated every beaver in their immediate trapping area along the Bear River and its many adjacent waterways. Soon all that remained in the numerous beaver ponds were a few muskrats, river otter and arriving pairs of waterfowl ready to begin another nesting season. Then as the Barnes Clan and Jim Bridger began compressing and bundling up their remaining beaver skins and wolf pelts, Kanti and Nuttah began the process of closing up their camp in preparation for heading to the upcoming Bear Lake Rendezvous. The final tally of beaver skins was 293 taken during the fall trapping season and 313 taken during the spring trapping season, for a total of 606 beaver pelts and 48 wolf pelts trapped and ready for sale at the rendezvous. It was more than apparent that Bridger had been correct in selecting the Bear River area as their beaver trapping grounds based on the numbers of trapped beaver, and that the trapping expertise of Bridger and Wallace Barnes was nothing short of outstanding!

Come the first day of June, the Barnes Clan and Jim Bridger left their camp near the Bear River and headed back up to the Bear Lake area in current-day Utah for the upcoming rendezvous. Four days of easy travel found the clan and Bridger moving into the rendezvous site which was already holding several dozen camps and their trappers, who were low on provisions and more than ready for the arrival of the pack train bringing in the needed supplies for the coming trapping seasons. Moving into the same grove of cottonwood trees they had camped under during the previous rendezvous, the horses were unpacked and unsaddled, hobbled so they would not mix with other trappers or friendly Indians' horses and let out to water and graze. As Otis cleaned out the leaves and other debris from his previous year's firepit, the rest of the group collected up all the loose firewood they could find before it was all gone and placed it near their firepit. Then Bridger, Cloud and Feather constructed a temporary meat pole from one of the cottonwoods and hung the two freshly killed antelope taken by Bridger and Otis that morning while traveling into the rendezvous area. As the men skinned out the animals so they could cool out, glaze and by so doing, make the meat taste less strongly, Kanti and Nuttah laid out the group's sleeping furs under the cottonwoods. Then they routinely laid out all of their packs around the sleeping area in a defensive position just in case trouble was to come their way. Finished with that work, the group brought their saddles into the main campsite near the campfire so they would have something to sit on or lay against when sitting or eating around the firepit. Then it was time to walk around the existing campsites and see who had 'kept their hair' and see who had 'gone under' the previous year among their friends. It was also time to see how a number of trappers had fared when it came to their annual harvest of beaver and other skins. Additionally, Wallace and Bridger took the time to put the word out regarding the availability of a large number of horses and mules from the large herd of Blackfeet and trappers' horses they had captured in their earlier battles. It did not take long for numerous trappers and several Indians who were 'horse short', to trade in a number of their pelts for the more than 25 Blackfeet and trappers' horses, much to the satisfaction and enrichment of Jim Bridger and Wallace Barnes's group of trappers.

By the middle of June, the rendezvous supply train, including heavily loaded wagons for the first time, had traversed across from St. Louis, up the Mississippi River to the Missouri River, up the Missouri River to the Platte River to the North Platte River, then on to the Sweetwater River, past Devil's Gate, across the Continental Divide via South Pass, then across the Green River Valley and into the Bear Lake area, the designated site of the rendezvous. Their arrival called for much celebration and hell-raising, especially when the kegs of rum and whiskey were unloaded from the wagons and made available to those trappers gathered around and those friendly Indians arriving into the rendezvous site in greater and greater numbers on a daily basis.

On day three since their arrival, the yells of "INDIANS! INDIANS!" rang through the rendezvous settlement early one morning after the traders had arrived. With those yells of danger hanging in the air, that was then immediately followed by a flurry of shooting as about 20 Blackfeet Indians rained down on the trappers camped along the outer edges of the rendezvous site! For many moments the sounds of yelling, whooping of attacking Indians and gunfire rang throughout the area! But soon, the larger numbers of trappers, traders and friendly Indians had recovered from the shock of a bold daylight attack by the Blackfeet and those Indians were quickly driven off with a few of their number left behind, along with a few dead surprised in their sleeping furs trappers as well! Then in celebration after the rout of the Blackfeet surprise hit and run attack had run its course, the wagons carrying the kegs of rum and whiskey were then heavily visited by the trappers and many a cup of the fiery liquid was consumed by those who had survived the raid and lived to tell about it...

However, instead of running to the battle in support of the other trappers being attacked along the edges of the rendezvous site, Bridger and the Barnes Clan just stood at the ready in their camp with their rifles in hand and their women hidden from view behind the packs of beaver pelts. There the group safely waited out the outcome of battle with the attacking Blackfeet. When the short battle was over, said and done, several returning trappers inquired why Bridger and the rest of his party had not joined them in the battle. Bridger just shrugged his shoulders saying, "We made our peace with Black Wolf of the Southern Band of the Bear River Blackfeet. I could see no advantage in killing those who now are our friends and kin of the women in our party. Had they attacked our party, we would have fought back. But in order not to kill those Indians who are now our friends and kin to our women, we just stood down and protected that which was ours. Asides, there were plenty of you straight shootin' trappers taking care of those Indians who were foolish enough to attack our group. So with that in mind, we did not get worried about being overrun and scalped, being camped way over here away from the scene of the battle." That explanation seemed to satisfy those inquiring trappers and the rest of that issue was left to 'the prairie winds'.

Later that evening after supper, Bridger and the rest of the clan gathered around their campfire with cups of the last of their rum until they could trade in some of their pelts for more of the fiery drink when they 'provisioned up'. That was when the normally quiet Wallace, after a time, spoke to an issue that had been in the backs of many of their minds. "Seems time we decide where we are a-going come this fall and the coming spring in which to trap beaver and further our trade. We can't go back to the "Bear" because we trapped that area out. And no matter where we end up, it must have good trappings because Feather and Cloud have made it very clear that when we quit trapping and head home to Missouri to buy some land, settle down and leave this dangerous life, they wish to go with us and remain as part of the family. When they do, they plan on taking Kanti and Nuttah with them so they can be baptized and married in the Catholic Church that Otis and I have been talking to them about so they can become good Christian men and women in the eyes of the Lord." For the longest time after Wallace had broached the subject of the coming year's trapping grounds so all of them could return to Missouri with enough money to purchase some good land and settle down, all one heard were noisy trappers celebrating off in the distance and the crackling of limb wood in their own fire.

That was when Jim Bridger spoke up and shocked everyone! "I have been meanin' to talk to all of you about this coming year, the fall and spring trappin' and all. I might as well spit out that which has been stickin' in my craw for some time now, so here it is. I plan on leaving the group and striking out on my own once again right after this here rendezvous! There is a lot of this here land I would like to see afore I 'go under' and I can't do that just by beaver trapping every day of my life in one place or another. I need to be free so I can roam as I see fit, eat whatever I can catch or shoot, and just cast my eyes upon all the new lands that lie further to the west. We can't do that as a group because all of you some-day want to quit this dangerous beaver trapping business, buy some good bottomland, raise some crops and settle down. Me, I don't hanker to do that until the good beaver trapping quits and I plumb wear out, get 'kilt' or have a chance to see whatever lays out there that I still ain't laid eyes on yet. After the success that all of us have had this trappin' season, I can take my share which will be more than enough and that which I have saved from previous years of trapping, which will allow me to stretch my wings and see what there is still to see out there with these tired old eyes that the good Lord has given me. Additionally, I have my share of the pelts traded to us for all of those Blackfeet and trappers' horses and mules we won fair and square in battle these last few months. What I get from that share of the pelts will give me at least another year in the back-country doin' what I like doin'."

Once those shocking words and revelations from Bridger were out and in the night air, the silence around the campfire was deafening! In one swoop, the Barnes Clan would be losing their Man of the Mountains and the innate knowledge of one of the most experienced Mountain Men in the Rocky Mountains! In Jim Bridger they would be losing a man with an uncanny survival sense and a wonderful breadth of geographic knowl-edge because of his previous years of travel and exploration while living out on the frontier. Lose in him a level of excellence and experience that had already been proven during their last year's trapping time and time again while out on the "Bear" under some of the most trying of circum-stances!

Sensing the shock and surprise felt by the clan over what he had just uttered, Bridger began speaking once again saying, "I know that is a shock to all of you but you have been honest and fair with me and I just figured it was time I was the same with all of you. Don't get me wrong. I love all of you like you were my own brothers and sisters. But the insides of me say I have to move on and see what is out there afore it is all gone, or I can no longer see and appreciate what the good Lord has laid out for me to experience. Therefore, once we settle up over what we have made with our furs and pelts from this trapping season, I plan on taking my share, purchasing what provisions I will need in my future travels and strike out on my own once again as I have done in years past and have come to love doin'. However, knowing you folks still need another good year of trapping in order to have enough money saved up so you can purchase enough good land back in Missouri for all of you to call home, I have a suggestion. Years back in some of my earlier wanderings about 12 days' travel due north of here above the Salt River Range, I came through an area I call the "Hoback". That area is beaver-rich and was named after John "Trapper John" Hoback, a fellow Mountain Man and old friend of mine. He traveled through that area with several men including a big fur man named John Astor looking for good beaver trapping grounds. To the best of my recollections, that area has not been trapped hardly at all, except by a few Indian trappers, is still full of beaver and just about any other kind of critter worth eating or selling. It has timber galore for building a cabin, plenty of good water and horse graze, and the only drawback I can think of are the damn cold and long winters. Well, those and the damn, mean as a stepped-on snake Gros Ventre Indians that call that area home in their wanderings. But if I remember correctly, the beaver are big Made Beaver for the most part, plenty in number and are in their prime more months than normally because of the cold found up there in those waters in that 'neck of the woods'. But there is money aplenty to be made up there if you can keep your hair and don't mind a little cold and some deep snows," said Bridger with the sound of high adventure now ringing in the tone and tenor of his voice.

Then looking at the clan seated around the campfire and seeing an interest on their faces and in their eyes over what he had just mentioned, Bridger grinned. Then he continued saying, "Now, I plan on heading west so I won't be able to show you folks the way to what I consider fabled beaver trapping grounds, but I can draw you a map on how to get there from my memory of having traveled all through that country in my earlier days. I would be more than willing to do so if you be interested. That is the least I can do for all of you good folks for what you have done for me," continued Bridger with another big grin from under his wide-brimmed hat.

"Well, Jim, if that is your decision, all of us would hate to lose your company but we would surely stand behind you and understand. We hate the idea of losing you being such a knowledgeable partner and all, but I am sure we all understand your need to see what is on the other side of what lays over the next mountain. As stated earlier, we still need another good year as near as I can figure from all of our previous Letters of Credit, especially now with our larger family to buy the amount of land we would need back in Missouri in order to make a right and proper living. Besides, it will be just a matter of time before Feather and Cloud are with family after they are married and will have even greater needs. So, we will give the frontier one more year of our lives and then head south and go back home to Missouri. We have already lost three of our much-loved brothers to this harsh land and I do not want to lose any more of our family. So if you say that area is heavy with large and prime Made Beaver, that is good enough for us to hang our hats on. I will get us some paper and pencil from my saddlebags and have you put to paper a map showing us how to get there. And knowing your good mind for the geography of this land of ours, that should be enough for us to locate the area on our own and make the rest of our fortune on the backs of the beaver that we catch," said Wallace, as the rest of the clan listened very intently to the conversation between the Man of the Mountains and the Patriarch of the Barnes Clan. For the next hour around the light of their campfire and using Wallace's side of his saddlebag as a 'table', Jim drew a very detailed map on a piece of paper on how to get into the Hoback country lying to the north and the fabled beaver trapping waiting for whoever, as described by Jim Bridger. As he did, every man in their group stood around observing what was being drawn on the piece of paper and had many questions. Then with many of those questions in mind, Bridger drew onto the map even more detail so the men could find their way to his land of promise by just using his document mapping out the way. When Bridger had finished, that map went into Wallace's 'saddlebag bank' for later use by his family come the end of the rendezvous, the trip there to the Hoback and the coming fall and spring beaver trapping season.

For the next few days, the Barnes Clan and Bridger continued visiting old friends and making many new acquaintances. Then it came time for all of the trappers to meet with the Rocky Mountain Fur Company traders, display their catches, have their pelts counted, graded and valued so they would have the wherewithal to purchase the coming trapping season's provisions. (Author's Note: Rocky Mountain Fur Company took over the American Fur Company, and became the largest fur company during that time.) When it came time for Bridger and the Barnes Clan to make their trades, they closely watched the graders, making sure their furs were not under graded because the Mountain Price per pound of beaver was only $3 that year! That was because the demand for beaver was waning in favor of the new silk hat craze in Europe and the eastern United States over that of a beaver hat. And as usual, the trappers, if they wanted to be resupplied with provisions for the coming year, they had to pay the high Mountain Prices for everything they needed!

Being that the Barnes Clan and Bridger had to split their catch of beaver that allowed each party to sell 303 beaver and 24 wolf pelts to the traders. In the end, that netted each party $1,363.50 for their beaver pelts and an additional $300 for their wolf pelts. Then the group was able to sell those furs they had received in trade for the Blackfeet Indian and French-Canadian trappers' horses and mules sold earlier, which netted each party an additional $450, for a total of $2,113.50 for their year of hard and often dangerous work as trappers! No two ways about it, netting $2,113.50 was a fortune in those days of dollars and cents!

Realizing the potential challenges the new Hoback country in general and the Gros Ventre Indians specifically represented to the Barnes Clan, the men carefully and in greater detail, discussed what the selection of their provisions should carefully represent. They had plenty of the cooking, shooting, cutting and gutting essentials when one counted their own gear as well as what they had acquired provision-wise from their earlier shootout with the Frenchies. With that in mind, the men made sure their provisions for a trip into a rugged and possible hostile country for their next beaver trapping season was well represented with the absolute survival 'necessaries', especially when it came to defending one's self!

That meant extra kegs of gunpowder, more pigs of lead, a good stock of heavy blankets for the snows Bridger had predicted, extra wool capotes for everyone including the two women, extra gloves, socks, felt hats with wide brims, flints, extra powder horns, gun worms to clean out fouling from the barrels, 20 extra one-pound metal canisters of DuPont FFg powder and ten one-pound canisters of DuPont FFFFg priming powder for their flintlock mechanisms to be carried in their 'Possibles bags', extra leggings for the trap setters to wear, extra Linsey-woolsy pants for everyone, extra parts for their pistols and rifles, bags of oiled patches, and two rifle ramrods.

Then Otis who was always the one who worried the most about the welfare of the folks, walked over to the firearms section of the Rocky Mountain Fur Company traders' displays and purchased two shotguns and four extra .54 caliber pistols. The caliber of the pistols Otis had just purchased was done so because they matched what everyone else in their party carried, making bullet casting simpler. When questioned by Wallace since they already had plenty of extra firearms, Otis pointed to Kanti and Nuttah. "Where we are going and the Indian varmints in that neck of the woods that hate the Blackfeet, both of those women are going to learn to shoot and shoot well for their own protection. I have purchased shotguns for the women so they don't have to aim well, just cover their target and pull the trigger towards any Indians who happen to break through our defenses and get at our women. They need to be able to defend themselves and well, that is why I have purchased a shotgun for each of them and two pistols each as well. That way with buck and ball in their pistols, they can once again defend themselves if anyone gets close to them with evil intentions on their minds! Remember, the Gros Ventre hold a bitter historical hatred towards the Blackfeet. If they can get to our women, they will suffer a fate worse than death because the Gros Ventre will gang rape each of them and then kill them! That ain't going to happen as long as I am alive," said Otis, as he handed the weapons just selected to the Rocky Mountain Fur Company Clerks to record and hold for the trappers as new purchases.

Then since they had plenty of hardware and other building and cutting necessaries, the men moved on to the food provision displays laid out on buffalo hides on makeshift log tables by the Rocky Mountain Fur Company wagons. There Otis made selection after selection so fast, that he kept Cloud, Feather and the Fur Company Clerks just a-hopping. Sack after sack of flour, beans, rice, green coffee beans, salt, red pepper flakes, black pepper, cinnamon, brown sugar cones, four jugs of honey, three jugs of bear grease, bag balm, six kegs of rum, dried raisins, dried apple slices, fire steels and the like soon amounted to a small mountain of goods he felt necessary for the coming year's survival of the clan.

Then Otis walked over to another wagon site where numerous wares were displayed in such a manner that they were meant to catch the trappers' eyes so such goods would be purchased for the trappers' Indian wives. There he instructed Kanti and Nuttah to select out several bolts of bright red cloth that struck their fancy for clothing, canisters of red, blue and green glass beads from Europe, a "Russel Wilson" made in England sheath knife apiece for everyday work they would be involved with as well as self-defense, awls, needles, spools of thread, spools of twine, several combs for their long black hair, a couple of mirrors, and some brightly colored women's capotes made from heavy red colored wool so they could be warm come winter when out wolf trapping with their menfolk. After all, Bridger said the winters in the Hoback could be brutal... When Otis had finished shopping for the women, he turned and all he could see were smiles across the faces of Kanti and Nuttah when it came to all the riches they had just been given. The looks on the faces of Cloud and Feather looked pretty pleased over the special treatment their womenfolk had just received as well from what they now considered their adopted father!

When all was said and done when it came to purchasing the needed goods and provisions for another year trapping in the backcountry, the company Clerk after some 'ciphering', advised Wallace their costs came to $910, Mountain Prices! Considering a working man in the United States in that day and age made between $200-400 per year, $910 for a year's supplies was considerable! After that amount had been deducted from the fur credit owed by the Rocky Mountain Fur Company for the men's furs, the Barnes Clan was issued a Letter of Credit to the tune of $1,203.50 for the balance of what they were owed. Once again, Wallace took that Letter of Credit and rolled it up with his other Letters of Credit from previous years of trapping and placed all of the valuable documents back safely into his saddlebags. Someday those Letters of Credit would be redeemed at the Rocky Mountain Fur Company fur house back in St. Louis. Then those monies would be applied to a land purchase that would in the future be able to care for Wallace, Otis, White Cloud, Spotted Feather and once married in the Catholic Church as Otis and Wallace demanded, their two wives Kanti and Nuttah and any of their future children.

That evening back at their campsite, the Barnes Clan and Jim Bridger, who had also been shopping with his share of the trapping proceeds, loaded their packs for travel when the day came for them to go their separate ways. Then as Otis prepared a celebratory supper of pinto beans, skewered venison, a sweet dish of rice, raisins, cinnamon and brown sugar, coffee and the ever-present Dutch oven biscuits, a keg of recently purchased rum was brought forth and a relaxing evening was had by all. For the next eleven days, the Barnes Clan and Jim Bridger made the rounds on-site celebrating with a number of their old and newly made trapper friends. There they took part in a number of the ongoing celebrations such as horse races, shooting contests, cook-offs, foot races, tomahawk and knife throwing contests and storytelling, all along with numerous cups of rum at every trapper's campsite visited. However, as to be expected, the men did not take part in any of the Indian wife swapping, buying or selling events…

Being that the next day was the Fourth of July, a great celebration was being prepared camp wide. The traders from the Rocky Mountain Fur Company had planned on killing two of their oxen, roasting the same over an open pit and providing a great feed along with ample supplies of rum for all of their trappers and peaceful Indians in camp. The next morning right at daylight, a cannon brought along by the fur company was fired and the day's Fourth of July celebrations began. There was more of the same revelry only more and louder, the rum flowed and come the afternoon when the oxen were fully roasted, a great feast was held and enjoyed by all present. Then as darkness fell, several men broke out their fiddles and a great dance was held around the fur company's campfires by the trappers dancing with each other since women were scarce on the frontier. Then even more rum was consumed as much more rifle fire broke out in celebration of the young Nation's Birthday. Before long, the rum began taking effect on many of the trappers and soon a number of men were happily staggering around, falling down, lying in piles sleeping off a drunk, or getting into fist fights over nothing in particular!

By the time the celebrations had gotten to that stage of craziness, Cloud and Feather had turned down at least a dozen trappers who wanted to buy Kanti and Nuttah! It was then that the Barnes Clan retired to their campsite for a quiet evening of celebration together. Meanwhile all around them the celebrations continued as the fur company's cannon was fired numerous times, there was much happy shooting into the air, along with much loud singing, yelling and shouting going on all around them, all fired up by the copious amounts of rum previously imbibed. Finally tiring after a long day, the Barnes Clan turned to their sleeping furs and called it a day. However, Jim Bridger did not come back to the campsite that evening due to his celebrating all night with other long-time fellow trappers like Smith, Jackson, "Bear Scat" Sutta, "Iron Hand" Warren, and James Beckwourth.

Come the next morning, with a very dry mouth and somewhat wobbly legs, Otis left his sleeping furs, built up his fire and put a pot of coffee on the hanging irons with an extra four handfuls of coffee beans being added for the extra kick many would need that morning just to 'get everyone's hearts working'. In so doing, he figured most everyone in their camp would be looking forward to such a strong brew after the long night and celebrations that had gone on into the wee hours of the morning. Soon, Kanti and Nuttah who had drunk very little if any of the rum, tumbled out from their sleeping furs and began giving Otis a hand in making breakfast for the group. Presently, the coffee was boiling away filling the cool morning air with great smells, the venison skewered on metal stakes was fat-sputtering away, the biscuit dough was ready to be put into the Dutch ovens for baking and the sweet rice and raisin dish Otis had prepared was warming and almost ready to eat. About then, Kanti and Nuttah walked over and got both Cloud and Feather up because breakfast was soon in coming. As the men washed up in the little stream near their camp, the women got out the plates and coffee cups and set them alongside the fire to warm up so the men's food would not get cold so fast when they plated up and decided to eat.

Since Wallace had not stirred and breakfast was almost ready, Otis walked over to where his brother was sleeping and gave him a nudge with the toe of his moccasin in order to gently wake him. Wallace, having drunk a considerable amount of rum the night before in celebration of the Nation's Birthday and other happy ongoing events, did not move. Grinning over his older brother sleeping so soundly, Otis gave him another nudge with the toe of his moccasin only that time making it a little more forceful. Once again, Wallace did not move, just continued laying there wrapped up in his sleeping furs like there was no tomorrow…

"Hey!" said Otis, as he reached down and bodily shook his brother in order to wake him. Plus now, Otis had to return to his baking biscuits or they would burn, so he shook his brother even more forcefully. THEN OTIS PULLED HIS HAND AWAY FROM HIS BROTHER IN ALARM! HIS HAND WAS COVERED IN COLD AND STICKY DARK BLOOD! REACHING BACK DOWN IN ALARM, OTIS LIFTED UP HIS BROTHER'S RIGHT ARM ONLY TO FIND THAT WALLACE WAS LYING IN A COLD POOL OF DARK, STICKY BLOOD AND IT WAS THEN THAT OTIS REALIZED THAT HIS BROTHER'S ARM WAS STIFF AND COLD TO THE TOUCH…

DROPPING TO HIS KNEES, OTIS ROLLED HIS BROTHER OVER IN HIS SLEEPING FURS

ONLY TO DISCOVER A BLUE-BLACK HOLE IN THE SIDE OF HIS HEAD WHERE HE HAD BEEN SHOT AND KILLED! DROPPING ONTO HIS BACKSIDE IN SHOCK, OTIS JUST SAT THERE LOOKING AT THE COLD BODY OF HIS BROTHER IN DISBELIEF! THEN OTIS BECAME AWARE OF KANTI STANDING SILENTLY BY HIS SIDE ABOUT TO TELL HIM HIS BISCUITS WERE BURNING AND THEN UPON SEEING ALL THE BLOOD, LET OUT A LOUD SCREAM! A SCREAM WHICH BROUGHT THE BARNES CAMP AND SEVERAL TRAPPERS FROM A NEARBY CAMP OVER TO THE GROUP'S SLEEPING FURS AT A DEAD RUN TO SEE WHAT WAS THE MATTER!

Soon, the whole rendezvous camp was in an uproar as news spread over the shooting death of Wallace as he slept! Since no one had come into the Barnes Clan's camp that night and purposely shot Wallace, Otis began examining the scene of death. Upon looking more closely, it became apparent from a deep bullet's gouge in the dirt next to where Wallace's head had laid in his sleeping furs that a fired projectile had struck right into the dirt next to a sleeping Wallace. Then that projectile had ricocheted upwards and struck Wallace in his temple as he laid there sleeping, killing him instantly! As it turned out, the killing appeared to have been caused by nothing more than a stray round probably fired from within the rendezvous camp in drunken celebration the night before. In so doing, that round had gone low, hit the ground, and ricocheted directly into a sleeping Wallace's head by horrible accident! And from the cold touch of his body and stiffness to touch, he had been killed earlier in the evening and even those sleeping around him had not known of what had happened until the following morning's discovery.

After the news about the tragedy of Wallace's untimely death had spun its ways throughout the rendezvous, a great sadness and stillness moved silently throughout the camp in respect for the death of one of their own caused by an unknown, unfortunate and unknowing hand. Within an hour, Wallace's old friends had gathered around and with Otis's sad permission, had dug a grave in the cottonwood grove in which the Barnes's had traditionally made their camp during the rendezvous. Therein Wallace was then and without fanfare, quietly laid to rest. Those present all too sadly realized that Wallace had escaped drowning, freezing to death during the frontier's harsh winters, escaped injury from horse wrecks, being eaten by a grizzly bear and avoided a speeding lead ball or steel-tipped arrow from a number of angry Indians, only to die in his sleep from a trapper's stray bullet fired in celebration of his nation's birth. Then the real irony sunk in even further into the surrounding trappers over the revelation that Wallace had died on the day of his nation's birth, which also just so happened to be the dead trapper's own birthday as well...

That morning, Otis's breakfast cooked earlier for his group remained largely uneaten since the coffee had boiled away to thick sludge, the biscuits were burned black and the fancy rice dish he had so painstakingly prepared in celebration of another new and happy day had turned rock hard from being overcooked. Somehow, no one seemed to mind going hungry that morning as they laid a dear friend and family member to a rest in an unmarked grave, like many other hundreds of trappers would experience across the West while pursuing their dreams out on the always dangerous and many times violently life ending frontier...

For the longest time after the last shovelful of dirt had been respectfully shoveled onto Wallace's grave, Otis just sat by his older brother on the ground, 'speaking' to him through silently moving lips, accompanied with tear filled eyes and a broken heart that would be long in healing... Now Otis slowly realized he was the last of the Barnes Clan and the dreams that he and his brothers had spoken about so many times earlier when finally back on their own farm in Missouri, were only that, just dreams of dust. Finally having said his final good-byes to his brother, Otis looked up through tear filled eyes only to see Spotted Feather, White Cloud, Kanti, Nuttah and Jim Bridger quietly sitting underneath the

cottonwood trees a few yards distant, waiting
for their turns to share their grief with their dear
friend... It was then that tough, stern and man of
few words Otis Barnes broke down and immediately found he was being held by five other tearful
ones, whose tears of love dropped and splashed
dark blotches all over the grieving man's buckskin
shirt as they held his grief stricken and emotionally shaking body...

The following morning after Otis had fixed
breakfast for the rest of the Barnes Clan, he looked
at Feather and Cloud saying, "Today, Bridger and
I will be teaching Kanti and Nuttah how to shoot,
load the same and care for their shotguns and pistols. In the meantime, I need you two boys to take
all of our horses and Jim Bridger's as well over
to where Cooter Krentz has set up his blacksmith
shop by the Rocky Mountain Fur Company's wagons holding all of the kegs of rum. There I need
for the two of you to get all of those horses shoed
with new shoes for this coming year and have him
check their teeth to see if any of them need to have
them 'floated'. If so, get it done so we don't have
any teething problems while out on the trail."
With those words, the tough old Irishman named
Otis Barnes, the last of the Barnes Clan bloodline,
moved on and enjoyed his blessings being around
those he loved and over seeing another sunrise on
the beautiful frontier, mixed with the great smells
of baking biscuits and the invigorating smells of
coffee in the early morning's cool air...

After breakfast and Cloud and Feather had left with the group's entire horse herd to have them shod, Otis and Jim Bridger gathered up Kanti and Nuttah and walked off a ways from the main rendezvous campsite so they would not disturb the remaining few trappers with their shooting. In their hands the men carried several shotguns and pistols. In the hands of Kanti and Nuttah were carried several powder horns, a bag full of shot and lead balls and cleaning equipment for those weapons being carried by the two men. For the next two hours, Otis and Jim taught the two Indian women how to load and effectively hold and shoot their shotguns and pistols. As they did, the two men found the women very attentive to what they were being taught, were astute observers and as it turned out, excellent learners. In fact, the two trappers figured that since the two Indian women had never fired a weapon, they had learned no bad habits and in so doing, quickly learned another necessary facet of frontier survival. Kanti and Nuttah realizing that if they were ever recaptured by renegade trappers or Indian enemies again, they would suffer as they once had greatly at the hands of their captors. With those thoughts in mind and after having previously experienced the same, paid close attention to what they were being taught. Therefore, the Indian women made every attempt to learn and learn correctly on how to use and care for their weapons. By the end of their lessons at the hands of the two experts themselves, they, in the eyes of their teachers, had during their periods of instruction almost mastered the sometimes deadly trade of weapons use and maybe the instruments of their survival. Now, only time would tell…

In fact the two women had gotten so comfortable with their new shotguns, that on the way back to their campsite at the rendezvous, the teachers and 'students' jumped a large covey of greater sage grouse. Before the black powder smoke had cleared away and the remnants of the covey had sailed off onto several faraway sagebrush ridges, four of the larger male birds had been killed by the quick-shooting and now surprisingly well-trained women! Then the women were given another lesson by the two expert trappers. Right then and there in the field, the women were taught that they needed to immediately clean their freshly killed sage grouse and by so doing, that made for a much-less strong and tastier meal. As the two women began cleaning the strongly smelling sage grouse, Bridger taught the women that the species of bird just killed ate a lot of sagebrush leaves and buds. As a result, the meat from such birds could be strong tasting if not immediately picked and cleaned so they could quickly cool out. So as Bridger and Otis walked back to their distant campsite, the two women walking along picked and cleaned the birds while the two men carried their new shooting gear. Come supper time that evening along with beans and biscuits, the group feasted on quartered up and freshly killed sage grouse, rolled in flour, pepper and salt, and fried in bear grease in their three-legged cast iron frying pans over low coals from their campfire. As promised by Bridger and Otis, the birds were not as good eating as was the meat from a buffalo. However, by the end of their supper, none of their sage grouse parts remained in their frying pans... Then the next day, Otis and Bridger made leather slings for the women's shotguns which enabled the women to carry their weapons slung over their shoulders while on horseback for quick and easy retrieval in case they were needed for close-in acts of self-defense. That or plunking a much-better tasting blue grouse off a limb or from off the ground while out on the trail...

The following morning, the Barnes Clan was up early and while Cloud and Feather assisted Jim Bridger in the loading of his packhorses, Otis and the women cooked up a large breakfast since Jim was not sure when he would stop for his next meal while out on the trail. Breakfast was mostly eaten in silence that morning as the friends realized there would soon be one less number in their closely knit group and more than likely, in all of their future travels. When breakfast was all too quickly finished and done, the group said their good-byes and soon the man named Jim Bridger, the Man of the Mountains, was but a dot on the horizon as he and his pack string headed back into his beloved mountains as he put it, "To see what God had arranged for him to see this fine day…"

The rest of that day was quietly spent in making ready for the Barnes Clan to depart the rendezvous as other trappers and traders were in the process of also doing. That evening after supper as the women cleaned up around the camp and made ready for the morrow, Otis took the time to remove Wallace's saddlebags from his old saddle. Opening up one of the flaps of the saddlebag, Otis removed the maps Jim Bridger had drawn for them so they could find the fabled beaver trapping grounds in the Hoback. He then moved over near the campfire for the light it offered and committed to memory as he had done earlier the scribbled drawings Jim had left for them to follow. Because Jim had never learned to write or read, Otis only had his crude drawings and the verbal directions given when the map had been drawn up for them to go by. But Bridger's verbal directions were still clear in his mind and so well presented, that he was not worried over being able to locate the trapping grounds that Bridger had so highly thought of and so clearly described through his scribblings on paper.

As Otis finished up on his breakfast makings the next morning for the group, Cloud and Feather finished up with the saddling of the all of their riding horses and the packing of their packhorses.

Then after a quick breakfast, the last of the breakfast cooking implements were carefully packed away. Then the group made ready to leave the rendezvous and head for the Hoback country for hopefully the clan's last year of trapping before they headed for Missouri and began what was to become the start of their new lives. As everyone checked the cinches on their saddles, and made ready to leave, Otis took the time to walk over to Wallace's grave for the last time and just stood there for a few minutes in the morning's cool air. Looking down at the fresh dirt underneath his feet where his brother lay, Otis once again felt the tears flooding his eyes with many emotions crowding by his soul of better times when all of his clan was together as a family of brothers. First the loss of his father Rufous to a heart attack in Missouri, his brother Sterling to quicksand along the Platte, his brother Oliver to a rotted tree that fell on him in the wind just before the shootout with The Wolverine and his lot, the arrow into his brother Cedrick's stomach when they had been ambushed en route a rendezvous, and lastly, the stray bullet that had 'found' his brother Wallace as he slept. It just didn't seem right at that moment in time when they all had started off in 1822 by signing up with General Ashley for the opportunity and fur trapping adventure of a lifetime on the frontier. Now the brothers were all 'dust' save for the exception of one Otis Barnes, the last of the Barnes Clan bloodline...

"Good-bye, my brother. Wish me luck and allow me to be the leader that you were through thick and thin. Pray that we all make it home and that I am able to provide for White Cloud, Spotted Feather, Kanti and Nuttah," said Otis out loud to himself and hopefully to the good Lord above listening to his prayer... Then wiping the tears from his eyes so that sign of abject loss would not affect the others, Otis turned, mounted up onto his horse and with Kanti and Nuttah trailing him leading their four packhorses each, he had Cloud and Feather fall in behind trailing their four extra riding horses, for the protections they offered in case of an Indian attack from the rear of their caravan. Then with Bridger's map burned into the annals of his mind, Otis turned his group away from the rendezvous grounds and headed them towards the northeast to the Salt River Range and from there, hopefully onto to the Hoback and what adventures laid in wait...

Chapter Fourteen

"HO" TO THE "HOBACK"...

FOR THE NEXT TWELVE DAYS of slow travel after leaving the rendezvous, the Barnes Clan headed first to the northeast and then almost due north towards what had been described by Jim Bridger as "the Hoback country". Throughout the way, Otis was amazed at how closely the map and Bridger's verbally given geographic descriptions matched the landscape through which they were currently traveling. In fact, one evening the group stayed in Bridger's old cabin in the Salt River Range where he and his two partners had trapped beaver during one fall and spring trapping season. Remarkably once again, Otis following the map and verbal directions Bridger had given him, located Bridger's old cabin just like he had drawn it out on his map and had verbally described its very location beneath a bluff of rocks!

Then it was another whole new world upon leaving Bridger's cabin in the Salt River Range. Up, up and up they traveled into the mountainous and heavily timbered north country. Once again, it was like traveling through the Wind River Range, only seemingly higher in elevation. But once there they were surrounded with the lordly moose, herds of elk at every turn with many bull elk still in velvet, dainty mule deer in every brush patch, blue grouse scattered throughout the many game trails they traveled, and pristine trout streams full of the surprised silver flashes of trout darting for cover when their horses forded such waters. Like when they had crossed through the Wind River Mountains, the game was such that every night the group feasted on a different flavor of meat, including the occasional buffalo discovered living in the mountain range's timbered glens.

But the part of the landscape that captured everyone's heart and soul were the spectacular mountains of many thousands of feet in height that when roundabout traversed, bighorn sheep and mountain goats abounded, which added new meal and sight experiences plus much mountain beauty to one's amazed eyes! Once again, the many referrals to Bridger's scrawlings on his map of the area led the Barnes Clan easily through the passes and into the mountain meadows so delineated on the 'guiding paper'. And with a geographic accuracy that made Otis's head just spin on many of the findings relative to the descriptions on what to find or expect! More than once, Otis found his head spinning over the absolutely accurate geographic descriptions Bridger had committed to the map being used, all from memories committed to his mind observed years earlier during his travels through the same country!

Then one morning after several hours of travel from their last campsite, Otis all of a sudden sat even further upright in his saddle in amazement! When he did, he raised his hand for the group to stop and just intently looked over the terrain lying just below from where he sat on his horse. The bend in the river below looked so familiar from Bridger's much-rumpled map that it looked as if he, Otis, had been there before! Removing the rumpled and much-used map from his buckskin shirt pocket, Otis stared intently at the riverine system lying below him and then moved his eyes back to the map as if in disbelief. There below him lay the exact place that Bridger had drawn on his map and had explained in such great detail back at the rendezvous as the area he felt would be a beaver trapping wonderland! Looking once again at the area lying out below him, Otis could faintly see even from the distance from where he was sitting on his horse the numerous watered areas along the huge bend in the previously described and mapped out "Snake River". Additionally, he observed many tiny conical shaped beaver houses, mud and stick dams stitched across many of the waterways, and acres of some of the finest beaver looking waters he had ever seen since his arrival on the frontier!

Looking once again at the scribblings on the much-rumpled map, Otis could see an "X" plainly marked off onto one corner of the map. Looking down at the landscape below him where he figured the "X" would have been located on the map, Otis could see a large meadow inset in heavy timber just off what had been described as the Snake River. On each side of the meadow running into the Snake River drainage appeared to be two streams if the sun's silvery glint and sheen off the vigorously moving waters below were true. Looking back at his line of weary travelers, Otis pointed down into the river plain located several hundred yards away and below the trail upon which they now sat. Then he kicked his horse in its flank and slowly and carefully began the descent into the lowlands below, so as not to cripple up his mount on the loose scree on the mountainside that abounded under his horse's hooves.

Leading his caravan into the lush meadow 'sided' by the two vigorously running streams somewhat later, Otis stopped his horse and intently looked the area over even more closely. To his frontier experienced way of thinking, the location would be perfect for the building of their new cabin. The meadow was sided on three sides with heavy timber, their cabin could be built below a long ridge lying to the northwest that would block the worst of the winter winds, there was plenty of water and good graze, and off to its north side was a perfect place in a grove of aspens in which to build a new horse corral. Otis just shook his head as he realized they were where Jim Bridger had marked where "X" marked the 'spot' for their new campsite...

Nudging his horse in its flanks one more time, Otis headed for the head of the meadow and the small rocky bluff so he could get a closer look at the potential building site in his 'mind's eye'. When he arrived at the base of the interesting looking rocky bluff as a potential backdrop to a future cabin, Otis dismounted, turned and said, "This is the spot for our new home!" With tired but happy looking grins all around, Cloud, Feather, Kanti and Nuttah dismounted and after a long day's ride through rather steep mountainous terrain, were glad to be on foot on solid ground once again.

Within moments after their arrival, the trappers in routine practiced moves began unpacking the packhorses and unsaddling their riding stock. A 100' cotton rope was soon unwound from a spool taken from one of the packs and woven around and through the grove of aspens bordering the area for the shade it offered the horses. Then after leading the horses so they could water in the nearby fast flowing creek, the horses were 'long-tethered' to the winding cotton rope so they could graze under the watchful eyes of the group. Under the watchful eyes of the group because they were deep in the territory of the dreaded Gros Ventre, and no telling what eyes had been watching their long and slow descent down the scree-covered mountainside and into the meadow where they now stood.

Then with the horses cared for, the men routinely began hauling all of their loaded packs into the aspens and as they always did, arranged them into a defensive circle for the protections it would offer in case they were suddenly attacked by any Gros Ventre in the area. As they did, Kanti and Nuttah removed all of the group's sleeping furs from the packs and laid them out behind the protective circle of loaded packs so upon the arrival of nightfall they would have a comfortable place to sleep. With those chores out of the way, the men walked over to a spot near the rocky overhang and decided that would be an ideal place for a permanent outdoor firepit and cooking area. Without another word, Cloud with a shovel removed from one of the packs, began scraping out a cooking area as Otis and Feather hauled over their riding saddles and arranged them around the soon to be developed firepit so the group would have something to sit upon come mealtime. As Otis and Cloud continued digging out a firepit and arranging the needed stonework with rocks from the two nearby creeks for their outdoor eating area, the women began unpacking the packs holding the cooking and eating implements and brought them over to where the men were constructing their firepit.

Finally finished with his shovel and rockwork around the firepit, Cloud, with Otis's input on where their nearby cabin should be located and its outside dimensions, began digging out the several years' accumulation of fir cones, pine needles and other duff from seasonally falling aspen leaves down to the soil level so the future cabin's log foundation would have a solid base upon which to be laid. All of a sudden, Kanti gave a shout and made a run for her saddle lying by the recently dug firepit and her new shotgun! When she did and the men seeing the same frantic moves, also made moves to grab up their rifles expecting an Indian attack at any moment! Grabbing up her shotgun, Kanti yelled over to Nuttah saying something in the Blackfoot language and when she did, Nuttah made a run for her shotgun as well! By now, the men were frantically looking all around at the open end of the meadow expecting to see a number of Gros Ventre horsemen riding 'hell-bent for leather' right at the trapper trespassers! Then as the two Indian women ran into the aspen grove carrying their shotguns, powder horns and 'Possibles bags', they left the men standing there wondering what the hell was going on…

Moments later, the men heard two shots from the women's shotguns! Somewhat later, they heard two more shots from the women's shotguns being fired from deeper down into the aspen grove and then nothing more followed but silence. THAT DID IT! The men took off cautiously moving for the large aspen grove into which the women had run just moments earlier, disappeared and then began shooting! As they did, they heard two more shots even deeper in the dense aspen grove from the women's shotguns. Then just the sounds of rustling aspen leaves could be heard, as the men anxiously strained their ears for any other concerning sounds coming from the women. Shortly thereafter, they could hear the women squealing in delight deep in the aspen grove and by now, the three anxious men had no idea as to what the hell was happening. Moments later as the men headed deeper into the aspen grove once again, they finally saw the two women coming their way. When they observed the women coming their way, the men could see that THEY WERE ALRIGHT!

Lowering their rifles from the 'ready' positions having expected the worst, the three men saw two happily talking among themselves women working their way through the dense aspen grove carrying something flopping in their hands. As the women got closer, the still concerned men finally realized what the women had done in the way of causing such worry and concern among their menfolk. That was when Kanti held up her right hand containing three dead blue grouse to show the men! Taking that as her cue, Nuttah held up her right hand and therein were clutched four more dead blue grouse as well! Then it dawned on Otis and his adopted 'sons' that Kanti had spied several blue grouse in the aspen leaf litter scratching away for bugs. Realizing the excellent supper fare the grouse potentially represented, she had grabbed up her shotgun and taken off after them. When she did, she had the foresight to call her sister 'to arms' as well, and the two women without a thought about the worry back at camp they would generate with such an explosion of females 'roaring' through the timber, had gone thoughtfully blue grouse hunting in the aspen grove for the group's supper!

His concerns now subsiding, Otis just grinned from ear to ear over what he and Jim Bridger had created back at the rendezvous site with the two ladies by giving them their own shotguns and teaching them how to use them... As for Cloud and Feather, also greatly relieved over the safety of their two wives to be, grinned broadly over what they were seeing as well. Later that evening after a supper of coffee, Dutch oven biscuits and fried in bear grease, flour, salt and peppered blue grouse, the group sat back against their saddles arranged around their firepit and relaxed with full bellies. That and a cup of rum for each of the men finished their new day at a new home site and then into their sleeping furs the group tiredly went. That they did, full well realizing the next two to three weeks they would be running from daylight to dark as they worked hard in establishing a new home site before the fall beaver trapping season arrived.

After a breakfast of biscuits and coffee the following morning, the men picked up their rifles and headed off into the timber behind their new campsite to see what they could kill for the much-needed high energy camp meat they would soon be needing in their meals over the next few days of hard cabin building work that lay ahead. In the meantime, the two women with their shotguns in hand, took all of their hobbled horse herd out into their huge meadow and watched over them as they contentedly grazed in the deep grasses and got used to their new pasture area. About an hour after the three men had left their campsite on their meat hunting trip, the ladies heard one faraway shot and then silence. Two hours later, they saw Otis bent over and carrying the full hindquarter and backstrap of an elk as he entered the head of their new meadow, soon followed by Feather carrying another hindquarter and backstrap over his shoulder as well. Right behind the two laboring men walked Cloud carrying all of the men's rifles and 'Possibles bags' doing guard duty on the lookout for any signs of danger.

Walking into the cooling shade of the aspen grove, the two tired men carrying the heavy bull elk's hindquarters and backstraps laid them down in a bed of leaves and then headed for the stream to wash up and get a drink. Finished with their clean-ups, they walked over to give Cloud an assist in the cutting down of several nearby hell-for-stout aspens. With that, Feather, carrying several lengths of rope, shinned up two equally hell-for-stout aspens and roped up a cross member from one of a smaller of the two just cut aspens between the two larger and now limbed trees. Soon, the two elk quarters were swinging in the aspen grove's cooling breezes from the group's new meat pole, which was their first structural addition to their new home site. That night, the hardworking men feasted on all the spitted and roasted tender elk backstrap steak they could eat, along with a pot of beans that had been soaking and cooked during the afternoon by Kanti, and some of Otis's Dutch oven biscuits and hot coffee. Then it was a trip to the stream just before dark for all of the men. That they did with all of the usual 'suspects', their friends the small in size but hard biting mountain mosquitoes swarming about them everywhere! There the sweaty men washed up and shaved before heading off to their sleeping furs.

For the next two weeks, the three men with a single buck saw and axes fell, limbed and bucked up pine and fir logs of various sizes for the construction of their new cabin. One more week of hard labor by everyone including the women helping and a new cabin stood in the clearing! The new cabin was 20 by 20 feet with a doorway and two window openings in the front for defense and a window facing the soon to be built horse corral at the end of the cabin to shoot from to help ensure the safety of their horse herd from theft!

Then once again, Otis, the best carpenter of the group, using his smaller saw, hammer and more of his nail spikes, showed the boys how to face the window and door openings with split logs and build a spiked heavy log front door to prevent any kind of unauthorized entry unless those inside the cabin deemed it appropriate and had released the inside latch. The spiked front door idea that Otis had dreamed up was to keep grizzly bears or attacking Indians from pushing in the door and attacking those trappers inside. That he accomplished by driving two dozen 12" spikes he had procured back at the rendezvous, through the front door from inside the cabin with the sharpened ends facing outward. With that defensive configuration, any bear or Indians pushing against the front door attempting to get inside the cabin would find themselves impaled upon the sharpened spikes! Then with the outside of the cabin mostly completed, the group moved in all of their provisions, saddles and the like to prevent any kind of ruination from the ever-increasing afternoon thunderstorms, destruction from local animals chewing on the sweat soaked pieces of leather for the salt contained therein, or theft from wandering Indians when the trappers might be away from the campsite.

Then only broken by a hunting trip or two in order to bring in the much high energy camp meat, the men ventured back into the woods and began felling, limbing and cutting to length smaller logs for construction of a storage shed adjacent their cabin for their furs, and a corral for all of their horses which had been up until that time held at bay by just rope picket lines strung among the many aspen trees near their campsite. Finally with the completion of a corral and the much-needed storage shed, the horses were as safely ensconced as possible and many of the not needed right away provisions were moved from inside the cabin into the outside storage shed so there would be more living space in the cabin. Therein went the pack saddles, extra tools, sacks of food items hung from the storage shed's rafters so the mice and such would not eat or destroy them, as well as the extra kegs of gunpowder, rum and the like.

Once all of those tasks were accomplished, Otis with hammer and saw once again set about making log tables, chairs and bedframes for use inside the cabin. Finishing those necessaries, Otis, Cloud and Feather set about making log shutters for the cabin's three outside windows, covering the same with Kanti and Nuttah's 'brain-tanned' and shaved deerskins. That way, the 'brain-tanned' deer hide coverings could let in some light but mainly keep out the cold, snows and rains during the fall and winter months. Following those labors, Otis cut a hole in the wall at the east end of their cabin. Then for the next week, Otis, Cloud and Feather constructed a stone, mud and stick fireplace and chimney. That they did with the help of Kanti and Nuttah bringing in heaps of mud from the creeks to aid in the building of the structure. Letting the mud in the walls and chimney of the new fireplace dry for another week, a quick fire inside the fireplace proved that the chimney was of sufficient height so that once a fire was built inside the fireplace come the cooler months, it would 'draw' perfectly and not smoke up the inside of the cabin.

Still not finished, the men went back into the forest and began cutting down with their four-foot-long single buck saw a number of the nearby bug infested and lightning killed trees. Then once again, the two women using the team of horses as Otis had taught them to safely do, hauled down the dead and dry logs and set them off to one side of the cabin so they could be used as a winter wood supply once the snows became too deep to easily gather in much-needed firewood. Still not done and totally ready for the winter, the men built another meat pole set-up and adjacent meat smoking racks so they could make the much-needed jerky for when they were out on the trail for extended periods of time either hunting elk, mule deer and the few buffalo found in the area, or wolf or beaver trapping.

Lastly, Otis constructed an inside wall at one end of their cabin making a room so the two women would have a private place of their own in which to dress and sleep. To his way of thinking being a strict Catholic and all, Cloud and Feather, even though madly in love with the two women and they them, would not be sleeping with Kanti and Nuttah until they were baptized and married in the Church, all right and proper-like and everyone knew it!

That outside work accomplished, the men built up the group's sleeping areas with log bedframes so they would not be sleeping on the damp dirt floor of their cabin. Then the inside walls were drilled and pegged with numerous wooden pegs for hanging their clothing, winter gear, 'Possibles bags', firearms, bags of provisions, cooking implements and the like inside the cabin.

Finally, the three men were just about ready for the fall beaver trapping season. Thankfully, up until that time, the group had not observed any new 'neighbors' other than a few nosy black bears and were beginning to wonder about Jim Bridger's assessments regarding the very real dangers from the much-dreaded Gros Ventre. Of course, Jim Bridger had been as 'right as rain' up until now… Now all the group had was the 'good work' facing them. Since their arrival, they had observed several smaller herds of buffalo quietly feeding and living in the wooded timber and grassy areas adjacent the Snake River and every one of them longed for the meat provided by such animals. So now with the meat poles up and the smoking racks built, the group prepared to go out on a hunt for some buffalo with which to grace their meat poles and smoking racks and fill those empty jerky bags hanging from the pegs in their cabin.

Come the morning of the planned buffalo hunt, the Barnes Clan made ready to leave their camp-site and 'scratch the itch' all of them had for the excellent taste of fresh buffalo meat. With Otis in the lead and followed by Kanti and Nuttah lead-ing six packhorses, Cloud and Feather brought up the rear doing guard duty. Two hours later, the men had killed two buffalo bulls they had discovered living near their cabin along the Snake River. When they did, they did so with the four shots it took to kill the huge old bulls. For a short while after the shooting, Otis made sure he kept a sharp eye on the ridgelines and along the river and its many game trails for anyone of the Gros Ventre ilk who had heard such unfamiliar shooting in the area and were coming over to investigate such unnatural sounds for the area.

Seeing no arriving threats coming in from along the river or mountainsides, all caution was soon forgotten when the first buffalo was opened up and the mineral starved group got to feast on their favorite meat from the buffalo, namely the raw and still warm and bloody liver. So much so, almost the entire liver was eaten from the first buffalo killed by the liver famished group! Then mindful just how fast a freshly killed buffalo would spoil unless cooled out and allowing the meat to glaze, the group set to the extensive butchering chores at hand. Soon, the six packhorses found their panniers almost filled with butchered out chunks of the energy rich meat. Leaving the rest of the carcass remains for the critters of the land, the clan slowly headed back to their cabin so as not to stress out their heavily loaded packhorses.

Once safely back at their campsite and with Otis beginning to prepare the group's supper, Kanti, Nuttah, Cloud and Feather began cutting the rich meat from the two old and tough buffalo into thin strips to facilitate the necessary smoking process. Then once the low heat smoking fires were lit, they began placing the meat over the smoking racks so it could smoke and dry out into the much-loved jerky. Shortly thereafter with the smoking fires going, more and more meat was heaped upon the racks until they groaned under the quickly drying and smoking weight of the meat.

In celebration of the 'buffalo discovery event in their neck of the woods', the men stayed up all night tending and fueling the low heat smoking fires so the meat would be properly cured for the jerky to come and not be overcooked. In the meantime, Kanti and Nuttah waited until the dark of the evening had descended in their quest for decency, and then walked over to their nearby stream near the corral, disrobed and bathed. That they did so they could remove all of the buffalo's juices, sweat, blood and smell from all of the butchering. Then as the two sisters talked and reveled in being clean once again, they took turns washing and combing out each other's long and beautifully colored black hair, as the ever-present mosquitoes enjoyed the females' evening's bathing events as well...

Come daylight, a smoke caused and sleepless night, bleary-eyed Otis commenced with his breakfast making duties for the group. That morning he had planned a surprise for his hard-working clan and a throwback to the days of his brother Cedrick! Come breakfast time when everyone was gathered around for the morning meal, they were surprised to find on their plates Otis's special Dutch oven biscuits full of previously soaked and plumped-up raisins, intermixed with cinnamon and covered with heaps of crystalized brown sugar! That morning was mixed with much happiness over the unusual treat accompanied with a number of sad memories over what had once been another more joyous time with another family member now long-lost to the annals of time... Seeing the sadness spreading over the faces of the rest of the Barnes Clan regarding the memories his brand of biscuits brought back, Otis decided his treat that morning wasn't so special after all...

For the next two weeks the group traveled along the Snake River checking out the myriad of scattered beaver trapping waters along the way. Every day of travel, the group became more and more amazed at the beaver trapping riches that lay along the river's many and varied waterways. So much so that Otis had difficulty in picking out a spot for the beginning of his new trap line. About two weeks later, the men decided with the advent of the colder weather that it was now time to begin their fall trapping season. With that, they set about smoking their beaver traps over a rotten cottonwood fire (creates the most dense smoke) to get rid of the man smells, filled their saddlebags with freshly made jerky, checked and loaded their 'Possibles bags', refilled their powder horns with fresh powder, and readied two of their best packhorses and their panniers for the first day of the fall beaver trapping season in the Hoback.

Come the first frosty day of the anointed start of the fall beaver trapping season, the men and women were up early. Otis soon had breakfast for the group and as they enjoyed the spitted venison, Dutch oven biscuits and strong trapper's style of coffee, the two women announced they would not be coming along that day. They advised they had bathing they wished to do without the men being around, clothing to repair and needed to start making new and heavier duty winter moccasins for all of the men. That being said and the men knowing their strong-willed women had other things they wanted to get done, acquiesced and planned on starting their trapping season with just the three of them. Leaving the women to guard their remaining horse herd and with warnings to be careful and on the alert at all times, the three men soon filed out from their campsite en route the beaver trapping grounds previously decided upon to begin running their first fall trap line.

An hour later of riding and the three men arrived at the planned start of their first Hoback beaver trap line. Dismounting, Otis stripped down by removing his heavier wool pants and put on his buckskin leggings and breechclout for the wet work that came with the setting of beaver traps and anchor poles. Then followed by Cloud with the beaver traps, anchor poles, bottle of castoreum and small hand ax, Otis headed for his first promising looking beaver slide area in which to set his first trap. As the two men prepared for the beaver trapping to follow, Feather remained in the saddle on his horse as the trappers' lone sentry guarding against any kind of a surprise attack from hostile Indians or irritated grizzly bears. As he did, upon following the foot progress of the two men walking along the various waterways and doing all of the trapping, Feather also trailed all of the men's riding horses and their two packhorses as well.

For the next six hours, Otis and Cloud set all 30 of their beaver traps in promising looking slide areas and along several freshly built beaver dams. Then the men moved their horses and themselves into an adjacent grove of aspens, dismounted and sat upon the ground, watching their back trail while they feasted upon some of their tough but delicious tasting buffalo jerky. After relaxing in the aspens for about two hours and in the process letting their livestock graze close by, the three trappers prepared to backtrack their previously set trap line in order to check to see if they had already caught any beaver. If so, those would be removed, skinned out on the spot, the carcasses left for the critters to eat, their traps reset, and then they would continue along checking the rest of the entire previously set trap line until finished.

Back at the campsite and inside the trappers' cabin, Kanti stepped out from the large wash basin previously filled with heated water after taking her much longed for warm bath. Wiping off her trim body, she sat down at the kitchen table as her sister Nuttah, taking another pan of warmed water, washed out Kanti's long and thick black hair. When finished, Kanti wrapped her wet hair in a towel and then Nuttah undressed and began bathing in another large wash basin of warm water. Later upon finishing, Nuttah stepped out from her wash pan of heated water and wiped herself off. Then she too sat down at the table in front of a warm fire in the fireplace and had Kanti wash out her long black hair as she had done for her sister. Then as Nuttah wrapped her hair in a towel so it could begin drying off, Kanti, still as nude as a baby robin, picked up one of the large wash pans full of used wash water, walked over to the front door of their cabin, lifted the indoor latch with her foot, let the door swing open and careful not to spill any wash water inside the cabin, gave a big heave, tossing the liquid out through the open front door.

When she did, instead of tossing the wash water out into the front yard, SHE DISCOVERED THAT SHE HAD TOSSED IT RIGHT INTO THE FACE OF A GROS VENTRE INDIAN STANDING THERE HOLDING A RIFLE! A MAN WHO HAD SNEAKED RIGHT UP TO THE FRONT DOOR OF THE CABIN AND WAS ABOUT TO BURST INSIDE HAD HE NOT EXPERIENCED HAVING A PAN OF SOAPY WATER BEING TOSSED INTO HIS FACE! KANTI, STANDING THERE COMPLETELY NUDE GASPING IN SHOCK OVER WHAT HAD JUST HAPPENED, THEN SAW THE GROS VENTRE INDIAN DROPPING HIS RIFLE AND STAGGERING AWAY FROM THE FRONT DOOR OPENING, TRYING TO CLEAR THE STINGING SOAPY WASH WATER FROM HIS EYES WITH BOTH OF HIS HANDS...

LOOKING UP, SHE THEN SAW SITTING THERE IN FRONT OF THE CABIN ON

THEIR HORSES, ANOTHER FOUR GROS VENTRE INDIANS, WHO WERE ALSO COMPLETELY SURPRISED OVER WHAT HAD JUST HAPPENED! THIS AFTER THEY HAD SNEAKED UP TO THE CABIN ON THEIR HORSES IN ORDER TO SURPRISE THE TWO INDIAN WOMEN THAT THEY HAD EARLIER OBSERVED FROM THEIR PLACE OF HIDING.

QUICKLY CLEARING THE SOAPY WASH WATER FROM HIS FACE AND EYES WITH HIS HANDS, THE GROS VENTRE INDIAN JUMPED BACK IN FRONT OF THE OPEN DOORWAY IN A WILD AND ALMOST UNCONTROLLABLE RAGE OVER BEING SO SURPRISED WITH A FACEFUL OF WARM WASH WATER IN FRONT OF HIS FELLOW WARRIORS!

Hearing her sister gasp loudly in extreme shock after she had opened up the front door of the cabin and tossed out the wash water, Nuttah's 20,000 years of inbred Native American survival instincts immediately kicked in! Realizing her always stoic and staid sister, one who was normally as tough as a horseshoe nail and usually as 'quiet as a mouse pissin' on a ball of cotton', had apparently just been intensely shocked over something of great danger! Jumping up from the kitchen table, a still nude Nuttah ran for the front door of the cabin and as she passed the door jamb, she reached out and grabbed her shotgun propped up alongside the wall. A shotgun so placed which Otis had always preached to the two women about their placement in such positions in case of emergencies when the menfolk were not at hand to protect them. As she did and once again as taught by Otis and Jim Bridger earlier back at the rendezvous, that in times of emergency, quickly cock the hammer when raising up her shotgun all in the same fluid motion when facing any real or perceived danger. That frontier 'trick of the trade' would save her life someday by being ready in the face of danger Otis and Bridger had counseled during her and her sister's 'earlier use of firearms' training session.

SHOVING HER SISTER FORCEFULLY AWAY FROM THE DOORWAY WITH HER LEFT HAND, NUTTAH STEPPED INTO THE DOOR'S OPENING WHERE KANTI HAD BEEN STANDING IN SHOCK AND WAS ALSO SURPRISED TO SEE THE LEERING FACE OF A GROS VENTRE INDIAN, WHO WAS JUST IN THE PROCESS OF REACHING OUT FOR HER SISTER WITH HIS HAND! A HAND WHICH WAS JUST INCHES AWAY FROM THE FACE OF HER SISTER STILL STANDING IN THE OPEN DOORWAY IN SHOCK, BEFORE SHE HAD BEEN FORCEFULLY SHOVED ASIDE BY HER SISTER!

BOOM! WENT NUTTAH'S SHOTGUN AND THE FORCE OF THE BLAST FROM JUST TWO FEET AWAY FROM THE INDIAN'S LEERING FACE WAS SUCH THAT HIS HEAD

DISAPPEARED INTO A WHITE CLOUD OF BLACK POWDER SMOKE WHICH WAS FOLLOWED BY A DEADLY STREAM OF LEAD BIRDSHOT! THAT STREAM OF LEAD BIRDSHOT CAUSED HIS HEAD TO EXPLODE INTO A BRILLIANT BRIGHT RED SPEW IN THE MORNING'S SUNLIGHT, CREATING A MOMENTARY RAINBOW IN THE PROCESS! THE IMPACT OF THAT EXPLOSION BLEW THAT INDIAN'S BODY OUT THE OPEN DOORWAY AND ONTO THE GROUND IN FRONT OF THE CABIN! BUT NOT BEFORE THE EXPLODED BRIGHT RED SPEW OF HIS BODILY ESSENCE WAS SPRAYED ONTO HIS COHORTS' BODIES CALMLY SITTING ON THEIR HORSES LOOKING ON AT ONE OF THEIR OWN ENTERING A TRAPPERS' CABIN!

THEN THE INDIAN SITTING ON HIS HORSE DIRECTLY BEHIND THE ONE WHO HAD JUST LOST HIS HEAD TO NUTTAH'S SHOTGUN BLAST, FOUND HIMSELF VIOLENTLY PITCHED TO THE GROUND OVER THE PLUNGING HEAD OF HIS HORSE! PLUNGING OVER THE HEAD OF HIS HORSE BECAUSE THE TIGHT PATTERN OF STREAMING LEAD PELLETS JUST FIRED BY NUTTAH BLEW THROUGH THAT FIRST INDIAN'S HEAD STANDING IN THE DOORWAY A FEW FEET AWAY, OUT THE OTHER SIDE OF HIS SKULL AND STRUCK HIS NEARBY COHORT'S HORSE IN THE FOREHEAD! WHEN THAT

HAPPENED, THAT STREAM OF LEAD PELLETS DROPPED THAT ANIMAL IN ITS TRACKS, KILLING IT INSTANTLY AND IN SO DOING, VIOLENTLY TOSSED ITS RIDER HEAD OVER HEELS OVER HIS HORSE'S NECK AND ONTO THE GROUND!

Then all hell broke loose as a hastily thrown tomahawk from another surprised Indian sitting on horseback in front of the cabin, zipped by the side of Nuttah's head so closely that it caused her to instinctively duck back behind the safety of the log walls of the cabin! Simultaneously, **BOOM!** went the sound and **ZZIPPP!** went the shot fired from a rifle of another sitting Indian on his now nervous 'crow-hopping' horse. A 'crow-hopping' horse now terrorized because of all of the shooting and movement action to its forefront, plus the now intensely vaporized smell of fresh blood drifting in the air! Fortunately, that shot aimed and taken at Nuttah missed because the earlier closely thrown tomahawk had caused her to instinctively duck behind the cabin's log wall from the direction she had just come in order to help her sister. In so doing, that shot meant for Nuttah for shooting one of his fellow warriors, went harmlessly through the open doorway and lodged itself into the cabin's back wall...

JUST THEN ANOTHER INDIAN BAILED OFF HIS HORSE AND WITH AN UPRAISED TOMAHAWK, RAN RIGHT THROUGH THE CABIN'S OPEN DOORWAY! WHEN

HE DID, HE RAN RIGHT INTO THE NOW RECOVERED KANTI AND THE BLAST FROM HER SHOTGUN JUST RETRIEVED FROM ITS PLACE LYING AGAINST THE CABIN'S INSIDE WALL RIGHT NEXT TO THE DOORWAY! **BOOM!** WENT THAT BLAST FROM JUST TWO FEET AWAY INTO THE SIDE OF THE FACE OF THE INDIAN CHARGING INSIDE THE CABIN WITH HIS UPRAISED TOMAHAWK! WHEN KANTI FIRED, INSTANTLY CLEAR OVER BY THE OPPOSITE SIDE OF THE OPEN DOORWAY BY THEIR FIREPLACE, A FLYING MOUTHFUL AND PARTIAL JAWBONE OF THE ATTACKING INDIAN'S TEETH EMBEDDED THEMSELVES INTO THE LOG WALLS. THERE THEY STUCK, EMBEDDING THEMSELVES INTO THE WALL'S LOGS LIKE WHITE AND BLOOD RED-FLECKED DECORATIONS! THE REST OF THAT INDIAN'S ESSENCE FROM HIS EXPLODED HEAD SPEWED CLEAR ACROSS THE CABIN'S FLOOR AND ALL OVER THE FRONT OF THE TABLE AND FIREPLACE! When that close-in shot was taken by short in stature Kanti, that stream of lead birdshot streamed through the Indian's head and just over the top of still bent-over Nuttah, who was in the process of retrieving her .54 caliber pistol from the small bench located alongside the still open doorway! Had she not been bent over in the act of going for one of her pistols loaded with buck and ball, Kanti's just fired stream of lead from the face-shot Indian would have cut her in half from such close range! Rising up with blood, bone chips, bits of teeth and brain matter spattered all over her just washed and still naked body, Nuttah desperately aimed her pistol loaded with buck and ball towards the open doorway for what danger might still be coming through the open doorway!

As the next Indian burst through the door's opening with an upraised rifle aimed at Kanti who was now standing there almost in shock over the man she had just blown apart at such close range, her sister Nuttah seeing the danger, screamed out in rage! Her sister's scream broke through Kanti's fog of shock and instantly realizing her danger looking at the business end of a rifle barrel, quickly dropped to the floor as she went for her brace of .54 caliber pistols loaded with buck and ball lying on the log bench right next to her side of the open doorway! Once again, she had always kept her pistols by the doorway like her sister for quick retrieval, as Otis had so instructed the young women to do just for times of danger when the men were not around to protect them.

Fortunately Nuttah's scream of panic combined with sisterly rage, momentarily distracted the Gros Ventre aiming his rifle at Kanti, which was just enough of a distraction so that it 'placed' him on his way to also joining his own 'Cloud People' as the Gros Ventre called their dead ancestors. **BOOM!** went Nuttah's pistol loaded with buck and ball at a distance of about six feet, dropping the chest-shot Indian dead as the head-shot horse he had just stepped off from when it had been killed earlier in the battle! In so doing, he fell right on top of the still bent over Kanti trying to retrieve one of her pistols from the log bench near the door and cock it for the needed action she was sure was soon to follow!

Scrambling out from under the dead and bloody as all get-out Indian's body that had just fallen on top of her, Kanti struggled upwards with pistol in hand, only now with her own menacing look of desperation and 'fight' in her beautiful black eyes. Looking quickly around the door jamb and out the open doorway of the cabin knowing there were more Indians in front, Kanti saw the other two Indians still trying to get control over their bucking horses! Bucking horses now spooked over all the close-in shooting, spews of human essence flying their ways, white clouds of black powder smoke rolling over them, along with their Indian riders desperately jerking their horses' reins every which way in surprise and panic over the 'the naked female cyclones' they had just unleashed from inside the trappers' cabin!

BOOM! went Kanti's pistol from such close range, but in her hurry she shot low! However, she still managed to knock both Indians from their saddles with the charge of buck and ball in her pistol! One of the two Indians was gutshot and found himself blasted from the saddle and moments later, lying on the ground writhing around in abject pain as his insides began hemorrhaging, causing him to begin bleeding out! The other Indian off to one side and a little further back in line was just hit in the point of his hip bone! However, the ball's impact also blew also him from his saddle! Hitting the ground, the man painfully but quickly scrambled back to his feet. Then by some miracle, he managed to drag himself back into his saddle onto his now almost out of his mind in fear, horse! Jerking his horse's head around, that Gros Ventre tried to get his panicked horse under control so he could ride off and away from the danger spewing forth from the cabin's open doorway! Just then, **BOOM!** went a shot of buck and ball from Nuttah's second pistol, spilling the frightened and now badly back shot Indian from his saddle! That time he laid still in death after hitting the ground!

Moments later quickly looking outside and seeing the danger was over, Kanti emerged from the cabin still naked as a baby jay bird, calmly walked right up to the previously gutshot Gros Ventre still writhing around on the ground in agony, and shot him in the head with a load of buck and ball from her second pistol! Then she vomited up the remains of her breakfast right on top of the now dead Indian, as the contents from his blown open head splattered out all over

Kanti's bare feet! Then that potential moment of terror from the potential rape and death by the five Gros Ventre Indians had passed and quiet once again reigned over the trappers' campsite...

After losing the last of her breakfast, Kanti took a look around their campsite for any other signs of danger. Seeing none, she walked back to the cabin and then the two sisters fell into one another's arms and bawled like babies over the abject terror and violence they had just been subjected to and had to participate in for survival's sake. Finally after a good cry over surviving the potential of being gang raped and then killed by their own kind, a quiet and determined 'frontier' calm began manifesting itself in the two sisters. Pausing and then looking deeply at one another, they made a vow between the two of them that they would never ever again be separated and if faced with the potential 'hell' of rape and death like they had just experienced, they would face it as they just had, and kill until the danger had passed or until they themselves were killed... Then with even more calmness now that the terror was done and with increasing wonderment over what they had accomplished by themselves and with the little weapons training they had earlier received from Otis and Bridger, their own strong survival realizations began manifesting themselves! And with those manifestations, they as survivors began feeling a very special kind of determination now filling their beings.

Then with stubborn determination born out of disgust, she and her sister managed to drag the dead Indians out from inside their cabin and laid them outside their cabin on top of the dead Indian's horse that had been inadvertently shot in the head. Following that, the two tiny women dragged the remaining dead Gros Ventre lying dead in front of the cabin over to the existing pile of dead Indians and left them lying there for the returning men to take care of their disposal when they had ventured back from their day's beaver trapping adventures...

With that, the two Indian women returned to their cabin, shut and latched the door. Once inside and as had been previously taught to them by Otis, they took the time to reload their shotguns and all four of their pistols and placed them back where they had found them for ready access in case the need ever arose, since they were in their new beaver trapping country in the Hoback, ancestral home of the deadly Gros Ventre...

Then dressing back up into their dirty clothing, both ladies warmed up more water and began cleaning up the blood, brain material and bits and pieces of bone material blown throughout the inside of their cabin during the fight. However, both women decided after washing them off a bit, they would leave the one-foot-long row of glistening white teeth blown from a Gros Ventre's head and implanted into the log timbers across the room! These they would leave as a reminder of how well they had learned their survival lessons from Jim Bridger and Otis Barnes in how to use their firearms… An hour later, the cabin had been cleaned up of all the 'human spew and essence' with the use and aid of a lot of wash water, using some of their precious soap and leaving all of the windows and reopening the front door. That they did, so all traces of the smell of death were washed away and the acrid smell of black powder smoke could dissipate.

Those chores completed, more pans of water were then heated and Kanti once again bathed and had her sister wash her long and beautiful black hair. Once Kanti had bathed and dressed in clean clothing, Nuttah took her warm bath and had her sister wash her long black hair as well. Then when dressed in clean clothing, both women calmly set to cutting out foot patterns from a tanned bull buffalo hide and began the process of making their menfolk new and heavier duty winter moccasins from the bull's thicker hide…

In the meantime, too far away to hear the shooting back at their cabin because of the distance involved, the dampening effects from all the heavy timber surrounding the men, and the sounds of the nearby Snake River's rushing waters, Otis, Cloud and Feather mounted up from their short respite in the aspen grove. Then once again they began running their recently set trap line in the reverse to ascertain if any beaver had been trapped in their absence since the traps were first set. Sure as shooting, out of the 30 traps set, there were so many beaver in the area that the men had caught 16 beaver in their first settings! Those numbers represented the most beaver caught by the clan since they had been trapping just after the traps had been set and upon making a return check! As Otis checked, cleared and re-set each trap that had successfully caught a beaver, Cloud quickly skinned out their catches. Finally by late afternoon, the men had finished their rather lengthy first day of beaver trapping and skinning, and were finally on their way back to their campsite after Otis had changed out from his buckskins and breechclout into his warmer Linsey-woolsy pants and dry moccasins.

Later in the afternoon as the tired men turned up into the bottom of their meadow leading into their campsite with their horses, Cloud all of a sudden stopped his horse! When he did, Otis and Feather, trailing Cloud, reined up their horses as well. Leaning over and looking down at the soft ground, Cloud instantly had a mask of worry fly across his face! Then quickly looking up towards their cabin in alarm after seeing the unshod horses' hoofprint 'story' in the damp soils, he thankfully saw the two women moving around by their outdoor campfire adding some more wood to it. When Cloud saw the women moving around the campfire, the earlier mark of worry on his face over the unknown unshod horse tracks lessened but not in its entirety. Pointing down towards the fresh horses' unshod hoofprints, he said to Otis and Feather, "Unshod horses!" Then spurring his horse into a trot, Cloud led the men up to the area of their cabin and as he did, he stopped once again! There he looked hard at something suspicious lying in the front of their cabin. Then Cloud broke his horse into a gallop and headed straight away towards the two women working around the cabin, realizing there HAD BEEN a very serious problem earlier in the day!

Jumping from his horse and taking a quick look around at all the dead Gros Ventre Indians piled up at his feet, Cloud ran right up to Kanti, scooped her up into his arms saying, "Are you alright? Did they hurt you or Nuttah?"

About then Otis reined up arriving behind Cloud and Feather because he was leading the slower and fully loaded packhorses with all of the fresh furs and the partial carcass of a three-point mule deer the men had killed en route the cabin for camp meat. By then, Nuttah was also in Feather's arms and he was asking questions as to her well-being as well as well. It was then that Otis's eyes moved from the two men hugging their choices for wives over to a bloody pile of dead Gros Ventre Indians and an obviously dead headshot horse! "What the hell in tarnation happened here? Who shot all of these Indians?" he asked, looking around with disbelief spelled clear across his face as he looked at tiny little Kanti and Nuttah…

"They came when we were bathing and we shot them," said Nuttah rather flatly, like it was nothing more than stepping on a small bug...

"Are you ladies alright?" Otis asked, still in disbelief over what he was seeing lying in a bloody pile in front of their cabin. "Hells Bells, I count five of these son-of-a-bitches in this pile. How the hell did you two ladies manage to kill all of them and one of their horses as well and then come to not be injured yourselves?" he asked, still in disbelief over what he was observing and yet thankful that the two ladies and what he considered his 'adopted' daughters were alright.

Moments later, the two ladies shared their morning of terror with the three still disbelieving men. When they had finished, Otis took a closer look at the dead Indians and it was then that he noticed how many of them had been headshot! "From what I am seeing, these men were shot at very close ranges. Are you ladies sure you are not hurt? Did any of these bastards lay a hand on either of you?" asked a still incredulous-looking Otis.

"We are fine," said Kanti. "We sisters had good teachers on how to use our guns and how to reload them. We just did what you and Jim taught us to do when we were alone, and trappers or other Indians tried to have their way with us or capture and take us away. These dead men tried to attack us. However, what you and Jim taught us back at the rendezvous when we were in the field practicing our shooting and reloading worked very well. So, we just did as you told us."

Still hardly believing the ladies' stories but when faced with the proof of what they had experienced and accomplished in the face of extreme danger, made Otis just continue shaking his head in wonder. As for Cloud and Feather, they not for a moment since they had arrived back at the cabin had let either of the loves of their lives out from their arms. Then Otis said, "We need to rid ourselves of these bastards. I suggest we leave these fresh beaver pelts in the hands of the ladies to begin their processing and we best be getting rid of what they left us to clean up."

An hour later, the three men had dumped the five now stripped-naked Gros Ventre men into the raging Snake River for it to dispose of the evidence regarding their rather violent demise. Then the trappers released the remaining four Indians' horses back to the wild so they would disappear in such a manner making it difficult for any other Gros Ventre to retrieve them and from that, try and discover what happened to their owners or blame any trappers for their absence. Finally the men returned to their cabin, quartered up the headshot horse saving the hindquarters for additional camp meat and then with their packhorses, hauled off the rest of the quartered-up horse, dumping its remains into the Snake River for nature's disposal as well.

Come the fall of darkness, the three men had

returned and while Otis prepared supper for the clan, Cloud and Feather tended to all of their horses. After supper, the group retreated into their cabin and spent several hours finishing the skinning, defatting and hooping of the 16 beaver skins they had removed from the beaver they had trapped their very first day of the fall trapping season. During one session of hooping the fresh pelt he was working with, Otis noticed something unusual in the cabin. Then after a long look at the object of his interest, laid down his fresh pelt and walked over to the middle of their cabin along the back wall. There he quietly removed a tomahawk that had been thrown at Nuttah earlier in the fight, had missed and lodged itself into a log in the back wall of their cabin… Walking over to the two sisters who were also busily hooping beaver skins, Otis looking down at the two women quietly said, "Here is something from this morning meant for one of you I suppose. I suggest one of you keep this memento of your fight in case you have use for it sometime down the line." Then walking back to his unfinished beaver skin, Otis sat back down on his log stool and as he did, glanced over at the fireplace wall noticing something else that had not been there earlier in the morning. Getting up once again, Otis walked over to a string of busted up teeth that had been explosively driven into the log wall by some unknown violent force! "I suppose there is some sort of explanation associated with this string of broken human teeth driven into the logs of this here wall. Dare I ask?" he continued with a questioning look spreading clear across his face. Cloud and Feather now noticing what Otis was talking about, like Otis, looked first at the row of teeth and then over at the two ladies with obvious questions in their eyes as well. Neither of the ladies even looked up from their pelting duties like what had just been asked of them was no big deal. Sensing that the row of teeth was now a closed issue, Otis just shrugged his shoulders, shook his head in disbelief, sat back down and finished hooping his fresh beaver pelt. Cloud and Feather, seeing that Otis seemed to be satisfied with the women's reluctance to talk about the row of human teeth blown into the log's wall, satisfied them as well and they then continued pelting out their fresh pelts not daring to pursue the issue of the teeth any further... Nuttah was right. Kanti was as tough as a horseshoe nail. Truth be known, both women had now become so...

For the next four weeks, the men continued beaver trapping until just before freeze-up. Then just before the first hard freeze made the pulling of their beaver traps difficult, they pulled their beaver traps and called an end to their fall trapping season in the Hoback. However, the Hoback held another surprise for the men but just not one as deadly as it had been for the women. Numerous times throughout the last four weeks of their fall beaver trapping season, the men had seen many small groups of Indians moving about. Indians who appeared to be looking for something but in so doing, never discovered the small and careful group of three trappers and to the trappers' way of thinking, the Indians didn't appear to find what they were looking for either. The three trappers just thanked their lucky stars that it was not them or the five Indians that had attacked their cabin and had been killed in the process that the many small groups of Indians appeared to be looking for and did not discover.

Another Hoback surprise was that after the 'women's battle at the cabin', Kanti and Nuttah never rode with the men on a number of their many beaver trapping adventures. They had discovered a certain kind of independence among themselves after that deadly fight and acumen the men were never quite able to fathom. After that, the women preferred to remain back at the cabin when the men were away watching over their remaining herd of valuable horses and doing the work needing to be done around the cabin from the horse tending to the making and repairing of the men's clothing. Like Jim Bridger had advised earlier in the group's relationships, "Blackfeet women are damn hard workers." However, neither woman was now ever very far from the cabin without carrying her shotgun, at least one pistol lodged firmly in a sash worn around her waist, and with her 'Possibles bag' flung over a shoulder so she could reload her firearm if in the course of events it became necessary. Also, Otis discovered that the two women remained very attentive to his every need thereafter, almost as if a reward for trusting them enough to purchase them their own weapons and taking the time to teach them how to effectively use them. Cloud and Feather also noticed the positive change in their two women after their deadly battle at the cabin. A noticeable change in the women after that battle with the Gros Ventre that Cloud and Feather highly approved of when it came to the women utilizing their newfound brand of independence and utilization of their frontier skills in their daily lives. Cloud and Feather also appreciated even further what their adoptive father Otis Barnes, had done for the women as well in having the foresight to arm and train them so they could protect themselves when the men weren't there to do so.

After freeze-up, the men counted the beaver taken after completing their fall trapping season. They discovered that they had trapped a total of 51 'blanket-sized' beaver, 142 Made Beaver and another 33 smaller in size beaver for a total catch of 226 beaver taken during their first season in the Hoback. *Jim Bridger had been right in his assessment of the numbers and quality of the beaver potential in the Hoback,* thought Otis with a satisfied grin. In fact, if their spring haul of beaver was anything like their fall catch, they should now have enough money from their future sales in St. Louis, in combination with those monies guaranteed with their Letters of Credit from previous years of trapping, to buy enough land back in Missouri for all the members of the clan to settle down upon and live comfortably for the rest of their lives.

Stepping out from the cabin early one winter morning, Otis stopped for a moment and looking skyward, surveyed the morning's elements to ascertain the day's weather. The morning was unusually warm for a winter day, there was a soft wind blowing out from the northwest from whence came most of their storms and there was a moisture-softness in the air that proclaimed a major weather change was coming. Heeding those familiar 'weather tells' of an oncoming weather change, Otis scrambled around the outside firepit getting a roaring fire going in order to produce the much-needed biscuit making coals for the clan's breakfast. Then he made a trip over to the camp's meat poles and cut a number of chunks of meat off an elk's hindquarter, brushed off the bird poop from the always visiting black-billed magpies and Northern chickadees who had been helping themselves to a meaty meal, and then headed back to his firepit. There he washed the meat off, cut it into smaller chunks and spitted the meat on metal skewers over the edge of the fire for cooking after peppering the hell out of it with some white pepper. Then another trip was made to their creek for water and then back to his fire. There he made up a pot of coffee and while it was beginning to boil on its hanging rod, Otis whipped up some biscuit dough in preparation for the baking to come in his two Dutch ovens.

About then, out from the cabin tumbled Kanti and Nuttah, who immediately walked over to Otis 'cooking away' around the firepit. Once there, they each gave him a good morning kiss on his cheek, then headed for the aspen grove to take care of a call of nature and finally to the stream so they could wash up. Moments later Cloud and Feather emerged from the cabin as Otis banged a large cooking spoon on the backside of one of his cooking pots announcing that breakfast was almost ready. Those kettle-banging noises soon brought the group to their sitting logs around the firepit where they began enjoying their break-fasts. As they did, Otis cast his practiced eye on each of his 'charges', noticing approvingly that each person had a firearm perched alongside where he or she was sitting that morning just in case and at least one pistol tucked away in their sashes.

After breakfast, Otis shared his 'read' of the coming weather with the clan and then the group with his 'weather' read in mind, accordingly set about their morning's chores. More wood was cut for their winter woodpile with Cloud wield-ing their single buck saw making long logs into short rounds ready for splitting. Feather took the short rounds and split them into useable sized chunks of firewood with his six-pound maul, as Kanti and Nuttah hauled the wood chunks into their cabin and stacked it by their fireplace in case the weather turned into their first snowstorm of the year as Otis had predicted. Then Otis hauled two wash pans and two coffee pots full of water into the cabin so it would not freeze in place if left outside and would be ready for the next day in case it snowed or the temperature dropped below freezing. The rest of that morning was spent in making up a small mountain of .54 caliber bullets for their pistols and rifles and refilling all of their powder horns with fresh powder from one of their powder kegs. Come the afternoon, the men, armed with their rifles, let the entire horse herd out to water and graze in their meadow and watched over the same, making sure they were not disturbed by any wandering horse hungry Indians or a grizzly bear hungry for a horse meat meal prior to going into hibernation for the next few months.

As they did, Otis could not help but notice the blue-black clouds scudding their way from out of the northwest, the quickly dropping temperatures and that the air had turned from its early morning softness to one with an ominous cold sharpness in it. With those changes being felt, the men herded back to the corral their riding and packhorses, shut the gate and then walked over to their meat pole. There they cut down a hindquarter from a moose, brought it back to their cabin and laid it on top of their nearby meat smoking rack for easy access in the evening and following morning for future meals in case it snowed. Turning back to the front door of their cabin, it was then that the men noticed the first snowflakes of winter softly falling. Winter concerns had finally come to the Hoback, ending the fall beaver trapping season which had been a good one for the trappers with 226 beaver taken and a bad one for the rodents they had been pursuing...

The next morning when Otis opened up the cabin's door and looked out, he could see about 12" of fresh snow on the ground with more on the way. Stepping outside and closing the cabin's door so the warmth from its indoor fire in the fireplace would continue warming up the cabin, he just grinned. *Being raised up with his Indian friends as a young man sure had its advantages*, he thought with a satisfied grin. *Learning from his Indian friends "The Way" when he was a young man, especially in learning on how to read the signs of the weather and its changes sure had its advantages*, he smiled, as his eyes checked their horses in the corral and then went back inside to tend the fire and make the rest of the breakfast for his 'kids'.

For the rest of that day, the men compressed and bundled up their beaver furs, clad those bundles in tanned deerskins to keep them clean in transit back to the rendezvous and their eventual trip to St. Louis for the higher prices offered and then had them tightly bound. Come later in the afternoon when the winter snows had finally subsided, the men dressed for the cold, grabbed up their rifles and pistols, released their horses so they could dig down through the freshly fallen snows and feed, and then stood by in the area of the feeding livestock so they would not wander off or disappear into the hands of others. Later, once their horses were back in their corral after those who wanted to water had done so, the men hustled back into their warm cabin and once again after warming up a bit, Otis made the group their supper of roasted moose meat, a cast iron pot of pinto beans loaded with red pepper flakes, Dutch oven biscuits soon to be slathered in honey from one of their jugs, and traditional coffee made strong enough to stand a horseshoe up in their metal cups without having it falling over and hitting the sides.

Being lower in meat than they wanted with only one moose quarter in camp, the men dressed for the cold weather the following day, saddled up their horses and leaving the women behind in the warm cabin, struck out looking for a 'slow-moving' elk as a fresh source of camp meat. Moving along the Snake River, the men were surprised when they ran into a small herd of buffalo and soon had two of the shaggy beasts cooling out in the snows. After a short interlude in which the three men feasted on some warm buffalo liver, they commenced butchering out the two animals, taking their hindquarters and backstraps. The rest of the buffalo carcasses they left but only after setting ten of their wolf traps around the carcasses in the hopes that the wolves' hunger would overcome their usual wariness when moving around the 'man-trap' smells. Then on their way home, the men observed ten Gros Ventre Indians moving along a distant ridgeline and thankful for a finger of firs and pines, the Barnes Clan moved into that cover and remained there until the safety of darkness overcame the men and their horses.

Not wanting to brave below freezing temperatures overnight, Otis finally cautiously led his little band out from where they had hidden in the timber and into the bright moonlight of a half-moon. Banking on the Gros Ventre not staying around nearby in the sub-zero temperatures, the Barnes Clan made directly for home without attempting to hide their trails. That they did in the hopes the winds now swirling around them would bury their horse tracks and not provide any evidence of their shod horses' hoofprints or a direct route they had traveled to their more or less secluded cabin. Arriving later that night from their travels, the men upon their arrival let the women know they were home so they would not start shooting in their direction, hoisted the freshly killed buffalo quarters high onto the meat poles so any non-hibernating grizzly would not find an easy dinner, corralled their hungry horses and adjoined to their warm cabin.

The next morning right at daylight, the men arose, dressed for the cold weather, released their horses and escorted them into their nearby meadow so the animals could feed. Skipping their own breakfasts, the men let their valuable horses graze until the later part of the afternoon. Then it was back into their corrals as the half-frozen men adjourned to their warm cabin but only after cutting up some more wood to replenish their cabin's indoor fireplace wood supply. Supper that evening was one of beans cooked with generous chunks of buffalo, Dutch oven biscuits and hot coffee, all prepared by two very worried ladies over the men's late arrival but extremely happy over the news of fresh buffalo meat. Not surprisingly, supper did not end that evening without the men imbibing several cups of their fiery rum for 'medicinal purposes'! The next morning after finishing breakfast, the men adjourned to their storage shed and dug out a number of pine marten traps they had taken from the Frenchies' camp many months earlier when they had shot hell out of things and then discovered they had also 'acquired' Kanti and Nuttah as the newest members of the Barnes Clan...

The rest of that afternoon, the men spent their time after grazing their horse herd, cutting off the tails from the mule deerskins previously wrapped around the compressed bundles of beaver skins ready for transport to the rendezvous and then on to St. Louis. Those dried tails were to be used later as lures placed near the pine marten pole traps to lure that species of animal to the uniquely set traps as would be required.

The following morning after having breakfast, the entire Barnes Clan set out on their first trapping session for pine marten. That day Kanti and Nuttah, not familiar with the trapping of such animals, wanted to go along to see how it was done and now rode with their men. This Otis had allowed since their travels would be confined to the surrounding coniferous forests and not be out in the open like they would normally be when trapping beaver or wolves and exposed to those eyes of the hostile Gros Ventre Indians who might be out and about. Otis, having learned about the proper pine marten trapping techniques from other trappers at the rendezvous who trapped such animals, would be the one setting the traps with the other members of his party sitting on their horses watching out for any signs of danger as well as learning the correct trap-setting methods.

As the rest of the Barnes Clan soon learned, pine marten traps are set in trees in such a manner along major branches whereby the animal has to run along the limb, over the trap, in order to get to the fluttering deer's tail lure on the end of the limb. Or the trapper places a pole at an angle several feet above the ground in the timber and ties a marten trap about three-fourths of the way up along the pole. Then a bird's wing or deer's tail is attached to the top end of the angled pole. The theory being the marten sees the fluttering object at the end of the angled pole, and runs along the pole or tree limb to get to the object of its interest. However, in so doing, it has to run across the open-faced jaw trap and is caught. After a number of trials and errors, Otis finally had the proper trapping method down, and soon the group had set 20 traps in the tree branches and on angled poles in the hopes of catching such an elusive animal and valuable fur bearer. Then with all of the Barnes Clan keeping their eyes on the open meadows within the forests and along the exposed ridges looking for any sign of Indians, the group made it home safely without being discovered or being chance-attacked on their first day of pine marten trapping. Then with the ladies back in the cabin trying to get warm, the rest of the men let out their horse herd to graze in several windswept meadows where the dried grasses were readily available to the horses, without them having to 'paw' their ways down through the snows in order to get enough graze to keep them fed, warm and healthy as well.

The next day, the men returned to the two partially butchered out buffalo carcasses only to be disappointed. Five of their wolf traps showed signs of having trapped a wolf only to have that animal killed and partially eaten from the trap by a large, what appeared from its footprint, boar grizzly bear not yet in hibernation. Additionally, the bear had feasted on the buffalo carcasses and then partially covered them with nearby grasses and limbs from adjacent trees. With that grizzly bear destruction of their valuable wolf carcasses in mind, the three men removed their wolf traps and headed back to their cabin. There they picked up the two women and once again headed out to their previously set pine marten trap line in the dense timber above their cabin. After running that unusual trap line for the first time, the men discovered they had trapped nine pine marten and had another one killed and eaten out from the trap by a fisher, another arboreal member of the weasel family only larger and more elusive than the pine marten. With those successes under their belts, the Barnes Clan returned to their cabin and while Cloud and Feather tended to the horses grazing in the nearby meadow, Otis showed Kanti and Nuttah how to properly skin and stretch out on a board a pine marten skin so that it could correctly dry in a manner that would be the most valuable when it was sold to a fur buyer.

Way before daylight the following morning, found the three men from the Barnes Clan shivering in a stand of pines in a foot of snow while quietly watching the remains of their buffalo carcasses. Once daylight arrived, the men could see a huge yellowish-brown moving mound of what appeared to be a feeding grizzly bear on the two buffalo carcass remains! Quietly moving in behind the great bear in the snow so the men would not be heard, Otis took careful aim and headshot the unsuspecting giant who was too busy eating to be aware of the approaching danger from behind! With that one shot from Otis's heavy .54 caliber rifle bullet, its deadly impact flattened the huge specimen of a bear where he stood eating! After giving the bear time to show any more signs of life after being shot and seeing none, the three men cautiously and with their rifles held at the ready in case the bear was not dead, advanced upon the most ferocious predator in the Hoback. After poking the bear in his rump with the end of a rifle barrel to make sure he was dead, the men rejoiced in finding Otis's shot made for a one-shot kill!

Standing there, the men were amazed over the mountain of a bear that had just been killed! It had to weigh at least almost as much as one of their horses and its pelt was thick, not rubbed, and luxurious! An hour later, the three men had removed the beautiful bear skin with ideas in their heads of making a valuable bear skin robe from the wolf and buffalo eating creature. Then taking advantage of the situation, the men re-set their wolf traps around the carcasses of the two buffalo and now mound of bear flesh and left with a very nervous packhorse dragging a huge, bloody bear pelt behind it in the snow on the way back to their cabin. The men discovered that neither packhorse they had brought along would carry the fresh 'bear' smelling hide in their panniers. So they improvised and dragged the pelt in the freshly fallen snow at the end of a long rope so the bear smell would not be as bothersome to their chosen packhorse towing the flopping pelt. However, that was just about as bad, especially when the packhorse dragging the huge pelt saw it flopping around in the snow behind it... But after a few false starts and much 'crow-hopping' on the part of the horse, the men were finally successful in getting the pelt back to their cabin, cleaned from being dragged in the freshly fallen snows and undamaged. Upon their arrival, the two women were very pleased over the huge and prime bear's pelt. Then without further ado, the men left to check their pine marten traps while Kanti and Nuttah worked their magic on the massive bear's pelt defatting, fleshing and stretching out the same so it could begin drying.

Two hours later found the men running their pine marten trap line, catching 11 marten in their 20 traps! But they found that they also had a problem! Right at the far end of their pine marten trap line they discovered from the tracks left behind that a wolverine had discovered their traps. In so doing, it had discovered a live and struggling pine marten in a trap. Being the fierce predator it was, it had climbed out along the angled pole holding the trapped marten, killed and eaten the same except for its bony feet! The next morning, the men arrived on their marten trap line, ran it and discovered that the clever wolverine had now backtracked the men and their horses as they ran their trap line. In so doing, the wolverine had discovered three more trapped marten and had eaten them as well! Frustrated over their trap losses, Otis had come prepared figuring the wolverine was now 'with them' come 'hell or high water', and now he was bringing the 'high water' part of his plan on how to trap the highly intelligent wolverine.

When Kanti and Nuttah had defatted and fleshed out the bear's huge pelt, they had collected several pounds of bloody meat and fatty scraps. Figuring he had a real problem and an outstanding and clever trap robber in the wolverine unless controlled, Otis had asked the ladies to save their remaining bear pelt's fleshing scraps. Otis had purposely left a dead and frozen pine marten in trap number nine in the middle of their trap line. Otis figured that trap number nine would more than likely be the next victim of the glutinous wolverine and therein he began laying his plan to catch the extremely clever and damaging larger member of the weasel family. Underneath trap number nine, Otis planned on deliberately leaving the just caught dead pine marten hanging down off the angled pole to act as a lure and attractant for any wandering by and hungry wolverine. Then Otis laid the bear's flesh and fat scraping in a pile directly underneath the dead and hanging down pine marten. Lastly, around the bear scraps which were placed directly underneath the dead and hanging down pine marten, went Otis's choice for his 'hell or high water' surprise for that damned old trap line running, pine marten eating, wolverine! Twenty minutes later, five toothed wolf traps lay cleverly concealed beneath the snow in a circle around and underneath the dead hanging marten! Then the men got the hell out of the area for fear of running off the wolverine if they were observed in the area or because of all of the human and horse smells left in the area.

Then it was back down to the buffalo and bear carcass dumpsite to check the rest of their wolf traps. As it just so happened, there were three wolves caught in the previously set leg-hold traps and after being dispatched, the men found that one of the wolves weighed about 130 pounds and possessed a beautiful solid gray and very valuable pelt! Those traps were reset and the men hightailed out from that area being out in the open and not wanting to be discovered by any close at hand Gros Ventre. Arriving back at their cabin, all of the men stood guard over their just released from the corral and now grazing horses until dark. Then once the horses were watered and back in their corral, the men washed up in that part of their fast running creek that was not frozen and entered the cabin. There they were met with the warmth from the blazing fire in their fireplace and the smell of a supper already cooked by Kanti and Nuttah. It had been a long day and the cold and tired men gladly partook of the supper just produced, and then the men and women went their separate ways to their sleeping areas for the night.

The following morning, Otis fixed breakfast and got down a slab of buffalo meat from the meat pole for the women to cook for the men's evening supper since the moose meat was now all gone. As he did, Cloud saddled up their horses and soon the men were gone once again running their two diverse trap lines. Back up on the pine marten trap line, the men approached marten trap number nine with caution. They approached with caution because once they had gotten within earshot of the trap's location they could hear the growling sounds of all hell breaking loose. Could hear all hell breaking loose in the form of growling, snarling and one hell of a lot of brush being thrashed about along with several wolf traps being clanked together like there was no tomorrow! Dismounting a short distance away so the horses wouldn't be spooked, Otis unlimbered his rifle and began slowly walking towards where pine marten trap number nine was located. Sure as shootin', upon walking up closer to the trap site, Otis saw a small bear-like looking, dark in color animal hunkering down under the pine marten trap with two of its feet caught in two different wolf traps! The other thing Otis observed was that the sinister looking small snarling bear-like animal appeared to be all about bad attitude and a mouthful of flashing teeth! Now that the trapped animal saw Otis advancing, it hunkered down along the torn all to hell ground around the wolf traps and growled out a warning that if it ever got loose, it would totally eat the human thing now approaching it and be very happy to do so!

Realizing the fur value of the wolverine he now had in the trap, Otis continued cautiously approaching the vicious animal as it continued tearing against the two toothed wolf traps holding one hind foot and one front foot. THEN ALL OF A SUDDEN THE ANIMAL TORE ITS FRONT FOOT FREE FROM THE WOLF TRAP AND BEGAN LUNGING VIOLENTLY TOWARDS OTIS AGAINST THE TRAP HOLDING ITS ONE BACK FOOT! **BOOM!** went Otis's rifle and when it did and the white cloud of black powder smoke had drifted away from over the raging animal, it moved no more! Otis, to preserve its fur value, had cleanly shot the vicious animal in its head, leaving its beautiful body fur untouched. Then carefully walking up to the dead animal, Otis touched it with the toe of his new pair of heavy duty, bull buffalo hide winter moccasins recently made for him by Kanti. When he did, the previously raging animal moved no more.

Then Cloud and Feather brought up their horses and for a few moments, the men took the time to marvel at a small bear-like critter that had a reputation for such fierceness that it could take a fish away from the mouth of a feeding grizzly bear and live.

With that, the men removed the wolverine from the wolf trap and tossed the animal into one of the panniers that their two packhorses carried. Then trap number nine in the trap line was reset and mounting up, the men commenced checking the rest of their pine marten trap line and in so doing, removed another ten of the small fur bearers over the course of the entire line. Then it was down to their buffalo and grizzly bear carcass wolf trap sets where two more wolves that had been trapped were shot, skinned out and then those five traps were retrieved to be set elsewhere. That they did because for the most part, all three carcasses they had been using as attractors to their trap sets had been pretty much picked clean by the mammal and aerial predators, so the men moved on.

Thus passed the three trappers' winter months with many long and cold hours being spent trap setting for wolves and pine marten, occasional hunting trips to replenish the camp's meat supplies, tending to their horse herd, and cutting wood on a daily basis for cooking and warmth. Come the warming spring months and the advent of the spring beaver trapping season, the three trappers were more than ready for a change of pace. As it now stood, by the end of their 1828 fall beaver trapping season, they had trapped 226 beaver and their winter trap lines had produced 37 wolves, 116 pine marten pelts, one wolverine hide, and one beautiful grizzly bear hide, which only added to the men's Missouri farmland potential purchase incomes if and when they safely arrived back in St. Louis to sell their furs to the highest bidder. And they still had their spring beaver trapping results to be added to the above harvest which would provide even more potential income.

Stepping out from the cabin that first morning determined to be the start of the spring trapping season, found Otis standing there and 'scenting' the day's weather. The morning was cooler than normal, making the air heavy with moisture and dark foreboding gray skies from horizon to horizon in the form of wave clouds met his eyes. Shaking his head over what he had just 'read', he commenced with his breakfast makings around the outdoor firepit before the oncoming weather dampened his efforts. As he busied himself with his biscuit making, Kanti and then Nuttah arrived and simultaneously each lady planted a kiss on each cheek of their cook and protector as a good morning greeting. Then off the two ladies flew to the creek so they could wash up and then help him with breakfast. Otis just grinned, glowing over the loving treatment he had just received from the two women whom he now considered his 'adopted daughters'. As he did, he vowed in his heart that he would die first before he would let anything bad ever happen to the two of them. Looking over at the corrals, Otis could see that his two 'adopted sons' had all of their horses saddled and ready to go, so he began plopping the biscuit dough into the two heated Dutch ovens. Finished with that chore, he placed their lids back on the Dutch ovens and heaped a mess of coals with a shovel onto the lid tops to aid in the baking process.

Waving to the two ladies somewhat later back at the front of the cabin, the three men trailing two packhorses carrying panniers loaded with all of their beaver trapping needs, left their meadow and headed for the watered areas adjacent the Snake River holding a number of beaver dams and houses. As they did, the cold winds blowing out from the northwest made Otis almost turn around and ride back to their warm cabin instead of thinking of changing into his buckskin leggings and breechclout in a few minutes and walking around in the spring's icy cold waters of a beaver pond. But Cloud and Feather were raring to go and get started with their spring beaver trapping season, so...

For the next four hours, Otis set 24 of their 30 beaver traps in a cold wind now flecked with snowflakes driven horizontal to the ground before he called a halt to the trap setting. Then barely able to mount his horse because of his intense cold and numbed legs, Otis, Cloud and Feather rode into some heavy timber in order to get out from the intensely chilling winds and the heavy wet snows now flying through the air. As Feather gathered up some dead leaves and sticks from under some trees and began making a fire, Otis changed out from his wet and almost frozen to his legs and pelvis area leggings and breech-clout. Then still hardly able to move because of his previous and long immersions in the icy cold waters, Otis was finally able to crawl into his warmer wool pants and dry moccasins. As their fire crackled away, the men continued gathering in more loose limbs and sticks from underneath the trees as the now horizontally driven snows turned into a full gale of winds and rapidly falling temperatures!

Two hours later, the three men found they were caught in a spring blizzard, heavy with wet snows and sub-zero freezing temperatures! Gathering their horses in even closer to the men so they would not wander away in the darkness, the three men sat huddled around the fire, thankful for the dense timber surrounding them blunting a lot of the freezing winds and wet snows. However by late night, the winds had increased to gale force, the temperatures had plunged to way below zero and by now, a lot of the wind driven snows were making their ways into the forest and covering the men now huddled together under their horse blankets for the body warmth they could provide to each other to avoid freezing to death…

Come daylight and with the men now out of any close at hand firewood, the three snow covered trappers rose, saddled their horses and with subsided winds and some sun poking through the scattering of clouds, they headed for their cabin. Twice in the long ride, Cloud, damn near frozen, fell off his horse and had to be helped back into his saddle by Feather and Otis. Finally, the men turned into their meadow and riding in two feet of freshly fallen and drifted snow, made their ways back to their corrals. Therein they placed their horses and then staggered like drunken men on frozen wooden peg-like legs to the cabin being nearly frozen clear through! Their initial physical appearances made both of the women scream in fright and then as the men stood there dripping in the warmth of the cabin, the women carefully began removing their rock-hard frozen clothing as it began thawing, allowing itself to be removed from the men's skins to which it had been partially frozen! Then as the three near naked men stood there in front of the now built up roaring fire in their fireplace, their bluish-looking icy bodies dripped so much water that they were soon standing in puddles created from the ice melting from their bodies!

Standing there shaking like a 'dog passing peach pits', Otis remembered he had thought twice about starting their first day of spring trapping based on what the 'weather Gods' were 'telling' him when he had stepped out from the cabin that morning. But he had caved to the excited requests of Cloud and Feather wanting to start their spring trapping season. In so doing, he had learned a valuable lesson, one that he would never forget. Especially in so doing and not paying attention to what the weather-looks were 'telling' him, he had just jeopardized the lives of all of his kids. Jeopardized their lives because the men could have frozen to death and then the girls, defenseless without any men around to protect them, would have fallen prey to any passing trapper or Indian. Right then and there, Otis resolved never again to threaten the lives of his 'kids' by going off and doing something foolish like trapping in the face of a weather front that could and did turn deadly.

It was another two weeks before the men felt secure enough weather-wise to return to the beaver trapping arena due to a series of spring snowstorms rolling through the Hoback. When they did, they found many dead beaver hanging in their previously set traps that they had to discard due to spoilage and predatory bird damage upon the carcasses that had floated to the surface in plain view of the predators. However, a lesson had been learned once again by all that the frontier could be unforgiving at times and that Jim Bridger had been more than right about the Hoback and its 'killer' winters…

With the increasing daylight, longer days with sunshine and waters still colder than 'Billy Hell', Otis continued setting and clearing their beaver traps. However, he now knew this was his last beaver trapping season due to the cold and indications that his body, because of all the long icy immersions in the beaver trapping waters, was breaking down. In fact, because of the extremely cold waters that he found himself wading around in on a daily basis, he sometimes would have to spend up to half-an-hour in front of a roaring fire in the fireplace or the outdoor firepit every morning just to get any kind of feeling back into his legs and feet before he could once again begin beaver trapping that day! And many a night he found sleep hard to come by, while trying to sleep with icy cold feet and legs for most of the night as his constant companion.

But their trapping continued because all of the men knew it was necessary to amass as many beaver pelts as they could so that when they took them to St. Louis in the coming summer, the money received for their efforts would go towards their future land purchases back in Missouri. Then the entire clan could settle down in an area where deadly animals, bad men and evil Indians would not become an everyday issue of trying to live until the next sunrise. So trap beaver they did during the spring trapping season and amass numerous beaver pelts as a result. Soon their storage shed was jammed clear full of bundled beaver, marten and wolf skins and now the clan was storing their extra bundles of furs in their getting more and more crowded cabin. This was because they had trapped 303 mostly Made Beaver, 29 prime wolf skins and 116 pine marten during the spring trapping season to date! To those numbers were also added 226 mostly Made Beaver that had been taken during the previous fall trapping season!

As the spring trapping season began winding down and the beaver were starting to slip out of their prime, the men decided they would make one more beaver trapping run in a new area along the Snake River and then call it quits. Then they would pack up their furs and other essentials and head for the upcoming rendezvous site to be held near the south end of what the trappers called Sweet Lake or Bear Lake, to be held sometime in July. Being that this would be the last beaver trapping done in the Hoback by the Barnes Clan, Kanti and Nuttah decided on that series of trips they would accompany the men and by working with them, speed up the skinning process and make easier the final days of their spring beaver trapping season.

The following morning, Otis exited the cabin and as he always did, looked skyward and 'scented' the weather. The sky was blue without a cloud anywhere, the smell of late spring was in the air, aspens were beginning to leaf out and the warm air was very inviting. Pleased, Otis headed for his outdoor firepit and began his breakfast duties as the rest of the clan took care of their individual calls of nature, washed up, shaved and began saddling their riding and packhorses. Out from the cabin pranced the two excited ladies and after giving Otis his morning kisses, breakfast was served. However that morning, not many were interested in doing a lot of talking as they ate because they wanted to be up and going on their last rounds of trapping.

Somewhat later, the Barnes Clan streamed out from their campsite with Otis in the lead and Kanti and Nuttah following leading a packhorse apiece. Cloud and Feather rode alongside each of their ladies talking all the way and in so doing, provided protection to the overall group from any surprise forms of attack. Shortly thereafter with the ladies off at a distance, Otis changed into his leggings and breechclout and Cloud gathered up all the needed trapping gear as he had always done. Feather in the meantime, sat astride his horse so he could watch out for any signs of danger a short distance away from the two near defenseless men setting their traps.

By late afternoon, all 30 beaver traps had been set and with that, the men adjoined to a nearby aspen grove, dismounted, broke out their jerky and visited. As they did, the ladies soon had fallen asleep on a patch of leaves and so had Cloud and Feather next to them. Otis however, remained the lone guard against any sign of danger and as he did, he took the time to enjoy the beauty of the country surrounding him. He felt a certain degree of sadness knowing this would be his last sojourn as a trapper in some of the most interesting and beautiful country he had ever lived in or seen. Then the losses of his brothers flooded across his mind and that caused him pause as a deep sadness now slowly flowed over and through him.

It was then that he noticed for the first time dark storm clouds building far to the northwest and realized they would eventually be coming their way. So with that, he roused the rest of the clan from their pleasant naps under the aspens and once again like they had always done when setting out their traps, began working their ways back along the just set trap line checking to see if they had caught any of the highly territorial beaver before they left for the day.

Soon Otis was pulling dead beaver from their traps and as he did, he kept a 'cocked' eye on the still ominous clouds building further to the northwest. But the beaver catching was good and soon the men had emptied 13 freshly caught beaver from their 30 traps and the ladies had skinned out the same. However by now, the rolling their way and threatening storm clouds were beginning to cool the day's previous warm air and sending gusts of cooling winds across the land. Picking up the pace on their trapping activities because Otis could now see that a late spring rainstorm was on its way, the clan hurried through the last of their trap checking activities.

Finally finishing, everyone mounted up and feeling a few cold raindrops beginning to fall, the group began trotting their horses back the way they had come towards their cabin. Shortly thereafter, the rain was starting to fall even more heavily so the clan began galloping their horses for home to avoid the cold soaking rain now coming their ways. By now, everyone was in a full gallop including the two packhorses as they rounded the familiar fingers of trees below their cabin and began heading up into their meadow.

BOOM-BOOM-BOOM-BOOM-BOOM! rang out five quick shots as the Barnes Clan rounded the finger of trees into their meadow, finding their group in the middle of a Gros Ventre Indian ambush! With that initial fusillade of shooting, Cloud was hit, spun off his horse and hit the ground hard! In that same fusillade of shots, Otis was instantly thrown over the head of his horse and to the ground when his animal was shot out from under him! Kanti had a bullet pass so close to her head that it blew off a swatch of her long hair! The shot taken at Feather fortunately missed and when the bullet 'whined' off into nothingness, he turned, unlimbered his rifle and killed a Gros Ventre standing by a pine tree trying to hurriedly reload his just fired rifle! **BOOM!** went Kanti's shotgun hitting a Gros Ventre sitting on his horse in the brush trying to hurriedly reload his just fired rifle and when she shot, the Indian's horse exploded from under him! Kanti's shot had gone low and partially hit the Indian and partially sprayed his horse full in the face with a load of birdshot, causing the horse to literally blow up in surprised pain! Nuttah was also missed in the initial shooting and that was a mistake on the part of her shooter. Realizing they had been ambushed, Nuttah quickly reined in her horse, turned in her saddle and shot a Gros Ventre off his horse as he rode yelling directly at her with his tomahawk upraised and ready to strike! The next shot fired came from Otis who had hit the ground hard when he had his horse surprisingly shot out from under him. However, when Otis hit the ground, the impact had broken the lock off his rifle making it useless for returning fire. No matter! Otis was a crack shot and when he fired his pistol at a Gros Ventre riding right at Kanti with an upraised tomahawk as she was trying to hurriedly reload her shotgun, that attacker was blown from his saddle with a solid body shot from Otis's .54 caliber pistol! Dropping that just fired pistol and quickly drawing his second pistol from his sash, Otis shot another hard charging Gros Ventre riding right at him with a downward pointing lance aimed right at his chest! When he was struck by Otis's heavy lead bullet from such close range, that Indian was blown backwards off his horse, over its rump and was dead before he had hit the ground!

Seeing his four fellow ambushers either killed or injured by the surprised but now accurate shooting trappers and their womenfolk, the fifth ambusher tried to sprint off on his horse and flee. Down through the meadow on his horse he stormed and when he turned the corner by the finger of trees, another rifle shot rang out fired by Feather who had just hurriedly reloaded and fired his rifle. When he did, it seemed that the fleeing Gros Ventre rode untouched for a number of yards and then having been gutshot, slowly leaned over and collapsed off his racing across the meadow horse, landing in a jumbled heap!

Otis, still hurriedly reloading his second pistol as he continued looking around for any more attackers and seeing none, finished loading his pistol and then ran over to a lying without any movement of any kind on the ground, Cloud! Reaching Cloud the same time Kanti did, they rolled him over only to find his entire face covered with blood! Kanti jerked off her shirt and attempted to frantically wipe the blood from Cloud's head and face. In so doing, Otis trying to ascertain the seriousness of Cloud's wound realized he would live. He would have a ringing head for a long time but as far as Otis could determine, the shot taken at Cloud who had ridden the closest to the ambushers, only had a head wound. But what a head wound it was! The bullet fired at Cloud as he had ridden right by the hidden ambushers, had left a deep fleshy gouge clear across his entire forehead! Cloud's wound was not serious but being a typical head wound, Cloud was bleeding like a 'stuck hog'! Then **BOOM!** another shot surprisingly rang out! Everyone who had gathered around Cloud to see if he was alright, turned and saw Feather in the process of reloading his pistol as he stood over what had been the badly wounded Gros Ventre that Kanti had shot with her shotgun loaded with birdshot and had not killed. Feather had just seen to it that that Gros Ventre seeing another sunrise was no longer a concern...

Feather then got back on his horse and rounded up the four valuable remaining Gros Ventre horses, including the one not seriously shot in the neck and head with birdshot by Kanti and herded them into their corral. At the same time, Otis lifted up the still madly bleeding Cloud and bodily carried him up to their cabin in the rainstorm now turned into a downpour. Once in the cabin, Cloud was laid on their table next to the fireplace as Kanti and Nuttah worked over him trying to get the bleeding stopped and bring the still unconscious Cloud back into the world of the living.

As the two sisters continued frantically working over Cloud, Otis and Feather brought all the rest of the Barnes Clan's horses up to the cabin and put them into the horse corral for safer keeping as well. Then the two men dragged the four dead Gros Ventre into the grove of pines from whence they had ambushed the Barnes Clan and left them to rot or for the critters to eat. Following that, with fully reloaded weapons, the two men walked down towards the remaining dead Gros Ventre killed with a long shot by Feather, dragged him into some brush and left him there for the critters to eat as well.

Quietly walking back to their cabin, Otis began thinking about what had just occurred. *They had just been ambushed by five Gros Ventre from out of nowhere. Of the five attackers, all now lay dead! However, one of the Gros Ventre's horses had gotten away and more than likely was en route the familiar herd of horses kept by the Indians near their encampment from whence it came. Now it would just be a matter of time before a number of the Gros Ventre from the five dead men's band, backtracked that horse to the trappers' secluded campsite and attacked once again only in larger numbers this time. And they would, seeing that the horse that had escaped would have blood all over its saddle and down the side of his horse from Feather's gutshot horse's rider. When that discovery was made, Otis knew they would not be so lucky to survive a second round of attacks and if any of them did, they would be horribly treated before they were finally killed and mutilated by their attackers.*

With those thoughts streaming through his mind, Otis came up with a plan that would keep all of them alive in the future. Especially if the rainstorm they were currently experiencing kept up its downpour. Because if the heavy downpour now being experienced continued, it would wash away most of the tracks the Gros Ventre would need in order to backtrack the dead Indian's horse and in the process, discover the trappers' cabin. Once that event occurred however, they would figure out what had happened and take the appropriate killing action on the entire trespassing and killing Barnes Clan...

With those concerning thoughts storming through Otis's mind, he decided what the clan's response actions would be. Once back at the cabin, Otis made sure everyone had reloaded every weapon they had. Then he checked up on Cloud only to see that the man's head wound had stopped bleeding so profusely and had been dressed but he was still unconscious from the almost fatal wound. Otis then gathered everyone around him and told the group they would be leaving just as soon as they pulled all of their beaver traps from the surrounding waterways, had emptied out their cabin, loaded all of their pack-horses and would be heading for the upcoming rendezvous site earlier than originally planned. That way he advised, they could possibly avoid being attacked by the Gros Ventre again once they had discovered that the dead Indian's horse had blood on its saddle, that its rider had come to an untimely end and then came looking for his killer or killers. He also hopefully suggested that with all the rain they were experiencing, maybe they would get lucky and the blood would be all washed off the dead Indian's saddle and horse before anyone from the band of Gros Ventre got any wiser, at least right away.

Right then and there after making sure once again that Cloud was alright, Otis and Feather saddled up their riding and packhorses and left for those beaver waters just trapped, downpour be damned! Once there, they removed their valuable beaver traps, tossed them into the pack-horse's panniers and returned to their cabin by another route so as to confuse anyone from the Gros Ventre band who might already be attempting to track them down. Come the following day, the Barnes Clan, minus Cloud who was awake but now suffering tremendous headaches and seeing halos in his eyes caused by his head wound, was a whirlwind of activity. As the ladies cleaned out their cabin and loaded those essentials into the packs ready for travel, Feather and Otis loaded all of their bundles of furs and other provisions from the storage shed into the packs ready for travel as well. That afternoon with Otis in the lead, a fully loaded pack string trailed by Kanti, Nuttah and a semi-revived Cloud leading the loaded animals left the trappers' campsite. In fact, even the four recovered horses from the Gros Ventre ambushers were loaded as well. Trailing the heavily loaded pack string was Feather making sure there would be no danger attacking the caravan from the rear without going through him first.

Backtracking their earlier route of travel into the Hoback from the Bear Lake Rendezvous site, back down through the Salt River Range and along the Hams River, found the slow moving and heavily loaded pack train stopping at their original cabin from the year before on the Hams some eleven days later. By then, other than still having a ringing head, especially anytime he quickly bent over, and halo lights at the top of his eyes on some days, Cloud had pretty much recovered from his almost fatal head wound. Pulling into their old cabin site on the Hams, Otis made the decision to spend several days resting up their horse herd and letting them graze from morning to night in order for them to get back their strength after such a long and exhausting trip out of the country of the Gros Ventre. Then the group set to cleaning a porcupine and its refuse out from their cabin and that from a pair of gray squirrels as well, so they could occupy it without any problems coming from the resident critters for the next few days.

Little did Otis realize that just two days after they had left their cabin back in the Hoback, over 30 Gros Ventre had discovered their dead band member's still saddled horse in among their tribe's free-ranging horse herd. Upon closer examination after removing that horse's saddle and discovering the original owner's blood on the underside of the saddle, the Gros Ventre band's best tracker was then put on that horse's back trail. Two days later, over 30 mounted Gros Ventre warriors had stormed into the old Barnes Clan's now empty campsite with 'blood in their eyes'! Now that same group of Indians, unbeknownst to the Barnes Clan, were following the very easy to follow trail of the trappers and their horses as they quickly headed south towards the upcoming rendezvous! This they did especially after finding the rest of their band's bodies, laid out, bloated and stinking near the Barnes Clan's recently deserted cabin! Now the Gros Ventre were hot on the trail of the white man killers with revenge in their hearts! However, the Barnes Clan had a two-day lead on the Gros Ventre, having left immediately after the ambush in accordance with Otis's plan to avoid retaliation. But in deciding to let their horses graze at their old cabin on the Hams for two days after the group had arrived to recover their strength, they may have sealed their doom by allowing the hard charging and tailing Gros Ventre the ability to make up the two-day gap in their chase after the killers of their five tribal members...

Later in the afternoon of the Barnes Clan's second day of rest and letting their herd of hard worked horses put on the 'feed bag', Otis, while preparing supper for the group, heard the whinny of a far off horse smelling the clan's horse herd and numerous fresh droppings now safely back in their old corral. When Otis heard that far off horse whinny, his survival instincts went into high alert! They were deep in Indian country and for one not to be alerted over such an animal's simple act, was to many times court injury or death! Looking up in the direction from whence he had heard the other horse's recognition call, Otis spotted the last four members of a string of Indians working their ways through the trees and slowly coming their way! Dropping his cooking gear, he grabbed up his rifle off his nearby sitting log and yelling for the rest of the group who had been sleeping to awaken, grab their guns and make ready for the uninvited company and an expected attack!

As Otis raced up to his old cabin's half-open front door, the wood on the door's frame exploded into a million splinters as a heavy caliber bullet narrowly missed his head and drove itself into the door's frame, splattering his face with wood chips! Bursting through the door into the now mass confusion inside the cabin by the rest of the now alerted clan, Otis yelled, "INDIANS AND A DAMN MESS OF THEM, I SUSPECT!" Turning around, Otis slammed the heavy log front door shut just as two more bullets smashed into the door, sending more wood chips and splinters flying! Within moments, the three men each manned one of the cabin's three windows in preparation for the obvious battle with the unknown Indians to come. **THUNK–THUNK–THUNK!** went three more bullets into the log walls of the sturdily built cabin, as Kanti and

Nuttah quickly laid out the men's 'Possibles bags' by each man along with their powder flasks and extra Indian Trade Rifles the group possessed, loaded with buck and ball from previous times of use.

That Kanti and Nuttah did just in time as about a dozen of the hard-pursuing Gros Ventre made a mad foot charge across the open ground for the cabin's front door before the trappers trapped inside could adequately prepare for the oncoming battle! That was a deadly mistake on the part of the Gros Ventre. Otis, Cloud and Feather then cleanly killed three Indians with their rifles, grabbed their near at hand Indian Trade rifles just laid against the wall by Kanti and Nuttah, and killed three more just as the now depleted ranks of cabin charging Indians reached the front door! Slamming into the front door as a group, the remaining attacking Indians jerked open the cabin's front door and plowed headlong into two shotgun blasts fired by Kanti and Nuttah! Four more Indians died where they stood in the entrance to the doorway and as the remaining two attackers tried to flee, they were cut down when Cloud and Feather back shot them with their pistols as they turned to run from the hail of gunfire coming from the cabin!

Chief "Runs-From-His-Horses" of the Band of Gros Ventre from the Hoback region, upon seeing the destruction of twelve of his men in a heartbeat, grimaced and then through narrowed hatred-filled eyes, swung his hand around in a signal for the rest of his warriors to surround the cabin and try attacking the trappers hidden inside from all sides. Immediately, his remaining 20 warriors circled the cabin from all sides and began pouring their concentrated rifle fire into the open doorway, through the windows and into its back and side walls. Inside the cabin, the inner walls flew into thousands of wood splinters as hot lead assailed the trappers and their women inside from just about every angle!

Inside the cabin, the men frantically reloaded every just fired rifle and pistol they had as did Kanti and Nuttah their shotguns. As the two women finished reloading their shotguns and after making sure both of their two pistols were loaded and ready for action, they fell into each other's arms in terror and hugged. They both realized that if their men were overrun and they had fired off all of their weapons, they would more than likely suffer gang rapes and eventually a horrific death as only the attacking Gros Ventre could conjure up. But the looks in the two women's eyes beyond the terror they initially felt said it all, namely, "Bring it on and plan on joining your Cloud People before the sun sets this day when you approach the two of us sisters..."

Then all of a sudden the Barnes Clan hunkering down in the cabin heard all kinds of yelling, rifle and pistol shots, then even more yelling and screaming from all around their cabin. Then after a short time of hearing such confusing and conflicting sounds, total silence surrounded the cabin. Taking a quick peek through his open window to see what the hell was happening, Otis saw almost 100 Indians swarming all around a mess of dead Indians lying scattered about everywhere outside the cabin! When he did, his heart sank! With that many foes swirling all around their cabin, there was no way they could survive so many attackers... Then looking again, he could see the 'sea' of new attackers were scalping and mutilating the previous group of Gros Ventre who had been tracking the trappers for days and had just attacked them. Then it dawned on Otis as to what was happening. Apparently the Gros Ventre were far away from their own territory and had inadvertently wandered into another hostile tribe's territory. Because the second group of attacking Indians far outnumbered the Gros Ventre, minus those killed by the trappers, they had been quickly annihilated to a man by the other yet to be identified attacking Indians!

Now the trappers and their women were really in trouble. There were upwards of 100 other Indians swirling around the cabin and the trapped trappers and their women inside! Otis knew that no matter how accurately they shot and killed the other attackers, there were just too many of them. They were all going to die before the day was over once they were overrun and then the real torture of any of the Barnes Clan who survived and the rape of their women would begin in earnest!

Then a number of mounted Indians from the band who had just killed off all of the Gros Ventre, rode up to the outskirts of the soon to be battle-field and just quietly sat there looking on out of rifle range, as the rest of their warriors took up their positions around the cabin and the trapped Mountain Men inside. Then all of a sudden, Otis and Feather positioned nearest the two women, heard the clattering of their two shotguns hitting the floor. Then they heard Kanti and Nuttah screaming, breaking into crying and OUT THE CABIN'S DOORWAY INTO THE FACE OF THE INDIAN MENACE THEY FLEW, TOTALLY UNARMED TO THE MEN'S HORROR BACK INSIDE THE CABIN!

Kanti and Nuttah raced across the open ground in front of the cabin towards the mounted warriors and as they did, seven braves from the latest attacking group stood up from their hidden positions behind the horse corral, raised their rifles to shoot the women down and then lowered them when one of the freshly arriving mounted Indians raised his hand in a signal for them to stop. That Indian then quickly dismounted and began walking towards the two women who were crying and running right at him! When that happened, Otis raised his rifle and took careful aim at the Indian walking towards the two de-fenseless running and crying women. He knew he only had one shot to kill the Indian walking towards the two running women, so he took very careful aim and…

Just then, Kanti and Nuttah flew into the outstretched arms of the lone Indian and it was then that Otis lowered his rifle, realizing what was happening. He then realized that the Indians surrounding them were Blackfeet and the lone Indian holding the two crying women was none other than Black Wolf, Chief of the Southern Bear River Band of the Blackfeet Tribe, and THE FATHER OF KANTI AND NUTTAH! Seeing that, Otis yelled out to Cloud and Feather not to shoot and put their weapons down and out of sight before they really got everyone in trouble. With that command, Otis also gave a quick explanation to the two surprised men as to why they were to lay down their weapons. Otis then laid down his rifle and taking a chance that he and the Indian holding the two crying women were still friends from the first time they had met, exited the cabin and boldly started walking towards Black Wolf.

"We meet again, Chief Black Wolf," said Otis a few moments later, as he raised his right hand in the Plains Indians' universal sign of peace.

For the longest moment in time, the great chief just held his two daughters and stared coldly at the white man who was so boldly confronting him. Then realizing who was confronting him, Black Wolf spoke saying "It is good to see my old friend and the one who cares for my two daughters. They have told me that they have remained pure this whole time under your care and that they love you like they love me. Because of your love for my daughters as a 'white-man father' and their love for you, you and yours shall live this day. But be aware, many of your kind are heading for the lake with all of the bears feeding along its shore (Bear or Sweet Lake) and my people are afraid. My people are afraid that your kind are like the locusts out on the prairie in the fall of the year and that if we don't stop you, you will soon be like the shoots of grass that come forth after the winter snows. Today we killed off the Gros Ventre who dared to enter our territory. Soon, my warriors will be attacking your kind when they arrive for the great white man gathering called the rendezvous. My only hope as a father is that you and your kind will not be a part of the great battle to come between the whites and my people."

Then turning to his two daughters still firmly clasped in his arms, Black Wolf spoke to them in the tongue of the Blackfeet. Then releasing his two daughters who his culture and tribal traditions still considered 'impure' because of what the trappers who had earlier captured them had done to them initially, turned towards Otis once more. " 'White-man father' to my daughters, please continue caring for them and see to it that they have a good life living with the people of the white race. They say you will soon be taking them and the two men they have fallen in love with to where your home is far to the south and away from here. Remember, they will care for you as you have cared for them. Because of the great battle to come between your arriving trappers and my people, I will not see you ever again. Until The Great Spirit comes for you, I want you to wear this necklace made from the claws of the 'Great Bear' (grizzly bear). If you do, they will protect you as they have me for all of these many moons." Then Black Wolf lifted a magnificent grizzly bear claw necklace from his neck, walked over and placed it around Otis's neck. He then took Otis's hand, shook it, turned and mounted his horse. With that he yelled out a command in the Blackfeet language and immediately his warriors began heading for their horses and mounted up. When all of Black Wolf's warriors had mounted, he paused, dismounted and walked over and gave each of his daughters a long and meaningful hug. Then he abruptly mounted his horse and with a wave of his hand, out from the cabin area rode a stream of gaily painted for battle Blackfoot 'horseflesh and humanity'. Soon only a small cloud of dust remained in the air as a remembrance of what had just happened between two very different cultures. Well, that and a 'remembrance' of a moment in time that left two young Blackfeet Indian women sobbing who realized they had just lost a father from one culture and had gained another...

With all of their horses refreshed after being allowed to do nothing but graze and water for two
full days, the trappers now found themselves
ready to continue their journey toward the vicinity of Bear Lake and the coming rendezvous.
Finally by noon, all the riding horses had been
saddled and the packhorses heavily loaded with
bundles of furs, the Barnes Clan's remaining provisions and all of the rest of their essential gear.
Two days later of slow travel so as not to stress
out their heavily loaded pack string, the Barnes
Clan entered the rendezvous campsite. There
they headed for a grove of trees for the shade
they offered and the nearness to a cold flowing
creek for the horses and camp water it offered.
For the next hour or so, the group unloaded all
of their horses and after letting them water in the
creek, picketed them in the adjoining grasslands
so they could feed. Then before all the 'drift or
dropped' wood had all but disappeared being
taken up by all the other arriving trappers and
friendly Indians, the group gathered up the
needed fuel supplies for their campfire while
at the rendezvous. Then as Otis scratched out a
firepit, assembled all of his hanging irons and
cooking essentials from the packs, Kanti and
Nuttah laid out everyone's sleeping furs under
the protective leaf cover of the grove of trees in
their camp. After filling up a coffee pot and bean
kettle in the nearby creek, Otis loaded the bean
pot full of pinto beans so they could soak and

soften up. Then taking one of his beloved Dutch ovens, built a small fire and roasted up a mess of green coffee beans so he could make coffee come nightfall. Then after Kanti and Nuttah had lain down on their sleeping furs and were soon fast asleep after an emotionally exhausting time, Otis took the time to sit down by the campfire, light up his pipe full of James River smoking tobacco and had a good and quiet smoke. A quiet smoke that was soon interrupted by Feather and Cloud bringing back a freshly killed mule deer doe for their camp meat. Otis, after knocking out the ash from his pipe's bowl, stuck the pipe back into his 'Possibles bag' and with the boys holding the doe's legs apart, set about skinning the animal out so it could cool out and glaze.

That evening as more and more trappers continued streaming into the rendezvous campsite, the night air soon filled with the sounds of happy gunfire, herds of horses not used to each other 'arguing' among themselves, shouts of joy and whooping sounds among much other quiet laughter around the many campsites recently being set up. Then as Otis cooked the group's supper, the quiet among their campsite was interrupted numerous times with the happy arrival of old friends getting reacquainted, seeing who had 'lost their hair' and who had 'gone under' among their old friends…

Soon, so many old friends showed up at the Barnes's camp that Otis found himself making

Dutch oven after Dutch oven full of biscuits and skewering more and more of the recently killed doe's meat on metal skewers that soon saw the entire deer consumed by many of their arriving and hungry friends at supper time. Finally around midnight, the crowd of old friends gathered around the Barnes's camp drifted back to their own campsites and then only the crackling of their fire and the 'celebrating' of a nearby pack of coyotes over a recent kill graced the evening's air. Then remembering Black Wolf's concerns over the white men trappers flooding into and around the Indians' homelands and the threat of an attack, all of the Barnes Clan slept that evening next to their firearms just in case...

For the next six or seven days, more and more trappers kept funneling into the 1828 Rendezvous campsite. Soon the campsite resembled a small city at night, there were so many campfires glowing in the darkness and the air, either at day or night, was filled with the constant hum of talking, shouts of glee over one's safe arrival, the sounds of drunken fights and the dust from friendly Indians' arriving horse herds. But all in all, the rendezvous rang out with a happiness literally 'felt' by hundreds of men who had braved the dangerous elements while out on the frontier, survived another year of difficult and often lonely work, many times without the sound of another human voice and were now among their own kind and did so with untold joy.

For the next several days, Otis and the boys circulated around the rendezvous campsite visiting with old friends and explaining to others they had not seen for years what had happened to Otis's brothers Wallace, Oliver and Cedrick. Cloud and Feather could see that when those moments involving the other brothers' whereabouts came up, a heartfelt sadness was evident in the face of their adoptive 'father' over his great family losses. But Otis, being the tough old Irishman that he was, always found a way to address the issue over the losses of his brothers and then moved on quickly to other more pleasant memories. Then the boys and Otis circulated around the Rocky Mountain Fur Company's campsite when those traders arrived and got surprised. There they found that the demand for the beaver fur was on a downhill slide even though their numbers of pelts showing up at rendezvous were in decline. Apparently the markets in Europe and the eastern United States were beginning to move away from the beaver hat to that made from a worm that came from China. It now seemed that wearing a beaver hat in public was 'old hat' and wearing a new silk hat was all the 'rage' in Europe and in the United States. That 'rage' for the new style of hat was also reflected in the Mountain Price being paid per pound of beaver fur. A price per pound for that of the Free Trappers for beaver pelts that year was around $3 per pound and even less for the few remaining company contract trappers still in the business. Also, the prices for many of the provisions needed for another year in the backcountry beaver trapping were just as high as ever, if not even higher! Once again, the Mountain Price threshold for goods and provisions was considered necessary because of the danger and inherent losses suffered by recent Blackfoot and Arikara Indian attacks, losses when making river crossings, horses being bitten by rattlesnakes and dying or left behind to die, destruction of horses by grizzly bears or by just damn old horse wrecks, and a lower market price for beaver fur...

"INDIANS! INDIANS!" yelled several trappers riding into the rendezvous site on horses heavily lathered up with sweat from having to run so far at such high speeds several days later. Soon the two exhausted trappers bearing the news of 'Indians' were swarmed by their own kind for any information relative to the attacks. The inquiring trappers were soon informed that about 300 Blackfeet had just attacked Robert Campbell's party of trappers heading for the rendezvous site and were just a few miles away and holed up in a desperate battle for survival! Soon the 'battle cry' was heard around the rendezvous site and moments later, about 70 trappers and some of their Indian allies stormed out from camp and headed for where the battle was raging between Robert Campbell's party of fur trappers and the much-dreaded Blackfeet! Four hours later, the men from the rendezvous site had turned the tide of battle between the Blackfeet and the holed-up trappers and now, all of the men included the embattled trappers, were thankfully and safely streaming into the rendezvous site.

However once again, upon hearing about the battle between the Blackfeet as Black Wolf had warned and the embattled trappers, Otis, Cloud and Feather stayed back at their campsite and there they awaited the outcome of the battle. Once again, Otis figured his group was not at war with the Blackfeet and he was not going to chance having any of his kids killed in battle or someone from his group ending up killing the girl's father, Black Wolf, in battle...

The Barnes Clan stayed throughout July at the rendezvous visiting old friends and buddies knowing it would be their last opportunity to do so. Would be their last opportunity with old friends because Otis had already made arrangements to join up with the returning to St. Louis, Rocky Mountain Fur Company fur train with his kids and their furs for the protection such a large group offered... Then with luck, they would travel back with the returning fur train to St. Louis, trade in their furs for better prices than offered out at the rendezvous and then after a few days in St. Louis celebrating and shopping for the clothing worn by those of the white community, head out. Head out with all of the monies owed the Barnes Clan via their several Letters of Credit from previous years of beaver and wolf pelt sales and see if the old Barnes farm was maybe for sale or could be purchased outright. Then the thought was the entire clan would settle down, the kids would get baptized and finally married in the Catholic Church, and then without all the dangers inherent out on the frontier beaver trapping, quietly settle down into their next life. If all of that could happen, then Otis already had a thought in mind that would more than pay for their lives to come when it came to being able to make a respectable living once back in Missouri…

Chapter Fifteen

MISSOURI "MOONSHINE-MADNESS"

BY THE END OF JULY, found the Rocky Mountain Fur Company fur traders strung out along the trail leading a heavily loaded horse and mule pack train heading for distant St. Louis. As part of that pack train and under the conditions that they would help guard and protect the valuable fur train, rode the Barnes Clan. On the morning of departure, Otis, Cloud now fully recovered from his head wound with the Gros Ventre, and Feather were up way before dawn. As the men began packing all of their horses with the bundles of beaver, wolf and pine marten skins, Kanti and Nuttah made breakfast and finished with the packing of the group's sleeping furs and cooking essentials.

Come daylight found the Barnes Clan patiently

sitting on their horses with their heavily loaded pack animals as they waited for the rest of the fur company's men to complete the last of their loading of their pack animals. Finally loaded and strung out along the trail, the order was given to 'move out' and the long trek back to St. Louis began. Falling in behind the company's long pack train, the Barnes Clan, as per previous arrangement with the fur company, brought up the rear along with other fur trappers quitting the fur trade and provided protection from being attacked in that section of the pack string.

Each evening along the trail, the fur company would send hunters on ahead of the long and slow moving pack train to kill several buffalo for camp meat for that evening's meal as well as locating a suitable and safe campsite. A campsite that not only offered good graze and water for the animals but one in which a defense could be mounted against any surprise attack by hostile Indians. Then when encamped, the company men would provide the day's meals as well as the numerous camp guards to protect the valuable horse herd, the packs of furs and the men moving such valuables. Then each morning way before daylight, the laborious job of packing all of the horses and mules hauling the bundles of fur and other equipment would begin anew. Once those packing duties were completed, another day would begin crossing the expansive Green River Valley (near Daniel, Wyoming), ascending the Big Sandy River, crossing the Continental Divide through historic South Pass, traveling along the Sweet Water River past Devils Gate and Independence Rock, down the North Platte River, along the mighty Platte River, then along the Missouri River, and finally down the mighty Mississippi River and into the city of St. Louis, the fabled 'Gateway to the West'. Leaving the rendezvous site the last of July in 1828, the great Rocky Mountain Fur Company fur train finally arrived in St. Louis near the end of October, after 79 days of travel through vast herds of buffalo along the way and seeing numerous bands of Indians along the trail watching from a distance. Numerous bands of Indians along the way of travel, who because of the fur train's great number of men providing overall protection, were not attacked or disturbed.

Come the much-anticipated morning of arrival in St. Louis, the entire pack train was hurried along even more forcefully by the eager company men. Soon the long pack string fresh from the frontier entered the city limits to many stares from its citizenry. Then a short time later, the entire pack string was drawn up in front of the company's main fur house to much excited greetings, laughter and excitement. It would be late afternoon before the Barnes Clan, being at the end of the pack string, was confronted by the Rocky Mountain Fur Company's graders and sorters so their load of furs could be evaluated.

By supper time the company's count was in and the Barnes Clan's inventory for their last fur trapping season was 529 beaver pelts, 66 wolf pelts, 332 prime pine marten pelts, one wolverine skin, and one monster-sized grizzly bear rug.

Just as Otis had suspected, their trip to St. Louis with all of their pelts was going to pay big dividends. Especially in light that the Mountain Prices being paid out at the rendezvous for beaver was only $3 per pound whereas in St. Louis, those same pelts were bringing $4 per pound! As a result, their beaver pelts brought forth $3,174, their wolf pelts at $30/pelt brought $1,980, and the marten pelts at $10/pelt brought another $3,320 for a Letter of Credit totaling $8,174, and an additional $300 in hard cash which Otis had requested! Realizing it was too late in the day to redeem all of his Letters of Credit, Otis had just requested $300 in hard cash so his party would have some spending money for food, lodging and celebration over their successful and safe trip home.

That evening after placing all of their horses in a livery, Otis took his family to "Ma Sylvia's Boarding House and Eatery" on 3rd Street, where he also took out lodging for himself, the two ladies and his two sons. All the while walking the streets to the livery and the boarding house, it was a good thing his kids had moveable heads on their necks. Since none of his family had ever been in a city, much less one as large as was St.

Louis, their heads were moving from side to side as they looked on in wonder at what new and unique things they were seeing, smelling and hearing, including numerous sounds from the steamboat whistles along the docks! Especially exciting to his family were all of the sights and sounds at every turn in the streets compared to the quiet beauty found out on the frontier. And even though every member of his family was armed, they were finding that there were no grizzly bears or hostile Indians at every bend in the roadways or on the street corners...

Then when they tried entering Ma Sylvia's Boarding House and Eatery, they found they were stopped at the front door by a very large and imposing figure of a man named Tom Davis, son to Ma Sylvia. There he politely informed the Barnes Clan they would have to remove the flints from their pistols and rifles before entering the eating establishment! Complying with Tom's request, the group entered the eating hall to find a noisy mixture of farmers, gaily dressed Indians from local tribes, frontiersmen of all sorts, noisy and rough talking river men, important looking businessmen dressed in coats, tails and beaver skin top hats, and a host of women carrying large trays of food to the numerous tables scattered throughout the noisy and lively eatery! As they did, Otis had to smile at his kids. Once again the kids' heads were moving from side to side drinking in all of the new sights, sounds and smells associated with such a mix of humanity. In fact, having lived for so many years out on the frontier with its many forms of silence and then entering such a facility with all the noise of its hustle and bustle, almost hurt one's ears...

Taking their places at a table, the Barnes Clan was soon confronted with a pert and pretty little gal named "Miss Betsy" as she called herself, who called upon the family to select what they would like to eat from the menu. His kids not being familiar with a menu, Otis ordered for the whole family and when the huge trays of great smelling food begin arriving, he once again saw the wonder in his kids' eyes over so much food being served so fast and having so many great choices and smells! It didn't take the very hungry family members long to bury themselves in the mounds of numerous great tasting food dishes, especially when it came to Ma Sylvia's home-made pies! Once again, Otis included, just could not seem to get enough of the homemade pies and breads being served in such amounts and right out from the ovens in the kitchen. It was about then that the family's faces reflected great joy over what the life in a city like St. Louis could offer over that of the mosquito ridden and many times dangerous frontier...

Then the surprises did not end there. Otis saw to it that all of the family members, even though their clothing showed the signs of many days' use and abuse while living out on the frontier, were all treated to hot baths! Then back into their old clothes smelling of sweat, smoke from a campfire and grease drippings from eating fatty slabs of buffalo meat, they went as they were then treated to another surprise. The family was shown to their rooms where the ladies had one room, the two young men another and finally another room for Otis. After that evening's rest, when they got back together the next morning for breakfast, they all agreed it was better to sleep out on the ground in their sleeping furs over the smelly and bed-bug infested beds recently used by other sweaty and smelly clients.

Following breakfast, the family went to an emporium where they purchased new clothing commonly worn by white folks in the area to replace their worn and filthy buckskins. There the ladies found they liked wearing the clothing of men over some of the frilly things the women of the day wore, and purchased accordingly. Then the clan headed back to the Rocky Mountain Fur Company's main fur house, where Otis handed in his several Letters of Credit so they could be redeemed. When he did, the Letters of Credit from the many years the Barnes Clan had trapped beaver, wolves and pine marten came to $22,271.00, or a small fortune in that day and age! Then the Rocky Mountain Fur Company's Clerk made out a single Letter of Credit to be drawn on "The First Mercantile and Agriculture Bank of St. Louis" for the amount of $22,271.00. After receiving instructions on how to find the bank, the clan went to the bank and had the bank's president draw Otis up a Promissory Bank Note for that amount. With that note placed securely into his saddlebag which he carried everywhere he went and used as a pillow to protect its contents, Otis made sure the flint was placed back into both of the pistols that he was carrying in his sash, as did White Cloud and Spotted Feather, just in case.

Returning to the livery, the Barnes Clan retrieved all of their livestock, settled up with the liveryman and headed west to the town of Matson, Missouri. Matson being the location of the last known residence of the Barnes Clan when they were all alive and when they lived with Rufous Barnes, Patriarch of the Clan before his untimely death. Arriving in Matson just in time for the last Mass at the Catholic Church, Otis hustled his kids into Church and there they sat through a Mass, the first one Otis had sat through in a number of years and the first for his kids.

At the end of the Mass, Otis and the rest of the clan stood around outside the Church waiting for the Priest to meet and greet his Parishioners as he always did at the end of every Mass. It was then that Otis was surprised to hear a familiar voice speaking out to him from a nearby group of visiting neighbors after the celebration of the Mass.

"Well, I'll be damned! Otis Barnes, how the hell are you? Damn, I thought you were out west somewhere trapping beaver with your brothers!" bellowed out Sheriff Bill Clemmens.

Hearing the familiar voice of an old family friend, Otis turned and was surprised to see the sheriff pushing his way through a group of people and coming his way. "Hello, Bill. Good to see you, my old friend, after all these years. How the hell have you been, and your family, are they well?" asked Otis.

"Damn, it is good to see that you 'kept your hair'! When did you get back in country and how are the rest of your brothers?" Sheriff Clemmens asked as he vigorously shook Otis's hand.

"Just got back this morning in time for Church and as for my brothers, they all left their bones back out on the frontier," Otis quietly replied.

"Damn, all of your brothers are gone? They were a tough bunch. I can't believe some damn Indian got all of them. I am sorry to hear that, Otis," replied the sheriff. Then realizing the loss of his brothers was a sad subject, the sheriff continued on with his line of questions saying, "What brings you back to this neck of the woods, my old friend?"

"Me and my new family here plan on settling down and purchasing a good piece of ground in this area as the site of our new home," replied Otis.

Then Otis saw Sheriff Clemmens's eyes 'fly' to that of Kanti and Nuttah and then back to Otis with a scowl on his face. "Damn, Otis, them is sure pretty Indian women but you damn well know a man in Missouri kain't have but one wife!" said Sheriff Clemmens, reverting back to his old law enforcement self.

Hearing those words of concern coming from the local sheriff set Otis to smiling. "Bill, I am sorry for my poor manners. These here two boys are named White Cloud and Spotted Feather. They are my now adopted sons. These two pretty ladies are also my adopted daughters as well, named Kanti and Nuttah. They have been with me through 'thick and thin' and all of us once finished with trapping out on the frontier came back to Missouri to start our lives over. But before all of that happens, I need to get all four of these kids baptized and then married in the eyes of this here Catholic Church, so they will be all legal-like not only in the eyes of the Church but the State of Missouri as well," Otis continued.

"Well, hell, why didn't you say so earlier? My wife and I just figured you had gone rogue and were running around with them two Indian squaws and I was going to have to set you straight as to the laws of this here state. I am very happy to hear what you have to say about getting them all married and legal-like. That way I don't have to pay you a visit and put you in the 'calaboose' for breaking the State's laws about having more than one wife," continued Sheriff Clemmens with a grin of relief spread clear across his face. "Especially in light of the fact that the Barnes Clan were always fighters if crossed and Otis, you was one of the very best when it came to slinging his fist and being able to take a punch," continued Sheriff Clemmens.

"Nope, don't want to cause anyone any trouble, least of all with the law. I am just waiting for the Priest to get clear of all of the 'meeting and greeting' things he has to do and then get him to baptize my kids and marry them at the same time if that is possible. That way, the four of them can get on with their lives and start living together and raising their own families," said Otis.

"Well, hell, this is your lucky day, Otis! Old Man DeWitt who bought your old man's farm after you boys lost it and left for the frontier because of the back whiskey taxes your old man owed the Federal Government, is selling out! His wife choked to death on a piece of pork fat and now he is selling out and heading back to Pennsylvania just as soon as he can, so his mom and dad can help him in the raising of his six kids," said Sheriff Clemmens, with a lilt of hope sounding in his voice for his old friend.

Upon hearing those words, Otis's ears perked up and his heart skipped a beat! "What does Old Man DeWitt want for my old man's farm?" asked Otis cautiously.

"Last I heard was that he wanted $10 an acre for the land and another $1,000 for the buildings. Also as I understand it, he was going to throw in all of his farming equipment as a bonus for whoever buys the land. Well, I can't say all of that. He is keeping all of his horses and one wagon. That way he can take his whole family back to his folks' house in Pennsylvania in the back of that hay filled wagon," replied Sheriff Clemmens.

With those words, the thought of buying back his father's old farm and starting out fresh roared through Otis's mind! If he could do so, the first part of what he planned on doing with the rest of his and his adoptive kids' lives was already on its way to fruition to his way of thinking, along with the rest of the future thoughts now 'stampeding' through his mind as well! That was when he saw that the Priest was through with his 'greeting' duties and upon spotting Otis, one of his oldest Parishioners from the past, walked his way with a big smile of recognition spelled clear across his face!

"Excuse me, Sheriff, we will have to catch up on our pasts later. Right now I have some very important business to conduct with the Priest," said Otis. Then after shaking the sheriff's hand, they parted just as Father Paul walked up to Otis.

"Otis Barnes, Me Boy! I haven't laid eyes upon your old hearted black soul in so many Sundays that I have lost count and almost given up earthly hope of saving your black hearted carcass. Are you home from your trapping on the frontier with all of your brothers?" But before Otis could reply to the Priest's question, he found another one already was coming his way from the now very excited Priest, happy to see an old friend. "Say, Me Boy, where are the rest of your brothers? After all, their hearts are just as black as yours after missing so many of my Masses," said Father Paul with a big grin.

"They all be dead, Father," said Otis quietly.

Upon hearing those sad words, Father Paul quickly made the sign of the cross and then said, "How can that be, Otis, My Son? You and your brothers were as tough as horseshoe nails and God fearin' as well near as I can remember. What happened to such a tough bunch that they are all dead before their time?" he asked.

After hearing Otis's sad tale of woe, Father Paul just shook his head and made the sign of the cross once again as he mumbled a barely audible prayer for the lost Barnes brothers' souls. "Otis, to my way of thinking, today is still a happy day. You are back and I hope you will be another loyal soul and attending my Masses from now on regular like as a good Christian should. What are your plans now that you are home where you belong once again, My Son?" asked Father Paul.

"Father, these four young people standing behind me are my new adopted family members. This is White Cloud and Spotted Feather and these two lovely young ladies are named Kanti and Nuttah," said a proud Otis as he introduced his 'family' to his Parish Priest. "They have expressed to me many times that they wished to meet the white man's God and become a part of what the rest of the white men believe in. Because of their wishes expressed to me those many times, that is why I am here this morning," said Otis. However, when Otis introduced his kids to Father Paul, he saw a look of concern fly across the good Padre's face... "Have these children been living in sin all of this time, My Son?" he asked.

"No, Father! They are all in love with one another but in keeping with my earlier Catholic teachings, I have made these four live as the Catholic Church dictates and as my father raised us boys up to believe. That is why I am here today. We five plan to make this area our new home now that I am back from my days as a fur trapper on the frontier. With that in mind, I need to have you baptize these four kids of mine into the Church and then marry them so they can get on with the rest of their lives. Lives that they have held all these many months in abeyance at my request until they were baptized and married in the eyes of the Church," said Otis.

Upon hearing those words, Father Paul's face just beamed and then he said, "Otis, Me Boy, you are in luck. I am done with my churchly duties for this day and could think of nothing better than baptizing these children and then marrying them in the eyes of the Church so they will not be living in sin while they are living among us."

For the next four hours, the lives of the Barnes Clan were like they were living in a whirlwind!

First Father Paul sat down with White Cloud, Spotted Feather, Kanti and Nuttah and provided instruction into what was required in a good marriage and offered a lengthy explanation of the teachings of the Catholic Church and what would be expected of them now as good Christians. Then all four were instructed in the rites of Confession and attended their each and own confessions with Father Paul. Then Father Paul after some more preparing of the celebrants in the faith, married White Cloud and Kanti and Spotted Feather and Nuttah in the 'eyes of the Catholic Church'. This all the while as Otis proudly and with much happiness in his heart stood as a witness to the ceremony. Then with the good Father's blessings, the Barnes Clan went out from the local Catholic Church with their heads just a-whirling as to how quickly their lives had changed…

But their whirlwind day was not yet done! Otis and his new family rode out to the old Barnes family farm and there Otis met up with Charles DeWitt, its current owner. Within the hour, Otis had pledged $4,000 for his old father's farmstead and DeWitt had agreed. Otis also advised DeWitt that his Promissory Bank Note would be deposited in the "Hagar State Bank of Missouri" in Matson come Monday morning. After that, he could draw out his $4,000 and be on his way to Pennsylvania. As a surprise, DeWitt advised Otis that the five-bedroom farmhouse that had once belonged to his father Rufous, would be left as it was. DeWitt advised that they were leaving everything, beds and cookware included and just taking their clothing, one wagon full of hay for his family to ride upon and two-span of horses in which to pull their wagon. He also advised they could be out of their old home within two days because DeWitt needed to get his kids to his parents' place where he could get some help in raising them, especially the two youngest children, ages three and four.

Otis could hardly believe his ears! Here they would have a 'move-in' home and not have to fool around with furnishing it so they would have a decent place in which to live! Two days later, the Barnes Clan moved into Rufous Barnes's old farmstead and with it the first part of Otis's dream for their new lives was complete! When they did, Otis saw to it that one bedroom was designated for White Cloud and Kanti and another for Spotted Feather and Nuttah. Otis then took his father's old bedroom and for the first time in many years, he found a sound night's sleep unlike he had ever had while out on the frontier, not worrying about an attack from the Indians, meeting a grizzly bear or the long days of immersion in the cold waters of a beaver pond...

For the next two weeks, the Barnes Clan's 'whirlwind of life' never stopped whirling. First their new home was cleaned up from top to bottom by Kanti and Nuttah. Then the clan visited

"Lynn and Ernie's Emporium" in Matson and procured those supplies and provisions needed for living on a farmstead in Missouri. While there, Otis ordered a mountain of supplies from his old family friend Ernie Eaton that left White Cloud and Spotted Feather wondering what Otis had in mind by ordering so many sacks of field corn, sacks of wheat, oaken casks, numerous sacks of sugar, copper sheeting, copper tubing, 200 feet of cast iron water pipe, two cast iron wood stoves, 100 stoneware gallon jugs, fire bricks, canisters of yeast, and on and on the ordering went. With all of that ordering also went a large amount of the group's beaver, wolf and pine marten monies as well…

Then back home with the family's living quarters brought up to 'snuff', Otis and the boys set to cleaning out and up the old family barn. Finally one night after a supper prepared by Kanti and Nuttah, Otis shared his plans for the rest of their lives with the family. There he advised they were going into the whiskey or Moonshine making business as his father had called it! Those words alone required an extensive amount of explanation in order to satisfy Cloud and Feather's open-eyed amazement. They would start with the one barn as their first still house and once business got better, they would have another and larger barn built on their farmstead that would become "Still House #2"! Like in the old days, they would make their whiskey, jug it on the place and then transport it to St. Louis for immediate sale in the saloons, and to the vast array of "River Men" operating the vast and rapidly expanding shipping industry along the Mississippi River and around the docks of St. Louis. In addition, they were going to 'oaken cask' for some of their whiskey for aging and downriver transport. Then Otis announced that once they had become established, they would ship their brand of whiskey in those oaken casks down the Mississippi River to even bigger markets in a city called New Orleans! By now, White Cloud and Spotted Feather had eyes the size of dinner plates! The only liquor either of them had ever tasted came from a rum keg purchased at a rendezvous. Now here Otis, their adopted father, was talking about making hundreds of gallons of whiskey and selling it in St. Louis and even to a place they had never heard of called New Orleans. Then Otis, all caught up in his grand scheme of things for him and his kids, announced that they would be using his father's recipe for making West Tennessee "Moonshine" with one change. It was then he told his family the story about an old German whiskey maker who back in Tennessee used to burn out the insides of his oaken barrels, then clean out the charred wood leaving a layer of charcoal char in each barrel, and then store his whiskey in such barrels for a period of time as it aged because he felt it made the whiskey more colorful and smoother to the taste. Otis having tasted such whiskey as a young man then advised his family that is why he had purchased the numerous oaken barrels and would be experimenting with them. About then Otis seemed in his excitement of the moment to run down on what he had to say about the grand scheme of things he had for his family.

With a big smile on his weathered face over sharing his plans with his kids, he sat back in his rocking chair and then quietly said, "If we can make this work, you boys will eventually never have to work another day in your lives, and Kanti and Nuttah will be treated in our society as the ladies they are and deserve to be. All of you had to endure some rough times when younger and I can't erase those hard times. But if I have my way and the good Lord takes a liking to us, your lives will be better for it and you will never again have to look back on those bad times in your earlier lives..."

Two weeks later, Ernie had the men working for him at his emporium begin delivering Otis's expensive mountain of supplies, which it now being wintertime was stored in "Still Barn #1" for safer keeping. Then under Otis's keen eye and direction from memory, the three men built three very large whiskey making stills from the sheet copper and copper tubing received from Lynn and Ernie's Emporium. Collaterally, two large cast iron stoves were erected in the front and rear of the still barn for the warmth needed in making Shine during the cold Missouri winter months and then come springtime, the three men would run the 200 feet of cast iron pipe from their cold water spring behind their farmhouse which ran all year, from an oaken tank at the spring site all the way down and into the planned still barns so the whiskey making process would have a dependable supply of cold and clean water for all of their stills.

Come springtime, Ernie's men delivered sacks of corn, wheat, corks, stoneware jugs, canisters of yeast and sacks of sugar to the Still Barn as Otis had ordered. When they did, Ernie, driving one of the number of wagons carrying all of the supplies said to Otis with a big smile, "Otis, if this Shine is as good as your old man's used to be, there had better be a jug or two set aside for Lynn and me for all the work you have had me and my men doing. You know my great little wife, Lynn. She likes to take a 'nip' every now and then, especially when "Old Man Winter" and his cold comes nosing around. In fact, she keeps a jug of whiskey right at the foot of her bed for whatever ails her right now, but it is not of the quality like your old man used to make."

Otis just smiled over his friend's request saying, "If the boys and I can pull this off, you can tell "Miss Lynn" she will always have a jug of our Shine under her end of the bed whenever she wants. And also let her know we won't be saying anything to anyone, especially her group of stuffy old ladies at the Church, that she likes her

Shine for other than medicinal purposes…" With that, the two friends shook hands on 'Lynn's jug a month' deal, as over $12,000 changed hands in payment for most of Ernie's supplies. That left only $7,000 more needed to finish paying the whole bill, an amount that Ernie was willing to let slide for his old friend until the profits from his whiskey making business began rolling in.

By now, White Cloud and Spotted Feather were all eyes and ears when it came to learning the whiskey-making trade. In fact, both of the two young men found the idea of making Shine one hell of a lot better than watching out for mean-assed grizzly bears, hostile Indians, walking around in freezing water, and skinning out and hooping smelly beaver and pine marten skins…

Finally the day arrived when under Otis's careful instructions White Cloud and Spotted Feather completed making their first batches of Shine in their three large stills. Then the waiting game occurred until the finished product began dripping from the cooled copper coils into a two-gallon crock. There they learned the very first of the 'witches' brew' they were making was not good to drink but must be tossed. Shortly there-after, the 'real McCoy' began dripping from the copper coils and after a short 'run', it came time for the testing. Otis took the first sip and after a low whistle describing the excellence of the brew they had just created, the men began jugging up the Shine for later sales in St. Louis and surrounding areas so Otis could pay off the rest of his creditors!

For the next four months, the three men made gallon after gallon of Moonshine, hauled the jugs of their product into St. Louis and soon had more demand for their product than they could make. Soon word got around about Otis's excellent brand of Moonshine called "The Old Trapper"! Under that name brand they produced two lines of Moonshine, one labeled "The Old Beaver", and the other labeled "Black Wolf" (in honor of Kanti and Nuttah's Blackfoot warrior chief's father). Soon both lines of The Old Trapper whiskies had a reputation for being "Smoother than a Schoolmarm's Thigh"!

Presently the reputation of the whiskey became so well-known and respected, that Lynn and Ernie's Emporium was soon shipping oaken cask after oaken cask to the eating and drinking establishments all the way down to New Orleans! And sure as God made crickets good fish bait, Otis's process of aging his whiskey in oaken barrels that had been slightly burned out inside leaving a charcoal coating, and then filled with his brand of Shine, was not only more colorful but met the smoothness of great tasting "West Tennessee Sour Mash"!

With the money rolling in, soon there was enough left plus using the last of their trapping funds, to build a second Still Barn, and Otis committed all of their funds and some of his bank's in order to do so. Soon the second Still Barn had been built and in the process, additional stills were now being contemplated and constructed in "Still Barn #3"! Then even more happiness was forthcoming with the announcements of the soon to be arrival of children, one from Kanti and the other from Nuttah! Soon every Sunday when the Barnes Clan showed up for Church, they found themselves, just as Otis had predicted, even though his kids being of Indian stock, were becoming more and more respected and accepted by the St. Louis and Matson societies! There was no two ways about it, becoming respected distillers in and of their own right, had propelled the Barnes Family into local prominence, if not slightly overspent and over committed.

Finishing up another still in Still Barn #2 one morning, White Cloud was holding a heavy sheet of copper up for Otis to attach to the top of their last still. As Otis fumbled with the heavy sheet of copper, he found his grizzly bear necklace getting in the way every time he leaned over. The one and same grizzly bear necklace that had been given to him by Chief Black Wolf for caring for his two daughters, Kanti and Nuttah. The one and same necklace blessed by The Great Spirit that had brought the chief good luck in his life and had protected him during battle. In removing the sacred necklace from his own neck and placing it around Otis's, Black Wolf told him that having been blessed by The Great Spirit, great things would always come to the wearer of said protective necklace. Without paying heed to Black Wolf's exact words, Otis removed the necklace so he could more easily work with the heavy sheet of copper and set it off to one side. He then hefted up the huge sheet of copper and immediately the scaffold upon which he and White Cloud were standing collapsed under the combined weight of the copper sheeting and the two men! White Cloud's fall was broken when he fell onto several dozen sacks of corn and other than badly bruised, he was alright. Otis however, fell underneath the falling sheet of copper and his head was crushed! Within moments, Otis's body was being cradled by his distraught and sobbing adopted kids... There they cradled the body of an old fur trapper who had withstood grizzly bear attacks, fights with hostile Indians, shootouts with trap-stealing French-Canadians from the Hudson's Bay Company, avoided freezing to death in blizzards, survived horse wrecks and managed to trap hundreds of beaver while immersed in icy cold waters, but had been killed by a damn falling sheet of copper...

The surviving members of the Barnes Clan soon discovered their losses were just starting one week after Otis had been killed and later buried alongside Rufous Barnes, his father. It was shortly thereafter that Sheriff Clemmens arrived one morning unexpectedly on their property. Accompanying him were two Federal Revenuers with bad news. According to the federal men, Otis, in his haste to build a life for his new family, had forgotten to pay a 25% Whiskey Tax on the thousands of gallons of Moonshine they had been making and sold over the last number of months! White Cloud and Spotted Feather soon discovered, according to the Federal Revenuers, that Otis owed over $4,500 in back federal excise taxes for the Moonshine whiskey they had made and sold throughout the Mississippi River system!

Taxes that if not paid immediately, they were authorized to seize the farm under federal law and sell all of its holdings and other assets at auction in order to settle the bill owed the Federal and the State of Missouri Governments! It was then that White Cloud realized that they did not have the money to pay the huge bill owed the Federal Government. Otis and the clan had just invested every dollar they had accrued from the sale of their brand of Moonshine to pay for most of the materials and labor to build the second and third large Still Barns and for the materials needed to build the new stills within the barns! They also knew they did not have the money to pay the tax bill because Otis had always been a stickler on paying up front what he owed and had done so when the bills for the new barn and still had been submitted to him. In so doing, his coffers were basically empty for the moment.

Then the next 'ax' fell upon the remaining

Barnes Clan. Otis had not had the time to legally adopt White Cloud, Spotted Feather, Kanti and Nuttah. As such, no legal papers had been filed in the local courthouse making all four of them legally his children! Therefore, Sheriff Clemmens sadly advised the four that they had no legal rights to continue selling any of Otis's whiskey stocks to pay the Whiskey Excise Taxes since he was the rightful owner and now dead! Nor could they attempt to liquidate any of the farm's holdings in order to pay off the back whiskey taxes because the farm was in the name of and had been purchased by Otis Barnes. Since they were not legally adopted and since no will had been drawn up deeding the farm and its assets over to the four of them, they were only legally considered 'hired hands' and had no legal standing, Sheriff Clemmens sadly advised the still in shock kids! Still in shock kids who really did not understand such workings in this new white man's world...

Then the Federal Revenuers advised the sheriff that being the case, they had no other option other than serving the legal writ they possessed to seize the land and all of its assets and hold them for a public auction in order to settle up what was owed in back Whiskey Excise Taxes! Then the sheriff was requested to throw the 'Indian squatters' off the land now owned by the Federal Government! Turning to the four shocked members of the Barnes Clan, the sheriff sadly told

THE SAGA OF THE BARNES' CLAN, MOUNTAIN MEN | 685

them that there was nothing he could do but order them off the land now owned by the government. Then Sheriff Clemmens got mad over the unfair legal action being foisted on Otis's kids, turned facing the federal men saying, "I will not just up and throw these folks off the land! Otis was my friend and I know he loved these four like his own kids. I realize there is nothing I can do for them legally as far as their rightful hold on the land, but I am telling you federal people they can stay until they at least get their things together so they can move on. Can't you see that the two women are pregnant and just cannot up and leave this very moment," he said.

"Sheriff, you know the law. Our hands are tied as well. We are holding a Federal Court Order confiscating this land since it now is obvious there is no money available to settle up this tax bill. They have to go because this is now government property, so do your job or we will get someone who will!" said Federal Revenue Agent Bob Tilletson.

"You can shove your court order!" said Sheriff Clemmens. "White Cloud and Spotted Feather, you can take what time you need in order to get your things together so you can leave in an orderly fashion," said Sheriff Clemmens. "That is the least that I can do for my friend Otis and you folks as well. Now 'Mr. Revenue Agents', you can mount up and ride off and leave these good God-fearing folks to do what they have to do."

That night after a quiet and sad supper, White Cloud and Spotted Feather decided what was to be done. The next morning way before daylight found every horse loaded with provisions, necessaries and equipment just like they had in the days as Barnes Clan trappers. They were taking with them every horse on the place, firearm and 30 beaver traps that had been hung in the barn from their days as trappers. Then still before daylight, they rode by Ernie and Lynn's Emporium, leaving six of their last jugs of The Old Trapper whiskey as Otis had promised his good friend Ernie for Miss Lynn as her private stock of 'medicinals'. Then before they were stopped from taking assets off the land now owned by the government, the pack string and their four riders, two of them pregnant, headed out towards the north and west...

Three months later on the trail, White Cloud, Spotted Feather, Kanti, Nuttah and two newborn babies rode into a surprised but welcoming Black Wolf's Band of Southern Bear River Blackfeet Indians. When they did, they were cheerfully welcomed into the band by Chief Black Wolf, who was surprisingly handed back his valuable and sacred grizzly bear necklace by Kanti, his long-lost and now found daughter, with an explanation. After that, Otis's kids and grandkids' life histories, like many others from the country's many times deceived and lied-to Indian nations, disappeared forever into the annals and 'dustbins' of time...

Out of rebellion by the Missouri locals over

what the Federal Government had done and in fond remembrance of the Barnes Clan and what was right by the people of the day, NO ONE STEPPED FORWARD TO PURCHASE THE BARNES'S FARM AND ITS PROPERTIES AT THE SUBSEQUENT GOVERNMENT AUCTIONS, NOR HAVE THEY TO THIS DAY! LOCAL LORE AND LEGEND IS THAT ANYONE WHO PURCHASES THE GOVERNMENT'S TAINTED LANDS AND ATTEMPTS TO RAISE ANY CROPS ON SUCH LANDS WILL BE DOGGED BY BAD LUCK. IT IS SAID BY MANY OF THE LOCALS TO THIS DAY IN THE MATSON AREA, THAT ANY CROPS BEING RAISED AND NOT USED TO MAKE WEST TENNESSEE MOONSHINE, WILL SOON FIND WHAT IS GROWING IN THEIR FIELDS TO BE WITHERING AND DYING...

TODAY, THAT SAME FARM IS NOW OWNED BY THE STATE OF MISSOURI AND IS SAID TO BE BY MANY OF THE LOCALS, STILL ROAMED BY TWO MOONSHINE-MAKING IRISHMEN GHOSTS, WHO FOR WHATEVER REASON, FOUND IT THEIR RIGHT TO QUIETLY MAKE THEIR BRAND OF MOONSHINE WITHOUT THE 'HANDS' OF GOVERNMENT SPOILING THE 'SMOOTHNESS OF ITS TASTE'... THAT RUFOUS DID, AFTER SERVING HIS COUNTRY IN A TIME OF WAR, AND AS OTIS HAD DONE IN HELPING TO OPEN UP THE UNTAMED WEST TO ALL OF THOSE WHO

DESIRED TO FOLLOW THEIR DREAMS, AS DID THE BARNES CLAN... HOWEVER, TIME, GOOD LUCK AND DECENCY HAD GOTTEN AWAY FROM THEM... AS OTIS OFTENTIMES SAID WHEN THE CHIPS WERE DOWN, "SOMETIMES YOU EAT THE BEAR AND SOMETIMES HE EATS YOU"…………..

THE BARNES'CLAN

A Look At "Buck Snort" Toni And "Wind Horse", Mountain Men

BY TERRY GROSZ

IN 1806, the return to St. Louis of Lewis and Clark from their epic journey across the unexplored American West with their tales of untold abundance of valuable furbearers, especially beaver, excited the populace! Men like General Ashley and Major Henry responded to such tales of valuable furbearers in abundance by forming a fur company, employing 100 adventurous young men as company trappers, and keelboating up the Missouri River to the Yellowstone to establish a fort and trading post. There they initiated trade with the Indians, the principal harvesters of animal furs in America, and sent their own company trappers out to harvest valuable furbearers, especially beaver.

Thus begins Vince "Buck Snort" Toni and his Indian "Brother", Wind Horse's lives, first as orphans at a 'hellhole' orphanage, which by fate, exploded them into a life as fur trappers in the beautiful but dangerous largely unexplored American West! In the adventurous years that followed, Buck Snort Toni and Wind Horse trapped beaver and wolves along the Bighorn River facing freezing waters, violent "Ball Lightning" thunderstorms, buffalo stampedes, a deadly Frontier web of revenge, "Winter Bears", vicious Northern Arapaho 'Sons of the Prairies', renegade Hudson Bay fur trappers, dangerous 'pasts' from their earlier days in the orphanage, killed horse thieves, and joined the brotherhood of adventurous fur trappers known today as "Mountain Men". Then when Fate forced them from the field, they discovered a 'circle of life' surrounded by a Frontier Grace…

"Buck Snort" Toni and "Wind Horse", Mountain Men is an epic story of two intertwined lives, formed by destiny, forged in the fires of the American West and ultimately framed in "Frontier Grace".

Available now from Terry Grosz and Wolfpack Publishing.

ABOUT THE AUTHOR

Terry Grosz was born in June of 1941 in Toppenish, Washington. He graduated from Quincy High School in 1959, and attended Humboldt State College where he earned his Bachelor of Science Degree in Wildlife Management in 1964, and his Master of Science Degree in Wildlife Management in 1966. He was a California State Fish and Game Warden from 1966 until 1970, based first in Eureka, California, and then in Colusa, California, in the Northern Sacramento Valley. He then joined the U.S. Fish and Wildlife Service in 1970, first serving in California as a U.S. Game Management Agent and later as a Special Agent Criminal Investigator until 1974. In 1974, he was promoted to Senior

Resident Agent over the States of North and South Dakota where he served until 1976. In 1976, he was promoted to Senior Special Agent and transferred to Washington, DC. There he served as the Endangered Species Desk Officer and Foreign Liaison Officer until 1979. In 1979, he was transferred to Minneapolis, Minnesota, where he served as the Assistant Special Agent in Charge until 1981. In 1981, Terry was promoted and transferred to Denver, Colorado, as the Special Agent in Charge over the wildlife resource-rich eight-state region of the Service's Region 6, encompassing over 750,000 square miles in the States of North Dakota, South Dakota, Nebraska, Kansas, Montana, Wyoming, Colorado, and Utah. He retired from the U.S. Fish and Wildlife Service in 1998, after a 32-year career in state and federal wildlife law enforcement.

In 1999, Terry began his second career as a writer, with the publishing of his first wildlife law enforcement true-life adventures book titled, **"WILDLIFE WARS"**, which won a National Outdoor Book Award in the Nature and Environment category. He has since had 13 additional wildlife law enforcement adventure books published, titled, **For Love Of Wildness, Defending Our Wildlife Heritage, A Sword For Mother Nature, No Safe Refuge, The Thin**

Green Line, Genesis Of A Duck Cop, Slaughter In The Sacramento Valley, Wildlife's Quiet War, Wildlife Heritage On The Edge, Wildlife Dies Without Making a Sound (Volumes 1 and 2), and Flowers And Tombstones Of A Conservation Officer (Volumes 1 and 2).

Additionally, he has written five Western novels, titled, Crossed Arrows, Curse of the Spanish Gold, The Saga of Harlan Waugh, The Adventures of the Brothers Dent, and The Adventures of Hatchet Jack, and five Mountain Man novels, titled, The Adventurous Life of Tom "Iron Hand" Warren, Josiah Pike, Hell or High Water, Elliott "Bear Scat" Sutta, Mountain Man, and The Saga of the Barnes Clan, Mountain Men.

Also, Terry has a two-hour film credit on the reality-based TV series of "Animal Planet" titled, "WILDLIFE WARS", filmed in 2003 and released nationwide, based on a number of Terry's true-life wildlife law enforcement adventures during his career as a state and federal wildlife officer.

Terry has earned many awards and honors during his lengthy career, including the U.S. Fish and Wildlife Service's Meritorious Service Award in 1996 – Honored as one of the "Top Ten" employees of the U.S. Fish and Wildlife Service under Service Director Frank Dunkle

– The first federal officer to be honored with the "Guy Bradley Award" presented by the National Fish and Wildlife Foundation in 1989 for "Outstanding Wildlife Law Enforcement Service" – Colorado Conservationist of the Year Award in 1984 – The Conservation Achievement Award for Law Enforcement from the National Wildlife Federation in 1995 (the first law enforcement officer so honored by that organization) – Special Achievement Award for Law Enforcement Excellence from the U.S. Department of Justice in 1998 – Distinguished Alumnus, College of Natural Resources, Humboldt State University, 1995 – Humboldt State University Distinguished Alumnus Award, 2008 – Distinguished Achievement Award from the Native American Fish and Wildlife Society, 1992 – Received the Service's highest Annual Performance Ratings under five different supervisors from 1983-1998 – Unity College in Maine awarded Terry an Honorary Doctorate Degree in Environmental Stewardship in 2002.

Terry resides in Evergreen, Colorado, with his high school Sweetheart and Bride of 56 years.

Find more great titles by Terry Grosz and Wolfpack Publishing at http://wolfpackpub-lishing.com/terry-grosz/